THE MESSIAH FCA

Anthony Scrimgeour

The Book Guild Ltd
Sussex, England

First published in Great Britain in 2001 by
The Book Guild Ltd
25 High Street
Lewes, East Sussex
BN7 2LU

Copyright © Anthony Scrimgeour 2001

The right of Anthony Scrimgeour to be identified as the author of
this work has been asserted by him in accordance with the
Copyright, Designs and Patents Act 1988.

All rights reserved. No part of this publication may be
reproduced, transmitted, or stored in a retrieval system, in
any form, or by any means, without permission in writing
from the publishers, nor be otherwise circulated in any form
of binding or cover other than that in wich it is published
and without a similar condition being imposed on the
subsequent purchaser.

Although several of the dignitaries described in the text actually exist – for example
the Pope, the Queen, the President of the United States, an ayatollah and several
prime ministers – the meetings described never actually took place and the persons
portrayed holding these positions have no relationship whatsoever to real people.
All other characters are entirely fictitious

Typesetting in Baskerville by
SetSystems Ltd, Saffron Walden, Essex

Printed in Great Britain by
Antony Rowe Ltd, Chippenham, Wiltshire

A catalogue record for this book is
available from the British Library

ISBN 1 85776 554 0

CONTENTS

1	Kylb	1
2	Genesis	25
3	Exodus	41
4	Reflectus	64
5	Miraculus	76
6	Committicus	98
7	Abacus	119
8	Calculus	133
9	Consultus	147
10	Matthew	172
11	Eclipsus	195
12	Publicus	224
13	Panicus	247
14	Regina	274
15	Terminus	296

The Council meeting chamber had lost its customary harmonious hum. Electrons, neutrons and mega-molecules vibrated with unusual intensity in spite of the protective magnetic vacuum. Static electricity crackled, irritating the iactrochemical logic circuits of those present. Kylb glanced towards his colleague, Alaap. Not surprisingly, the latter was petrified. Only the absence of faeces in his bio-physical composition was preventing the defilement of his undergarments. The mighty # was xxlyco ('exasperated' for those not familiar with Council communication terminology). Area Manager Alaap was responsible for overseeing Zone Bµ219XL2–1, colloquially called the 'Milky Way' by one of its indigenous neo-biological subspecies, its appearance apparently resembled excretion emanating from twin protuberances adorning their female's outer casings, a relationship totally baffling to those present in the meeting chamber.

Everything was running smoothly in Zone Bµ219XL2–1, in perfect conformity with Zy-eecep (loosely translated as 'internal control procedures'). Except on Bl-zzziii-5, an inhospitable bacterially infested planet named 'Earth' by a neo-biological life form inhabiting its solidified outer crust, the very same whose females spontaneously secreted opaque fluid as part of some molecular redistribution process, known to them as a 'reproduction cycle', whatever that was.

'Alaap,' boomed forth the mighty #, 'you have aaaabz'. (The nearest transposition into human communication terminology is 'made a mess of things', although the concept can be expressed otherwise.) 'Kylb,' continued the mighty #, 'due to the gravity of the situation I have postponed your scheduled micro-circuitry rephasing. We need your experience to ensure Zy-eecep are rapidly imposed, that there are no more inexcusable deviations from regularity. You are henceforth nominated Senior Area Manager for Zone B219XL2–1, assignment priority being the irredeemable elimination of nonconformities on Bl-zzziii-5. Report back to me in 3pz' (about 18 months in human existential terminology). 'And I will expect to receive confirmation that your mission has been successful.'

Meeting adjourned.

1

Kylb

It was a mild, sunny morning. This was unusual, at least in Esher. Not that mild, sunny mornings were unknown in South-East England. They did occasionally occur, but normally between Mondays and Fridays when George McHenderson was ensconced at the office, unable to benefit from the multifarious pleasures of the suburban Surrey countryside. Come Saturday or Sunday and you could be certain clouds would gather, the wind would rise, the temperature would drop and the humidity level would surge. In other words, it would rain. To be frank, nature's generosity in this windswept corner of the world was irritatingly parsimonious.

But not today.

He smiled for the first time since ... well since far too long.

'Come on, Beatrice, let's go!'

Beatrice wagged her tail and woofed in excitement. Sunday morning 'walkies' with her master were the highlight of her life. Although of extremely dubious pedigree, she was his best friend and companion, his confidante, his alter ego, someone with whom he could relax, momentarily forget the insidious pressures of professionalism; someone to whom he could moan without being moaned at for incessantly moaning in the first place. Beatrice was of course not Mrs McHenderson, since few housewives woof with excitement when their husbands call to them. Mrs McHenderson, Gladys Joyce McHenderson, née Smythe-Carstairs, all 93 kilos of her, was at that moment driving to the local sports' club where she was organising the Annual

Surrey Bowls Championships, including the accompanying tombola and buffet lunch.

He continued to smile as he strode towards the woods. He was clearly not contemplating Gladys Joyce, otherwise his face would have exuded a pained scowl. In fact, having successfully removed his wife from his thoughts, he was subconsciously trying to prevent her from infiltrating back into them. Gladys, that tall, bouncy, big-bosomed blonde beauty he had married 28 years ago, she of the Surrey county hockey team and whose uncle was a lord, she who, from the day of their nuptials, had progressively expanded into a mountain of arrogant and exceedingly pretentious suburban socialite; she who in 1977, after beating him at tennis in straight sets, gleefully announced the Honourable Freddie Fender had proposed to her, although she preferred him. He had one week to make a counter-proposal, otherwise she would become Mrs Gladys Fender. His mother insisted the niece of a lord would make a wonderful wife, whereas his father lauded her family's real estate holdings. He himself, young, healthy, naïve and heterosexual, was more interested in securing unbridled access to her mammoth mammaries. Freddie was a pompous twit who, in spite of inherent mental deficiencies, regularly bowled him out at cricket. Marrying Gladys would enable him to wreak his revenge on Freddie and claim that tremendous torso for himself. So he had proposed and was duly married to Gladys Joyce with much pomp and ceremony, not forgetting the circumstance.

Twenty-eight years later he was also trying to forget about Charles Dewey.

The person in question, managing director of one of his firm's major clients, had joined Gladys in the recesses of his subconscious at the beginning of the walk, but had not remained there for long. Noting the regrettable return of the incommodious Mr Dewey, his conscious mind instructed its module for muscular movements to command the pulling of selected facial strings. His face dutifully stopped smiling as he and Beatrice advanced towards Claremont Woods. He groaned, both inwardly and outwardly, as he recalled the events of the previous Thursday afternoon.

'But George,' Charles had intoned in his petulant, superior-than-anyone-else, you're-wasting-my-time tone of voice, 'you really must have worked in the timber industry and lived in Africa to fully understand the implications of the situation. You are undoubtedly a first-rate accountant, but it's just not possible for a theoretician like yourself to fully appreciate what is happening in the forests of Mozambique.'

A theoretician! He bristled with impotent fury. How the blazes could he be expected to understand what was happening in the mosquito-infested rainforests of equatorial Africa? Charles knew it, he knew it, and Charles knew that he knew it. It was for Charles, the company's managing director, to explain to George, his external auditor, what was taking place in those soggy jungles thousands of miles away. However, the supercilious bastard was certainly not spilling the beans. But exactly what beans were not being spilled? He admitted to himself, for once agreeing with Charles Dewey, that he knew damn all about the economic peculiarities of Mozambique's forested hinterlands. He was a professional accountant, a bean-counter, albeit a very senior one, but to count beans one had to be provided with beans to count, preferably spilled ones.

The other middle-aged businessmen and female secretary sitting in the wood-panelled boardroom of the East Africa Timber Corporation Plc waited for Charles Dewey to proceed. None dared speak, let alone interrupt their company's managing director, especially when he was haranguing his external auditor.

'You see, George, following the disastrous floods in Eastern Africa, there is an immense need for timber to reconstruct devastated towns and villages, not forgetting the transportation networks. As even you will have heard, this will be financed by the World Bank. So our year-end inventories which, as you have rightly pointed out, are larger than normal and could only be sold on the depressed European market at discounted rates, will now be in great demand locally, selling at excellent prices. Which means, my dear George, that there is absolutely no need to reduce our inventory valuations.'

The four impeccably dressed senior managers of the East Africa Timber Corporation attending the meeting nodded in agreement, an agreement nurtured by the knowledge that their annual bonuses increased in direct proportion to the company's profits, which in turn depended on maximising the valuation of prodigious stockpiles of timber lying around rain-soaked Mozambique.

He, George McHenderson, Harrow, BA Oxford, four 'A' levels plus nine 'O' levels and Chartered Accountant, gloomily studied his audit files. To economise travel expenses he had vetoed a second visit to Mozambique to perform the year-end physical inventory. As a consequence he could not possibly prove Charles was withholding information. Yet his gut feeling, his instinct borne out of nearly 30 years of auditing, told him the company was desperate to boost its profits. Everything depended upon those inventories. Concocting reasons for not reducing their value needed imagination, combined with an absence of professional integrity. Charles Dewey had both. More precisely, he had the imagination and he lacked the professional integrity. Of this his external auditor was convinced, but how the damnation could he prove it?

And in the boardroom of the East Africa Timber Corporation, the above-mentioned Charles Dewey was glaring at him, waiting impatiently for a reply.

'Well, Charles,' he had finally answered, 'I'll review the situation with my fellow partners.' In other words, 'Once again you've got your own way, you conniving little bastard.' The only silver lining to the exceedingly large grey cloud hanging over his head was that if he could not disprove Charles Dewey's inventory valuations, then it was extremely unlikely anyone else would. His firm's reputation therefore would be secure.

'I'll buy you a drink at the golf club,' Charles had proposed, glancing at him with a expression more akin to a sneer of derision than a smile. Both knew the cost of one gin and tonic was minimal compared to the value of Charles's potential year-end bonus. However, swallowing his pride, he accepted the offer gracefully. He was a true professional and knew how to behave towards his clients, just so long as he did not have to play a round, a distinct possibility since both were members of Esher Golf Club.

As he approached the woods he was feeling extremely dissatisfied with his professional performance, after all a Chartered Accountant should effortlessly outmanoeuvre a mere timber merchant. More than that, the honour of the Institute was at stake.

The Institute of Chartered Accountants in England and Wales had existed since 1880 to combat the Charles Deweys of the nation. Scotland, in one of its recurring fits of nationalistic pride, founded its own Institute, one considered infinitely inferior by the English and Welsh. Chartered Accountants are exemplary members of society, dedicated to ensuring that the nation's companies respect the laws of the land. They are fully aware of their regrettable reputation for being boring, outstandingly boring, when conversing with normal human beings. Of course accountants are not even remotely boring. They find themselves extremely good company. Yet society irrevocably accursed them with the unjustified burden of bombastic boredom. But why? He, when contemplating such social inequity, concluding that Chartered Accountants simply did not consider it necessary to expostulate their exhilarating intellectual aplomb to other members of society.

Concerning the particular case of the East Africa Timber Corporation Plc, the Institute, its reputation, traditions and professional ethics were being represented by himself, George McHenderson. And, that Thursday afternoon in the company's teak-panelled boardroom, he had been struggling pitifully.

As the sound of traffic diminished he heard the twittering of birds. Spring was in the air, but the state of his mind remained autumnal. As senior partner of the reputable London firm of Christie, Wainwright, Steinway and Company, 56 years old, Chairman of the Institute's Disiplinary Committee, Associate Member of the British Institute of Management, he was indeed a distinguished component of British industry, and justifiably proud of his achievements. But for some time, long before the previous Thursday's disastrous meeting with Charles Dewey, he had not been entirely satisfied with himself. He wasn't exactly unhappy, but in recent months he had experienced nagging doubts as to his social and professional infallibility.

At the office, his work was increasingly stressful. He was a first-rate accountant and auditor. He was an excellent manager of people. He had created an enviable team spirit in the firm and he knew how to charm clients, Charles Dewey excepted, such that the firm had steadily expanded over the years. His problems, at least the most recurring ones, arose from computers. Although born after the first data processing machine saw the light of day in the early 1940s, he was simply not IBM compatible, even less Digital, Apple or Compaq. Each time a client adopted a more sophisticated accounting system, he felt less able to master the situation as accounting transactions whizzed round in nanobytes instead of solid, comforting bits of paper. Yet he personally had to sign the audit reports stating whether, in his opinion, those accounting systems were reliable.

He was a computer misfit, a dinosaur of a business world run by modems and floppy disks, someone ever-increasingly incongruous with the office environment in which he worked. His ignominious performances on the golf course in past months, his total lack of sex life, an embarrassing bout of lumbago, his futile attempts to outmanoeuvre Charles Dewey, all had added to the self-doubting of his abilities, the hesitations, the nagging lack of self-confidence.

To put it bluntly, he was not getting any younger.

'Woof!'

Beatrice, feeling more than somewhat ignored by her master, had wandered off in search of exciting new smells. Either she had scented a rabbit or fox or, best of all, had encountered a fresh turd deposited by one of her doggy neighbours. He momentarily forgot about over-voluminous timber inventories and indeterminable computer listings. Breathing in the mild moist air, he looked around for his canine companion.

'Come on, Beatrice!' he shouted as he plunged into the semi-darkness of the wood.

'Morning, George.'

'Morning, Cedric.'

It was Cedric Saint-Johns, one of his near neighbours, walking his Labrador. Cedric was a stockbroker, not particularly surprising since Esher was in the heart of the stockbroker belt, an area of beautiful wooded countryside dotted with spacious and tasteful mansions designed for the rich, albeit not necessarily respected members of British society. Between the houses sprouted tennis clubs and golf courses, those essential appendages of a civilised social existence. Admittedly a few ultra-rich pop stars had vulgarised some of the estates, one referred to houses with gardens as *estates* in this part of the world, but Esher still remained undeniably civilised, quaintly old-fashioned and highly exclusive, distinctly unlike its neighbouring communities, especially Hounslow which resembled a disreputable Bombay suburb more than an English country town.

Naturally most of the people expressing such opinions had never visited Bombay, at least not since India's undisciplined independence. He was more broad-minded on such matters, often being shocked by the arbitrary condemnation of the non-Anglo-Saxon world by some of his social peers. His coloured acquaintances were intelligent and delightful company. Consequently, he failed to understand what all this racist fuss was about. Dr Zighani, an Iranian who lived nearby, was extremely brilliant, although a hopeless golfer, and the rest of his family were utterly charming. Yet local wags maliciously insinuated the Zighani house was the most valuable in the area: it was the only one without a 'darkie' as a neighbour.

When social conversation turned to such matters as skin pigmentation he remained silent. He had enough problems battling the complexities of computerised accountancy without worrying about the inequities of racism.

He exchanged a few pleasantries with Cedric about nothing in particular, obligatory neighbourly niceties, whilst their respective dogs attentively sniffed each other's rear ends. Beatrice was a bit miffed at the antics of Arthur the Labrador. Of course it was perfectly correct canine etiquette to sniff each other's anuses, familiarising themselves with each other's scent. Could you imagine having to shake paws or rub mouths as their masters did? But did Arthur have to sniff quite so low down? He was off target and bordering on an area socially off limits since she was not on heat. Admittedly his legs were shorter than hers, but couldn't he stretch a bit higher? Like a well-trained bitch, she would show no sign of outward upset so long as their masters were present, but next time they were alone she would have a polite woof with Arthur. In the meantime she bent her two back knees slightly, forcing his nose up to the socially correct sniffing position.

A cheerful wave and master and accompanying bitch were able to continue their morning constitutional, adventuring ever deeper into the Surrey wood.

He felt it coming, tried to stop it. But the thought in question was extremely stubborn. He gave in.

The golf club was short of money and the clubhouse desperately required rewiring before the whole place short-circuited and burned to the ground. Cirus B. Howenberger, (where did Americans acquire their names?) one of the more flamboyant club members, had offered to finance the whole deal as a gesture of friendship. But was it genuine goodwill or an attempt to buy influence? The Club Committee could not dilly-dally any longer, a decision had to be taken at the next meeting. And several members were making noises in his direction, insinuating it was for the club's Treasurer to resolve such matters. But what if their so-called benefactor, subsequent to disgorging his generosity, insisted, for example, on replacing Watney's Red Barrel with Budweiser and imposing 'hot dog specials' for Sunday lunch instead of steak and kidney pie? Damnation, why did today's problems no longer have any solutions?

'Good morning.'

Golf club ruminations were unceremoniously shoved to the back of his mind.

'Good morning!'

His hand was moving up to his head, an automatic reaction when meeting a lady. He stopped just in time, realising he had decided against wearing his deerstalker that morning.

He did not know her name. He assumed she lived nearby, several times he had caught glimpses of her walking in the neighbourhood. This, however, was the first time he had encountered her at close range. She had a husband, he surmised by the ring on her finger, although today's digital trinkets no longer necessarily symbolised marital fidelity. Anyway, most attractive, desirable woman of her age were securely married. And she was decidedly attractive and eminently desirable. Her body, at least the front half facing him, was sublime. But, frustratingly, she was gone before he could properly admire her contours, she had barely slowed down.

Should he turn and admire the other half? No, there was no point, such delicacies were no longer available to him, he was old enough to be her father and it would be foolish to kindle latent desires that would never be satiated. Furthermore, if she realised she was being eyed she would inevitably smirk with female self-satisfaction. Even worse she might tell her friends, women spent most of their lives gossiping about such matters, and he had his reputation to maintain.

Blast women, he thought to himself. Why were those you

would most like to possess those you were most unlikely to impress?

'Woof!' replied Beatrice.

'Ah, Beatrice,' he murmured fondly to his companion, 'if only women could be as generous as you in the pursuits of procreation. No, on second thoughts, that would be pushing things too far.'

He capitulated, turned to have one last lingering look at the gloriously moulded track suit, but it had already disappeared from view.

'Damnation!'

Not for the first time in his life he learned that when walking in woods one should look ahead at trees and not behind at behinds.

'Woof,' said Beatrice in consolation.

His brain changed subjects, although very slightly. When had he last made love? Best to forget his last two experiences, so carefully planned yet so disastrously accomplished. To be pedantic, so disastrously not accomplished at all. The last near-miss, he smiled at his unintentional pun, had been ten years earlier with Sheila, secretary to the Financial Director of A.G.P. Chemicals. Of course it was strictly forbidden to have licentious relations with client personnel. However, the lady in question was a temporary, so he had authorised himself to circumnavigate the rules slightly. About 40, not that bad looking, she was obviously as frustrated as a March hare in November. Unfortunately, as she hastily discarded her garments, his nasal senses had been increasingly overcome with over-powering bodily odours, those associated with an absence of soap. His masculinity, expectantly admiring the ceiling, was soon disdainfully studying the coffee stains on her carpet. Crying with frustration Sheila had turfed him out of her flat, not even inquiring whether he had reserved a hotel room. Luckily, never one to count his chickens before they were hatched when it came to women, he had a reservation at the local Ramada Inn.

And then there had been Samantha. The person in

question, he somehow felt the designation 'lady' misplaced, was a member of some conservationist association, an extremely sexually active member. But during their evening together her activity, more precisely her planned activity, i.e. to 'make it' with a Chartered Accountant for the first time, stopped dramatically when she realised the male about to ravish her was two years older than her father, was a member of the Conservative Party and had no condoms. Her thighs clamped resolutely together, barring access to his rising glory, leaving the male member of the male member of the Conservative Party in incongruous limbo.

Women!

Why had God or Nature, or Whatever, having endowed women with such biological delights, decided to make them so stingy when sharing themselves with males? Even Scots were more generous with their coins than women with their loins. He sighed, admitting the inevitable. Sports champions retired gracefully when they could no longer compete successfully, he should therefore do likewise, accept the situation and devote his energies to pursuits more compatible with his age and social self-esteem.

He strode on deep in thought, ignoring Beatrice. Sexually inactive he might be, but for 56 he was extremely fit physically, a reasonable skier, and he could still defend himself on the squash court against practically anyone. In two weeks he was leaving for Pontresina to spend his annual skiing holiday with Muriel and John, plus James, a bachelor friend of his. Life, he mused, wasn't that bad, Esher wasn't Sarajevo, Bagdad or Kosovo.

'Woof,' replied Beatrice trying to be helpful.

Breathing in the moist sweet-smelling air he looked around him. Although leaves had not yet started to sprout on the trees, a few green shoots were forcing their way through the earthbound debris remaining from last autumn. It was going to be a good year for bluebells. A squirrel scurried along the branch of an elm tree. He calmed down. After lunch he would play golf at the club, a useful and necessary means to digesting Gladys' cooking since his wife believed intuitively in quantity. Something only logical in view of her 93 kilos, after all a Chieftan tank consumed considerably more petrol than a Renault Twingo. Poor Gladys, she protruded in profusion where women were meant to protrude, but convexed even more contagiously where she was meant to concave. He realised it was not her fault, but this hardly solved the problem, her problem, their problem.

After the golf they were invited to the Hutchinson's for tea and no doubt a game of croquet. Then they would return home for a light supper before selecting a video from their vast collection. Apart from the news and *Panorama*, they rarely looked at the unmitigated rubbish served up on live television. He rather fancied watching *Basic Instinct* again, but Gladys disapproved of Sharon Stone. Intuition told him he would suffer a rerun of *Howards End* or *Out of Africa*. They had discussed buying a second television but, however minimal their domestic existence, something told them if they were unable to occasionally watch a film in each other's company then nothing whatsoever remained of their marriage. Luckily their tastes frequently coincided, so that Mr and Mrs George McHenderson managed to spend a few quiet evenings together, even sharing the same sofa, although sitting discreetly at opposite ends.

Yet another sigh escaped from between his lips. He determined to enjoy his walk, make the most of a sunny Sunday in Esher. With an extra-deep gulp of morning air he successfully zapped his trials and tribulations into the deepest recesses of his subconscious, shouted to Beatrice and charged after his canine companion.

'Woof!'

'Woof! Woof! Woof!'

No doubt a rabbit, or even a fox. He strode towards the sound of the woofs. Beatrice was standing in a small clearing, her tail wagging and her mouth barking furiously. He blinked in the blinding light. The sun was extremely strong even for late March. But the light was not emanating from the sun. It came from the opposite side of the clearing, an iridescent white, almost colourless shimmering brilliance, a sheen of unnatural bioluminescence. Presumably some film company making a television commercial for toilet products, one of those claiming to fill your lavatory with the fragrance of a mountain forest or, in this case, a Surrey wood.

'George Alistair Benson McHenderson.'

The voice seemed to be coming from behind the shimmering light. So it wasn't a television commercial. It must be the team from that goddam-awful *This Is Your Life*. At any moment Eamon Andrews would step into view clutching that leather-bound book. No, wait a minute, the BBC did not invest fortunes prying into the suburban sagas of Chartered Accountants, unless Gladys had bribed them to make a fool out of him. In any case, wasn't Eamon Andrews dead?

Candid Camera! But there were no people to be seen. The light must be operated by remote control.

'George Alistair Benson McHenderson,' the voice repeated.

Voice? It sounded like a voice, he was hearing words, but it wasn't exactly a voice. Yet his brain had clearly registered someone speaking his name. Benson! Who the damnation knew of his third given name, a dark secret and cause of much humiliation in his youth? His parents had adamantly refused to explain their choice; they both chain-smoked but he would be George Alistair Players McHenderson if that had been the source of their inspiration.

'George Alistair Benson McHenderson, can you hear me?'

'Errr . . . yes,' he mumbled, not quite certain to whom he was admitting to being a Benson.

'Good, now let's get down to business. Oh, by the way, don't be frightened, I can assure you that my intentions are peaceful.'

Kylb had to be careful. That stupid Jewish peasant had nearly killed himself falling down the mountain when he encountered Alaap's glowing form.

Hardly comforted by this declaration of goodwill, in fact decidedly alarmed by the words of consolation, he took a couple of steps backward. Surely that was the kind of soothing falsity Rambo uttered before shredding everyone in sight with a mobile howitzer.

'Please, George,' the voice said.

He stopped retreating. Rambo never said 'please' to anyone, so there was perhaps some hope of redemption. Did he have any enemies? He could think of several Esher residents who probably didn't exactly appreciate him. Furthermore, he had been excessively supercilious to his local bank manager the previous week, how dare he charge commissions on Euro bank transfers, but Barclays was not in the habit of eliminating garrulous clients. He had recently qualified two audit reports, but neither of the companies was run by Arabs. And none of them knew about Benson.

'Who are you?' he called out bravely. 'I can't see anything because of your damned headlights.'

Drat, car headlights in the middle of a wood on a sunny morning was pretty stupid, the kind of remark made by those pathetic victims of *Candid Camera.*

'I am Kylb, Senior Area Manager for Zone *B219XL2-1*. I represent #, Vice President Galaxy Control of AAA.'

'I'm terribly sorry, but I don't quite understand,' he replied, feeling even more confused than he sounded.

'AAA', strange name for a company, definitely not one of his clients. And none of his friends spoke with that vacuum-like unemotional tone.

'I'm not surprised,' replied Kylb, who himself was not exactly at ease. So much depended upon the correct choice of local agent to ensure the success of his mission. 'Let me explain in more detail. I represent the authority that oversees what you refer to as the Universe. The word commonly used when referring to our organisation, although your concept is somewhat misplaced, is God. My role is to ascertain what is happening on the various planets in my sector, at least those where life forms have evolved, and intervene as and when problems arise.'

'Then you must be the Angel Gabriel?' he asked, immediately regretting his crass stupidity, his gullibility.

He would not only be seen on *Candid Camera*, he would be included in the video of its most hilarious moments.

'If you wish,' replied Kylb with total seriousness, without the slightest trace of mockery or amusement. 'I am here because your planet is once again causing consternation. Your particular species, through greed and selfishness, is wantonly exterminating other terrestrial life forms. You are polluting and destroying the environment so that practically all biological structures, including your own, face premature extinction. You are permitted to do this to your own species, this is authorised by our Procedure 63–3C, but it is distinctly forbidden by subsection C574-E to suppress other species in the process. And another thing, it is equally against regulations to communicate with other centres of life. Naturally nobody could possibly interpret, let alone understand, what you are transmitting, but the practice creates interference and must cease. And finally, will you please stop flinging those metallic bits of junk into space. It's sufficiently cluttered up with asteroids and other galactic debris without your wretched satellites.'

Kylb almost sounded emotional. However, if he had displayed symptoms of one of the more common aberrations occurring in lower biomolecular life forms, his logic transposer would have automatically intervened to interrupt the manifestation. Even Senior Area Managers were no more than lowly mobile neutron condensers, designated an extremely limited logic capacitor. Emotions and imposing internal control procedures were not only incompatible but irrelevant.

'So, as a result of the current situation, I have been instructed to eliminate the problem,' Kylb continued more calmly.

Silence.

Several half-formulated questions circulated inside his

forehead but he hesitated. He had better remain silent in case there was a microphone hidden behind the light.

Kylb broke the silence.

'Our policy is not to intervene directly. We don't have adequate local knowledge let alone necessary resources. We select local life forms, neo-biological in the case of your planet, to act on our behalf. You call it sub-contracting. To put it bluntly, the current mess is partly our fault since our previous local agents, especially the most recent ones, have hardly been the most judicious choices.'

He understood the logic. After all, his firm engaged local auditing companies to control his clients' overseas subsidiaries. He wasn't himself going to verify Argentinian, Hong Kong and Italian books of account, especially Italian. He didn't want a Mafia knife in his back simply because he had unearthed a numbered bank account in Switzerland. However, the idea of appointing local agents to solve intergalactic problems somehow didn't make sense.

'You refer to them rather grandly as Messiahs,' explained Kylb.

His ingrained auditor's instincts for self-survival deserted him, but only momentarily.

'Can you please come out from behind the head . . . from behind the light so I can see you?' he requested politely.

'Sorry,' responded Kylb. 'I have no shape or form, at least nothing your optical sensory devices could ascertain. In simplistic terms, I am the light.'

Charlton Heston! No, Moses. He had watched the video with Gladys a few months ago. She adored romantic biblical epics. Moses had seen a ball of flame at the top of that desert mountain. Mount Sinai, that was it.

'Yes, he was one of our local agents,' said Kylb.

He was pleased with himself. He had guessed right first time. Then he froze, the pit of his stomach performing an imperfectly executed somersault. He had not spoken a word, he had merely thought about Moses and the Ten Commandments.

'Don't panic,' said Kylb. 'I am not literally hearing your

words, I am deciphering thought pulsations within your logic generator, your brain. You do not actually need to speak in order to communicate with me, although I appreciate it is more natural to actually mouth the words. Also, I am not speaking to you, I am transmitting thought messages directly to your brain lobes, which automatically process the messages even though they have bypassed your sound reception intake. That's why I appear to be speaking in your local dialectal speech form. You refer to it as English.'

Didn't they do that in *Star Trek*? No, it was *Star Wars*. He had been about to complement Kylb on his impeccable English, his total lack of accent, but fortuitously decided it was not exactly the moment. 'Local dialectal speech form', how dare he! He, George McHenderson, was one of the few people living on the planet speaking English as it should be spoken, without the slightest trace of accent, the purity of Harrow and Oxford. If he hadn't become an accountant he would have been perfect as a BBC announcer, no ITN, they seriously needed to improve the quality of their news broadcasts which had become disturbingly sloppy in recent years, their presenters afflicted with accents emanating from almost anywhere. He was just what they needed.

'Sorry to interrupt,' said Kylb.

Embarrassed at his display of impoliteness, he quickly concluded that the best form of defence was attack.

'Who were the other Messiahs?'

'The first human was Abdul, a very pleasant Mesopotamian, but his limited mental capacity prevented him from comprehending the nature of his assignment, let alone achieving any results. So we replaced him with that Moses you mentioned. Bright chap, but totally committed to the affairs of his particular tribe. He saved them all right, but he resolutely refused to help other members of your species, considering them inferior and not worth bothering about. His parting of the Red Sea was the highlight of his achievements, great intuition and quick thinking. But he was as stubborn as they come, insisted on taking notes whilst Alaap waited. Took him hours. Next there was a Chinese. Whenever possible we try to select our agents from different subsections of your species. He was followed by Davli the Tibetan and Mohammed the Arab. All three were ineffective, spending most of their time meditating in the desert instead of achieving anything constructive. Admittedly, the latter has been very successful from a marketing standpoint and the procedures manual he initiated, you call it the *Koran*, has a lot of intelligent ideas, although also some pretty crackpot ones. The main inconsistency with all three was the limited regional influence they achieved, whereas the identified problems and corresponding solutions concern your entire species.

'Then there was Joan of Arc, but he rushed around all over the place rubbing everyone up the wrong way, achieving nothing. Too Latin. So next we chose a Germanic, someone meticulous and well-organised. Adolf Hitler started off remarkably well, but then something went drastically wrong. He was the first to take population control seriously but his efforts were inappropriate, too selective and highly obnoxious in their philosophy. We are extremely ashamed of him. His internal procedures manual, *Mein Kampf* he called it, was hopelessly theoretical and full of intellectual deformities. All very regrettable. However, at the time we were experiencing budgetary restrictions which limited our ability to supervise ongoing field work.

'And that's the lot.'

'But that's not many.'

'Of course not. We cannot visit your planet frequently. It's a minor outlying life centre far distant from our main areas of involvement. Even so, if it makes you happy, your planet has given us more trouble than entire solar systems, some infinitely more complex than yours. We nearly eliminated your planet once due to the misguided efforts of one of our pre-human agents.'

'Who was he?' he inquired. 'No, I mean what was he?'

'A dinosaur. You see, we always choose our agents from the dominant species and, at the time, dinosaurs were omnipresent on your planet. But the one we chose went completely berserk, totally uncontrollable, so in exasperation we decided to eliminate not only him but the entire species, deviated an asteroid, quite cunning in fact, although we unintentionally created a serious geophysical disorder and regrettably wiped out numerous other life forms in the process. Still, I suppose it was better than our intervention on Mars, when we inadvertently and permanently eradicated all existence due to an excessive disintegration discharge. Now we apply molecular redistribution. Regrettably your solar system has been the source of multifarious deviations from *Zy-eecep*.'

Something was bothering him, something was not quite as it should be. Suddenly he realised what was bugging him.

'Haven't you missed out one of your Messiahs, one of the human ones?'

'No, that's the entire list.'

'But what about Jesus Christ?'

'Oh, him,' responded Kylb sullenly.

'You don't seem very proud of him,' he commented. 'What did he do wrong?'

'Damnable impostor,' replied Kylb 'Nothing more than a peasant charlatan, although admittedly brilliantly intelligent and a remarkable visionary. And, to add insult to injury, he becomes more successful than all our official local agents combined.'

This was not exactly going to please the Pope, reflected the recently appointed Local Agent. But at least he could seek revenge on Gladys, a devout Church of England believer and stalwart of the local Christian Union, who sarcastically derided her husband's less than committed stance on the Holy Trinity and its over-flamboyant trappings. He supposed he believed in God, at least in some outside force of creation, that which had formed the universe. AAA Corporation according to Kylb. But he had always considered the story of nocturnal donkey rides by a Jewish carpenter and his pregnant wife more than far-fetched, however full of love and understanding the various gospels might be.

What upset him about religion in general, Christians had no monopoly in such matters, was how its leaders so often spawned mistrust and hatred, defied social progress and used their respective churches more as personal ego-building and fund-raising organisations than distributors of goodwill: Northern Ireland, Iran, Afghanistan, Jehovah's Witnesses and the multitude of sinister sects whose only saving grace was their tendency to participate in mass suicides. If you studied history, most wars seemed to have been started by some religious nutcase. In Belfast you machine-gunned your neighbour in front of his wife and children because he was Catholic and not Protestant, or *vice versa*, which was the equivalent of someone from Esher eliminating a member of the tennis club because he shopped at Tesco instead of Sainsburys. Meanwhile, in Algeria, grown men sliced the throats of teenage schoolgirls for not wearing a scarf, all in God's name.

Kylb, listening to his local agent's reflections, was pleased. His candidate appeared to be taking things seriously, he was already formulating interesting ideas.

And yet, suddenly thought his recently selected Local Agent, could Jesus really have been an impostor? Supposing AAA had competition, a different heavenly organisation with equal authority to police the Universe. Who had sub-contracted some urgent problem-solving to a carpenter's son?

Kylb commenced short-circuiting. Thought patterns about possible AAA competitors were listed in his logic sensor's 'unsanctioned' control file which, when activated, disrupted his operating mode with static, causing a form of electro-arthritis. He automatically evacuated the censored neuroimpulses from the earthling's brain before the latter arrived at any discordant conclusions.

Still thinking hard, unaware of the redirecting of his thoughts, the Local Agent's mind turned to more pragmatic issues.

'Yes, George, you are right. I must fully explain why you have been chosen and what exactly we require of you.

'Your overall mission is to ensure that, within a reasonable time frame, your planet once again fully respects our internal control procedures, especially the respecting and preserving of other life forms coexisting with you. This will inevitably require dramatic population reductions of your species, down from the current ridiculous seven billion to no more than one billion entities. I assure you even that total is very generous, but we are prepared to accept it on condition your planet's atmosphere and outer crust do not suffer further degradation. Remember your planet belongs to the AAA corporation, you are only its tenants. In fact, since the advent of your species arose from an unintended biophysical reaction, legally speaking you are unwanted squatters.

'It is not our policy to issue detailed instructions on how to achieve our goals, that is your responsibility. We entrust you with certain powers although, following mishaps with previous agents, these will be somewhat more restricted in scope than usual.'

'Powers?' interrupted George.

'You refer to them as the ability to perform miracles.'

The Local Agent considered the implications.

'Well, if you really want to create visions of choirs performing operatic works from clouds, there is nothing to stop you. But, frankly, I don't see how this could achieve your objectives. We chose you because, following our earlier mistakes, we believe you have the necessary qualifications. You are male, biologically mature, conceived in wedlock, infertile and a senior member of an organisation whose role is to ensure your own society's internal procedures are respected, an experience that should be extremely useful. Also, you are used to managing people and you are familiar with the problems facing your planet, even though to date you have shown little inclination to implement solutions.'

'Why do you insist on a male?'

He was as chauvinistic as most males, although perhaps less so than the average accountant. His question was posed out of curiosity, not outrage at an affront to the female half of the human race.

'Well,' Kylb was slightly nonplussed. 'Males, as you call them, constitute the more dominant component of your societies, they furnish most of your leaders. We consider their logic circuits more stable, consequently their ideas are more likely to be pragmatic and implementable. We are ready to be proven wrong, we were with that idiot Jean who changed his name to Joan, dressed like a man and then pretended to be a woman, but we will need a lot of convincing. Your planet is one of only two centres in the Universe where the renewal process is not auto-generated, so we are consequently unsure how to handle the situation. After all, 'split entity procreation', sex as you call it, is not only illogical in its concept, it is extremely inefficient in practice, it complicates evolution and distracts you from the prime purpose of your existence. Cyclical cloning is infinitely more straightforward and predictable. Your reproduction practices have been the subject of one of our scientific seminars. Although slightly less ludicrous than those of the planet Yuujx, where they suffer three separate sexual components, we are mystified by the whole phenomenon. Something clearly went awry in your planet's early evolutionary cycle, but it's difficult at this advanced stage to re-establish normality. Nothing in our procedures actually prohibits sexual activity, presumably because those compiling the rules were never aware of its potential existence.'

'How do you reproduce?'

'That is beyond the scope of my mission,' retorted Kylb.

In fact, he had no idea how he reproduced himself, assuming of course Area Managers did reproduce, but he wasn't going to admit this to a member of a lower subspecies of existence.

'The thought of Local Agents renewing themselves was most alarming, so we decided to eliminate all possible danger by selecting sterile candidates. Inevitably, any choice of agent is a gamble, but we must attempt to minimise the risk factors.'

The sterile member of a lower subspecies of existence pondered. He had in fact been pondering intensely since meeting Kylb. Yes, he supposed, there was little risk of his disappearing into the nearest desert to meditate for 30 years, nor insulting the English and being burnt at the stake. But he was an accountant, not a saviour of mankind, even less the protector of millions of other biological species, most of which he had never even heard of. Perhaps he should decline the offer.

'George, we are relying on you to bring your planet back into conformity with our internal procedures. We spent considerable effort on the selection process before finally choosing you. Please don't disappoint us. I will return in about one year, as defined by your planetary time measurement system. Although I do not expect the mission to be fully completed, I expect a status report detailing your accomplishments, also an action plan explaining how and when outstanding tasks will be accomplished. Otherwise, however fascinating and unique your sub-species might be, I will be obliged to apply Procedure 99–2 and efface you.'

'Er, Keeb?' he queried, mispronouncing the Senior Area Manager's name rather dramatically. Kylb remained unperturbed. He was used to such travesties of phonetic justice.

'Yes, George?'

A short silence ensued. He had innumerable half-formed ideas he desperately needed to discuss with Kylb, so many he did not know where to commence.

'There are over 70,000 other Chartered Accountants in Britain, why did you choose me?'

'Well, not many members of the Institute are sterile. You form part of the Disciplinary Committee which should be an invaluable experience and, well, it was sort of the luck of the draw.'

He was relieved to learn most Chartered Accountants were able to reproduce normally although, if he was a typical case, the main problem facing male accountants was not sterility but finding a female partner willing to be impregnated. That, however, was hardly the point. He needed some detailed guidelines from Kylb.

'Woof,' went Beatrice.

'Quiet,' he shouted, extremely exasperated at being interrupted at such a critical moment. He turned back to the source of light for further counselling.

But it was no longer there.

Whenever possible Kylb avoided providing practical guidelines to his local agents for the simple reason he was far from competent. He also risked sharing responsibility for their failures.

So he had departed.

Without even saying goodbye.

2

Genesis

He walked back through Claremont Woods in a highly disturbed state of mind. He had carefully searched the clearing for electric cables and scorch marks, indeed any tell-tale evidence that something unusual had taken place, that someone or something, Kylb, poltergeist, the ghost of Eamon Andrews or whatever, had been present. Preferably a live television production crew.

But it or they had not. Or, more strictly speaking, his search had revealed nothing other than a typical grassy glade in a Surrey wood. It wasn't rag week at the nearby University of Kingston, nor could camera crews disappear in seconds without leaving signs of their passage. Had he said anything incriminating during the interview, or should that be 'seance'? He supposed he must have made a complete fool of himself. If this became public knowledge he would never dare return to the golf club.

As he and Beatrice walked homewards in silence, the latter extremely miffed at a master who refused to throw any sticks for her to chase, his trained analytical auditor's mind progressively compiled a simple synopsis of the situation, of the events of the past 30 minutes. It enumerated three possible explanations:

- He was asleep in bed. He occasionally experienced strange dreams, he assumed most people did, but this one had seemed so real. Of course, if he had dreamed his meeting with Kylb, the dream in question was still happening and he was still in the midst of it. He was, therefore, at this very moment dreaming about walking

in the woods with Beatrice wondering whether or not he was dreaming about walking in the woods with Beatrice. If only the alarm would ring. Blast! It was Sunday. He would have to rely on Gladys's snoring to wake him up.
- He had suffered a seizure of some kind and was hallucinating from brain damage, hopefully something of a temporary nature.
- He was the Messiah.

None of the options were particularly appealing, only the first would not occasion long-term side effects. Although, admittedly, feeling relieved to see Gladys lying in the adjacent bed when waking up would be an alarmingly unusual experience.

'Morning, George!'

Jonothan Edwards, his rotund next-door neighbour, greeted him affably.

'Discovered any good frauds lately?'

Silence.

'I say, you look singularly peaky. Touch of the 'flu, or an over-indulgence in twelve-year old single malt?'

'No.'

He finally found his voice, although the literary flair of his response lacked a certain evidence of panache.

'Well, keep on trying, we need people like you to keep Britain's companies on the straight and narrow. See you!'

And Jonothan was gone, leaving him alone in the woods with Beatrice. Or dreaming he was alone in the woods with Beatrice. The sudden return to normality of his dream, if dream it was, worried him considerably more than its initial uncanniness. Was he or was he not dreaming? In films people pinched themselves, except they were normally awake trying to prove they were not asleep, not dreaming trying to prove they were awake.

Ouch!

When he woke up, assuming he would soon be waking up, he would inspect his arm for traces of a pinch mark. No, there would be no point. If he were to wake up he would have irrefutable proof he had been dreaming, therefore he would only have dreamed about pinching himself. Unless, in spite of being asleep, his brain had actually ordered his right hand to pinch his left arm. Dream or not, he would still exhibit a pinch mark and nothing would be proven.

Damnation.

He sniffed the moist air. At least his nostrils appeared to be functioning normally. Supposing he wasn't dreaming, he must have suffered a sudden fit, apoplexy, wasn't that the medical terminology? He sighed with relief until realising that being prone to episodic weird dreams was unquestionably preferable to potentially chronic brain malfunction.

UFOs. He glanced around, half expecting E.T. to emerge from behind a tree trunk riding a bicycle. He rapidly eliminated the possibility, how could a Martian know he was called Benson?

He recollected his encounter with the woman, the owner of a remarkably contoured tracksuit, although this was not his reason for remembering her. Hadn't he tripped whilst – well, never mind why he had tripped. He had hit his head on a tree trunk. Instead of seeing stars, as one is apparently supposed to do in such circumstances, he had witnessed a single blinding source of light and hallucinated. That was it! Greatly relieved, he shouted to Beatrice and strode towards the generous-sized mansion he called home.

The Granada, Gladys needed a spacious car even for short journeys, was parked in the driveway. He had never dreamed of his wife, at least not for decades, so encountering her would settle for once and for ever that he was wide awake.

'George, you still haven't mowed the lawn!' His better, or rather larger half emerged through the garage door. 'You've just got enough time before lunch.'

He said nothing.

'Are you all right? You look extremely pale.'

He wondered whether his wife's sudden concern was for the state of his health or for the possibility of their lawn remaining unmown.

'Hit my head on a tree.'

'Well, if you won't watch where you are going. Let me look. Absolutely nothing.'

Yet her husband really was as white as a sheet and acting peculiarly.

'You had better go and sit down,' his wife decided on their behalf.

Gladys, having completed a Girl Guide first-aid course, considered herself a fully competent medical practitioner.

For once he was happy to oblige his wife, he really was feeling light-headed. A quiet sit would do him good, the lawn could wait another week, after all it was not even the end of March.

'Yes, dear,' he replied to his wife as he headed for the living room.

Collapsing into his favourite armchair he closed his eyes briefly, then opened them again. He really did seem to be awake, he felt awake. He picked up the newspaper lying on the table. Sunday 21 March, 2005. An East European nuclear power plant had blown up and Liverpool had overtaken Arsenal at the top of the Premier League. Now, if he were dreaming, it was still Saturday night, the Sunday papers had not yet been delivered. He felt the texture of the paper, it undeniably had the touch of *The Sunday Telegraph*. Gladys was in the garden. He turned on the television and swiftly zapped, the programmes definitely corresponded to those announced in the newspaper. He switched off the set and sat contemplating the blank screen. He could not possibly be reading the Sunday morning newspaper in a Saturday night dream.

What the darnation had happened in that wood? He felt his head. As Gladys had diagnosed, there was nothing, no bump, no scratch, no clotted blood. Surely one does not encounter a tree trunk with sufficient force to hallucinate without leaving some trace on one's scalp? He eyed the mantelpiece clock. It was still too early for a gin and tonic, yet he felt he needed one. He really felt ill, no, not ill, just abnormal. A heart attack, he had suffered a heart attack. The blood supply had ceased pumping oxygen to his brain and he had momentarily experienced visions, perfectly normal in such circumstances. Except there was a glaring contradiction of logic to his supposition; people suffering a major heart attack do not habitually walk four miles back home, chasing after a dog, without realising they have flirted with death. He felt his heart. It was thumping away as regularly as ever.

Puzzled, perplexed and perturbed, he sat staring upwards. Finding little solace in the decidedly grimy ceiling, they would have to redecorate the lounge shortly, he decided to read the paper in order to take his mind off the morning's traumas. The world really was in a mess, with natural disasters occurring practically anywhere, pervading endemic corruption in high places, AIDS spreading faster than ever, another major drug haul, a series of assassinations and car bombs, hundreds of democracy demonstrators jailed in Hong Kong, race riots, polluted lakes and the Prime Minister insisting the latest Mad Cow crisis wasn't really a crisis at all. True, he reflected, the mad cows weren't the crisis, it was the Prime Minister. If they really wanted a mad cow crisis, the voters should re-elect Maggie Thatcher . . .

Kylb was right, the world really was in a terrible mess.

Kylb!

No, this was ridiculous. It was nearly 11.30, he could justify a gin and tonic. Five minutes later, halfway through his second glass, he felt distinctly better, almost back to his customary convivial self.

'Ah, George, are you feeling well enough to lay the table?'

Gladys had entered the room to adjudicate on her husband's state of health.

'Your face has returned to normal, in fact you appear fully recovered,' she pronounced with a wistful glance at the unmown lawn.

He resigned himself to laying the table, arguing would have been useless even if perchance Gladys had failed to notice his empty glass on the table. He selected one of his better bottles of Australian white Chardonnay and, whilst struggling with the corkscrew, managed to reflect upon matters other than incandescent globes commanding him to save civilisation from imminent extraterrestrial extermination.

Sunday evening in Esher. He was once again sitting in his favourite armchair, gazing out of the window, listening to Vivaldi's *Four Seasons* whilst sipping a glass of Glenlivet 12-year old single malt. He should have been relaxed and contented, he usually was when settled into, almost snuggled into, his extremely comfortable albeit faded armchair, appreciating one of the less pompous works of classical music. But tonight was an exception. The music was pleasantly unpompous and the whisky sublime, but he was far from relaxed. Charles Dewey and Kylb kept penetrating his thoughts, distracting him from the lilting melodies of Sr Vivaldi. He had to admit he was no longer certain which season he was listening to.

Lunch had been like most other Sunday lunches in the McHenderson household, with Gladys doing practically all the talking. It was their weekly exchange of gossip and practical information, a post-mortem of the week ended and a planning session for that soon to commence. Issues such as stratospheric ozone deficiency and perennial drought in the sub-Saharan continent were absent from the agenda. Her interpretation of the word 'exchange' differed significantly from the Oxford Dictionary, it had even less in common with the definition carefully crafted by the literary boffins at Collins and Harrap's. 'Exchange' to Gladys meant one person doing all the telling and her husband monopolising the listening. The dry-cleaner had been very pessimistic about removing the stain from his dinner jacket, just what had he been eating? Muriel Braithewaite's *au pair* girl was rumoured to be pregnant, apparently by a neighbour's son and not by Eric her husband. And the upstairs toilet leak was worsening, should she call the plumber or would George inspect it after lunch? Of course, only if he had fully recovered from his encounter with a tree. He dutifully promised to inspect the leak. Like a well-trained auditor, he did not promise actually to mend it, just take a look. Gladys alluded once again to the lawn, rather tactfully for her, so he agreed to extract the lawn-mower from its winter hibernation in the garage. Ever the professional accountant, he did not promise to mow the lawn, merely investigate the lawn-mower.

First things first. Sunday lunch was inevitably followed by his weekly round of golf with Ted, Jimmy and Jean-François, a Swiss lawyer from Geneva currently working in the City. A couple of hours outdoor exercise immediately following Sunday lunch had not initially enthralled him, but Jean-François insisted it prevented overdosing on calories around the dining-table and overdozing on the drawing-room settee afterwards. And since few other Esherites seemed keen to save their livers from urea-saturation and arteries from cholesterol clogging, the golf course was almost empty, enabling the quartet to dawdle along the fairways, chatter animatedly and thoroughly enjoy themselves.

As they arrived at the eighteenth green Jean-François was leading. Nothing unusual, he generally was ahead as they approached the sanctuary of the clubhouse. His partners suffered this recurring ignominy with stoicism, wreaking their revenge by pitilessly mocking his questionable English. He himself was several holes down, inhabitually trailing his opponents. His swing was fine, he thumped the ball with gusto, but his putting was demoralisingly askew; he had difficulty sending his stupid little ball anywhere near the ridiculously minuscule holes, which, in his opinion, had purposefully been placed in totally illogical parts of the greens.

'Oh, go in you little bugger,' he swore to himself silently and with proper golfing decorum as he miss-hit yet another putt.

The 'little bugger' in question swerved to the left and obliged. Jimmy advanced onto the green and started to prepare himself for a leisurely three-foot putt, twitching his legs and waggling his buttocks as all serious golfers should do.

'Miss,' he mouthed silently in an inhabitual display of unsporting pique. The ball, moving unswervingly across the green towards its destination, shuddered to a grinding halt at the edge of the hole.

Returning home he combined 'spending a penny', as Gladys would say, with concluding that the loo leak warranted the expertise of a professional plumber. True to his word, he inspected the lawn-mower. Although working perfectly last October, it was now suffering from acute constipation: nothing exited from its exhaust pipe. After briefly considering the matter he decided against repairing the machine himself, he was not a garage mechanic but an accountant who had no intention whatsoever of arriving at the office the following morning with oil-stained hands and broken fingernails. He loaded the offending contrivance into the Granada's boot; Gladys had the whole week to deliver it to the local repair shop. Meanwhile the lawn could grow in uninhibited abundance whilst celebrating the momentary demise of the ever-lurking petrol-driven horticultural guillotine.

Tea with the Simpsons had been most pleasurable. He surreptitiously observed their latest *au pair* girl without anyone noticing his discerning study of the Austrian physique. After careful inspection he concluded, with her cropped hair and tattered jeans plus a ring piercing her left nostril, that her appearance was radically un-Austrian, nothing like the children in *The Sound of Music*, which proved how little he probably knew about Austria.

'George, you're a financial wizard. Why can't the Government lower interest rates and eliminate taxes, thereby boosting consumption so unemployment will disappear?'

Like many of his ex-public school socialist acquaintances, Gerald Simpson displayed a distinctly utopian approach to life, spending none of his personal fortune on those less fortunate than himself. Perhaps his conscience obliged him to occasionally debate the problems confronting mankind, thereby convincing others he was not totally insensitive to such things as social inequities.

As a Chartered Accountant he was used to such interrogations. He answered Gerald patiently, explaining if taxes were reduced a huge national deficit would accumulate which could only be financed by government borrowing. In order to attract lenders interest rates would be raised, defeating the purpose of reduced taxes. Before long there would be no money left for the government to borrow. One solution would be to print extra bank notes, which would lead inexorably to galloping inflation. The cost of imports would soar, for example the prices of BMWs and Toyotas, not forgetting the petrol to drive them.

'So people would buy British cars, further helping the national economy,' Edwina Simpson interjected. 'Unemployment would disappear altogether!'

'Perhaps for a short while,' he countered, 'but there would be a run on the pound forcing the government to further hike interest rates and clamp down on the economy.'

'Why?'

'Since no one would be purchasing Sterling we would no longer be able to pay our imports.'

'So what?' Edwina was as enthusiastically socialist as her husband but her notions of budgetary control were limited to asking Gerald to transfer generous funds to her e-commerce credit account. 'We wouldn't buy any more imports, Gerald could exchange the Mercedes for a Jaguar.'

'Other countries would retaliate, we would be kicked out of the European Monetary Union,' he argued, realising this was going to be an uphill struggle.

'So what?' chorused both Gerald and Edwina.

'Damn good thing,' Gladys echoed. 'In any case,' she continued, 'if every country reduced its interest rates, the economy would boom globally and there would be no need for backhanded backlashes against Britain from those uppity foreigners.'

He thought he could explain why this wouldn't work, but he wasn't totally certain. In any case, successfully explaining economic technicalities was one thing, convincing Gladys was a totally different matter. He had been about to launch into an attempt when Edwina interrupted him.

'It's the fault of you males for playing stupid political games with our economies. Even currencies have boys' names.'

'Pardon?'

'What about the Frank, the Mark and Sterling?'

'Sterling?'

'You've all heard of Stirling Moss?'

They had.

Edwina's attentions turned to other matters. A new fishmonger was opening in the High Street, so with a suppressed sigh he relinquished the task of elucidating the enigma of world economics. Dear Edwina, early forties, pleasant, kind-hearted and delightful company. And that was it. She wasn't pretty or sexy, nor was she ugly. She was simply Edwina, wife of Gerald. Apart from an occasional 'good morning' he had only ever met her in Gerald's company, in perfect conformity with the propriety of Esher's social mores.

'Another cup of tea, George?' inquired his neighbour and unsuspecting subject of his ruminations as she passed him a plate of cucumber sandwiches.

The world's economic and socio-sexual problems were left to solve themselves without assistance from the Esher Debating Society, Sunday Afternoon Sub-committee.

Gladys flushing the upstairs toilet returned him to the practical realities of evening life in Esher. He counted slowly: five, four, three, two . . .

'George, it's still leaking.'

The bedroom door slammed shut, not because Gladys was particularly irritated by the leaking loo but because she was inveterately unable to close doors gently.

He was once again alone with his music. Sr Vivaldi had reached Autumn, about the middle of October. He recalled the morning's worrisome events. If this is a dream, he mused, it was an unusually long one. Infuriatingly, the one witness to his possible meeting with Kylb could only wag her tail and go 'woof'. Perhaps he should undergo a medical examination, it might happen again. A brain-seizure, not a reappearance of Kylb, since presumably no one hallucinated twice about the same thing. Next time he might be in the middle of a business meeting, his career could be irrevocably ruined. He would ask Gladys to organise something, she was very efficient at such matters and the BUPA would pay.

He attempted to remember, purely out of intellectual interest of course, the exact words 'spoken' by Kylb. He hardly needed to try. He could recall every damn syllable with startling clarity.

Reduce the world's human population from seven to one billion. Even massive floods in China, AIDS and influenza epidemics combined would hardly make a dent. Mass sterilisation? He was infertile, so why not everyone else? Kylb hadn't specified a time limit so the objective could perhaps be achieved painlessly over several centuries. He smiled, there would soon be a crisis in maternity hospitals then, before long, in primary schools. They would be forced to make thousands of teachers redundant. Serve them bloody well right, over-pampered civil servants, it would be just retribution for striking last year. He stopped smiling. Reducing the world's population by six billion would not only not be easy. It would be horrendous. Perhaps he should have negotiated. No, even two billion would be impossible to achieve. He decided to rephrase his last thought: 'that it would have been impossible to achieve if Kylb had existed'. Which of course he did not. Yet, damn it, he had undeniably witnessed something unusual that morning in the wood. Or had he only imagined it?

He sighed, refilled his glass with twelve-year old single malt. Vivaldi wafted harmoniously through the lounge, it was early November, at least musically. Dream or not, there was certainly a painful logic to Kylb's words, the human race was definitely losing control of itself, not only its unimpeded population explosion but the egocentric desecration of the planet it shared with multitudinous other life forms. Perhaps he should resign from the Conservative Party to join the Greens. No, he would be unceremoniously ejected from the golf club as well as numerous other privileged local institutions. Gladys would disown him.

He abruptly sat upright in his chair, nearly spilling his whisky. Of course! That would settle things for once and for all! He simply had to perform, more appropriately fail to perform a miracle. Damnation, why hadn't he thought of that earlier?

He remembered the fairy tale, was it Grimm or Andersen? where some idiot had been granted three wishes and had totally blown it. He would have to tread carefully. Suddenly ending starvation in Africa was a noble thought, but people would start realising something was afoot. In any case, it would take ages to determine if he really had achieved a miracle. The attempt should be conducted discreetly, a mini-miracle, simple and unobtrusive. Imagine he were to announce the end of all disease and nothing happened, he would be the laughing stock of the whole of Esher. His colleagues would never let him forget his impromptu moment of madness, he could never again confront a client, assuming any remained. The Disciplinary Committee of the Institute would withdraw his membership, even though there was nothing in the section on professional conduct specifically barring members from claiming they were Messiahs. They would probably oust him for improper advertising. Also, since Kylb had categorically ordained that he must reduce the human population, eliminating sickness and starvation was not exactly a step in the right direction. Just imagine if millions of barren trees suddenly bore fruit, dried up river beds flowed with sparkling water and empty warehouses were filled overnight with grain. Why not *champagne* and *foie gras*?, might as well do the job properly. Play havoc with world commodity prices. Just imagine those poor dealers trying to explain why their books didn't balance. And there would be another problem, far more appalling to contemplate. He would become instantly famous, mobbed, turned into a hybrid Billy Graham-come-Michael Jackson. Everyone would be pleading with him to perform individual miracles, curing their arthritis and rheumatism, making them wealthy, even reducing their golf handicaps. He would require a full-time personal bodyguard. Gladys would go bananas.

He needed time. He liked the idea of the mini-miracle, something no one else would notice but something sufficiently impressive to convince himself he really was Kylb's appointed Local Agent, or should that be Messiah? After due consideration he decided he preferred the title of Messiah, definitely more appropriate in view of the awesome responsibilities he would be inheriting. From Adolf.

He gazed ceiling-wards again. Vivaldi had reached December 31 and had ceased composing, the room was in silence. The loo leak! But how exactly does one perform a miracle? He tried to recall how Jesus achieved his, but the Bible was sparing on technical details. In any case, Jesus had been a fake. That pretty witch in the television series twitched her nose like a rabbit. Most unseemly, not suitable for a Messiah. Perhaps he should get down on his knees and pray? But to God, to Kylb or to whom?

How about closing his eyes and chanting?

> 'Upstairs loo,
> However do you do,
> It is to thee I speak
> Stop your bloody leak.'

No, this was to be taken seriously.

He closed his eyes and muttered under his breath 'Upstairs toilet, I request that you immediately stop leaking.'

Not very elegant, but the message was unambiguous. He glanced at the ceiling, half expecting to witness blinding lights as in *Close Encounters of the Third Kind*. But nothing happened, no celestial choir singing 'Glory Alleluia', not even the sound of flushing from the toilet to confirm it had received the message. At least no water was pouring down the stairs.

He suddenly tensed, her light had been turned on. He genuinely enjoyed listening to music before retiring to bed, but there was an added attraction. The drawing room bay window overlooked the bedroom of delectable 17-year-old Jennifer, daughter of Jonothan Edwards whom he had met during his morning constitutional. During the day there was nothing special to observe, but Jennifer slept with her curtains open, which was not exactly the point that interested him. Every evening the delectable young lady arrived in her bedroom, turned on the light and proceeded to undress. With a pair of binoculars strategically available in the drawer of his desk, Gladys never looked inside, he was able to follow the ritual in vivid detail. Except for one major inconvenience. Every time she was about to start removing her garments Jennifer moved out of sight, only returning into the vision of the waiting binoculars when safely clad in her pyjamas. Twice, just a miserly two times in years of waiting, she had obliged by starting to remove her blouse before disappearing out of sight. On both occasions he had muttered something impolite and totally unjustified, because Jennifer was a charming young girl with no canine connections whatsoever.

Tonight she was wearing a tight-fitting green jumper and blue jeans. Simple but inspiring. Okay Kylb, he said to himself, show me what your so-called AAA Corporation is capable of. I want a full strip and no tease.

When Jennifer finally walked naked towards her dresser, after having displayed two perfectly sculptured breasts and a delectable dark triangle of pubic hair, his binoculars were trembling. He was uncertain whether this was due to his wishes finally coming true after hundreds of wasted evenings, or the fact he had possibly performed his first miracle. Since he could hardly phone Jennifer to request her opinion on the matter, he was no further advanced in his attempts to confirm the existence of that dratted Kylb. Quick! How about an encore? Across the garden, Jennifer realised her pyjamas were still hanging on the hook near the bedroom door. Frowning, she crossed the room to collect them, then made for the bathroom.

Click, click, click. The record was still turning on the hi-fi system. He stood up, walked across the lounge, carefully placed his treasured record in its sleeve, it was the original 1963 pressing, and turned off the player. He then realised that Messiahs should be able to achieve this without moving, even without an automatic control. On second thoughts, it would be unwise risking one of his valuable vinyls for the mere sake of confirming the existence of a kylbian blob of extraterrestrial luminosity. Tomorrow he would select one of Gladys' records, Engelbert Humperdinck would be perfect.

'Woof, woof, woof!!!' Beatrice, locked up for the night in the pantry by Gladys, must have heard a noise.

'Shut up, you silly little bitch,' her master commanded silently.

And Beatrice shut up.

Feeling disinclined to inspect upstairs water pipes for signs of miracle interventions from nocturnal plumbers, he performed his late night pee in the downstairs toilet. Oh blast, Gladys was snoring again.

'Shut up, you silly big bitch,' he muttered.

A rasp, a snort, a gurgle followed by a swallow and noise of uncertain origin, and Mrs Gladys McHenderson settled down peacefully for the remainder of the night. Her husband, however, was far from joining her in relaxed slumber, the sudden cessation of Gladys' nocturnal gurgitations had achieved the opposite effect to that intended. The unnatural quiet, sign of yet another miracle, no, an as yet unexplained and rather mystifying occurrence, had only worsened his state of agitation. He decided that he would have to perform a whopping humdinger of a miracle, something to convince him unequivocally, without the slightest shadow of doubt, that he was the Chosen One. How about reducing Gladys's weight by about 20 kilos? Or replacing Gladys with the woman in the woods?

Visions of Jennifer's lace brassiere and the adorable little breasts that snuggled inside it increasingly interfered with his quest for the perfect miracle. Tomorrow evening he would command a full frontal followed by a ... what was the opposite of a full frontal? Finally, wondering whether 20 kilos was enough to reduce Gladys to a satisfactory circumference and how the remaining volume should be redistributed, he drifted into the world of dreamless sleep.

3

Exodus

Drrring!

6.45 on Monday morning.

'Sleep well, dear?' inquired Gladys as she heaved herself off the bed.

Without waiting for a reply she advanced towards the bathroom door, which was still wide enough to accommodate her both simultaneously and at the same time.

His brain converted to daytime mode. Obviously Gladys had not shed 20 kilos during the night nor, regrettably, had the gorgeous woman in the woods materialised to replace her. Although, he quickly recalled, he had not formally requested that this should happen, which was probably just as well, it would be a daytime nightmare explaining to Gladys how his unexpected bedmate had happened to materialise from nowhere. Gladys would . . . well what would she do? Catching sight of a voluptuous female fondling her husband, she would hardly ask politely if he had slept well before ambling off to clean her teeth. He then recalled the intention had been for the woman in the woods to replace Gladys, there would be no Gladys to worry about. Well, not quite. His wife would presumably be waking up somewhere, possibly alongside the husband of the woman in the woods. He tried to imagine the scene when the poor fellow discovered he was seeing double, not the same delectable wife twice, but Gladys once. He, George, would be charged with abduction by an enraged neighbour whilst Gladys would sue the innocent husband for nocturnal kidnapping. The scandal! Breakfast would be missed and there was a train to catch.

A train to catch! He hurriedly climbed out of bed and made for the bathroom, recently evacuated by Gladys. As he shaved he concluded that performing miracles wasn't as simple as it sounded, he would have to be excessively careful. Then he grinned at himself in the mirror. Performing bloody miracles! Humbug! The week was about to start. He had three major deadlines to respect before Thursday noon, one articled clerk to fire and another to hire, and Charles Dewey to sort out. Although, being realistic, it was more probably that Mr Dewey would be making mincemeat out of him.

Blast, he had cut himself shaving. It was all Gladys's fault. She was sitting on the toilet, at least he presumed she was because that is what women supposedly did in such places, when suddenly she screamed through the oak-panelled door.

'George, I think the leak's stopped!'

His razor, instead of smoothly following the contours of his Adam's apple, as in television commercials, attempted to amputate it, removing a sliver of skin in the process.

Damn, where was that special stick to stop the bleeding? No, he was not going to ordain his blood to stop flowing. He had suffered enough bloody 'miracles' for the time being. Although, he mused, this one would presumably be bloodless.

'Cut yourself shaving?' inquired Gladys, proud of her powers of reasoning, powers so extensive she was able to deduce a man descending to breakfast clutching a pad of red cotton wool to his throat had just circumcised part of his neck with a razor.

'I keep telling you to buy an electric razor.'

Yes, he thought, you do keep telling me.

He parked his car in its usual place outside Esher station. One of the advantages of departing early was the ability to park where one wished, in his case only yards from the platform entrance. The station clock announced to the world it was 7.44, he had nearly ten minutes to wait for the 7.52 fast train to Waterloo. Theoretically that is, he reflected as he waited on the platform, since South West Trains published timetable warranted classification under science fiction. Admittedly, on the rare mornings he inadvertently arrived a few seconds late, the 7.52 had left precisely at 7.52, abandoning him and numerous other city commuters who shared his presumption that their train would never actually leave on time.

In spite of the timetable's inherent flexibility, he always tried to arrive at the station in good time to buy his newspaper, amble onto the platform and catch his train in a relaxed frame of mind, at whatever time it eventually condescended to put in an appearance.

It was cool but not cold. After all yesterday had been gloriously warm, nearly like summer. No, it normally rained in July and August, nearly like what summer should be like. As usual the platform was crowded, mostly with well-groomed males in dark business suits, stockbrokers, insurance brokers, bankers and company directors, all setting off to manipulate the planet's markets whilst surviving another day in the financial anarchy of the City.

She was there!

Waiting for a train is not the world's most exhilarating occupation. At Esher, thanks to the vagaries of South West Trains, loitering impatiently on a platform was more an integral part of daily life than a transient pasttime, with an element of suspense thrown in for good measure. Having announced the late arrival of the train, which standard excuse would they use to explain the delay? Thanks to the imagination of certain South West Trains employees, some of the excuses had an undeniable entertainment value that alleviated the feeling of frustration.

During these enforced pauses he enjoyed surreptitiously observing his fellow travellers, trying to deduce their professions, imagine what they were thinking. Some passengers he knew vaguely, enough to accord a nod or mumble a quick 'good morning'. However, trains, especially commuter trains, were for reading or ruminating, for dozing or dreaming, for planning how to survive the working day that lay ahead, not for polite smalltalk. It would be disastrous to inadvertently start up a conversation with someone at Esher and be lumbered with him all the way to Waterloo.

There was usually a smattering of women standing forlornly on the platform. Emancipation had attained even the inner sanctum of the City. Women. Not ladies. Female commuters were women. Ladies did not rush to catch the 7.52 to Waterloo, they were still enjoying a relaxed breakfast in their mansions before settling down to the day's socialising. Like Gladys.

The 'she' who had caught his attention that morning may not have been a lady, but she was a superb specimen of womanhood. About 25 and a regular commuter, she invariably dressed to overemphasise her physical assets. She was a miniskirt connoisseur, knowing how to create the maximum effect from the minimum of material, displaying exactly what she wanted everyone to see, never exposing a centimetre more than was acceptable, acceptable to her way of seeing things or, more to the point, of not seeing things. She must have been aware of his glances, plus those of the majority of male commuters who habitually caught the 7.52. He could never quite conclude whether she wanted to be watched. Which was more impolite, to goggle appreciatively at her cherubic charms or to ostentatiously ignore her hyperbolic hips? The anti-chauvinist little prick-teaser, she deserved to be taught a lesson for repeatedly taunting half the members of the London Stock Exchange, Lloyd's and the Bank of England. Her morning antics were probably creating more disruption to the City's money markets than the inept politicking of the current Chancellor of the Exchequer. Yes, revenge would be sweet, but how? Moses, one of his former colleagues he reminded himself sardonically, had parted the Red Sea. Perhaps he, calling upon the unbridled powers of nature, could also do a little parting of his own? A puff of wind, just enough to lift the offending hemline . . .

The owner of the miniskirt, in sweet innocence of the improbable and theoretically impossible ignominy about to ascend upon her, was preening herself whilst surreptitiously eyeing her fellow passengers, seeking out those studying her curvaceous contours as they eagerly awaited a glimpse of lace, or should that be Lycra? Whilst studiously pretending to read their newspapers.

For the honour and vindication of masculine mankind, he briefly closed his eyes and silently chanted:

'Miss Prick-teaser, you right little bint
We don't want a glance, not a mere hint
All of us gentlemen, city slickers
Want a full blown look at your sweet little knickers.'

Highly ashamed of his literary achievements, he waited. Nothing happened. Nothing whatsoever. The miniskirt clung steadfastly to its owner's upper thighs. Although tremendously relieved at not being the Messiah, he was also mildly disappointed, having become increasingly intrigued with the possibilities afforded by his kylbian powers, which included pleasurably anticipating his *rendezvous* with Jennifer that evening.

The Portsmouth express, even later than usual, entered the station at high speed. A violent gust of wind blew along the platform, surrounded the prick-teaser and swirled heavenwards, except that heaven, at least for the male population of Esher station, was a mere three feet from the ground as a delightful pair of white minibriefs came into view and, for several lovely lingering seconds, remained there. The woman uttered a cry of distress, successfully attracting the attention of those not already admiring the womanly manifestation. She desperately turned away from the crowd of spectators, providing them with an encore, one sublime rump her briefs failed dismally to camouflage.

The Portsmouth express continued its onward journey, the force of gravity regained control of the circumstances, permitting the miniskirt to return to its normal protective position concealing its owner's nether regions. And the commuters of Esher returned to pretending to read their newspapers.

'Well,' he said to himself, smirking seditiously, 'I did ask for a "full blown" look. Thanks, Kylb!'

A train arrived. It was not the 7.52 a mere eight minutes late, it was the 7.36 over half an hour behind schedule. Realising that in the world of South West Trains one must be thankful for small mercies, he joined the jostling crowd and, thanks to a combination of experience and some astute below the belt shoving, secured a coveted window seat. After smiling knowingly at fellow passengers who had witnessed the same lycrean delights as himself, he settled down to reading *The Daily Telegraph*. It was hardly inspiring. Declining educational standards combined with violence in classrooms, more mad cows, unemployment rising steadily towards 4,000,000 which, the government proudly insisted, was considerably lower than in either France or Germany. More floods, this time in Peru, had made thousands homeless, the hole in the ozone layer was now the size of Wales although, luckily for the Welsh, it was still situated somewhere over Antarctica. Japan's stock market was collapsing whereas Hong Kong no longer owned one, cholera and tuberculosis were again rampant not only in Africa but in several European countries, Russia's latest president was no longer able to walk upright and the United Nations peace-keeping forces in Hungary were continually unearthing scenes of Serbian sadism. The world, to quote Kylb, really seemed to be heading for disaster. Even worse, the human race was far from behaving as if prepared to lead itself, plus the rest of the planet's multifarious life forms, towards a safer future.

Then there was the Pope declaring that the 60-year-old woman pregnant with eight foetuses, subsequent to taking fertility drugs, should have none aborted even if it meant certain death for them all. This really infuriated him. Poor pathetic woman, desperately swallowing procreation pills to have a child and now condemned to die for displaying her maternal instincts. Nature provided lionesses with eight teats. They were equipped to have large litters. Women, with only two breasts, were presumably meant to produce no more than twins. That pompous pontificating Pontiff in Rome deserved to be taught a lesson. How would he react if his own wife was about to die? No, that was hardly likely. Notwithstanding, how dare he preach God's will to mankind on matters he presumably little understood, at least from a practical point of view. It would be interesting to learn Kylb's opinions on contraception. On second thoughts, his occult visitor didn't seem particularly cognisant on such matters although, apart from the process of procreation, he had proven remarkably familiar with the sorry state of the world. Unless, he immediately corrected himself, his own brain was still short-circuiting subsequent to its sharp contact with a wooden tree trunk.

The train pulled into Waterloo Station two minutes early. No, at the risk of sounding pedantic, he pronounced it nearly 20 minutes late since this was the 7.36 and not the 7.52. He descended with the jostling crowd, ready for the eight minute saunter to his office.

As he walked he became increasingly frustrated and despondent. Kylb or no Kylb, his fellow human beings did seem to be riding the fast lane to an early extinction, taking thousands of other innocent species with them. Kylb's words made sense, the timing of his visit made sense, it was just Kylb that didn't make sense. Also, choosing a Chartered Accountant was surely pushing matters to the outer limits of the credibility gap. Or was it? There was nothing wrong with accountants. Who could trust a lawyer? Knowing their devious twisted minds, the one chosen would use miracles to create inextricable conflicts all over the place, disputes that could only be settled by highly-paid lawyers. A doctor or banker would be useless. Both existed in blinkered dream worlds. Of course, nothing could be worse than a politician. Anyone disagreeing with their egotistical ideological idiosyncrasies would be ripe for rapid biomolecular disintegration. There would soon be fewer Britons left than giant pandas, which would presumably displease Kylb, who had pronounced strongly against selective elimination. Accountants, after all, were highly respectable citizens, fair-minded and totally dependable. One should be proud to add the initials FCA after one's name since this did not imply 'fucking chartered accountant', as numerous brainless idiots had joked to him over the years. Bright chap that Kylb, he and his fellow Institute members could be counted on to solve the crises facing Mother Earth.

Assuming the Senior Area manager from AAA Corporation existed. For, without his support, even the nation's Chartered Accountants would assuredly fail to save the planet from the scourges of mankind.

He walked past one of London's many churches. Slowing down, he gazed towards the impressive building, half-expecting to hear sweet music pour forth as angels fluttered around the spire singing in perfect operatic hallelujahrial harmony. Instead, pigeons wandered around the worn and pollution-stained gravestones and a decrepit old tramp sat alone on a bench, staring bleary-eyed at nothing in particular.

Was he or was he not the Messiah? Ascertaining that two nubile females wore white undergarments, stopping Beatrice from barking and Gladys from snoring, plus possibly mending a Shanks toilet, did not constitute unequivocal proof of his new identity, his new messianic mission in life. If he continued like this he was more likely to be arrested for sexual misdemeanours. Messiah or not, he, George McHenderson FCA, still had his personal reputation to consider. If only Kylb had left some proof of his passage, a visiting card or portable telephone where he could be contacted in case of emergencies. Supposing he got himself into deep water, would Kylb come to his assistance? Unlikely. He must tread very carefully.

Not treading carefully enough, he stepped in a dog turd just before arriving at the entrance to his office.

'Morning, George.'
  'Morning, Richard.'
  'Morning, Mr McHenderson.'
  'Morning, Sally.'
  'Morning, sir.' (from a newly recruited articled clerk)
  'Morning.'
  'Morning, Janet.'
  Janet was already sitting at her desk. Dear Janet. Early forties, a bit short and plump, she wore glasses and unfashionable clothes, yet she radiated a natural charm and friendliness. Dear Janet, when hired ten years earlier she had been delightfully carefree and extremely pretty. Time, however, had been harsh on her. Her marriage disintegrated, she then lived with a married man who radically changed his mind about divorcing his wife when Janet joyously announced a happy event. He even refused to pay his share of the abortion, the one that left her sterile. He himself knew about this because Janet was more than a secretary, she was a friend, strictly a business friend. They never met outside the office context. She was someone he trusted implicitly, depended upon, could confide in and, exaggerating only marginally, was the woman who replaced the daughter he had never achieved and the wife he never should have married. He related the antics of the prick-teaser at Esher station, which is possibly why she always wore such long dresses. But he never mentioned Jennifer, feeling highly ashamed of his disposition towards voyeurism. He had occasionally wondered what Janet was like as a woman, but this was idle curiosity. She was a lovely person, someone to be treated with respect, as a fellow human being and not as a female. Prying into her sexuality would break the spell that bound them together.
  He had just finished thumbing through the mail when Janet arrived with the coffee. She smiled at the four piles on the desk. She knew the procedure well:
  Pile 1: Waste paper basket
  Pile 2: Transmit to someone else for action
  Pile 3: Immediate filing

Pile 4: To be read again more carefully
'A pleasant weekend?'

Janet never referred to her boss as either George or Mr McHenderson when they were alone. With clients and junior staff he was 'Mr McHenderson' with a slight Scottish accent, although her boss had not the faintest notion where the 'Mc' had originated. With longstanding members of staff who referred to their Senior Partner as George, Janet was equally at ease using her boss's first name. He was always relaxed in her company. They made a good team, especially during moments of crisis which, as in most accounting firms, were far from infrequent. He occasionally invited her to lunch, a simple affair in the nearby pizzeria, certainly nothing ostentatious, not because of his being stingy but because anything extravagant could be wrongly interpreted by the other members of staff and by Janet herself. Mostly they chatted in his office over morning coffee or afternoon tea, or whilst sorting through routine administrative matters.

If he were to tell anyone about Kylb he would first confide in Janet. But, before explaining matters to her, he still needed to convince himself whether he was the chosen leader of mankind or an accountant suffering from a rapidly spreading brain tumour or aggravated middle-age crisis. He was still searching for the ideal maxi-miracle to perform when the phone rang.

One of the senior auditors had discovered some unusual accounting entries in a computer listing and she wanted urgent advice before tackling the Foreign Exchange Manager of the bank concerned. The audit manager was on vacation, so her call had been redirected to the senior partner. With the Nick Leeson scandal at the forefront of his mind, he thought he should perhaps investigate the matter personally. Also, the trip to the canyons of the City would take his mind off more esoteric matters.

He returned to his office at noon, pleased and relieved. He was pleased because the strange accounting entries were the result of a parasite in the computer system, a minor glitch and not some major currency speculation that had gone horribly awry. When presented with yards of computer listing that could have been edited in ancient Egyptian, he had desperately scoured the jumble of figures, despairingly pretending to understand what the hieroglyphics were meant to signify. Encountering figures printed slightly more to the left than others, he placed his finger in the middle of the muddle and asked petulantly the reason for the inconsistency. It had taken the highly impressed auditor 30 minutes to trace the origins of the problem. He was also relieved because the last thing he relished, with Kylb and Charles Dewey lurking ominously at the back of his mind, was another major auditing crisis.

Meanwhile, back in the confines of the bank, the senior auditor was bitterly disappointed. She had imagined herself being interviewed on CNN explaining to the world how she had unearthed the fraud of the century.

Janet was waiting for him, looking extremely grim. What now? She handed him a fax from Charles Dewey:

'Urgently need audit clearance on inventory valuation so we can proceed with publication of financial reports.
   Very best wishes,
      Charles'

The bastard.

He stared out of the window seeking inspiration. There were no flashes, no blinding lights, just the faceless windows of the office block on the opposite side of the street.

'How can I nail the dishonest, thieving niggardly little villain?' he asked himself desperately.

Something clicked in his head. It didn't feel like a brain tumour exploding but, endowed with meagre experience in such medical matters, he was far from convinced and braced himself for the worst. However, no grey matter started oozing from his ears and he felt perfectly normal.

But of course! It was so obvious! The floods in Africa had wiped out homes and railways, but also road networks. The water had submerged whole tracts of land, especially low-lying areas along river banks, exactly the sort of place timber companies sited their saw mills and warehouses. Wood warped and rotted, especially when it had been cut into planks ready for shipment, except there was nothing to ship them along. The rivers were unnavigable, the roads and railways no longer existed. And, idiot that he was, he had not even reacted to the article in *The Daily Telegraph* which told of guerrilla uprisings in Eastern Africa, the insurgents profiting from the confusion and misery caused by the floods. A World Bank official had announced aid would be frozen until the democratically elected authorities had regained full control of the territories concerned. In layman's language, the promised funds would remain in the bank's vaults for years to come.

He sat down, reached for a blank fax form, picked up his fountain pen, and wrote:

Dear Charles,

Agree on urgency to confirm inventory situation. However require dated photo confirmation and back-up certified report from your local plant manager that timber stocks have not been washed away or otherwise damaged by floods. Also that the Kuambali-Banbulu and Huanki-Freetown roads are operating normally so that finished goods can be shipped (photocopy of newspaper articles will suffice). Also confirmation that World Bank financial aid to Mozambique has been validated so railway reconstruction work can proceed without delay.

Sorry to be a little pedantic but I am certain you will agree that the issue is of vital importance from an audit viewpoint.

As soon as requested documents received will issue unqualified audit report.

Very best wishes,
George

P.S. Haven't the UFM rebels recently taken Huli, which is only ten miles from the Kani regional depot?

He showed the fax to Janet.
'By George,' she whistled.
Her boss presumed she was referring to one of the nation's ex-kings or a certain dragon-slaying saint, not to himself. He smiled maliciously at his secretary.
'Show it to Richard and, if he agrees, transmit it straight away.'
The fax was indeed transmitted straight away.

No reply had been received from Charles Dewey when he left the office to commute back to the pleasant pastures of Esher. For once he had no early-evening committee meeting or business dinner, he could therefore catch the 17.58 from Waterloo. His train left on time. Strange, South West Trains seemed to work better in the evening. She wasn't on the train. She never was. He had never seen the delightful owner of provocative miniskirts during the return trip to Esher. A mystery, she must arrive home somehow. It was going to be interesting to see what she was wearing the following morning, assuming she dared make an appearance at the station.

In his compartment there was no one worth studying. The older passengers were silently reading newspapers whilst two of the younger commuters were avidly tapping away on portable computers. It was difficult to guess what was plugged into whom. He idly wondered whether the youngsters concerned could survive unattached to their keyboards or, if you unhooked them, they collapsed from instantaneous megabyte starvation. He managed to catch a glance at one of the screens: *Death Invader* had scored 6,000 points as he advanced towards annihilating the *Trolls of Govenderland* but *Shining Man* was fighting back with his *Patrionic Shield*. His computerised commuter companion was unlikely to be an accountant.

The scenery was as boring as the previous Friday evening and no doubt as depressing as it would be the following morning, relentlessly uninspiring until you reached Wimbledon. With nothing to distract him, he gazed unseeingly out of the window, his eyes half-focusing on blurred images as London's soot-stained inner suburbs flashed past the train. His mind, however, was anything but inactive. He must solve the problem of Kylb for once and for all, preferably before he made a public fool of himself. But how? Stop the earth revolving? Make the River Thames flow backwards? No, he was not yet ready for public manifestations. Turn Gladys into a frog? On second thoughts, a toad? Ah Gladys! Would you be as irritating, as infuriating, as mind-bogglingly supercilious if you only weighed 60 kilos?, 60 kilos of delightful wanton womanhood, sculptured like the day I married you, no you married me. I've often wanted to cut you down to size, perhaps thanks to Kylb my wish will finally come true. Supposing, just supposing, you did transform into the Gladys of 1987, would I again climb into your bed and ..? Perhaps he should first repair her chipped tooth and remove the mole from her chin. There was nothing wrong with perfection. But would he, could he, should he ..? As the train clattered its way through Wandsworth he thought back to their nuptials, that first night at the hotel in Basingstoke. In those days three sets of squash had been less tiring than one Gladys love session, also considerably less dangerous.

The train screeched and shuddered to a halt in Esher. One of the more distinguished passengers descending from his carriage had not only failed to identify his perfect miracle, he had forsaken all attempts during the latter half of the journey.

On the way back from the station he visited the St Francis of Assisi Home for Children. He knew Gladys disapproved of his involvement. She admitted the home provided a worthwhile service to the community, but it was run by

Catholics. One had to be very careful with Catholics. The thought of her husband conversing with nuns genuinely troubled her, although she could not explain why, merely stating he and Sisters of Mercy did not intermingle. She assured him she was not expecting him to seduce the younger nuns, nor them to convert him to their Papist ways, but the whole thing distressed her.

Several years previously one of the golf club members had asked him to assist the home. It was undergoing a tax investigation and the inspector was threatening dire penalties if it failed to rapidly provide valid accounting documents. The nuns had been ready to confess their sins and be pardoned, but the tax inspector was Methodist and unmoved by their pleas for clemency. So he had spent a weekend and several evenings sorting out the confusion. Catholic or not, the sins were hardly cardinal, originating from a filing system which insured every document was filed religiously rather than logically. Consequently, not even the most earnest prayers could unearth the invoices requested by the tax inspector.

Having saved the home a modest fortune, he had been invited by the person in charge, someone irredeemably inferior at accounting but eminently superior at mothering, to tour the centre and meet some of her flock. He hesitated, frightened of the unknown, for he rarely associated with children, let alone deformed ones. But nuns can be very persuasive. He found himself deeply moved by his encounter with the pathetic misshapen forms known as inmates, children born human beings and subsisting as human beings, yet not considered human beings by other human beings. Initially he had been ill at ease, shying away from contact, but the children suffered few such inhibitions. They smiled at him, they came to hold his hand, they eagerly wanted to show him their toys, their paintings, where they slept. They enthusiastically attempted to communicate with him. In some cases the Mother Superior was able to decipher their sounds, thereby permitting some form of rudimentary understanding.

Without the slightest trace of offence he had likened them to Beatrice, their trust, their simplicity, their joy and excitement at the slightest chance to demonstrate anything. He was soon pushing them on swings, playing ball, talking to them, even though he doubted they could comprehend. When a couple of the more severe cases shrank from him in terror, he felt slighted. The others he piggybacked before allowing himself to be commandeered for some boisterous ring-a-ring-a-roses. Away from the tension of the office and the social claustrophobia of the golf club he found he could relax and before long he was almost one of them.

He had offered the home permanent tax and accounting assistance. Over the years he never lost his strong reaction to the children's physical appearance, but he became very fond of several of the inmates. Always hurt when rejected, he realised it was nothing personal. He had enormous admiration for the nuns, the way they sacrificed their lives, rarely seeing progress, knowing intimately they probably never would.

Although he visited regularly, it was always on business. Somehow, he felt purely social calls would be committing himself too deeply. But he always played with the children before leaving. And felt tears welling in his eyes when he once saw a drawing of himself adorning one of the playrooms.

A recent occurrence had shocked and moved him profoundly. One of the teenage girls, a dwarf and amongst the most seriously mentally retarded inmates, yet one of the more demonstrative and affectionate, had suddenly advanced on him, trying to embrace him passionately. He had struggled until she ran away screaming. The Mother Superior explained that, under their physically deformed exteriors, most of the adolescents developed normal romantic urges, urges that could not be satisfied, more accurately urges that should never be allowed to be satisfied. Sally, the girl in question, had to be permanently drugged to prevent sexual activity leading to impregnation. Being a Catholic institution, there was no question of abortion if their precautions failed.

'You see Mr McHenderson, you might not perceive her misshapen body as belonging to a woman, but she sees you as a male. It's not love, it's a simple and very powerful animal need.'

'But surely, because you refuse to accept contraception, you are condemning Sally to a form of medical sterilisation.'

'Perhaps. All we can do is pray that we are doing what is best. God, in his wisdom, will make the final judgement.'

He had said nothing but, as his body aged ungracefully, he could share Sally's frustrations. He considered Gladys with her chronic weight deformity, sensing some comprehension of her possible anguish, but he never found the courage to take the necessary reconciliatory steps to make amends with his wife. If only Gladys had not been so rigid, imperial and unyielding, perhaps things would have been different. He never described his visits in detail, sensing stories of gallivanting with children, however deformed, would only hurt her feelings. After all, her childlessness was entirely his responsibility. She had sacrificed motherhood out of respect for her marriage vows.

The next time he encountered Sally she was once again fully under the influence of her drugs, he could therefore return to playing the role of 'Uncle Georgie' to her and the other members of his adoptive family.

The drive was empty, Gladys was not yet home from wherever she had gone. Monday. She was at the Christian Union, she was helping prepare the church fête which was to take place the following Saturday. No, not helping, Gladys never helped. Running the church fête.

He looked around the garden. The grass really did require mowing and the apple trees urgently needed pruning. Quick, there was no one in sight. He closed his eyes and wished his lawn mown and the apple trees pruned to perfection, something even Percy Thrower would admire.

He took a deep breath and opened his eyes.
It was.
They had been.
He was the Messiah.
Oh, Holy Shit!
Which reminded him that he had an urgent need to attend to.

On returning to the garden he inspected the Granny Smiths and Bramleys. They were trimmed exquisitely, even he could not have pruned them more expertly. The Williams and Conferences were still in a sorrowfully bedraggled state, but then Williams and Conferences produce pears and he had only specified apple trees. A quick closing of the eyes and the offending trees were clipped as professionally as their apple cousins. He heard a car approaching. He knew by the way it changed gears, practically without assistance from the clutch, that the driver was Gladys. Panic! The lawn and fruit trees, what to do with them?

He closed his eyes and pleaded.

'George, you really must mow the lawn next weekend.'

Gladys was back, harassed and bothered by the innumerable idiots who thought they knew how to organise a church fête. And, when she finally arrives home, what sight greets her? That pretentious husband of hers gazing in admiration at his overgrown, weed-ridden garden.

'Yes, dear,' he replied as he made his way towards the gin decanter.

Having listened patiently throughout dinner whilst Gladys carefully explained in excruciating detail why the fête would be better organised if she were given absolute control, he finally managed to escape to the lounge. Having suffered the news, he was listening to the weather forecast. The announcer was excitedly promising heavy showers over Wales and the Midlands when one of his viewers concocted an amusing little prank. The broadcast was live, so how about moving those nasty little black cloud symbols over to the East Coast whilst the weather man was looking into the camera, his back to the chart? The forecaster gulped in astonishment when he saw Newcastle was suddenly destined for a rain-soaked afternoon, whereas Cardiff was now promised blue skies and bright sunshine. A few muttered mumbles about cloud and rain towards the end of the week and the next programme was being announced. He smiled, wondering which weather prediction, the Meteorological Office or the McHenderson variant, would be the more accurate.

He switched off the television and sat down at his desk. Some serious thinking was required. He had been selected to save the world. No, he must not jump to hasty conclusions. It seemed increasingly possible that he had been chosen by an extraterrestrial organisation to perform an important task. Assuming this was true, just for the moment, strictly within the context of that evening's theorising, he would somehow have to convince the rest of the world of his appointment. He still had serious misgivings about being escorted ignominiously to the local institution for gentle folk, also known as the Esher 'funny farm', where he could no doubt spend the rest of his days exchanging experiences with Napoleons and a wide variety of other demented souls from Julius Caesar to Robespierre. He must not precipitate matters. He tried to imagine his reaction if Gladys were to suddenly announce she was the chosen one, before launching into instantaneous lawn-mowing, nocturnal fixing of loo leaks and . . . No, it was unlikely that the male population of Esher would suddenly find their trousers around their ankles, with Y-fronts exposed for the ladies to admire. What would she fabricate? He shuddered inwardly as he imagined himself led upstairs by a sex-starved Messiah to discharge his conjugal obligations. His life would be in danger. No it wouldn't, she would never choose him. Who would be the lucky suitor? The vicar? The milkman? Her best bet would be Mike Tyson or a Japanese sumo wrestler. He shuddered again and returned to more immediate problems.

True to his audit training, the newly appointed Local Agent decided to establish a job description. For nearly an hour he pondered, scribbled, pondered, erased, scratched out and pondered. Rereading his jottings, he had the distinct impression that things were far from clear in his mind. Another ten minutes pondering clarified somewhat the situation, things were indeed definitely far from clear in his mind.

LOCAL AGENT AAA CORPORATION

Mission
Save the human race from being unceremoniously zapped out of existence by # or . . . • . (sorry about probable incorrect spelling)

Deadline
Not quite certain but at least one year.

Team
Myself.

Essential Goals To Be Achieved
Reduce human population to about one billion.
Stop polluting planet.
Stop eliminating other life forms.
Stop launching satellites into space
Stop sending radio messages which attempt to communicate with other centres of life.

Budget
Not certain.

Action Plan
Various approaches seem possible:
* Go it alone, enforcing objectives by threats and performing miracles. Effective but undemocratic.
* Enlist help of friends, create an ad hoc committee. Problem of deciding whom to select as members.
* Submit the problem to the competent authorities. For example: British Government, Church of England, Nato, United Nations, The Queen, Institute of Chartered Accountants In England and Wales. (Not very reassuring, apart

from the ICAEW. Are any of the above authorities competent? Kylb presumably does not think so.)
Step one: *Perform discreet maxi-miracle*
Step two: *Decide which of three approaches to adopt (see above)*
Step three: *Not quite certain, to be honest not certain at all. Suggest completing first two steps before deciding on how to tackle Step Three.*

Other Comments
* *Must keep this confidential for the time being.*
* *How to deal with religious authorities? Mecca and Dalai Lama should be fairly friendly, but Rome likely to be upset. Is the Pope capable of ordering me to be eliminated by some Franciscan hit squad à la* Salman Rushdie? *Even if Rome proves amenable, the Rev. Paisley and those IRA fanatics might decide to eradicate me. Thought: if they did blow me up, am I immortal? How to determine whether I am? Best not to try for the time being.*
* *How to eliminate six billion people and remain popular?*
* *As a business perk do I qualify for inclusion in the surviving billion?*
* *What species need to be saved? Don't most of them live in the Amazon and are they not nasty insects, priority candidates for a good dose of insecticide? Cannot see any point in saving them. Better consult David Attenborough.*
* *Don't see how I can avoid becoming famous. I'll need a new suit and haircut. What about a publicity manager, not forgetting a damn good lawyer?*
* *Most world leaders have sophisticated wives. Gladys makes even Nikita Kruschev's wife look stylish. I couldn't possibly arrive for a diplomatic reception at Buckingham Palace or the White House with her in tow. Should I pursue my idea to remodel her? The biggest danger is that she will try and take over. And probably succeed. After all, anyone who can run a church fête as well as she thinks she does must be a natural for the job of Messiah.*
PS: What is a female Messiah called? Messiahess? Obviously

2,000 years ago no one considered the possibility of female incumbents.

'Working late, dear?' the recently rejected candidate for the position of Saviour inquired after her husband.
'Yes, I have an important meeting tomorrow and the bloody figures don't add up.'
'Don't swear, George. How many times have I told you it's not dignified.'
He did not answer. He had lost count years ago.
Instead he muttered, 'Sorry, dear'.
Not that he was, but it was the most effective way of sending Gladys Joyce bedwards in the minimum of time.
'Goodnight.'
'Goodnight.'
Once again alone, he reread his jottings. When elaborating audit programmes, he had his manuals and Institute guidelines to provide the answers. One simply applied the rules. Surely the AAA Corporation could have at least supplied an instructions manual. With or without guidelines, apparently without guidelines, he seemed to have been lumbered with a goddam-almighty mission to perform, and there seemed to be no obvious way to squirm out of the imbroglio. Blast Kylb. If only he did not exist. But then perhaps he didn't. But then again if he did, and his Local Agent ignored the fact, the day of reckoning would be infinitely worse than a confrontation with Charles Dewey.

He selected a record, Rimsky-Korsakov's *Scheherazade* with Pierre Monteux conducting the London Symphony Orchestra. The record was old and numerous scratches had infiltrated into the Russian's original score, but he preferred this recording to all others. After careful consideration, he selected a glass of Armagnac Fine Champagne to accompany the relaxing yet scintillating melodies of the opus and sank despondently into his armchair.

The music was filling his senses, taking his mind to the world of Arabian nights and unveiled nymphets, when Jennifer's light came on. Jennifer! He had forgotten the encore he promised himself. Dare he? It would be dastardly unfair to the poor girl, she was taking her GCSE exams shortly. Yet he needed something to distract his mind from Franciscan terror squads joining with the R.U.C. to make instant mincemeat out of him. He finally gave in to temptation.

Her Marks and Spencer T-shirt substituted for seven veils as Jennifer danced an extremely energetic and outrageously erotic belly-dance, especially the *grande finale*. Rimsky-Korsakov would have been proud of her.

Putting the record back in its sleeve, he glanced at the photo of the Arabian-looking lady on the cover. She seemed to be pretty upset about something, her smile was more a snarl.

'Cheer up,' he whispered and the scowl changed into a radiant smile.

He thought about removing the scratches from the record, but decided they were now an integral part of the orchestra's performance and should remain.

Hiding his messianic 'action plan' in his desk, tucked away from the prying eyes of Gladys and the cleaning lady, he switched off the lamp then glanced briefly towards Jennifer's window. There was nothing to see. He assumed the poor girl had already collapsed exhausted into her bed and turned off the light. Pleasantly distracted from his awesome responsibilities, he relieved himself in the upstairs no longer leaking loo and headed towards the bedroom.

4

Reflectus

Breakfast. Gladys, recovered from her frustrations of the previous evening, had returned to her usual bumptious bossy self. She was almost bouncy, metaphorically speaking, of course. No doubt the thought of further terrorising nincompoop church helpers had rekindled her ingrained vivacity.

'Oh, by the way, George, the vicar wants to see you.'

He nearly choked on a cornflake. How had the vicar found out about Kylb? Perhaps Jesus hadn't been a fake and was mounting a counter-attack.

'George, don't panic. He's not going to ask you to confess your sins, he's C. of E., not a damned Papist. Can you please try to phone him sometime today.'

When Gladys pronounced the word 'can' in such a way, he knew from bitter experience that closing the phrase with a question mark was redundant. This was no polite request, no inquiry into whether, perhaps, her husband could possibly find the time to contact the Reverend Jeffrey Marsh, at his convenience of course, sometime during the day.

With the matter closed, as far as she was concerned, Gladys sailed out of the kitchen, not gracefully like some eighteenth-century clipper but more like the *Torrey Canyon*.

What the devil could the local vicar want of him? The Devil! Perhaps Lucifer had decided to transfer his corporate headquarters to Planet Earth, its polluted environment being more conducive than Hades for running his business ventures. Or his Milky Way Mafia wished to claim blood money. Alternatively, and less alarmingly, the intergalactic securities commission was about to investigate AAA Corporation's earthbound activities, the Reverend Marsh was their newly-appointed local inspector. Well, there was only one way to find out. He would phone the Reverend once he reached the office.

As he munched his toast and marmalade his thoughts returned momentarily to Jennifer, making him feel distinctly guilty, it had been an extremely energetic and immeasurably unveiled belly dance. The poor girl must be feeling more than a little stiff. How on earth would she explain a hernia to her parents?

Time to leave for the office.

Although the station platform was as crowded as ever, one person was conspicuously absent, the owner of numerous extremely short miniskirts and one delectable rump.

'The 7.52 to Waterloo will be arriving approximately fifteen minutes late,' intoned South West Trains, not even offering an excuse for the delay.

He swore under his breath. Long live competition. If your train arrived late you fired the driver for incompetence instead of suffering supercilious smirks emanating from the safety of his cabin. Now here was a challenge, a real maxi-miracle to perform; make South West Trains run on time. On the other hand, perhaps not. Kylb had indicated his powers would be limited, so sorting out South West Trains could well be overly ambitious. Another thing, was the miracle theoretically possible? What would happen if every train suddenly respected the published timetable? Would there be an almighty pile-up at Clapham Junction as dozens of trains arrived exactly when they were theoretically supposed but never seriously expected to arrive? Surely the railway authorities had not published a timetable that could not work in practice?

As promised, the 7.52 arrived 15 minutes late, resulting in a quarter of an hour's boredom since Miss Prick-teaser's curvaceous contours were not available to occupy one's optical senses. However, when settling into his seat waiting for the train to depart, he espied the owner of the miniskirt emerge from the car-park and surreptitiously sneak into the rear coach of the train. The elongated tweed skirt she was wearing must have been bought by her mother in about 1950.

The Daily Telegraph was even more depressing than the previous day: epidemics, famine, chemical plants blowing up, economic crises deepening. One of the seven remaining brown bears in the Pyrenees was attacking sheep, local farmers had vowed to shoot it, even though the animal was protected. Now here was a worthy cause to defend, a species to be saved. Applying Kylb's philosophy, he should unhesitatingly intervene on behalf of the downtrodden bears. English farmers were garrulous enough, French ones were insufferably worse. Not only did they attack trucks importing best quality British lamb into France, they stank of garlic, so a reduction in their population would definitely benefit mankind. Having made sure he was unobserved, he discreetly closed his eyes. From now on, each time a Froggie farmer took a pot-shot at those innocent little bears, his gun would explode in his face. Messy, but efficient.

The 7.52 arrived at Waterloo 15 minutes behind schedule.

He had decided against mixing messiahing and accounting, considering miracles and office administration intrinsically incompatible and highly unethical. In any case, if he applied his extrasensory powers to auditing he would unfailingly uncover every minor fraud, tax dodge and bending of the rules performed by his clients. He would lose them all. What would happen if it became common knowledge that the firm's senior partner was moonlighting as a Messiah? He could hang up a sign outside the office:

By Appointment
Chartered Accountants
and Miracle Makers

The Disciplinary Committee of the Institute would have a fit.

Perhaps he should instead join Scotland Yard, help unravel unsolved murder mysteries or tackle the swine who ran organised crime.

In spite of his resolve to separate the affairs of Kylb and those of Christie, Wainwright, Steinway & Company, he performed five miracles during office hours:

- Janet had run out of coffee until, at his bidding, she searched behind the photocopying machine. It was her boss's favourite blend.
- The fax machine had broken down yet again. Or had it? When Janet tried to transmit an urgent letter at the senior partner's bidding, the fax was transmitted without the slightest glitch.
- Mrs Jones, the firm's bookkeeper, was going berserk looking for a difference of £1.80 in her accounts ledger until he pointed out that an invoice for £270.27 had been recorded as £272.07.
- Three clients settled overdue accounts. This would only be confirmed the following morning when their cheques arrived in the mail.
- Janet's migraine attack suddenly disappeared.

Initially he was delighted to have been of service to his beloved secretary, but a few minutes later, back in his office, he experienced second thoughts. For the first time he had cured an illness, at least he supposed so, since the pills Janet habitually swallowed never worked. If he could cure migraine, what about meningitis, arthritis, cancer? If word escaped about his powers of healing he would be pursued by millions of sufferers. Esher would make Mecca and Lourdes seem like ... Words failed him. The Kingston bypass would be choked with true believers desperate to touch his healing hands, except that the Kingston bypass was one big traffic jam anyway. He had better sell his shares in Glaxo and Beechams. Consumption of medicines would plummet dramatically.

He just couldn't cure millions of sick people, even supposing he could. He was panicking. What he meant, he told himself, is that even supposing medically, or should that be non-medically, he could cure illnesses, he had been told to exterminate – no, he didn't like the word, it reminded him of Adolf Hitler and the Daleks – remove, yes that was a little less unpleasant, remove six billion people from the planet. How about curing non-fatal diseases such as lumbago and arthritis, whilst allowing patients with heart disease and strokes to die naturally?

The British Medical Council were not going to be happy about this, in spite of reducing the interminable waiting lists of the National Heath Service.

He had visions of Esher choked with ambulances and wheelchairs as the crippled converged on his house, desperately seeking a chance to pursue a normal life. Nature was indeed pitiless, allowing heart-wrenching diseases to debilitate millions of innocent souls. The Church intoned blandly it was 'God's will', thereby conveniently washing its hands of the problem. No self-respecting God would impose such suffering on anyone, let alone innocent children. Only a devil incarnate, not forgetting the Devil himself, could consciously deform children like those in the St Francis of Assisi home. Kylb could. Well, not quite. Although his attitude towards the human race had not exactly abounded with love and understanding, he had not displayed any sadistic tendencies.

'I must remain anonymous,' he mouthed to himself. 'I must at all costs remain anonymous.'

He decided a few mini-medical miracles should be an urgent priority, there was no point in suffering nightmares about heavenly healing powers if he were unable to cure the common cold. And he still had to select his maxi-miracle. Perhaps he could prevent a natural disaster from happening, but how to know which disasters were about to happen? Then, if the one chosen failed to materialise, how to confirm whether it would have happened if he hadn't intervened? Chernobyl! That would be a good start. He would decontaminate that blasted nuclear reactor. Also, thinking back to Scotland Yard, he resolved to unravel some really nasty crimes.

Blast, his tea had gone cold.

But not for long.

Before leaving the office he nearly performed a seventh miracle. One of the temporary secretaries was sitting opposite him in the computer room, her mini-skirt riding high up her thighs. If only she would turn towards him, just a few degrees. He never did discern the colour of the plump young lady's undergarment because something deep down inside was nagging him. The possibility he could cure millions of sick people combined with thirty-mile traffic jams converging on Esher, turning his neighbourhood into a mass of pleading pilgrims, had sobered him. The implications were mind-boggling. It was no longer the moment to selfishly pry into the secrets of young ladies' lingerie.

He left the office at the usual time, inadvertently descending in the lift with the aforementioned rotund temporary secretary, trying to think of something polite and intelligent to say. He normally avoided lift conversations. On the rare occasions you started an interesting exchange of ideas you invariably arrived at your destination in midsentence. Then you had to decide whether to continue the discussion outside the lift, or run for it.

Preoccupied with contemplating elevator social etiquette, he forgot he had never glimpsed the article of ladies' lingerie protecting the modesty of the plump employee standing alongside him.

'Goodnight, Susan.'

'Goodnight, Mr McHenderson,' replied the young lady.

His 17.58 to Guildford had been cancelled. Fulminating he swore that, from that very instant in time, South West Trains, bloody South West Trains, would run on time, exactly on time, regardless of wrongly-shaped snowflakes that gunged up points, wet leaves that flew across the tracks and signals that failed, usually during the rush hour. Still seething with frustration, he strode off to purchase something to read, oblivious of having performed his greatest miracle to date, because, from that moment onwards, points ceased failing and trains stopped breaking down, resulting in enforced redundancies in the railway's maintenance department, whereas leaves and snowflakes, at least wrongly-shaped ones, obligingly obeyed his recommendations and avoided railway lines. It was proven, fortuitously, that the computer programmers who compiled railway timetables knew the tools of their trade. There were no pile-ups at Clapham Junction, nor anywhere else, as trains running in perfect synchronisation avoided colliding with themselves exactly as planned. And, although no one, not even himself, realised it that Tuesday evening, the standard list of excuses for explaining the late arrival of trains was destined for the dustbin.

This, however, was yet to happen. Not yet aware of the revolution about to descend upon the world of commuter trains, he and hundreds of other passengers waited impatiently on platform 18. The 17.58 remained resolutely cancelled. Even Local Agents were unable to perform miracles retroactively.

The 6.16 sped towards suburbia. In the crowded compartment he stared unseeingly through the opaquely dirty window of the red and blue coach, contemplating the complications of life. He had not been appointed senior partner of a respectable accounting firm through chance or skulduggery, nor by careful selection of the right parents. Hard work, an active mind and an inborn ability to avoid rubbing up people the wrong way, had enabled him to rise from articled clerk to senior partner in just over 20 years. He was by no means afraid of a challenge. In fact, he usually welcomed the opportunity to show off his mettle, Gladys and Charles Dewey excepted.

He glanced through *The Evening News* looking for worthwhile crimes to solve. He really must cease his underwear exposing pranks since all sorts of biographies would inevitably be written about his assignment, whether *The Gospel According to St George*, as published by the Oxford University Press, or *The News of The World*'s serialisation of the *Sensational Adventures of the Knickers' Crazy Messiah*. Anyway, he said to himself in his defence, admiring scantily-clad feminine posteriors was in no way perverted. It was perfectly normal behaviour for hot-blooded males like himself. It was just that, for some obscure reason, society disagreed that one of its halves should be allowed to experience pleasure from admiring the interlaced intimacies of its other half. On the other hand, a touch of salacious sex would be perfect for the film version of Kylb's visit, boosting box-office sales dramatically. Who the hell would accept the part of Gladys? Hattie Jacques was dead, for that matter so was Cecil B. de Mille . . .

Glancing through the inside pages of the newspaper he unearthed two suitable crimes to solve:

- A hit-and-run driver had seriously injured a mother and child at a road crossing. The mother was in an irreversible coma, her seven-year-old daughter crippled for life. He grimly promised that the drunken wretch responsible for ruining those two lives would never drive again.
- A 16-year-old girl had been raped and strangled in Richmond. He couldn't bring the girl back to life, or could he? No, even if he could, he wouldn't. But he would identify the perverted bastard who had sadistically murdered a fun-loving schoolgirl, insure he paid fully for his heinous actions.

He was quite worked up. He admitted to not being a role model for sexual decorum, the Pope would certainly disapprove of his past diversions beyond the moral confines of marital fidelity. Tough luck on the Pope, who would soon be experiencing some major ecumenical upsets and a serious setback to his professional career. He imagined the frail old man queuing in a Rome unemployment agency. With his experience at handing out wine and wafers he should easily qualify for a job at McDonalds. No, he was past retirement age.

He remembered one of the neighbour's cats had gone missing. Sascha would be found and returned to her loving owners.

Then there was PanAm Flight 103. The gutless terrorists who had disintegrated it over Scotland had never been brought to justice; nor those who torpedoed that cruise ship in the Caribbean, nor those who placed the bomb in Manchester, nor ... The list was endless. Then there was the health miracle he had decided to perform. Why not two or three, just to be on the safe side? At least Janet would never have another migraine. How about that poor vodka-sodden neo-communist democratic President of Russia. He appeared to be the least worst of a bad lot, the best hope for Russia and therefore for the world in general. His sudden disintoxication and a refurbishing of his heart could only be beneficial to mankind, not forgetting his wife who presumably had to live with him.

What about that poor boy with leukaemia? He had forgotten his name, the one who had asked everyone to send postcards and now had rooms full of them. His eyes had moistened when the lad was interviewed on television. Although he himself had never become a father, he could envisage the despair experienced by parents as their child withered away towards a totally unmerited premature death. What on earth would the parents do with all the postcards if the boy suddenly recovered and went back to school?

The train pulled into Esher station, which was just as well. He had already accumulated an alarmingly ambitious evening's miracle-making.

Gladys was still out, no doubt bossing those incompetent church fête helpers, a modern Boudicca saving the day for

Britain and St George. Jennifer arrived home. The poor girl looked most dejected and was limping slightly.

A note was waiting for him next to the gin decanter. When Gladys wanted her husband to receive her messages she took no chances.

Vicar will see you at 8.30 p.m. in the Vicarage. I'll be back 7.00 p.m. approx.
G.'

He had completely forgotten to phone the Reverend from the office. Trust Gladys to assume that he would forget and phone on his behalf.

Drat the vicar.

The tonic sizzled gently in his glass, two ice cubes bobbing on top of the translucent liquid. He took a large sip and then another. He installed himself in his favourite armchair and decided he might as well perform his chosen miracles before supper. He would have little time afterwards. He quickly scribbled his list of requests, realising he had already forgotten the cat's appellation. Would a name be necessary? He knew which cat he meant but would, well whatever it was, the force that actually produced the miracles, manage to decode his message and produce the right cat? He vaguely wondered how the miracles were carried out, presumably the AAA Corporation had a technical and logistics department. He concluded, however, that such matters were not his concern, he had enough on his hands without getting embroiled in extragalactic scientific biophysical paranormal manipulations. Whatever that meant, but it sounded impressive. He wrote down the name of the family that owned the absentee cat and their full postal address, not forgetting the postal code.

How should he perform the miracles? In spite of his earlier successes he still wished Kylb had volunteered practical guidelines. He agreed he should close his eyes, as he had instinctively done so far, but should he also sit and face Rome or Mecca, or the clearing in the wood? Did he have to pronounce the text of the miracles or was thinking them sufficient? Must they be requested individually or could he consolidate them into one maxi-miracle? Perhaps Esher Public Library had an instruction manual, in the section on witches and black magic. He finally opted for expediency and efficiency. Closing his eyes, holding the piece of paper in one hand and the gin and tonic in the other, he simply asked, most politely, that all miracles as per the enclosed list be performed as requested. He opened his eyes and took another gulp of gin and tonic, nearly swallowing an ice cube in the process, then waited. Nothing happened, nothing whatsoever, not even a miaow. At least when you transmitted a fax you received confirmation the message had been received.

Supper was a hurried affair since Gladys had promised to design the church fête posters in time for delivery to the printer the following morning. And George, as she reminded him yet again, had a meeting with the Reverend Jeffrey Marsh at 8.30 p.m.

'Is it about the bazaar?' he inquired innocently, hoping to glean some useful information from his wife.

'George, we are not Arabs, it's a fête not a bazaar. No, I've no idea what's on his mind.'

Before leaving he turned on the CNN news. There was no mention of a sudden change in the behavioural patterns of Russia's President, nor were any repentant terrorists begging for forgiveness. Arsenal were playing the return leg of their EUFA football match at Highbury Park, two goals down after their trip to Italy a fortnight earlier.

'Win,' he ordained.

Walking to his car he realised he had omitted to specify time limits for the execution of his miracles. He looked heavenwards, hoping the head office of the AAA Corporation was somewhere in that direction, and sent a mental postscript to whomever it might concern.

'Asap,' he intoned.

'And three-nil for Arsenal.'

And finally, having recalled the simple words of womanly wisdom bespoken repeatedly by his mother:

'Please.'

Now for the vicar. What on earth did he want? Should he take the plunge and talk about Kylb? He was still debating the matter as he rang the vicarage doorbell.

'Coffee and a glass of port?'

The Reverend Jeffrey Marsh was about 40 years old, married to a remarkably attractive woman, at least for a vicar's wife, and was the proud father of three children. Enthusiastic and energetic, certainly not rigidly old-fashioned, an excellent bowler, one could talk to him man to man about the problems of the day without feeling embarrassed. Apart from the dog collar around his neck he was a normal, likeable human being.

'George, we need the benefit of your vast experience. How should we control the cash receipts during the fête? It's not that I mistrust anyone, Christians or otherwise, but we need some means of safeguarding our money.'

He sighed with relief. He was not about to witness the revenge of the Holy Trinity. He quickly assumed the role of a Chartered Accountant and gave the vicar the benefit of 25 years' auditing experience.

By the time the Reverend Marsh had mastered the intricacies of the cash handling procedure it was getting late, too late to broach the subject of Kylb. In any case, it would be wiser to wait for the results of his evening's miracle-making. He still wasn't sufficiently confident to announce to a man of God that a Chartered Accountant was the appointed successor to the Führer and Mohammed. But when the moment was opportune, he would definitely consult his local vicar. Something told him that Jeffrey would be a worthwhile ally, someone who would offer him sound advice.

He was nearly home when a cat ran across the road in front of him. He slammed on his brakes, swerved and ran straight over Sascha.

5

Miraculus

The following morning the 7.52 to Waterloo entered Esher Station precisely on time.

As was wont to happen on these infrequent occasions, numerous *habitués* of South West Trains were parking their cars or patiently queuing to buy their morning newspapers. The inevitable panic ensued. City-clad gentlemen, the *crème de la crème* of London's financial elite, momentarily forgot the manipulation of world commodity markets or the mounting of offshore hedging operations, and ran for it. Accustomed to eighteen holes of leisurely golf and genteel tennis with the ladies, their determination and efforts were hardly compensated by velocity, pin-stripes, umbrellas and briefcases combining to further hamper progress towards those momentarily open carriage doors. The only athletic achievement of note was performed by a Lloyd's insurance broker who, accelerating at remarkable speed for someone his size, tripped on a step and almost bettered Carl Lewis's long jump record.

The train pulled out of the station exactly on schedule, abandoning numerous enraged and cursing financial dignitaries on the platform. One of these, the long jumper, was dismally inspecting the tear in his trousers through which protruded one bloodied knee.

The scales of moral justice can be harshly unfair to railway companies, even in sedate Anglo-Saxon suburbia. The 7.52 received more vociferous oaths that morning for leaving at 7.52 than it had mustered the previous day for its tardy 8.07 performance. One of the passengers dismally watching the rear-end of the train disappear towards the grime of the

City was a 25-year-old miss, owner of an exceptional assortment of miniskirts. The ankle-length dress she was wearing, bought the previous day at Selfridges, so restricted her leg movements she was still unsteadily waddling her way across the car park when the train whistle blew.

Safely installed in his seat, gazing backwards towards the platform, he was relieved to see her. Having noticed her absence he had been worried. Prick-teaser she might be, but he had a heart, albeit only an Anglo-Saxon accountant's one, and he did not wish to cause her undue suffering.

Sandwiched between two portly city executives, he cursed himself for failing to procure a window seat, a situation most undignified for an erstwhile Messiah. Luckily all four passengers opposite him were reading newspapers, there was little danger of accidentally making embarrassing eye contact. Two of the four were engrossed in *The Financial Times*, one *The Guardian*, whilst the person sitting directly opposite him was reading page two of *The Sun*, which meant page three was spread before his eyes. She was grotesque, they were enormous. He recalled some university maths students who proved statistically that the size of a woman's breasts was inversely proportional to their owner's intellectual ability. The creature grinning at him must be moronic. Naturally there were exceptions to every rule, in this case a very notable one: Gladys. In spite of her many faults, his wife was remarkably intelligent. For example, she always found the missing word when he was stuck doing a crossword puzzle. Not to be sexist, the same group of students had conducted a similar study into the length of a certain extension to the male anatomy. Much to his eternal regret, he was in total conformity with the findings.

The owner of *The Sun* finished page two and turned to page three, he himself could concentrate on other matters. He recalled his fit of rage the previous evening at Waterloo station and his ensuing supplication for the sorting out of South West Trains. Could it be, could it possibly be, that his impromptu cry of frustration had been received up above, that trains were now condemned to run on time? Was this the dawn of a new stress-less era for the commuters of London? Or were 40 trains at this very moment hurtling towards their doom as they converged inexorably on Clapham Junction?

Time would tell. He closed his eyes and included an addendum to his miracle, if miracle there had been. Henceforth there would be a comfortable window seat waiting whenever his train arrived.

Trying, and nearly succeeding in opening his newspaper without disturbing his fellow passengers, why did they print the pages so wide, he scrutinised the headlines. Nothing indicated that his attempts at redesigning the world had been taken seriously. Admittedly the newspaper was printed during the night, so it was presumably presumptuous to already expect confirmation of his messianic prowess. At least Sascha had returned home. On the way to the station, whilst driving past the place of their regrettable encounter, he had tried not to scrutinise the road surface. And failed. A tabby brown and red flattened heap bore witness to the miraculous return of the prodigal cat. Was it his fault? Should he have been more precise in his miracle-making? Should he have insisted Sascha return home 'safely'? He shuddered to think what might have befallen the Russian President and those Muslim terrorists. What had been his precise words? He had forgotten, he would just have to await events. After all he was still only a novice. He recalled the Mickey Mouse cartoon of Dukas's *Sorcerer's Apprentice*, where splinters of magic broom created uncontrollable havoc. It was deplorable, the AAA Corporation should at least offer its appointees a crash training course before disembarking them on their respective missions.

He returned to the newspaper.

Arsenal had won 3–0! But Liverpool had been ignominiously eliminated by Real Madrid. Why hadn't he remembered them last night? The only consolation, as the sport's commentator reminded his readers, was that the Spanish team had fielded more English players than its Merseyside adversary.

The drought in North-East Africa was worsening. Over one million people were expected to die from malnutrition in the next twelve months. How many humans would be born in the same period? There were seven billion humans on earth, therefore about one billion females of child-bearing age. Supposing one in five produced a child, that meant two hundred million babies were going to put in an appearance before Kylb returned. Should he help those starving Ethiopians, send a few Scottish weather systems down their way? It was ironic, a few hundred miles further south they were suffering the worst floods for over a century. Surely he could justify saving 1,000,000 existing lives if, in exchange, he prevented 1,000,000 pregnancies from occurring? But even 1,000,000 was a mere drop in the ocean as far as Kylb was concerned. People joked about the reproduction capabilities of rabbits, yet humans were equally prolific, breeding themselves towards a suffocating extinction. He recalled a Catholic friend commenting that the Pope's job would become infinitely less frustrating and decidedly more relevant if religious scholars discovered a misprint in the scriptures, confirming the Angel Gabriel had in fact ordained an 'immaculate contraception'.

One step at a time. First he would wait for the results of the previous day's batch of miracles. After all, he tried to convince himself, he still had no absolute, undeniable, irrefutable proof of his kylbian powers.

The office mood was upbeat. Three major clients had unexpectedly paid long-overdue accounts. Janet was full of the joys of life. He studied her surreptitiously, realising he was extremely fond of her, that she would be a wonderful companion with whom to share his remaining years. More pertinently, someone to help him through the difficult months ahead. The thought of waking in the morning to find her lying beside him made him smile with anticipation. But what could he do with Gladys? The verger was a bachelor. He would make them fall madly in love, allowing he and Gladys to divorce on the grounds of her infidelity, and each couple would live happily ever after. Well perhaps not the verger. There was however a potential snag: he had no inkling how Janet viewed him. Did she like him as a boss, a person, was she secretly in love with him, or were her sweetness and patience no more than sheer professionalism, nothing other than a coldly calculated front to ensure she retained her job and received generous pay increases each year-end? How should he broach the subject, what if she rejected him? He vowed he would never perform a miracle to make her love him, her affection must be genuine. If only he could read her mind, become telepathic. Perhaps he could, thanks to Kylb! Imagine being able to read people's thoughts, hear what they were thinking and not what they were saying. Party political broadcasts would at long last be worth listening to. In his youth he had devised the 'credibility gap', the divergence between a person's words and thoughts. It varied from 10% for some of his best friends to 100% for practically every member of the House of Commons and Charles Dewey. Gladys' rating was zero, she invariably expressed exactly what she was thinking.

Janet entered his office with some urgent papers to sign. He blinked and quickly ordained. But Janet's sentimental inclinations remained firmly inside her head. Messiah he might be, telepathic he was not.

He decided against a declaration of affection which, even if not interpreted as an underhand attempt to spend the night with her, would ruin their office relationship so carefully built up over the years. So Janet, the papers duly signed, returned unscathed to her office.

The woman in the woods! He would condone a mini-miracle to make her fall for him. Then, after the church fête, he would convince Gladys to visit her mother in Falmouth, the ocean climate would calm her extenuated nerves. The Archbishop of Canterbury and the Pope would presumably pontificate in dismay, but to hell with them, they were transmitting on the wrong wavelength. Mohammed, a fully accredited emissary he reminded himself, permitted males to have four wives. Surely he could stretch that to one wife and a mistress? It would be a messianic business perk which, if his own clients were a benchmark, would be perfectly in accordance with normal business practice.

Yet again, methodical and cautious to the extreme, he determined to progress in an orderly fashion. One step at a time. Firstly yesterday's miracles had to be proven. He must know for once and for all whether he was the guru to end all gurus. Then, and only then, would he would start worrying about saving mankind. The woman in the woods could wait a few more days, or should that be nights?

The 17.58 for Guildford left Waterloo at 17.58, with an eminent accountant comfortably settled into a window seat. He had only performed two office miracles that day. Mrs Reynolds, the chief accountant, was unaware that her unemployed husband had been offered the job he so desperately wanted. And Susan was travelling home on the Piccadilly Line, oblivious that her senior partner, having noticed an outburst of facial eczema when accompanying her in the lift the previous evening, had prescribed a cure infinitely more miraculous than those promised on the bottles of lotion she gullibly purchased at her local chemist.

As the train clattered its way towards suburbia he studied *The Evening News*, reading and re-reading every column.

Nothing. Nothing at all.

Was he sorry or relieved? Did he really want to be the Messiah? It would obviously be a great honour, even more prestigious than President of the Institute. Kylb had not mentioned remuneration. It must be an honorary position, although thanks to miracle-making there was plentiful potential for free entertainment, Jennifer and Miss Prickteaser included. On the other hand, once his appointment became public knowledge, it would create havoc with his social life, no one would dare play golf with him. Did he really want the previous evening's miracles to be performed? No, that was not the fundamental issue, his personal wishes were irrelevant, there was something far greater at stake, the lives of six billion people. If Kylb was an invention, mankind's excessive population could contentedly contemplate senior citizenship whereas, if Kylb really had visited that grassy glade in the wood, their future was bleak indeed. Kylb, he concluded, must be nothing more than a figment of his overblown imagination.

Unless of course you were one of billions of insects and other life forms threatened with extinction by humanity's hyperbolic population expansion prospects.

The train screeched to a halt at Esher.

Gladys was home when he arrived. He had to feign amazement, sorrow, consideration and finally patience as his wife recounted the incredible return of Sascha, the fleeting joy of her family, then the misery and heartache as the prodigal feline was scraped off the road and buried at the bottom of her owners' garden.

Equally astounding, the hit-and-run driver seriously injuring the mother and child in Princess Road had given himself up to the police, full of remorse. He claimed he had not been drinking. Of course, five days later, there was no way the police could prove otherwise. The poor mother was still in a coma, there seemed little hope for her, and the daughter would never walk again.

Lasagne. He wished it could be cooked a little less thoroughly than usual, still golden crunchy on top but unaccompanied by the solidified crust that normally weighed it down.

'The lasagne's not quite ready, dear. Shall I replace it in the oven?' inquired Gladys.

'Don't bother, dear, I'm certain it will be delicious just as it is.'

And delicious it was.

'*Here is the 8 p.m. news from CNN,*' shouted the excited voice.

He knew this was not necessarily a precursor of extraordinary events, at CNN they always sounded excited. The BBC nine o'clock news was far more relaxing, even though their bulletins were just as calamitous. Tonight, however, he was too impatient to want to wait an extra hour.

> *'President Gaddafi of Lybia astounds the world with his unconditional offer to hand over the terrorists who blew up PanAm Flight 103 over Lockerbie, Scotland in 1992.*
> *'Violent floods in Somalia have killed thousands as refugee camps are washed away in the region's first rain for over a decade.*
> *'The Russian President, looking fitter and healthier, announces vigorous new measures to crack down on organised crime in Russia's cities.*
> *'The Prime Minister . . .'*

He did not hear the rest of the news. Instead he sat in a stupor, as realisation dawned that Kylb really had existed and that he, George McHenderson FCA, had irrevocably and irretrievably been selected to save humanity from a pre-emptive extradition to nowhere.

'George, you look peculiar. Are you sure that you haven't caught the 'flu?'

'No, dear, just digesting your delicious lasagne,' replied the Messiah.

He listened to the BBC's nine o'clock news. The Russian President looked positively effervescent, like someone from a yoghurt commercial. Perhaps he should revitalise the British Prime Minister who was looking his usual perplexed little-boy-lost self, trying to explain why the crisis wasn't really a crisis. By the time the right honourable gentleman had finished bemoaning the current situation and the Leader of the Opposition had finished bemoaning the Government's inability to do anything other than bemoan the current situation, he had forgotten what the crisis was, or hadn't been.

'Juventus football club is demanding an investigation following their three-nil thrashing by Arsenal. They claim some of the referee's decisions were blatantly biased against them. Sven Jöhanssen, Arsenal's manager, retorted that Italians should learn how to lose gracefully.

'Thames Valley Police announced this afternoon they are holding a man for questioning in connection with the rape and murder of 16 year-old Pamela Jones, whose naked mutilated body was found in Richmond Park last January.'

'Perverted bastard,' he gloated with satisfaction, 'hope your bloody balls fall off.'

After the weather forecast he switched off the television, deciding against commandeering a sunny weekend, he had enough worries without playing around with high pressure systems. Seated at his desk, he pulled out the notes written so laboriously the previous Sunday evening. Tearing up the page with his initial pathetic attempt at an Action Plan, he found a blank sheet of paper and wrote in capitals:

ACTION PLAN

For 30 futile minutes he failed to put pen to paper, in spite of the impressive number of thoughts flashing across his mind. The thoughts, however, merely piled problems on problems and added unanswered questions to unanswered questions. Six billion lives depended on him and his mind refused to function, no ideas were forthcoming, his brain was as blank as the notebook in front of him. No it was not, it was processing thoughts like an overloaded computer, regrettably its output unit was stubbornly refusing to conclude anything.

Jennifer's light came on. She appeared to have stopped limping. He watched languidly as she walked to the chest of drawers to undress and climb into her pyjamas, safely out of sight of his binoculars which lay undisturbed in their cache.

He renounced his attempts at writing the action plan, feeling fretful and deeply concerned, the horrendous responsibilities he had inherited and the unimaginable scope of the problems to be solved steadily pervading his mind. He turned off the lights and went up to bed meditating. He was convinced he had not requested an end to the droughts in Africa, he had certainly not ordained rainstorms let alone floods. What had gone wrong?

Gladys was still awake.

'I feel all sort of tense.' For once she wasn't complaining, she was almost confiding to her husband. 'I suppose it's the church fête, those stupid women helpers become more useless with every day that passes.'

'Don't worry, dear. Just count to ten and I'm certain you will fall sound asleep.'

And somewhere between nine and eleven Gladys sank into a deep relaxing dreamless and, most important of all, snoreless sleep. She was soon joined by her husband.

Several miles north-east of the slumbering McHendersons, Richmond-upon-Thames police station was full of activity.

'Er, James.'

Detective Superintendent James Foster looked up, greatly pleased with the day's events. ITN's *News at Ten* had already filmed an interview, the BBC were sending a camera crew the following morning. There was no doubt in his mind, he finally had the culprit under lock and key.

'Yes, Mike?'

'We've a problem with the Pamela Jones rapist. The doctor sent to collect the bugger's semen samples says he ain't got no sexual organs. Not only is the bastard a bleeding eunuch, he's a raving loony. Says he 'ad them when he woke up this morning but they disappeared after dinner. We'll have to let the bleeding motherfucker go.'

On the Wednesday evening he was invited to attend a banquet arising from his membership of a City livery company, a vestige of Britain's glory days of dominating world trade. He conceded a tendency towards good old-fashioned snobbism but livery functions pushed things beyond the limit. The association's all-male members were thoroughbred industrialised socialites, knights of British commerce, from Lords and Rt Honourables to Your Excellencies and Wing Commanders (Retired). The more initials one appended to one's name the more one was pompous, pious and impossible to converse with, the insufferable person condescendingly talking down at you, straight down his nose at you, a remarkable feat for some of the shorter members present. He reflected that many of those attending the dinner had simply sliced up a few Huns 60 years previously, presumably not as an act of outstanding bravery but to prevent themselves from being dismembered by those very same Huns. He, as a mundane Chartered Accountant whose closest encounter with Jerry was sitting in the cinema watching Americans single-handedly win the war, was an outsider. However, whatever his opinions concerning his fellow livery members might be, he was acutely aware that underneath their old-hat and generally geriatric exteriors they wielded the power and influence that made Britain tick. As such they could help him expand his firm's client base, in some cases they already had. So he smiled, pretended to enjoy himself, ate the atrocious cooking and appreciatively sipped the exquisite wine. He usually fled as early as possible, soon after the ceremonial toast to the Queen and Lord Mayor, just in time to catch the last train home to Esher.

He was particularly peeved with the evening's events. To start with, the Master of the Livery introduced him as 'George Henderson, one of our accountants'. Then, when finally given the honour of being introduced to the European Trade Minister, the left honourable gentleman, he was a Socialist, pointedly glanced away as he shook his hand and launched into a heated conversation with someone else. To add insult to ongoing injury, he spent the remainder of the evening lumbered with a timber merchant whose only ambition was to garner free tax advice.

On the way home in the train he mentally compiled a list of attendees he would volunteer for the six billion. With Gladys and Charles Dewey for company. Gladys? No that would be murder. He just could not eliminate her, whatever her faults she was his wife. As such she would be included in the billion. Along with Janet.

Saturday morning, the day of the church fête. It was unexpectedly bright and breezy. Gladys, not one to hide her emotions under an external veneer of passivity, had been becoming increasingly frenzied at the thought of her bonanza being squelched out of existence. So he had finally relented. The depression advancing steadily towards South Wales chose to spend the weekend in Brittany. Several scientists at the Meteorological Office's headquarters at Bracknell were extremely puzzled but the British public, used to forecasts based on fantasy rather that fact, didn't give the matter a second thought.

Against his better judgement he promised Gladys he would attend the fête, negotiating a late arrival. One hour was more than enough for him. Gladys acquiesced. One hour of George was more than enough for her. As usual, she would introduce him to newcomers never having previously met her husband. She was proud of being married to one of the City's top financial accountants and George looked the part, in small doses he could greatly impress people with his air of benign authority and self-importance. Also, it was important they occasionally be seen together, effectively pre-empting potentially salacious rumours concerning the state of their marriage.

Whilst Gladys was launching the church fête, rushing around simultaneously in all directions issuing orders to anyone having the misfortune to come within earshot, her husband was sitting at home recovering from mowing the lawn the old-fashioned human way, staring unseeingly at the blank piece of paper that represented his action plan. He wistfully contemplated the possibilities of using Kylb's powers to become a parent, wondering who should have the honour, or misfortune, to be the mother. He finally postponed the idea. He was going to be far too otherwise occupied for bottle-feeding and changing nappies, let alone fighting a probable paternity suit.

> *It was just as well he decided against a modern-day equivalent of the Immaculate Conception. Procedures established specifically for Bl-zzziii-5 were strict, any attempt by a Local Agent to procreate resulted in immediate de-molecularisation. Kylb would have been furious. He would have to recommence the hunt for a replacement and George had an ideally programmed thought processor, extremely appropriate for the job to be performed.*

Blissfully unaware of his near-encounter with instant inexistance, Kylb's recently appointed Local Agent drove to the church fête.

Gladys as usual chose the direct approach instead of time-consuming diplomacy.

'George, what's the matter with you? You were pathetic.'

He nodded. There was no point in starting an argument, he hadn't been his best. At the fête he discovered it was difficult to push Kylb and thousands of drowning Somalians from his mind whilst avoiding Jennifer and the grieving ex-owners of Sascha, or rather the grieving owners of ex-Sascha, whilst making polite conversation about motorway extensions, debating whether Tesco's wine selection was better than Sainsbury's and considering whether he should become Treasurer of the Esher Squash Club. He conjured up images of the Queen smiling serenely as she opened Parliament or a new hospital wing, she never closed anything, whilst her mind was churning over how to finance

Fergie's latest expense account, how to obtain a mortgage on Windsor Castle and how to prevent the ghost of Diana from hogging the headlines whilst keeping Charles away from them, not forgetting how to save the Monarchy from Wedgie Benn and Company. He had a suddenly surge of admiration for Her Majesty, perhaps they should congregate for a friendly chat. Since they were both religious leaders, he likened himself to an ecumenical ambassador at large, there should be plenty to discuss. He felt certain the Queen would provide sound advice, yes a *tête-à-tête* was definitely called for. But how exactly did one organise tea with the Queen, he couldn't simply phone Buckingham Palace and invite her and Philip for scones and Earl Grey next Sunday afternoon.

'And what is the purpose of the visit?' her equerry would ask. 'I see, the demise of the Church of England and how to save the Monarchy. Half past four at your place in Esher.'

'You hardly said a word, what you did mumble was garbled and insufferably boring. You behaved just like a . . . an accountant. I was ashamed of you.'

He avoided his wife's angry gaze, looked dejected, easy because he felt dejected, and wondered how much longer the recriminations would continue. Once Gladys really launched herself she could pour scorn on him for an eternity. He was saved by the bell, the telephone bell. Someone was calling to congratulate Gladys on her outstanding organisation of the fête, her brilliant leadership qualities, blah, blah, blah. Well, that should bolster her frame of mind for the rest of the evening.

Whilst Gladys was being lauded on the phone he plunged deeper into his reflections. The only person for whom he had felt any affinity amongst those attending the fête was the vicar himself. They had not only discussed the cash receipts system, it was working to perfection, but several other matters. The subjects themselves were of little consequence, it was the easy communication, the feeling he was conversing with someone who listened, who understood. He finally resolved he would confront the vicar. The Queen could wait awhile.

He arrived at two other important decisions. In order to protect his anonymity he would engage a spokesman, weren't they called press secretaries? Out of necessity it would be someone he had never encountered, thwarting the inevitable efforts of nosey-parker newspaper reporters to trace him. The other decision was to definitely send Gladys away for a few nights, she really did need a change of scenery. So did he, well not quite, he wished to retain the same scenery but without Gladys in the foreground constantly distracting him from his kylbian projects.

At Gladys' suggestion he invited her to one of the area's most exclusive restaurants, and most expensive. Between the *hors d'oeuvres* and the fish course he proposed that his wife spend the forthcoming week with her mother. Gossip and walking along the sea-front would recharge her batteries after the fête.

'George, for once you've had a good idea. Although something tells me you need a holiday more than I. Your week's skiing should perk you up.'

He was holding a glass of Pouilly Fuissé to his mouth. It was lucky he hadn't just taken a sip.

Damn!

He had completely forgotten his annual visit to Pontresina. The flight was booked for the following Saturday. But he couldn't abandon the fate of the world and disappear for a week's vacation. However, he did need a change, in fact the fresh mountain air would stimulate his mind, help with his meditations. Jesus, Mohammed and that Chinese fellow, they had all disappeared into the desert for years. Surely he could justify a mere eight days halfway up a Swiss mountain. Even so . . .

'George, are you or are you not going to drink that wine? You have been holding the glass to your lips for aeons without actually tasting anything.'

'Just appreciating the bouquet, dear.'

By the time he climbed wearily into bed he had committed himself to talking things over with the vicar. He would phone the following morning. As he drifted inexorably towards sleep, he muttered to himself.

'To ski or not to ski, that is the question.'

The rain promised for Saturday, after its surprise detour to Northern France, struck South-East England with a vengeance on Sunday morning. There would be no 'walkies' in the woods with Beatrice.

He was just about to pick up the receiver to call the vicar when the phone range.

'Doing your ski exercises, George?'

It was Muriel phoning to confirm everything was *au fait* for their departure. She had the tickets and her brother would drive them to Gatwick. The *rendezvous* was *chez* George at nine o'clock the following Saturday morning.

Why did she keep speaking French, Pontresina was in the German-speaking part of Switzerland.

He couldn't abandon his friends a mere week before their departure. So he capitulated. To ski it was to be.

The Reverend Jeffrey Marsh would be pleased to see him straight away. This was surprising, were not vicars meant to be extra busy on Sundays? The voice the other end of the line explained there was now only one Sunday service, Evensong. No one wished to worship in the mornings, it interfered with golf and car boot sales. His enthusiasm for cycling did not extend to getting drenched with spray flung up by cars, consequently he was at a loose end and would be delighted to welcome his respected accountant parishioner.

So at nine o'clock he drove through grim and grey rain-soaked Esher to try and convince the Reverend Jeffrey Marsh, Church of England, that he joined the wrong organisation, that a designer of cash receipt systems and member of Esher Golf Club was the latest addition to the Holy Trinity, which was now a quartet. In all those biblical epics

Jesus appeared so self-assured, preening himself, bursting with self-confidence, whereas he, George, was suffering from acute self-doubt as he approached the vicarage. He was used to professional confrontations, he never went to business meetings without well-prepared notes, confident he could demolish the opposition, knowing that in case of emergencies his audit manuals were readily available. But he was totally unprepared for the vicar, he had even forgotten to bring the jumbled jottings that served as an Action Plan. At least the rain had washed away the last remnants of Sascha.

'OK, George, I'm all ears. What can I do for the world's greatest designer of cash receipt systems?'

'George, Gladys says you have been working extremely hard at the office these past few weeks.'

Blast that marauding meddling wife of mine, he thought to himself, scowling internally yet smiling serenely at the vicar in a totally relaxed manner. The Queen would have been proud of him.

He had just finished relating his encounter with Kylb and subsequent miracle-making exploits, explaining in simple, clear and unadorned terms the events of the previous week, adding a little emotion to create credibility yet not overdoing the dramatics to avoid sounding hysterical. He had told the truth, the whole truth and nothing but the truth. Well, not quite. He had previously decided that any reference to nocturnal belly dancing and tornadoes uplifting hemlines at Esher Station, uplifting being a word the vicar used frequently although not quite in the same context, were irrelevant to the overall situation and would only distract his host from the crux of the problem.

'No more than usual,' he answered.

He had been expecting such a reaction and was ready to counterattack. He had noticed Jeffrey glance at the calendar and it had taken him a few moments to realise April the first was next week.

'George, what exactly do you want of me?'

'I'm not entirely certain,' replied his visitor. 'First I want you to believe me. You must believe me. Then I want the benefit of your professional training to help sort out the mess. Decide what needs to be done.'

'Well, you must realise that I'm going to need some convincing. Put yourself in my place. You cannot expect me to rush to the pulpit and announce to the world that Jesus was the world's greatest con artist and that the new Messiah is Gladys McHenderson's husband. I'd be defrocked, end up with you in the loony-bin. No one would believe me.'

George's normality was the most worrying. Even in sedate Esher, Jeffrey suffered his share of cranks, mostly old widows or neurotic teenagers, not middle-aged accountants. In ecclesiastic college he had been taught to take such people seriously, at least to pretend to, to try and calm them down, understand what was disturbing them. Useful advice, but George was already perfectly calm. He had visually inspected George's clothes for tell-tale signs of a hidden microphone, convincing the local vicar the Anointed One was not Jewish but an accountant living in Surrey would be the talking point of Esher for months. He would have to be transferred elsewhere. So what was this accountant, this somewhat pretentious yet rather likeable pillar of Esher society, trying to achieve? He must keep cool, pray for his soul or outwit him, whichever was more appropriate.

'Jeffrey, you are about to receive all the convincing you could possibly want.'

It must be said he was not totally unprepared for the meeting, having previously concocted a list of miracles that should convert the vicar to the gospel according to St Kylb, miracles intended to convincingly unchristianise him for once and for all. They were based on the principle that 'anything Jesus could do, George can do better'. Assuming he could. Well, he would soon know.

'Go and fetch a jug of water, a slice of bread and a couple of eggs.'

Jeffrey reasoned he had better continue to humour his guest, at least for the time being. Returning from the kitchen he laid the requested objects on the table, feeling exceedingly ill-at-ease.

'Bordeaux or Burgundy?' inquired his guest.

He knew wine served during Catholic mass was all but undrinkable, not because the Vatican was devoid of expertise in the art of viticulture but in order to keep consumption to a minimum and worshipers reasonably sober. No *vin de table* for me, he vowed, this is Esher.

The Nuits St Georges was exquisite, the freshly baked baguette crisp and crunchy, much appreciated by the two tiny chicks who had a few minutes earlier hatched from the eggs.

'That's just for starters,' he said cheering up, starting to enjoy the proceedings. 'Let's stroll down to your church.'

Neither spoke during the short walk to St Matthias Parish Church. He eyed the gravestones. How about the Esher version of Michael Jackson's *Thriller* video? Or *Morning of the Living Dead?* Better not, he had other plans in store for the Reverend Jeffrey. In any case, this was Esher and not Amityville.

The beautiful Norman stone church, with its delicate yet sober architecture, looked comfortingly peaceful, albeit forlorn and abandoned against the dark grey of the scurrying clouds. There was not a soul to be seen, human or heavenly. Inside he was flabbergasted, even he had not expected such a total transformation. Every painting, statue, carving and inscription to Jesus Christ had been metamorphosed into one of him. The church was overflowing with Georges. He had toyed with the idea of replacing the Virgin Mary with Gladys, but concluded the young maiden should simply disappear. Amongst the multitudes of Georges some had halos, most flattering, whereas others showed him with holes in his hands and feet, most disconcerting. All were illuminated by a glowing luminosity that originated elsewhere than Battersea Power Station. Kylb would have been proud of his latest Local Agent.

Back in his study, alone, the Reverend Jeffrey Marsh was sipping the Nuits St Georges. His mind was in a turmoil, his whole world crumbling around him. George had thankfully returned the church to its original state, thoughtfully repairing a few leaks in the process, but that was only a temporary relief. In a few hours he would preach his weekly sermon to the faithful, his flock of true believers. At least God existed, sort of. So had Jesus, sort of. But if George was for real, and he didn't seem to have much choice in the matter, then Joseph and Mary were no more than ordinary parents. A mummy and daddy. He looked miserably at the Nuits St Georges.

'Turn back to water,' he ordained.

The Nuits St Georges resolutely remained Nuits St Georges.

'Absolutely delicious,' his wife commented. She had returned from visiting parishioners, espied the wine and helped herself.

'Where did you get it from?'

'George McHenderson brought it this morning.'

'But why on earth is it in the water jug?'

A moment's hesitation.

'He wanted to keep the bottle.'

'What year is it?'

Her husband was flummoxed.

'Forgot to ask George,' he mumbled.

Something told him even George might have problems confirming the vintage.

'What on earth are those eggs doing on your table?'

He had forgotten to replace them in the refrigerator. 'We were discussing some theory of George's,' which was not entirely untrue.

'I'll put them back in the fridge.'

His wife picked them up and departed to the kitchen,

leaving her husband to his meditations. It was George's dehatching of the chicks that convinced the Reverend Jeffrey he had better start taking his visitor seriously. Either George was a mad hypnotist or the Messiah and both were impossible. Apart from the wine, all traces of the morning's 'seance' had vanished, except one. George had admired his beautiful Virgin Mary and Child, a family heirloom. The crack in the Virgin's leg, caused by his great-grandmother when she knocked over the statuette with her bustle, was no longer there. The chicks had also disappeared. Eggs tend to hatch. It is one of nature's mechanisms for the survival of certain species. He had watched all sorts of eggs hatch in television documentaries, from rugby ball-sized ostrich eggs to those of minuscule hummingbirds. In *Jurassic Park* even dinosaur eggs hatched. Watching chicken eggs break open to let two adorable chirping chicks emerge had therefore not totally unfazed him, even though the shells were stamped 'Farmer's Pride' and he himself had collected the eggs from the pantry. His Electrolux may have been a refrigerator, not an incubator, but even so eggs do have a tendency to hatch. However, watching the two little chicks climb back into the shells, which then proceeded to close up around them, had left him feeling faint. His subsequent prayers for guidance remained unanswered. Was he, Jeffrey, really broadcasting on the wrong wave length as George had insinuated?

He had asked for time to consider the implications, something his visitor had obviously been expecting. He reiterated the two options: either his visitor was endowed with extraordinary powers of hypnosis, such that his own brain imagined everything and was still imagining his Madonna's leg being repaired, or Kylb existed, in which case George really had been accosted by a messenger from elsewhere. Yet how could Jesus not be the true son of God, His messages of love and peace could only have been inspired in Heaven. George had retorted that neither Gandhi nor Nelson Mandela were the sons of God, nor were millions of other people who had committed acts of love and self-sacrifice throughout the history of mankind. But if Jesus had been an impostor, then Heaven was surreal. At least there would be no Hell to worry about.

He remembered one of George's more comforting comments, in fact his only comforting comment, that Son of God or counterfeit, Jesus's message to mankind could not be ignored, should never be ignored.

Both had agreed to a second meeting before consulting with anyone else, before taking any action. Jeffrey desperately wanted to confide in his wife, Margaret, but George had been adamant. So he sat alone in his study, acutely aware he had some serious thinking to accomplish. And his Sunday sermon to reconsider.

Lunchtime.

Whilst the Reverend and Mrs Marsh were eating an *omelette aux fines herbes*, the former with certain misgivings, the McHendersons were sitting down to roast beef and Yorkshire pudding. The beef was British since Gladys had no time for 'mad cow' scaremongers. She was convinced British cows were safer than anybody else's, especially French ones which always looked filthy and spent their lives wallowing in excrement. He ate the beef without qualms, judging the health risk purely hypothetical. Medically speaking, no virus or germ, whether British or French, had the slightest chance of surviving Gladys's overcooking of the meat.

'I phoned Mother whilst you were with the vicar, I leave Tuesday morning and return Friday afternoon. You don't mind, do you? I'll fill up at Safeways tomorrow, I presume you can remember how to use a tin-opener?'

There was no sarcasm in Gladys' voice. She really doubted her husband's ability to survive without her.

'I'll try and manage, dear.'

Cooking was going to be the least of his worries during Gladys's stay with her mother.

6

Committicus

'Morning George.'
'Morning Mr McHenderson.'
'Wow, that's one hell of a suntan!'

He was back at the office after a week's absence. His suntan was genuine, obtained without the aid of creams or ultra-violet lamps, just a little assistance from Kylb. It was indeed a truly remarkable tan because the glorious golden brown extended to parts of the anatomy never normally exposed during a skiing holiday, nor during any other kind of vacation.

As he settled into his office, the senior partner of Christie, Wainwright, Steinway and Company was not feeling as radiant as he looked. Admittedly his train had left Esher and arrived at Waterloo exactly on time, in spite of the strike called by the Transport and General Workers Union, which was remarkable. The vast majority of members intended to vote for immediate industrial action when entering the voting booth, yet over 90% had changed their minds before leaving it.

So he arrived at the office on time, after a comfortable journey sitting in a coveted window seat. However, the few remaining shreds of bonhomie surviving from his recent holiday dissipated into gloom as he entered the inner precincts of his office, to be greeted by voluminous piles of documents waiting to be handled personally by the senior partner. For years the pundits and IBM salesmen had sworn those wonderful electronic machines called computers would eliminate office paperwork. All that had happened, just as he had doggedly forecast would happen, was that the existing mass of paperwork had been supplemented, not supplanted, but by reams of back-breakingly bulky computer listings.

Groaning inwardly, he picked up the first piece of paper, took a sip of Janet's coffee, and settled down to the day's work.

From time to time, between telephone calls, meetings with stressed colleagues and dictating to Janet, he permitted himself reminiscences of his week's skiing in Pontresina. He had not injured himself on the slopes, in spite of risking his neck, tibias and the majority of other bones composing his skeleton whilst attempting acrobatic exploits normally reserved for cinema stuntmen. With Kylb on one's side who needed the Norwich Union or Europe Assistance? Of course he normally skied like a traditional English tourist, ploddingly determined with all the wrong muscles tensed, although with reasonable if not textbook style, at least until descending the steeper bits. However, on two occasions his companions excessively over-imbued themselves alcoholically, so their following morning was consecrated to 'relaxing', the term 'recovering' would have been more explicit. Whereas he was raring to tackle the *pistes*, in spite of *après-ski* activities decidedly more imaginative than those of his comrades. So twice he skied alone. Alberto Tomba and Luc Alphand would have gazed in amazement as a middle-aged superman – didn't he look rather English? – pulverised a few world records and surpassed the exploits of his fellow countryman, James Bond. He thought about producing a parachute but decided he was already attracting more attention than advisable.

Pride, they say, goes before a fall, especially in the world of skiing. At Pontresina he narrowly avoided two extremely well-deserved tumbles. The first close encounter with calamity occurred subsequent to his first kylb-assisted morning outing. As he steadily negotiated his way down a black run, caution taking precedence over speed and self-survival over style, and as a mogul that had been deposited in an incredibly stupid place caused his skis to depart in distinctly different directions with him following neither of them, a group of admirers of his morning's performance were extremely puzzled. One of them nearly plucked up courage to ask, in front of Muriel who had rushed to his assistance, whether he had an identical twin.

The other close encounter with catastrophe bore little relation to skiing. Having decided that, as Local Agent, he should become better acquainted with the rest of humanity, after all foreigners did represent an important component of the human race, and having subsequently considered it fitting to commence with the fairer sex, not that he had any arguments to support his strategy, he launched into the business of studying mankind with gay but heterosexual abandon: the wife of a German banker, two wives of a sheikh, a Japanese ice skater, a Russian ballet dancer and the daughter of an American senator, all of them were enthralled at his poetic eloquence when speaking their language. None could momentarily resist his romantically seductive charms.

Prior to meeting Kylb he was wont to boast of '0' levels not only in Latin but also in French, although his more than modest Grade C, resulting from pathetic stuttering during the orals, was conveniently overlooked. In any case, learning other languages was a purely academic exercise designed to confirm the superior intellectual ability of the British, who were never actually supposed to converse in alien dialects, this being an activity strictly reserved for foreigners. In his youth he occasionally sneaked into 'cultural' cinemas to watch the latest Brigitte Bardot film, confirming that an almost total lack of linguistic ability was not the slightest impediment to enjoying the artistic content of Monsieur Vadim's cinematographic masterpieces. So why suffer the humiliation of trying to speak the lingo?

Kylb, however, put Berlitz to shame as his latest prodigy mastered German, Arab, Japanese and Russian in the space of a week, five nights to be precise. Convincing Cathy, the American, required no linguistic accomplishments whatsoever. The more he emphasised the Englishness of his

English, the more enraptured became the big, beefy blonde from Texas. She was into karate and what she lacked in sexual finesse, at least at the beginning of the night, she made up in enthusiasm and sheer physical energy. By daybreak she was not only a black belt at judo but a black below-the-belt at something else. Recovering from his second orgasm, he smiled at the appropriateness of the event. For centuries had not religious leaders, praying for a visitation from the new Messiah, referred to the event as the 'Second Coming'?

He never forgot he was *après-skiing* in a strictly professional capacity, that he was broadening his horizons concerning that part of humanity having the misfortune to be born other than British. And he did gain important insight into how the other half of the world lived, although statisticians, even British ones, would tend to rephrase that as how the other 98.75% of the world lived. He conceded that the skiers of Pontresina were not entirely representative of the human race: visions of drowning Somalians and impoverished children toiling in paddy fields intermingled with those of mink coats, Ferraris and iced champagne. However, for the first time in 56 years and however underhand his methods of research, he felt he was achieving meaningful understanding of life beyond the shores of Skegness, Weston-super-Mare and Bournemouth. He realised that the human race, whatever its faults, was unimaginably varied and complex, infinitely fascinating and unfailingly incomprehensible. Gazing in wonderment at the pristine Alpine peaks, it was difficult to believe Planet Earth was being systematically destroyed by a species responsible for technological wonders of purest genius, artistic creations of exquisite beauty and cultural heritages of immense richness. A species capable of creating marble sculptures that breathed life, virtual reality computers, brain scanners, *foie gras*, designer clothes, throwaway nappies, instant meals and plastic shopping bags. And equally capable of converting them into seas of stinking sewage.

Regrettably, the insights he gleaned from his nocturnal

trysts were far from encouraging. Relaxing alongside one of the Arab wives, he realised she had no conversation, nothing other than nebulous words of endearment and practical technicalities related to prolonging their sexual nirvana. Coming from a relatively modest family, yet being strikingly attractive, she had been trained for the marital bedchamber from the moment of her first menstruation, had been dressed like a poodle preparing for Crufts, although in her case 'undressed' would be a more fitting term. Her sole reason for existing was to satiate her husband's carnal whims. He asked what they talked about. Nothing, what was there to discuss? was her reply. She was hardly more than a chattel, a supplier of erotica rented not by the hour, as in Soho, but contracted under a long-term non-redeemable leasing agreement. Men monopolised the intellectual, cultural, social and business aspects of her society, its women were brainless bodies serving their masters, domesticated livestock raised for breeding children. How different from Britain. How depleted his country would be without its fascinating, gloriously inventive, muddle-headed and infinitely infuriating female citizens enriching every aspect of its daily life. If he ever faced the unthinkable, the matter of the six billion, he vowed equal rights for women would be respected.

The second wife was less talented physically, nor did she have the same stamina, so that on a couple of occasions she interrupted the proceedings to recover her strength. It was during one of these intermissions, whilst she was smoking something little related to tobacco, that he asked about her country, the lack of democracy, the oppression of women, rampant poverty, child labour. Her only comment was that everyone should solve their own problems, tough luck on the 99% of her fellow citizens too lazy or stupid to nourish themselves. Surprisingly, she had been allowed a modest education, but only to render her more negotiable on the marriage market, her personal ambitions were irrelevant. In other words, women had the right to a brain only when necessary to complement physical deficiencies. And even the paltry intellect accorded by her self-indulgent masters was attuned exclusively to conserving their chauvinistic way of thinking.

Even so, he was shocked at her attitude. Whatever the nature of her education, she was a person, how could she be uninterested in the destiny of the vast majority of her fellow human beings? Was it pure selfishness, an 'I'm all right, Mohammed' attitude, or was she genuinely unaware of the glaring injustices in her country? He then ashamedly realised his involvement in the social problems of Wandsworth, Hounslow and Hammersmith was equally non-existent, had been non-existent, something told him things would radically alter when he returned to England.

During his next respite (Jamina had a little urgency to attend to) he reflected that his employees were hired purely on competence, their social standing was irrelevant. The father of one of his audit managers was an unemployed electrician. And there was Patricia. When they spoke on the phone to confirm the interview, she was applying for the position of articled clerk, he had been charmed by the purity of her English. When she walked into his office she was as Indian as the Gandhi family, only the sari was missing. She was now a senior auditor, one of the best, and would almost certainly become a partner. Racism and business did not mix well.

He knew extremely few coloured people, not from design, but from circumstance, which he now realised was regrettable. His narrow social existence, however refined, had seriously limited his awareness of life, his appreciation and understanding of the remarkable animal species to which he belonged.

Soberly he realised, whatever the pleasures involved in entertaining the female half of mankind, in the pursuit of his mission he would essentially have to deal with the husbands of humanity. But in the meantime Jamina had finished performing her little urgency...

The second aforementioned catastrophe nearly occurred the last morning of his vacation, when he was riding the *télécabine* with his three holidaying companions. Four pairs of skis away was the wife of the German banker, making eyes at him and mouthing something excitedly in her native tongue. He smiled weakly in her direction, pretended she was talking to someone else and, on reaching the summit, exited the cabin as rapidly as any stockbroker arriving at the City on the Bakerloo line.

Janet arrived with a batch of audit reports to be signed. He temporarily forgot *après-ski* activities, smiled at his secretary, and took hold of his fountain pen.

The reports safely returned to the capable hands of Janet, his thoughts wandered back to Pontresina and the German banker's wife. Notwithstanding his unsociable behaviour in the ski-lift, he had been charmed by her. She was so unexpected, so unlike how German bankers' wives should be, or any German wife for that matter because German wives were supposed to be big, beefy and blonde, only slightly diluted versions of Gladys. But they were not, at least Anita was not, nor were many of the other females in Pontresina who spoke and who were presumably German. Anita was exquisitely petite, well, not too petite, and beautifully brunette. He found he could relax in her company, the interludes of recovery were arguably more enjoyable than their amatory aphrodisiac antics. It was strange, she was a Hun, a Kraut and a Bosch, her grandfather had fought against the British until his U-Boat was sunk, but she behaved just like any normal human being. If she were not speaking German she could have been English.

Perhaps it was the contrast after his previous experiences, the thousand and two Arabian nights, but he really felt like talking, discovering the personality of his bed-companion. Anita was not always in agreement. Oral sex to her, ever the banker's wife, was represented by a number, one that could be found between 68 and 70, whereas he found the numerical position of 66 more practical for conversing. Although, ever the meticulous accountant and after careful examination of her Teutonic torso, he concluded 68 would be more mathematically correct. But who was he, British gentleman, to prevent the young lady from having her way with him, or was that having him in her way?

Once the conversation strayed into the rarefied domains of high finance; her husband was a Frankfurt investment banker raising interest rates to stave off inflation, although, to his untrained accountant's mind, he appeared to be more successful at increasing unemployment. She explained that Germany was still terrified of the economic mistakes made in the 1930s, errors which generated galloping inflation and facilitated the Nazi incursion. He argued this was the twenty-first century, millions were ensnared in the despairing abyss of unemployment because of a psychopathic reaction to the economic misjudgement of their grandparents. In any case, should not elected Governments decide on such matters, not bankers, however delectable their wives?

The conversation ceased as they moved into a position impossible to describe numerically.

After years of war films, from *The Dambusters* to *The Longest Day*, not forgetting *'Allo 'Allo*, he realised he had been brainwashed about Germans just as effectively as Herr Himmler had indoctrinated Hitler Youth about Fascism. After 60 years of peace did the British and Germans know each other better than in 1939, did they understand each other at all? Germany was Britain's neighbour, with the onward march towards European integration the two countries were practically marrying each other, without bothering to first familiarise themselves with themselves. How could human beings work together as one global civilisation, save themselves from Kylb, when man's greatest ignorance related to mankind itself?

He left Anita with fond memories, all too conscious he still had much to discover about his fellow Europeans. And that was before encountering a Spanish *señorita*, let alone a French *femme fatale*.

The Russian ballet dancer, Natasha, left him exhausted,

even more so mentally than physically. It was not a case of nonstop, it was stop-go, stop-go, go-stop, go, stop and then go again. Everything was all or nothing, wonderful or abysmal, glorious or disastrous, despairing or joyous. She exuded unbridled and continuous intellectual passion, her moods changing every few minutes from sobbing to delirious delight, from despair to ecstatic pleasure. Each change of mood, each thought that flashed though her mind, resulted in vocal aerobatics of rare intensity accompanied by hand flinging and facial contortions. She never stopped either starting or stopping. And between her outpouring of emotion she swigged copiously at a bottle of Smirnoff as if it were water. Once, assuming it was water, he took a generous swig himself. It was the only time his emotion level approached anywhere near to Natasha's.

As for communicating, he achieved nothing. As soon as he grasped what Natasha was getting overexcited about, she had changed subjects. Twice. She claimed most Russians were like her, also they were the most civilised people in the world. Notwithstanding, although her ballet training was perfect for the boudoir and he finally learnt what a *pas de deux* really entailed, by breakfast he was none the wiser about life east of the Polish border. Of course she could not be a typical Russian, a country of 200,000,000 Natashas was an anachronism, a socially and conceptually impossible possibility. For Natasha exuded unending egotistical egocentricity, only her immediate state of mind mattered, the rest of her world being divided into adulating ballet devotees and an irrelevant abstraction. Although biologically human, she did not qualify as socially human, living in a micro-universe existing inside her head but outside the parameters of everyday society. And presumably Natasha was by no means unique. Yet, unless mankind's individual members worked together as an united whole, was there any hope of salvation from Kylb?

Whereas Natasha was exhausting, Yoki the ice-skater was mind-numbing. Her thoughts and emotions camouflaged themselves behind shrouds, impenetrable shrouds of mental barriers that prevented contact with the person hidden within. Always assuming there was somebody inside her protective cocoon? Was Yoki no more than external wrapping composed of politeness, deference, consideration, and sensuality? But where did her sensuality come from? Surely only people with personalities were sensuous. Furthermore, making love was a two-way affair, as it had been with Anita. With Yoki it was one-way, which counter-balanced Natasha who had been multi-directional. Were other Japanese women as imperiously impersonal as Yoki? Impossible to learn from the adorable Asiatic. On reflection, was Yoki adorable? Anita had been, but then she was a person. Yoki was visually exquisite, socially she was a vacuum. What was the purpose of belonging to a society if one hermetically sealed oneself away from it? Societies only vibrated, catalysed and progressed through personal exchanges, the meeting, merging and confrontation of minds. Uniquely devoting one's life to pirouetting on expanses of frozen water was insufficient to claim a place in the greater order of things.

Having completed his polygamous tour of femininity, he dutifully commenced acquainting himself with their husbands, requesting a meeting with the sheikh, landlord of two of his recently recruited research assistants. The charade of his welcome was solely designed to impart the superiority of the host and the inconsequentiality of the intruding infidel wishing to consult with him. So much for hospitality, the art of graciously receiving strangers into one's abode. Swallowing his pride, he profusely thanked his excellency for receiving him and humbly requested information on how his country would adapt its economy if fossil fuels were replaced world-wide with non-polluting alternatives. Accused of being a miscreant agitator from one of those misguided revolutionary communities, who dared claim the status of political parties, he was ejected from the pedestal of personal power where democracy was evidently deemed an evil representation of social depravity. Although not expecting to be received as a prodigal harbinger of good news – without its oil revenues his host's country would be reduced to camel caravans plodding around sand dunes – he had expected at least an animated argument on how to avoid returning to the medieval misery of bygone centuries.

The husband of Natasha, the world-famous classical conductor, spoke music, thought music, breathed music and existed solely for music. Any attempt to discuss matters relating to the non-musical world were impolitely ignored. Here was a man respected by millions, yet who doggedly rejected the notion that music formed part of a greater whole. Music was music, part of an infinity of music. Were other famous musicians, including rock superstars, equally mono-minded in their perception of existence? If so, in spite of their international fame and ability to influence the minds of millions, they would be useless at helping him face the challenges imposed by Kylb's demands. And he desperately needed powerful allies in his quest for salvation.

Sunning himself on the last day of the holiday, he reviewed the week's events, tried to make sense of his *après-ski* encounters. Each of his six nocturnal companions had been so utterly different, not only from himself but from each other, their personalities even more than their physiques. What should a normal human being look like, female or otherwise? Were eyes meant to be blue and were men supposed to remain slim, or was it more socially correct to exhibit paunches and go bald in middle age? The British assumed they were rôle models for the world but so did the French and Chinese, presumably so did Pigmies and Maoris, with equal justification. Consequently, nobody could claim to be better or worse than anyone else since there was no global benchmark, no normal human being. Although plenty of abnormal ones. And that was only the physical consideration. Even more relevant, what was a normal average acceptable standard personality?

He groaned inwardly. The more he investigated the human race the less he understood the species to which he belonged. How could he possibly decide the fate of civilisation if he was unable to communicate with his brethren and their sisters, let alone understand them? Presumably they made equally little sense out of him. Nor did they seem motivated to try, which was probably the greatest tragedy. The penis and vagina seemed to be the only universal point of convergence of the human race. Which was hardly going to help advance his mission since, in the forthcoming months, he would be dealing essentially with the males of mankind. Which, if his encounters with the sheikh and conductor were a foretaste, promised to be a recurring nightmare.

Back in London a sigh emerged from the depths of the senior partner's office. Janet assumed he was reviewing the monthly update of office expenses.

As the 17.58 clattered its way through Battersea, heading towards Clapham and Wimbledon, he read *The Evening News*. Nothing much seemed to have changed in the world, the pages were littered with the same repetitive dismal stories. The latest meeting of the G7 powers plus Russia had achieved absolutely nothing. He was furious. How could politicians expect to save the world from economic decline when their policies were based entirely on out-manoeuvring everyone else, defending their countries' short-term individualistic interests in order to improve their re-election chances? Did they not have the slightest inkling as to the seriousness of the global situation, a situation that desperately required global solutions? Perhaps things would change for the better if Amazonian insects were given the vote.

The word 'bear' caught his eye.

'The long-awaited hunt organised by local French farmers to kill the brown bear recently attacking sheep, ended in disaster and confusion yesterday. Three farmers were killed and four were blinded for life when their guns blew up in their faces. Police suspect sabotage, although both the ETA and Greenpeace deny any involvement. Brigitte Bardot, active campaigner for animal rights, was quoted as saying it served the farmers right.

In the noise and confusion the bear managed to escape and has not been seen since.'

Before arriving at Esher he mentally reviewed his social calendar. Dinner with the Jacksons tomorrow night. The wife was one of the church fête helpers and, in adulation of Gladys, had invited the McHendersons to dinner. Drat Gladys and her bloody bazaars. His wife had been almost amenable since his return to the greyish gloom of Esher, but then she normally was bearable after a separation. Absence makes the heart grow fonder or, in her case, less objectionable. The truce usually lasted a couple of days, so the coming evening should be almost pleasant. Then she would recover her normal matrimonial self with a vengeance.

He was safe until Wednesday.

Fortunately, that evening he would be away from home; after various deliberations he and the Reverend Jeffrey had decided to establish a 'Kylb Committee', both agreeing they needed additional support in their crusade. Apart from the two founder members, the following people had agreed to attend the first gathering of the committee, although none had the faintest notion what was in store for them:

Simon Weizenblaum: Jeffrey vehemently vetoed the participation of any representative of the Catholic church, due to its unanimously reactionary, dogmatic, blinkered and infuriatingly infallible attitude to everything Protestant. Under duress he admitted that perhaps another of the various religions on offer should be represented, and Simon was not as retrograde as he looked. Also, politically, having a Jewish rabbi in the team should significantly improve their

image, bearing in mind George's immediate predecessor had been an Austrian named Adolf.
Selwyn Broadstairs MP: Both he and Jeffrey mistrusted politicians intuitively but, as Jeffrey pointed out, the saying 'set a thief to catch a thief' was based on pragmatic logic. And Selwyn had attended the same public school as George so that, under the politician's roughshod exterior, there hopefully remained some vestiges of an English gentleman.
Mrs Margaret Marsh: The vicar's wife had not been selected to represent the approximately 51% of humanity born female, none of Jesus's disciples had been women and his management strategy had worked remarkably well, but simply because she could type and, well, she lived in the vicarage where the meeting was to take place. Also, someone was needed to serve coffee.

That evening, after Gladys had ascended bedwards, he watched *The Bible*, hoping to gain useful insight into the art of messiahing. He soon realised that Hollywood's celluloid documentary-drama interpretation of biblical events bore little relevance to anything religious, past, present or future. He might as well have chosen Monty Python's *Life of Brian*. At least he would have enjoyed a relaxing chuckle.

On the Tuesday evening the Jacksons were unmitigatedly awful. He even admitted to himself that Gladys had her attributes compared to Phyllis and Roland. How could anyone, let alone both of them, manage to extol the virtues of his wife during three hours? Every time one of them exclaimed how he, George, was so remarkably lucky to be married to someone as wonderful as Gladys, he practically performed a mini-miracle of rare intensity. In desperation, he attempted to liven up the proceedings by asking whom, assuming, just assuming, that Jesus was not the son of God, whom did they think was the most likely candidate to replace him?

'Don't be silly, George, of course Jesus was the son of God.'

Pol Pot, he of the Cambodian killing fields, never brainwashed his troops as effectively as Christianity had indoctrinated Mr and Mrs Roland Jackson. It was not their faith in Jesus that incensed him, it was their refusal to consider alternatives, in other words their condemnation of the overwhelming majority of mankind who happened not to have opted for the Church of England as their vehicle to heavenly paradise. To cap it all, by the time he and Gladys finally arrived home, Jennifer had turned off her light and was safely snuggled up in bed.

But now it was Wednesday. Tonight's meeting was different, tonight was important. According to plan, five distinguished members of Esher society were congregated in the drawing room of the vicarage, sipping coffee. Three of them were wondering what George could wish to discuss that was so important, one was wondering how on earth George would manage to convince the others of Kylb's existence, (he had a jug of water and some Farmer's Pride eggs on standby), and the fifth member of the group was wondering whether these eminent people would proclaim him a duly appointed Local Agent or a raving lunatic.

He could not put off the moment of verity any longer.

He told the tale of Kylb just as he had presented it to Jeffrey two weeks earlier, omitting the same irrelevant erogenous passages. And when he had finished, just as with Jeffrey, there was a total and highly embarrassed silence.

He was ready for them.

'You are expected to require more than a little convincing. However, first I must insist that everything already said, plus the events of the rest of the evening, remain strictly between the five of us for the time being.'

Four heads nodded in unison.

'Simon, you look pale, a glass of something? What can I get you?'

Simon Weizenblaum was too preoccupied to remark that

one of the other guests, not his host, was proposing liquid refreshment.

'Some more coffee will be fine, thank you.'

'No, stay where you are Margaret,' he commanded as the vicar's wife, as expertly trained as any Pavlovian dog, was about to depart for the kitchen.

He poured a steaming cup of coffee from the water jug which he had noticed, with great amusement and pleasure, waiting next to the eggs.

'Selwyn, your turn.'

'Madeira, that's if you have some?'

The golden liquid gurgled out of the water jug, vintage to the very last drop.

'A glass of water please.'

'Perrier,' he commented as he handed Margaret a glass full of fizzing tonic. 'Sorry, there's no ice.'

'Jeffrey?'

'Cognac, please.'

'Careful, it's 1812 vintage, could be a little strong.'

Simon may have been a religious disciple and not a businessman, but he still possessed the inborn intellectual shrewdness deemed typical of his race.

'I've seen that trick performed on the Paul Daniels's Magic Show!'

He was handed the jug, once again full of Metropolitan Water Board standard quality issue.

'Watch.'

And the mixture of dissipated ooze, dead bacteria, live viruses, saline sediment and various man-made chemicals, some intentionally added to made the resultant fluid drinkable, others present by inadvertence, obediently metamorphosed into 1926 Taylor's port. Then, whilst Simon was tasting the port, the liquid in the jug transformed into his favourite brand of kosher wine, 1992, one of the best years since 1948. By the time he had sipped the velvet-like *kibbutz* vintage, apart from being very slightly tipsy, Simon was bordering on despair.

After the chicks had clambered back into their shells,

each covered with feathery down tinted with colours personally designated before they hatched, and the oil painting on the wall had kaleidoscoped with portraits of each of them as children, all of them were genuinely terrified, even Jeffrey for whom this was a repeat performance.

He eyed his companions.

'I am prepared to perform increasingly impressive miracles until you are all convinced.'

'No, that's just fine,' replied Margaret on behalf of the others.

'Are there any questions?'

Silence. The newly appointed members of the committee had insufficiently gathered their wits, let alone their composure, to be ready for supplementary information.

'George, do you believe in Kylb?'

'Yes, Margaret. After much hesitation, hoping he was an illusion and longing to find a rational explanation, I now have no choice other than to believe in his existence.'

Another silence ensued.

'I ask each of you reflect on tonight's happenings, especially what Kylb announced in the wood. I expect you to be plagued with doubts, I assure you I was. I simply ask you, for the time being at least, to assume Kylb does exist and give me the benefit of your cooperation. You are here this evening because I need your help. I propose we meet Saturday morning to start preparing some sort of joint solution to the mess I am in, that we are all in.'

'Are you serious about all this?'

Simon gazed straight at George with his piercing blue eyes. The latter met his gaze unflinchingly.

'Yes.'

'But we cannot exterminate most of the world's population, it would make the Holocaust pale in comparison. I refuse to have anything more to do with your totalitarian scenarios.'

Simon, not unnaturally, was extremely tense. His nerves, frayed by repeated references to the horrific events of half a century earlier, were causing an instinctive and violent reaction to the heresy spoken by this normal-looking accountant. He had intuitively calculated that there would be sufficient room for all the world's Jews in the surviving one billion, the entire Arab population would of course be included with the remaining six billion. Then, realising his approach to the problem was akin to Hitler's 'final solution' in reverse, he gave up and sat in silence. George must be a fake, a damn clever one. He could not be for real. For if he was . . .

Selwyn, phlegmatic like most politicians, confident of his ability to worm out of any situation by deceit or finding another to take the blame, initially decided that eliminating all those planning to vote socialist in the forthcoming general election would be a worthy start towards achieving Kylb's goal, even though, he reflected sourly, it would not leave many Britons alive. Perhaps he should simply ask George to arrange a Conservative victory, it would need a bloody amazing miracle and George seemed to have the necessary gifts. Also, if George really was the Messiah and he, Selwyn, was a founder member of this so-called 'Kylb Committee', he could asssuredly wangle a Cabinet post for himself. How about Minister for Religious Affairs? But if he went public and George was revealed to be a fraud then, safe seat or not, Selwyn Broadstairs would lose more than his deposit at the next elections.

Jeffrey, carefully studying the rabbi and member of parliament, concluded that although George might not have fully converted them, he had certainly sown the seeds of serious doubt. More than anything, he was relieved to no longer be the only person, other than George himself, aware of Kylb's presumed existence. He supposed he believed in Kylb. Or did he? George's powers were supernatural, he could not deny that, but was George telling them everything about Kylb? Equally important, had Kylb been telling the truth to George? And if not, what was the truth? Could Kylb be an emissary of the Devil? George had admitted to entertaining such reservations. But if so, why were his prayers to God not being answered? He was also conscious that duty called, the church had a hierarchy to respect and sooner or later, preferably sooner, he would be obliged to inform his bishop, the stupid, doddering old gaffer. Amongst those serving under his tutelage, the only difference of opinion concerning their superior's competence was whether words went in one ear and out of the other, or never even penetrated the first one. Persuading the Very Reverend Nicholas Fotheringay to take Kylb seriously would not be easy.

Margaret was also thinking fast. She had sensed something was bothering Jeffrey, that he had been withholding information from her. Now she understood. She was used to acting as secretary to meetings, but preparing today's minutes would be a major challenge. To start with she hadn't the faintest idea how to spell Kylb. She eyed the water jug and eggs. Performing similar domestic miracles could significantly reduce her grocery bills, also save on the family budget by replacing the charwoman. She had been enthralled by the portrait of herself as a child, she adored the blue dress and wondered if she dare ask George to recreate it permanently. She had never liked the grim ancestor who habitually stared down balefully from the drawing-room wall.

It was that time of the day when evening is almost over and night has already begun. The vicar and his wife were in bed, not like Selwyn who was lustily partaking of his 28-year-old Swedish girlfriend, nor like Simon who was pouring over the pages of the Koran. (Well if George was genuine then perhaps he had better brush up on Mohammed.) Jeffrey and Margaret were lying side by side with the reading light on, separated by a narrow stretch of sheet. At least for the time being. Both of them knew well the joys of marital fidelity, neither had experienced sex, not even a French kiss, with anyone else either before or subsequent to their marriage, nor were they inclined to changes matters. Tonight Jeffrey had decided he was going to take Margaret, whilst Margaret had decided she was going to be taken by Jeffrey. Perfect marital harmony.

In the meantime they were talking.

'Do you really believe in Kylb?'

'How can I not believe in him? We simply cannot deny that George is, well that George has suddenly acquired certain exceptional powers. Good or evil? Something tells me we are on the side of Good. We cannot deny the facts, refute what we both witnessed tonight, what I experienced in the church two weeks ago. We can only trust George, assume he is telling the truth about Kylb. If one thing convinces me Kylb is for real it is George's attitude, he seems overwhelmed with the situation and is desperately seeking our help. That's not the behaviour of a psychopath, nor a satanic spirit sent by Lucifer. And if Kylb is a fiction, how do you explain the beautiful portrait of you as a young girl hanging in the drawing-room?'

His wife could not.

Jeffrey gazed at his wife in his special way. She knew what he wanted. With a tingle in that very special place, a very prim, proper, marital tingle, eminently suited to a vicar's wife, she smiled to herself and turned off the light.

George and a glass of Glenmorangie twelve year-old single malt were sitting in his favourite armchair, the former gazing out of the window. He had missed Jennifer yet again. Not only had he missed seeing her, he had missed seeing her. It was nearly two weeks since their last visual *rendezvous*.

As he sipped, he cogitated. He was pleased with his handling of the meeting, he was no longer alone. He appreciated why Jesus had gathered disciples around him. Being a Messiah, officially designated by the proper authorities or self-appointed, or should that be self-anointed, was a harrowing experience. But he was no quitter. His public school upbringing had toughened him, prepared him to face the challenges of life. Reflecting on the name of his public school, could that be where the term 'harrowing' originated? He realised he was getting inextricably enmeshed in the affairs of Kylb but, having committed himself to accept the AAA Corporation's existence, the sooner things advanced rapidly the better. There was no longer any turning back.

Ah, dear Jennifer, he sighed.

The 17-year-old neighbour's daughter stirred, woke with a sudden urge. A brief trip to the toilet, then she decided the blue of her pyjamas clashed with the green of the sheets. Having removed the offending garments she stood staring out of her bedroom window, looking unseeingly at the stars whilst deciding what to wear for the rest of the night. Surely, nowhere in the Universe, could there be a more delectable spectacle to admire.

But he had already gone to bed.

7

Abacus

'I'm sorry, Jeremy, but we cannot manage our firm's financial affairs this way. It is ridiculous providing extensive professional services to companies, submitting excellent audit reports and being wined and dined by their managing directors, if they fail to settle our fees. How do you expect me to pay salaries and office overheads, not forgetting staff training schemes, if your clients cannot be bothered to respect their pecuniary engagements? And you cannot be bothered to insist that they do so.'

The senior partner of Christie, Wainwright, Steinway and Company remained cool, calm and collected as he gazed steadfastly at one of his junior managers. Politely but firmly he was laying down the law of the land, the first commandment being *'Clients their fees shall pay pronto'*.

The monthly management meeting was in full session. He chaired the proceedings with iron discipline, occasionally raising his voice in exasperation yet never bullying, insulting nor humiliating his management team. He hardly needed to, he was on home territory where debits were invariably found on the left and credits were systematically and safely deposited on the right. Furthermore, he knew, and they knew he knew, the office procedures better than anyone else, because he had written them. Computers excepted, he was lord and master, respected and hopefully liked by his staff. Computers, plus Charles Dewey and Gladys, were the banes of his life, not forgetting obstinate golf balls that refused to enter the minuscule muddy holes patiently waiting for them. A modest list to which misfortune had recently added another kind of ball, a luminous one calling itself Kylb. However, for the time being at least, his little banes were forgotten and he was enjoying himself.

As the reunion drew to its close he noticed the usual signs of boardroom fatigue, for example shifting one's backside to relieve the cramp, furtively sneaking glances at watches, shuffling one's papers, stifling a yawn or surreptitiously checking that cigarettes were readily available in one's pocket or handbag.

'I have one more thing to announce.'

Need for nicotine and congested blood circulation of the buttocks were instantly forgotten. Everyone knew the boss left the best, or the worst, for last.

'At last month's staff meeting we agreed I would personally handle the AEX Europe account, at least until we better understood the extent of potential audit problems. However, I am currently involved in a major study which, if confirmed, could lead to important demands on my time. The project is confidential so I cannot divulge details. I propose that John handles AEX whilst Consolidated Dairies and United Taxis are transferred to Richard. Alternatively, Richard handles AEX, but John's experience with Belgian clients and his resultant knowledge of Flemish could be invaluable, bearing in mind AEX's major manufacturing facilities are situated in South Africa. What do you think?'

He always sought his colleagues' opinions, he ran a team and not an army training corps, the respect of democracy was fundamental to his management philosophy. He did not necessarily accept their suggestions, he was after all the boss, but he always listened intently, knowing they appreciated participating in the management process.

John and Richard accepted that his proposals made sense, although perhaps David could replace John on a couple of minor assignments whose timing clashed with the AEX deadline.

Agreed.

It was time for their traditional Friday lunch at a nearby pizzeria, a *fruit de mer* for the two Catholics present. The senior partner led the group from the conference room, striding ahead as if commanding the Charge of the Light Brigade. In fact, his bladder was bursting.

That evening, in fact every evening that week, the 17.58 from Waterloo deposited him at Esher precisely on time. There were mumblings and grumblings from commuters using the Underground and North London train services. Why didn't their trains also run on schedule? Trade unions representing South West Trains threatened strike action if things did not return to normal. The situation was a clear case of exploitation of the workers.

He had been too preoccupied with the monthly management meeting and finalising his *Mission Statement* to perform any major miracles. However, in the heat of the moment, he managed to perform several spontaneous minor ones having no connection whatsoever with saving humanity from Kylb's fiery furnace:

- Desperately late for a business appointment, he ordered all traffic lights to turn green. The taxi driver, emanating from London's East End and who cultivated an accent making Eliza Doolittle, long before Professor Higgins redesigned her vocal chords, sound like the Duchess of Gloucester, could not believe his eyes. The words of bewildered wonderment, especially when a policeman brought an ambulance to a shuddering halt to allow them through, demonstrated the richness and variety of the dialect of London's Docklands. On arrival several minutes early, choking in a cloud of diesel fumes as his 'mate' drove away as if at Silverstone, hurtling at high speed towards a resolutely red traffic light, he looked upwards. From the pavement of Throgmorton Street it was impossible to distinguish whether the sky skulking above the toxic waste of mankind's most magnificent metropolis was blue or grey. At least there was no risk of catching skin cancer.
- After the Friday morning management meeting, whilst

experiencing agonies of delight in the office toilets, he over-concentrated on people's reactions to his confidential project and insufficiently on where he was aiming. A snap of the fingers and the cabinet instantly returned to its habitual state of carbolic cleanliness, even before the guilty party was replaced back inside his pair of Y-fronts.
- His toothpaste had run out until he whispered a few words of encouragement to the empty tube. He even managed to insert those wriggled red lines into the paste.
- The office lift doors closed just as he was racing towards them. The miracle was not that they reopened to let him in. The miracle was that, having vehemently muttered 'bugger it' under his breath, he had the presence of mind to cancel his instructions before anything untoward occurred.

As far as the Kylb mission was concerned, he had the impression he was making some progress. On the Thursday evening he worked solidly on the *Mission Statement*, the rather grandly named handwritten notes he intended to submit to the Kylb Committee the following Saturday. The text displayed overall coherence. He could present his ideas to the group with a certain level of confidence. Or was he fooling himself? He was making progress, but progress towards . . . That was exactly the problem. Towards what? His notes, did they represent the answer to everything or merely a series of ideas, hopes and illusions? Was he pursuing the right approach? Should he not be parading outside the House of Commons or chaining himself to the railings of the United Nations? What would Jesus have done? Probably set up shop at Speakers' Corner and proclaim the end of the world was nigh, prior to roughing up a few stockbrokers on the steps of the Stock Exchange. Public crucifixion on Hampstead Heath was unlikely. Instead, the judge would probably sentence him to 30 days' detention at Her Majesty's pleasure in Bow Street police station.

The Kylb Committee was the key to everything, and it desperately needed to broaden its representation. At Simon

Weizenblaum's suggestion a new member had been added. Not only was Dr Zighani a man of medicine but, according to Simon, he had performed several outstanding social studies in Bangladesh. He was also a Moslem, albeit an exceedingly restrained one. Simon explained that Jews and Arabs, as opposed to Zionists and Moslems, not infrequently socialised outside the confines of the Middle East. There was a touch of exoticism in these relationships, somewhat akin to a monk climbing a convent wall to converse with nuns, but sometimes a real friendship was formed. Both Simon and Aziz were convinced the Middle East, without politicians and religious leaders, would be as peaceful as West Sussex.

With George's permission, Simon briefed Aziz about Kylb. However, without the benefit of miracles to corroborate the facts, Aziz assumed the whole idea was a prank, in extremely doubtful taste, but he was intrigued by the multi-confessional nature of the committee. He had been brought up in Pakistan by strict parents so, in spite of his own more than fuzzy religious beliefs, (for example he considered the Koran as relevant to defining contemporary social behaviour as the abacus was to explaining the functioning of an IBM AS-4900 computer), he knew well the teachings of the Moslem faith. When you peeled away its ecclesiastical indoctrination, its basic philosophy was not dissimilar to Judaism, especially concerning social and family mores; also its messages of peace and tolerance and, regrettably, the frequent deformation of those messages by reactionary clerics for political purposes. Both creeds were strongly concerned with protecting society. For example, neither religion permitted the eating of pork for health reasons. Sadly, both religions were controlled exclusively by males who, under the guise of ensuring social stability, blatantly manipulated doctrine to keep females downtrodden and exploited. The Jews had been dramatically less successful than the Arabs in recent times, which is possibly why one small state of Israel could defend itself against a dozen belligerent neighbours.

In spite of their mutual respect, Aziz and Simon had very

different personalities. The latter, as Jeffrey had told George half-jokingly during their first meeting, was not as sinister as he looked. Admittedly thick horn-rimmed spectacles, a head completely bald on top but which sprouted long, black, decidedly greasy hair on each side, hair that cascaded down to merge with a luxuriant but unkempt beard, and clothes ubiquitously shiny jet-black apart from a generous sprinkling of dandruff, did little to convey an impression of Anglo-Saxon normality. In reality, Simon, underneath his 'retrograde' exterior, was a private and sensitive person, someone who had suffered and survived but only at the cost of cumulating numerous psychological scars. He accepted other races had their attributes but he was theologically committed to Jews being the chosen people. Like many other Jews, he was secretly proud Jesus had been one of them, in spite of rejecting his religious authenticity. If, as George claimed, Jesus really was the impostor and Mohammed the truly anointed, Arab nations would inevitably revive their belligerency, claim Jerusalem for themselves. The all-important Middle East peace process would once again be in jeopardy. If George, this gentleman gentile, was the Messiah then he, Simon, would have to convince him to defend Israel's interests at all costs. If he was the Messiah. If he was. If.

Aziz, freed from religious constraints, was far more relaxed about life. All he wanted was to practise medicine in England, be accepted by the British as part of one happy, multi-coloured family. Pragmatic and practical, in spite of his innocent idealism, he had an open mind and was ready to serve all members of the community whatever their skin colour. Aware that progress towards integrating his family into Esher society had so far proven frustratingly slow, his biggest concern was that Islamist extremism would infiltrate Britain. He was particularly horrified at the antics of the British Islamistic Society whose members, all proudly possessing British passports, talked like Iranian Mullahs and behaved as if living in the middle ages. If they expanded their activities, resorted to unconstitutional methods of persuasion, the country's entire Moslem population would be castigated as unwelcome intruders, including himself.

Whatever its real purpose, the Kylb committee, however distasteful its activities, should provide the Zighani family with all-important and long-awaited social introductions. So he would pretend to take them seriously. For the time being.

On the Thursday evening, whilst working studiously on the action plan, he realised he had failed to notice Jennifer's light. He must have been over-concentrating on his kylbian labours. Should he raise her from the depths of adolescent slumber? No, he must first complete the action plan, business came before pleasure.

So, whilst Jennifer slumbered peacefully, her distinguished neighbour struggled manfully with his attempt to accommodate the extraterrestrial edicts of his newly-acquired boss. It was almost midnight before the business was completed, leaving little time for the pleasure. So he went to bed.

Now it was Friday evening, an evening free from social engagements, a momentary respite before the following morning's Kylb Committee meeting. At dinner he explained to Gladys his involvement in a convoluted scheme to finance the church roof renovation, hence his need to meet the vicar and others involved with the project. However, the copious notes he waved in his wife's direction referred not even obliquely to cracked tiles and plumbing estimates. He realised he had made shamefully insignificant progress towards defining his objectives, let alone identifying practical solutions. If only he not had dallied with exposing feminine lingerie and savouring the delights found therein, he might be well on the way to countering Kylb's threats to humanity. A twinge of remorse caused him a moment's uneasiness. But now, armed with a clear concise synopsis ready to be presented to the other committee members, something to serve as a basis for discussion, as a starting point in the race to save *Homo sapiens*, he had finally achieved meaningful progress and could afford the luxury of relaxing for a few moments.

He leant back, stretched his legs and glanced towards the cocktail cabinet. Gladys had stopped clumping around upstairs. How was it possible for one single person to generate so much noise whilst preparing herself for a mere few hours' sleep? What in darnation did she do to herself in the process? The twanging of metal springs being tested marginally beyond their breaking point confirmed Gladys had finally heaved herself into bed. What would his wife say, how would she react, if he were to follow her upstairs and manifest marital ardour? Either he would be ignominiously ejected to the accompaniment of 'have you gone mad' or he would find himself entwined in a boa-constrictor embrace likely to permanently flatten his ribcage. He admitted he had no notion how Gladys would view the situation, something that caused him considerable anguish. He managed to push the troublesome thought from his mind, but not altogether, it remained in the inner recesses of his brain, ready to resurface. Because of Kylb, or in spite of him, his conscience had concluded the time was opportune to attempt a reconciliation with his wife. It did not know exactly how and it certainly would not attempt anything that night. But consciences can be contumacious in the extreme and his had no intention of abandoning the idea.

Meanwhile, he returned to musing about Kylb. He remembered, as an articled clerk, being taught that defining and understanding a problem was half the battle. Finding the solution became a mere formality. He hoped his ex-boss's philosophising extended to the activities of Senior Area Managers from somewhere beyond the Milky Way.

He stood up, walked to the hi-fi, carefully selected the evening's musical entertainment, moved to the cocktail cabinet where he contemplatively poured himself a wee dram of whisky, although to be honest the dram was anything but wee, and then sank back with a sigh in his favourite armchair. Whilst the soundtrack of *Doctor Zhivago* played gently and the level of Cragganmore twelve year-old single malt slowly lowered in his glass, he considered the practical problems of coping with Kylb and Gladys. How and when should he inform his wife of his newly acquired mission? Not yet. First he wanted to ensure everything was advancing satisfactorily, sufficiently to present her with a *fait accompli*, as the French would say. Otherwise, he knew what would happen. Predictably and inevitably Gladys would not only involve herself, she would take charge. This, however, was not a church fête or a county bowls' championship, six billion lives were at stake. Entrust the organisation to Gladys Joyce, and the Mighty # himself would come visiting to sort out the chaos. A visit whose agenda would no doubt include an *adieu* to the human race. If she treated Kylb the same way as her church helpers, the entire Milky Way would probably accompany mankind on the road to extinction. Dear Gladys, she was well-meaning but impervious to advice, insensitive to the concept of compromise. What would be her answers to his problems? How would she select those destined for elimination? And, by inverted mischance, would her solutions be superior to his?

His conscience, which conveniently spent frequent and lengthy periods in judicious hibernation but which that evening was experiencing an unusual burst of hyperactivity, having eavesdropped into the thoughts of the brain it chaperoned, realised it should prepare itself for a long uphill struggle in the months ahead.

The *Dr Zhivago* recording had come to an end. It took considerably less time to listen to the soundtrack than read the book. After his acoustic travels to the Russian Steppes, he opted to visit the barren deserts of the Middle East in the company of a certain English army officer. He temporarily abandoned the comfort of his chair, combining the changing of the record with topping up his glass. He had just settled back into his armchair and was sipping his whisky when Jennifer's light came on. He had temporarily forgotten his young neighbour in order to meditate about Kylb and then, as 'Lara's Theme' had played, to imagine sweet thoughts of Julie Christie until realising she was now over 70 and probably a grandmother. Feeling decidedly mellow, the whisky having successfully sent his conscience back into hibernation, he decided he had earned the right to a command performance. However, after due consideration for his neighbour's physical well-being, he ruled out a cancan or Cossack dance. Instead, having removed her clothes, the nubile neighbour found herself once again standing in front of the window gazing into the night, this time seeing nothing, hearing nothing, thinking about nothing.

He gazed in wonderment at the lovely body, the delicately sculptured vision standing before him. This was no low-level neo-biological structure, this could only be a creation of Mother Nature herself. This was sheer beauty, the perfect innocence of youth, pure and untainted by the demons of adulthood. Why did children grow up to become fat and flaccid, arrogant and selfish? Did they unsuspectingly, become like their parents, simply not knowing any better? How could some humans perform saintly acts of sacrifice whilst their brethren pillaged, raped, polluted and destroyed? Jennifer in her simple natural and unspoiled nakedness surely represented something uniquely special, something worth protecting, in fact something to be preserved at all costs. And yet she was one of billions, with further millions being born every year. However sublime she might be, the world contained far too many Jennifers. But how could anyone decide which should live and which should be compacted into pulsating piles of meaningless molecules?

Then, of course, for every Jennifer there was a Jeremy, a Johnny or a James. Males did not perhaps achieve the unadorned physical perfection of the female, but they were no less unique, no less special. And, according to Kylb, there were three billion too many of them.

He focused the binoculars on Jennifer's eyes. What

thoughts were concealed behind her shining orbs? Someone once said – was it George Bernard Shaw or Oscar Wilde? – that if a man managed to fully comprehend women he might as well transfer to heaven, no greater challenges remained on earth. But, rest assured, all males could anticipate a prolonged lifespan, there was no danger whatsoever of comprehending the workings of the female mind. Someone later commented, more than a little maliciously, this was because women were hopelessly unable to understand themselves. Was not this, however, part of their everlasting charm and fascination? No, perhaps not.

He lowered the binoculars slightly. Her breasts came into view. Jesus had supposedly performed a miracle when manna appeared from Heaven to feed the hungry. Yet those two finely moulded little mounds produced the milk that nurtured and sustained life. Erotic perfection, symbols of everything female and feminine, woman with all her force and her frailties, and highly efficient food dispensers.

The binoculars next focused on Jennifer's navel. Not only could she give life, she had been given life. By her mother. Evolution. It had taken about 650,000,000 years to advance from the first basic life form to achieving a Jennifer. Astonishingly, in that momentous time span, nature had failed to invent an efficient way of being born. Much to his regret, he had never attended a birth, but he occasionally glanced through medical journals. Hours of heaving pain, forceps, blood and placentas, there must be a better way. Mother Nature had very graciously granted women a clitoris to induce pleasure during impregnation, why had not she designed it to function throughout the prolonged trauma of delivery, thereby providing at least some pleasure to the otherwise agonising and humiliating proceedings? The little indent in Jennifer's stomach was a quaint indication of nature's surprisingly artisan approach to solving the practical problems of procreation. A tiny imperfection? Perhaps, but one that hardly dimmed the beauty of the whole, perhaps even adding a modicum of charm. Almost a billion years of creation to achieve a Jennifer, yet a shapeless ball of light calling himself Kylb was ready to undo everything for not respecting a few blasted internal control procedures.

A little lower down and the binoculars rested on Jennifer's dainty triangle of protective hair, that discreet curtain guarding the entrance to her treasures within. Strange, hair on the head is to be seen, to be admired, to be flaunted, but those tiny strands shading the lower stomach are condemned by society, perceived as indecent, shameful, their very existence refuted if for example you were a Watteau or a Botticelli. But why? In accordance with what rationale? He recalled his own adolescence, the age of biological discovery. He had graduated from *Amateur Photography* and *Health and Efficiency* to *Folies Parisiennes*, his purchases instigated by an inordinate curiosity concerning the female body. The most interesting parts. Those hidden by clothes. But never a pubic hair had adorned those ever so photogenic maidens. Thus, when his hands were finally allowed to explore the real thing, one by the name of Sandra, he had frozen in horror when his fingers encountered not the smooth nakedness on display in his magazines but a fuzzy unkempt beard. His first ever conquest and she had to be a freak, an escapee from the circus, the cousin to the bearded lady. Yet behind that modest and sweetly adorable little curtain of discretion was the origin of life, the source of creation itself. No more than a miniature maze of biological tissue, perhaps, but that was where the greatest miracle of all took place. Conception. Sadly those unique embryonic life forms grew up, multiplied by the million, destroyed and polluted all that surrounded them. Kylb was right, yet he was so terribly wrong.

There, between the thighs, was a wisp of cotton, witness to that special time of the month, another example of nature's medieval approach to solving the complexities of creation. How could a blob of light appreciate the heartaches, the frustrations, the joys and the monthly inconveniences of the human reproduction cycle? It was only on Earth, sometime in the infinitely distant past, that atoms had decided to combine into molecules, into cells, into something that contained not only mass but the wonder of existence. Into something that millions of years later had become a Jennifer. And even if Kylb did comprehend how Jennifer had been achieved, did he understand why? And if he did not, did anyone else? Who, other than mankind itself, had the authority to impose arbitrary and draconian measures affecting the outcome of the human phenomenon?

He wondered how his thoughts would differ if Jennifer's father had been standing in her place. Jonothan was jovial to the extreme and a good neighbour, a *bon vivant*, his absence of waist bearing witness to many a gastronomical excess. He was pear-shaped, not a Williams but more a Conference. At least his body was consistent, he sported a double chin and fleshy legs to accompany a pot belly that easliy overprotruded a nine-month pregnant mother-to-be, unless she was expecting twins. He himself, not unnaturally and thankfully, had never witnessed Jonothan as nature intended, although it was unlikely that nature had indeed intended quite such a miscarriage of bodily justice. Whereas Jennifer's sexuality radiated beauty her father's, represented by a dangling hairy mangled mess partly concealed by his bulging belly, would radiate ... well luckily it probably would not radiate anything. Even so, however unsightly it might be, it had the same power of creation as any woman's body. It was just that the male's sexual accessories were devised somewhat differently, more emphasis being given to practicality than aesthetics.

Of course, beauty was far from skin deep. Surely crinkled and shrivelled Mother Teresa was a more beautiful individual than those nauseating overstatements of silicone sex permeating Hollywood films? Who, or rather what, since he could not bring himself to consider Kylb as even remotely human, could possibly write an internal control procedure that condemned six billion persons to molecular disintegration? Yet, he was forced to admit, humans were methodically condemning millions of other life forms to extinction, an inexcusable unethical mass extermination of epidemic proportions. Kylb was right, humans deserved to be severely punished if they did not mend their egoistical ways.

Jennifer's body trembled, not from emotion since her mind was a blank, but from the cold. Goose pimples were forming over her arms and legs. He understood, he relented, sadly allowing the vision before his eyes to put on her pyjamas and snuggle into the welcoming warmth of her waiting bed.

The record had finished, Lawrence of Arabia was dead, killed in that stupid motorbike accident. The glass of whisky was no more than an empty glass. He lifted himself out of his chair and wended his way towards his own bed.

8

Calculus

'Why on earth have you invited a Moslem, a heathen worshipper of Mohammed, an Arab, to help with the church roof fund?'

Gladys was amazing. She knew every single item of gossip, every scandal, every happening of interest plus many of no interest whatsoever, that had taken place, was about to take place, or was no longer going to take place in Esher and the surrounding district.

'Not my idea,' he replied as he munched on a pancake oozing with maple syrup, a treat he reserved for weekends. 'Perhaps he wants to rent the church Friday mornings as a mosque, no one uses the building then. It would reduce costs, help us finance the roof repairs.' He stopped. As expected his wife was staring at him in mounting horror. Dare he? Yes, he dared. 'After all, cinemas double up very successfully as bingo halls. Excellent idea, sound management thinking. The crucifixes could be easily adapted, Jesus on one side Mohammed and some crescents on the other. After Friday morning prayers the mullah presses a button and hey presto! there is Jesus ready for the Christian nuptials of Saturday afternoon. Far better than erecting their minarets all over the place.'

Gladys was speechless, probably for the first time since her dental brace entangled itself and glued her mouth together on the eve of her sixteenth birthday.

By the time her jaw muscles had loosened themselves, her husband was safely on his way to the vicarage.

'It's still a bit early for coffee,' announced the Reverend Jeffrey to his guests, 'so I suggest we start the proceedings.'

The self-appointed Chairman of the committee handed a copy of his *Mission Statement* to each of the five other people present in the vicarage drawing-room: Simon, Selwyn, Jeffrey, Margaret and Aziz.

On arriving, the newcomer had stared at George somewhat longer than is normally considered polite. Aziz was extremely nervous. To start with, this was his first invitation inside a Christian dwelling apart from the standard guided tour of St Paul's Cathedral. Added to that he was sitting down with a vicar and his wife, a member of parliament and a rabbi, whilst making polite conversation to a Messiah. He realised, of course, that George was not really the Messiah, he was merely pretending to be one, something that only marginally eased his misgivings. He gazed lengthily at the delightful painting of Margaret as a girl but, unfamiliar with the drab original, was not the slightest bit impressed, just curious. He was impatiently intrigued to discover how long the charade would continue, how long until they announced the name of the game and revealed the real purpose of the meeting.

The Chairman opened the proceedings.

'I propose we start by reading the notes I have prepared. Please understand they do not constitute a final document, they simply represent a basis for discussion, an attempt to channel our ideas into a logical order.'

Silence ensued as the members of the Kylb Committee settled down to study the *Mission Statement*, so meticulously and laboriously compiled during the previous week.

Kylb Committee
Mission Statement

Following the 21 March 2005 visit of Kylb, Senior Area Manager for the Milky Way and representative of the AAA Corporation which, from what I was told, is responsible for managing the Universe, I, George McHenderson, have been appointed their 'Local Agent' on Planet Earth. My mission is to redress three designated nonconformities concerning the organisation's internal control procedures, namely:

- *the sending of satellites into space*
- *the emitting of radio waves intended to communicate with other civilisations*
- *the wilful elimination of other life forms co-existing with us on Earth*

The following document is prepared on the assumption that Kylb (a) existed and (b) meant exactly what he said. Which entails a possible elimination of the human race if we fail to comply to his demands.

* 1 Mission
Our mission is purely and simply to save humanity from total extinction.

* 2 The non-conformities and how to eliminate them

2.1: Stop sending satellites into space.
Kylb's concern is the cluttering up space with metal junk. Although not discussed in detail, we may assume that all missions to explore outer space must henceforth stop. There is presumably nothing we can do concerning satellites already launched which can neither be recalled to Earth nor destroyed in space. Furthermore, it would appear reasonable to suppose we can conserve low orbit satellites used solely for terrestrial applications e.g. weather forecasting and telecommunications.

The United States and Russia are the only two powers involved in space exploration. It should be relatively simple to request that their respective Governments immediately halt ongoing projects. If they refuse, we destroy their launching facilities.

A formal note to the American and Russian Ambassadors in London should suffice. There would be no compensation.

2.2: Stop emitting radio messages
Apart from the United States and Russia, the United Kingdom and possibly France, Japan, India, China, Canada and

Brazil might also be conducting experiments into space communication. This should be reasonably easy to confirm from appropriate Government agencies dealing with space research, or editors of magazines specialising in space technology.

Once offending countries are identified, the Committee can proceed as for satellites, preferably handling both concurrently.

2.3: Stop eliminating other life forms
Kylb not only identified the problem, he imposed the solution: ceasing industrial and domestic pollution and reducing the human population to one billion, a figure apparently obtained by applying some arbitrary AAA formula. However, and Kylb was formal, within an unspecified time frame the number of humans on this planet must not exceed one billion.

Project A: Population reduction
Could we avoid population reductions if Project B relating to protecting other life forms, as detailed below, is implemented before Kylb's return? In this context we must rapidly establish the complete list of species to be saved and undertake actions necessary to prove conclusively that humans are, or soon will be, in conformity with the relevant internal control procedure. That is assuming my 'powers' extend to cleaning up chemical dumps and exhaust emissions, also rapidly regrowing forests and stitching up holes in ozone layers. But Kylb was adamant. We may consider it preferable to avoid population restrictions, but he apparently does not. Can we negotiate with him? We obviously must try, but it would be extremely dangerous to predict success and disregard reducing population levels.

1: Birth control
This approach is the most natural and the least dramatic. Unfortunately, it requires over a century to accomplish and therefore may not be accepted by Kylb.

Several methods exist to achieve the required reductions. The final choice depends essentially on the deadline imposed by Kylb.

1.1 Sterilisation of parents after the birth of their first child. Couples already raising one or more offspring would be sterilised forthwith. World population should decrease as follows:

2005	*7 billion*
2025	*7 billion*
2050	*3.5 billion*
2075	*2 billion*
2100	*1 billion*

(One generation equals 25 years)
N.B. *Due to the enormous numbers of children already born, in some countries nearly 50% of the population are currently under 25, it is assumed that for one generation i.e. during the period when existing children grow up, marry and produce their child, global population remains stable. Net reductions thus only occur from 2025 onwards.*
(Nb: A similar policy has been applied in China for many years.)

This is my preferred solution but will Kylb allow 100 years to achieve his target? If, when he returns, draconian measures have already been introduced to protect other life forms, there might be improved prospects of his being flexible.

1.2 As for 1.1 although, assuming Kylb does not accept a 100 year time limit, only one couple in two (or three) will be allowed to have a child. The selection process must be totally random.

2: Population quotas
I have tried to keep the following text devoid of emotion, but it has not been easy. Fortunately, we should only resort to this approach if Kylb refuses to accept any other solution. Even so, I believe it imperative to be prepared for the worst case scenario, however unpleasant for everyone concerned.

2.1 Immediate Selective Population Realignment
This achieves Kylb's requirements in one ghastly step.

Immediate elimination of everyone over 40*	*2.5 billion*
Secondary reduction **	*3.5 billion*
Total reduction	*6.0 billion*

* *Adults should accept death so their children might live.*
** *Do we make the selection random, or should we apply some form of prioritisation? For example should all criminals and those dying from incurable illnesses be removed, so fully viable people can survive? Humans, when culling animals, for example rabbits, deer and kangaroos, usually apply some form of scientific approach.*

Selection should be based around households, not individuals, to avoid decimating families. I also propose equal numbers of males and females amongst the survivors.

We should ask Kylb to perform the actual eliminations in accordance with our guidelines. Let him perform the dirty work.

2.2 Population Realignment Combined With Birth Control
This option includes an immediate mass reduction as in 2.1 but only to an intermediate level, for example four billion. Starting from a lower global population, it should be possible to apply the rules in Section 1 above more easily and achieve the final goal of one billion with less disruption to our societies.

Project B: Protecting other life forms
The following measures should enable us to respect Kylb's wishes:

* *Massive cleansing of known chemical dumps and strict limitations on all forms of industrial waste.*

* *Suppression of vehicle exhaust emissions.*

* *Effective treatment of household refuse by obligatory recycling or incineration. This could be encouraged by imposing punitive taxes on throw-away packaging and offering state subsidies for recycling.*

* *Immediate halting of deforestation, especially in the Amazon, combined with the replanting of forests already destroyed.*

* *Immediate halting of the hunting of all endangered species whether for food (whales), pleasure (tigers) or greed (elephants).*

I reiterate the greater our efforts to protect other life forms the more chance there should be to negotiate smaller population reductions. Or avoid them altogether.

* 3 Action Plan
The calendar of events below assumes we have one year to prepare for Kylb's return. Also that we remain anonymous.

Step 1
Finalise the composition of the Committee. Do we need further members such as a scientist, economist, lawyer, etc.?
Completion date: April 30

Step 2
Select our spokesman. He must be someone with close connections to the media but none to any members of the Committee.
Completion date: May 15

Step 3
Authorise the spokesman to announce the situation to the world. To ensure he is taken seriously, I propose simultaneously performing a major miracle. For example:
 # extinguishing the sun for a short period of time
 # making everyone alter physically, e.g. turn their skin blue or tattoo 'Kylb' on their foreheads.

Before attempting this I must confirm the extent of my powers. I simply cannot announce the sun will forget to rise the following morning, only to discover that dawn occurs on schedule.

Step 4
Once the world is fully aware of the situation and its far-reaching implications, we organise meetings with world leaders. This should enable us to obtain an understanding of practical problems to be overcome and how best to deal with them.
  I propose contacting the following people:
  The Prime Minister and selected members of his Cabinet

The Archbishop of Canterbury
David Attenborough
The Queen
The European Commission in Brussels
University Professors specialising in subjects directly linked to the objectives to be achieved: economics, history, sociology.
The Pope
The Dalai Lama
Secretary General of the United Nations

For the moment I have no idea how we can involve these people whilst remaining anonymous. The meetings would presumably have to be handled by our spokesman.
Completion date: June 30

I do not feel ready to extend the action plan beyond this point due to the uncertainties facing us all.

* 4 Marketing Strategy
There is one important conceptual decision to be taken urgently. What image should we promote? Am I a religious leader with you as my disciples, or merely a Local Agent designated to perform some necessary logistical house-cleaning?

* 5 Conclusion
None. All I can say is that I have not enjoyed preparing this document and, if I could, I would sent Kylb to eternity.

Esher April 2005

Apart from the shuffling of papers and an occasional throat clearing, plus a series of tummy grumbles from Selwyn, what had he been eating for breakfast? there was silence in the room. His own stomach was also in a state of turmoil but no noises emanated from within: butterflies are notoriously silent creatures. Re-reading his notes, he found them less incisive than the previous evening, several paragraphs were inconsistent with the overall message. At the office he solved the problem by stamping *DRAFT* on the document, warning his colleagues of inherent deficiencies. He just hoped his committee members understood the gist of what he was attempting to communicate.

Margaret, the first to finish reading, left the room to prepare something to drink. She was well aware George could instantaneously produce coffee far superior to hers, but she needed to escape from the others, to be alone for a few moments. She desperately hoped the whole ghastly thing was a nightmare, but she knew it was not. Every time she saw her portrait on the wall she knew it was real. Kylb existed and it was horrible. Jeffrey was 43 years old, she was not yet 38. Would she soon become a widow, knowing her own days were numbered, that her children would soon be orphaned? She accepted that George, or rather Kylb, was right about human population levels getting out of hand and she had long believed global pollution, especially ozone holes and global warming, were far more serious than the authorities were prepared to admit, but there must be another solution to the problem. The coffee was far too strong and dark brown stains on the kitchen floor bore witness to her state of agitation.

Aziz was the next to finish reading. He was used to Monty Python and Jasper Carrott, but this was pushing satire beyond the limits of reprehensibility, the notes were not even amusing. Living in Iran and Pakistan had toughened him, atrocities were regrettably part of everyday life. On several occasions he had tried in vain to reassemble mangled parts of a human body into a semblance of a person so he could perform an autopsy. George, however, was play-acting about dismembering society as a whole. Who was to be on the receiving end of this practical joke? However developed the British sense of humour, no one could possibly find their prank the least bit amusing. Whatever the social connections to be garnered from the people sitting in the room, he would have absolutely no part in their project. As soon as possible he would invent an excuse to escape from these benign yet seriously misguided idiots.

And then, turning to accept the cup of coffee offered by

Margaret, he caught sight of the painting of himself, his parents and younger sister who had been killed in an automobile accident. In the background was the car that crushed the life out of her delicate body that summer's day in 1979.

Selwyn had taken part in many a dastardly political plot, gleefully doing the dirty on innocent victims with all the multitudinous skills of his trade, but George's document left him numb. It was the language. Whereas George's analytical mind was at that very moment concerned that his notes were more than a trifle meandering, the stark simplicity and unpardonable honesty of the text completely fazed Selwyn. No Government, not even the Social Democrats, would dare present such an unambiguous document to the electors. It would be political suicide. Merely circuitously insinuating about thinking about modestly raising minor unimportant unspecified taxes, however justified, was enough to get you hounded out of office. Most electors hated being reminded about real problems, and politicians were well advised to play along with the deceit. Which of course they did. The Conservatives might just buy George's plan, but then political suicide was one of their specialities. Unfortunately, he, Selwyn Broadstairs, would end up in the political graveyard with his mentors. Visions of his rise to fame as Minister of Religious Affairs evaporated, to be replaced by his nomination as Minister of Mass Extermination. It would hardly be a stepping stone to Number Ten, having recently celebrated his fiftieth birthday, his first duty would be to exterminate himself.

He knew perfectly well the human race was careering out of control down the fast lane, heading inexorably towards Armageddon. Practically all Governments of the civilised world knew it, but none had the guts to tell the electors, preferring to let their successors sort out the mess, as their predecessors had done to them. Some political leaders harboured fanciful illusions about somehow extricating civilisation from the mess. He himself, ever pragmatic, ridiculed the idea of a fairy godmother arriving in a golden coach waving her magic wand. Or had she just done so, calling herself Kylb? A person with gangrene accepted having an arm or leg amputated to save his life. Would humans accept a voluntary shrinking to save themselves from Kylb's 'final solution'? He doubted it. As such, George's talk of respecting democracy was ludicrous, the poor chap must be self-deluding. A crisis of this magnitude required military intervention, NATO for example, not the ineffective self-opinionated whining of pandering politicians, like himself. He, Selwyn, desperately needed more time to sift through the ramifications of the circumstances, to ensure that he ended up on the winning side, if there was to be one.

Jeffrey sat feeling dazed. Trained to accept the teachings of the Gospel as no less than gospel truth, he obediently accepted George's words at face value. His parish was limited to Surrey suburbia. There were deacons and bishops to deal with this scale of problem. He could no longer even pray for guidance since there was presumably no one listening in, nor ever had been. He felt abandoned, like a puppet whose strings fall around him in a tangled heap, no longer supporting but entangling him. He waited, sipping his coffee dejectedly, hoping the others would discover the right answers, the ones he himself was unable to provide.

Simon was the last to finish reading and the first to speak.

'This is outrageous, absolutely preposterous. I'll have nothing to do with your preposterous plans. I don't care how many millions you exterminate but you won't touch a hair on the head of one single Jew, you have my word for that. If you don't abandon the whole damn thing immediately I'll, I'll . . .'

Simon, in his fury, was about to threaten setting the Mossad onto them, before remembering its interventions were not generally publicised in advance, pre-emption being the preferred strategy applied by his cousins in Israel.

'In any case, if Hitler was one of your fucking Local Agents then Jews have already been through the elimination process.'

'Simon...'

'Don't Simon me. How do we know you've been telling the truth? And even if Kylb happens to be more than a figment of your imagination, we only have your word for what he postulated. How do we know you haven't invented everything to increase your own self-importance and play out your perverted fantasies? In any case, who says that Kylb is the Almighty? Why should we obey him blindly? Frankly, George, you are either horribly gullible or bloody perverted.'

'Calm down, Simon, please!'

The Reverend Jeffrey was used to excited members of his congregation but not emotional rabbis.

'I will not calm down! George wants to exterminate most of mankind including millions of Jews and you expect me to calm down? Do what you like to the rest of humanity, but leave us Jews out of your perverted schemes.'

Aziz, already on tenterhooks, exploded in fury.

'Will you please stop talking continually about Jews as if they were separate from the human race. There is not one problem for the Jews and another for the rest of us...'

'The Jews *are* special. We always have been and always will be. Kylb may be your God but he is not ours. You can volunteer your own people for extermination but not us. After the Holocaust we are immune from your blasted problems.'

'What is so special about the Jews?'

'Everything. We are different from the rest of you. That is why we have always been persecuted.'

'Other races have been persecuted.'

'That is their misfortune.'

'Hitler also exterminated a million Gypsies in his concentration camps.'

Jeffrey remembered being deeply shocked when Lech Walesa, at a ceremony commemorating the victims of Belsen, had paid tribute to both Jews and Gypsies. It was not the tribute which had shaken him, it was the violent protests of Jews present who resented being grouped together with Gypsies.

'Aziz is right. If the Jews are to be exempted, then the Gypsies should be treated likewise.'

'How dare you lump us together with a bunch of uncivilised thieving nomads!' Simon was almost screaming.

'Please everyone! I have already considered the implications and, strictly from a practical point of view, I support Aziz and Jeffrey. If we accept to treat the Jews differently, however justified their claims, we would have to apply the principle throughout history. As Jeffrey rightly says, Gypsies were also decimated by Hitler. But what about the Armenian ethnic cleansing by the Turks, the Croats and Serbs, the Russians under Stalin, the Red Indians in North America, the Maoris in New Zealand, the Cambodians under Pol Pot, the slaughter of the Anglo-Saxons by the Normans in 1066 if you really want to push things to the extreme. History is full of ethnic atrocities. Whatever Simon or anyone else might say, the Holocaust is only one of many, the most horrible because of the premeditation and the scientific way in which it was conducted, the most shocking because it was so recent and conducted in Europe on such a massive scale. But from a historical context it is, sadly, far from unique. In our mission it would be a practical impossibility to treat nations or races individually, whatever the justification. We would open a Pandora's Box of dissent and get bogged down in endlessly heartbreaking and fruitless debate.'

This was too much for Simon. In a flurry of dandruff he exited the room.

Aziz stood up. His moment had come. He looked at George briefly, but not briefly enough. The eyes that stared piercingly at him were no longer the eyes of a genial accountant. There was an intensity, an aura of authority that he had not witnessed since meeting the Ayatollah Khomeni in Qum. He glanced again at the painting of his beloved sister, then at George, sighed and sat down.

'I think we all need time to digest the contents of my

notes, collect our thoughts and start facing up to the stark realities of the situation. Let's meet again Monday evening. We must advance without any further delays. And don't worry, our raving rabbi friend will be back. He drives by his synagogue on his way home. One look inside, and he *will* look inside, and he'll return to the fold. Pleading.'

'Margaret, your coffee was delicious!'

And smiling broadly at his hostess he adjourned the meeting. He had promised Beatrice a walk, but it was he who required the fresh air and exercise considerably more than his tail-wagging companion.

9

Consultus

April is supposedly the month of showers. The supposition had come true, with a vengeance. Of course the Englishman is unique, the solitary subspecies of civilisation impervious to weather, especially rain. The true believers slosh their way round the country's golf courses, fearing only snow and bunkers, they await the dank mists of autumn before pursuing misshapen rugby balls in oozing mud, they insist upon howling Atlantic gales before deigning to put to sea in their frail little sailing boats. Only tennis players and cricketers bow to the caprices of Mother Nature, the former because the damp snaps their racket strings whereas the latter can claim no extenuating circumstances whatsoever to justify their atypical behaviour. Down in suburban Esher the lady bowlers did occasionally admit to heeding the elements. The rain played havoc with their hairdos.

Margot Steenboch, wife of the manager of one of Esher's more reputable high street banks and winner of the 2003 ladies' county championship, was chatting to her bowling partner as rivulets of rain descended outside the clubhouse window.

'Don't worry, Doreen, I have it on good authority the committee raising funds for St Matthias' roof is a sham. They only spread the rumour about converting the church into a mosque to deflect people from discovering their real intentions.'

'So what are they really up to?' Gossip was to Doreen as water was to a fish. Or in her case a shark. 'An Arab and a Jew in league with Selwyn Broadstairs, they can't be up to much good.'

'Look, there's Gladys, she'll know what's going on.'
'Gladys!'
A mere 92 kilos of McHenderson, the stress of the church fête had seriously upset her metabolism, stopped in front of her two cronies, both of them at the same time.
'Gladys, what's that husband of yours up to, attending secret meetings about imaginary leaks in church roofs?'

Meanwhile, safely installed elsewhere in Esher, although equally despondently watching the same shower soak much of South-West London, Gladys's unsuspecting spouse was about to open the latest proceedings of the aforementioned and so-called Church Roof Repair Committee. Its members had met twice since Simon's stormy exit in a cloud of dandruff, dedicating many hours in the intervening periods to churning over the insoluble problems facing them. He knew everyone had a lingering, niggling hope that they were wasting their time on some stupid wild-goose chase, although none were prepared to ignore the risk that somewhere, far distant from them, a pulsating ball of light had made a mental note in his electronic diary to return to *Bl-zzziii-5* sometime in the near future.

'Let's begin, please. There are three matters to be discussed, no not discussed, we cannot procrastinate any longer, we must make decisions, we simply must achieve something definite. Until now all we have accomplished is talk.'

There was a hint of despair in his voice. It was easier to prattle about what should be done than accomplish the actual doing part of being done, but they were not politicians and could hardly afford the luxury. Well, Selwyn was, but the Chairman had no intention of allowing the Member of Parliament to offer himself such an indulgence.

'Firstly, do we incorporate any new members into the committee? Secondly, the choice of spokesman. And finally, how to announce the situation to the world, with special reference to the image we wish to create and the choice of maxi-miracle to ensure we are taken seriously.'

'Simon, what about Jacky?'

Only he and Simon knew what the latter had witnessed in his synagogue two weeks previously. But Simon had changed. To start with he no longer suffered from dandruff. But, more important, he was subdued and appeared very much committed to the cause. He apologised for his aggressive behaviour, asking them to understand it was sometimes difficult for Jews to distinguish between criticism and racism.

'As you know, at Margaret's suggestion, we agreed to consider the possibility of adding a second woman to the team, someone with experience in the world of social services. Jacky works for Surrey County Council and has been involved for many years in town planning, especially the construction of council houses, and I know she is deeply committed to the problems of the aged.'

'In that case, George will soon render her redundant!'

Selwyn was in a jovial mood following his previous night's exertions. There was an embarrassing silence, during which Simon failed in trying to pretend he had not heard the remark. To everyone's relief he remembered he had been discussing Jacky.

'I consider her an ideal person to help us. She has close ties with the Home Office, which could procure necessary statistics on population levels and breakdowns by age group. There is one major drawback. She is Jewish and I suppose one is enough for the team.'

'No problem, Jesus had twelve on his committee.'

Selwyn was still in a good mood. Jeffrey intervened.

'Simon, I appreciate your concern, but we are here to save humanity. I don't believe Kylb would give a damn if she were Zulu or Mongolian, and by that I mean someone from North-Eastern China, so let's ignore such issues.'

'I agree with your logic,' Aziz commented 'but we must be extremely prudent. We personally might not care, but the Arab nations will howl.'

'Sod the Arab nations. Next we'll be inviting blind mandarin three-legged lesbian dwarfs to join us because their Government is distressed about unfair lack of representation. This isn't the United Nations.'

Margaret made her first contribution to the meeting.

'I fully support Jeffrey, not because he is my husband I hasten to add. We simply cannot afford to get bogged down in politics. I suggested a second woman on the committee, not to defend the cause of feminist rights but to reinforce our expertise in certain areas. If this committee room turns into the House of Commons, the human race is doomed.'

Selwyn considered defending his place of work, then realised Margaret was doubtlessly right. From what he had been informed about Jacky, she was apparently a raving leftist radical and a right little bitch, but she knew her stuff. Politics apart, she would definitely reinforce the team's ability.

'That's settled. Simon, will you ask her?'

'Couldn't you, George? A few miracles do tend to convince people more easily.'

Simon sighed as he spoke. He was speaking from bitter experience. Then, before Kylb's Local Agent could protest, the rabbi scrawled Jacky's full name and office telephone number on a piece of paper and placed it in front of him. He gave in.

'Do you think miraculously constructing several hundred council dwellings should do the trick?'

'Depends where they suddenly sprout forth. If they convert the Kingston bypass into a quiet residential area, I'm convinced she will take you seriously.'

'Anyone else?'

Silence.

'Too many cooks spoil the broth, especially in committees.'

Selwyn's professional training had taught him the most efficient way to kill a project was to concoct an *ad hoc* committee, a large *ad hoc* committee full of gregarious people with differing ideas. To eliminate all risk of decisions being taken, you added a couple of trade unionists. The project, however brilliant, was doomed to a leisurely suffocation under a morass of paperwork and failed compromises.

'Fine! Next point, the spokesman. I think we can kill two birds with one stone if we invite David Attenborough to represent us. He is extremely well known, appearing frequently on television, so he obviously knows how to handle the media. He is also highly respected as a naturalist, so he presumably knows which biological species need conserving. He lives nearby, only twenty minutes away. If there are no objections I'll contact him without delay.'

There were no objections, especially from Margaret who avidly watched his television documentaries although not especially interested in wildlife.

But there was a problem. Mr Attenborough was currently leading an expedition to some outlandishly inaccessible forsaken and forgotten barren peninsula, to observe whatever wildlife one dutifully observed in such locations. Jeremy proposed Carstairs Welsh as a replacement. Although not a national institution, he was a thoroughbred scientist and nature lover. He also demonstrated, whilst lecturing to students at Kingston University, the ability to mesmerise his audiences whilst teaching them. He resided in Petersham, even nearer than the absent Mr Attenborough.

Professor Welsh was unanimously elected their spokesman. Whether the vote would have been equally unanimous if the eminent professor had been in attendance failed to distract committee members from the advancement of their crusade.

'Next, how to announce the news to the world? I propose our spokesman makes a statement to the press, Reuters or whatever, informing them of Kylb's visit and his list of demands. He should simultaneously advise them of our designated maxi-miracle. But, before advancing further, we must agree amongst ourselves on the appropriate image to create. Am I the local representative of the AAA Corporation or the son of God and second cousin to Mohammed?'

'And Adolf.'
'Please, Selwyn, let's forget about him.'
So far Jeffrey had listened rather than contributed, he had been saving up for this moment.
'I strongly support what George identified in his notes as the 'business approach', for two reasons. Firstly, any hope of the world's church representatives rallying around George to save the world is an illusion, a pipe dream, because religious leaders, however saintly they might pronounce themselves, are depressingly hopeless at working in unison.'
'Worse than Conservative and Labour,' muttered Selwyn who knew all too well about such matters.
'For starters they don't serve the same God. Their internecine mistrust and self-centred ambitions are a sorry reflection on the often inspiring but sadly irrelevant theory of their dogmas. The Church of England is a rare exception, it has striven valiantly to promote greater respect and understanding between differing beliefs, regrettably with little success. If only church leaders practised what they preached. Since, according to Kylb, only Muslims and German Neo-Nazi parties have any claim to authenticity, hardly reassuring if you are Catholic or Hindu, we can expect religious infighting to break out, rendering our mission impossible to achieve. At least democratically. George must be as neutral, as innocuous, as secular as possible. We must not allow religious patriarchs to lead society into a deepening incompatible hotchpotch of feuding congregations adhering to the introspective visions of medieval reactionaries.' Jeffrey paused, considering his words impressive rhetoric for a country bumpkin of a parish vicar
'But they won't know it's me,' he countered.
'I think we are fooling ourselves about remaining anonymous.'
Simon doubted the sleuths of Fleet Street would readily unearth their committee; however Mossad would trace them instantly.

'Well, I'm going to damn well try,' he retorted. 'But I fully agree with Jeffrey, at least so far.'

'So far?'

'Yes, you said you had two reasons.'

Jeffrey remembered the second.

'Kylb had little time for religion, he appointed George as 'Local Agent' and not as the Angel Gabriel.'

The others were not entirely in agreement. Selwyn, ever the practised politician, reacted first.

'I don't think 'Local Agent' is going to impress many people. Unless George grows wings.'

After nearly 20 minutes of intense discussion it was agreed he retain the title of Messiah. Image would be vital to their ultimate success and the designation 'Messiah' better promoted the concept of all-powerful messenger, whereas 'Local Agent' was insipid and uninspiring. Also, they agreed Kylb could hardly give a damn what his agent was named so long as he achieved his goals.

'Now for the choice of maxi-miracle.' He repeated those included in the *Mission Statement*.

'I suggest everyone voices his opinion before we vote. Margaret, what about you?'

Margaret had already made up her mind. No one was going to turn her purple or green, all her clothes would clash. Nor was she going to accept wearing an engraving of Kylb on her forehead like Indian women, most undignified.

'I propose that the sun goes out for a day. It will have an enormous impact on everyone, also the sun has indirect links to religion which can only enhance the message we are trying to communicate.'

'Simon?'

'Frankly I have no preference, to be honest I don't like any of your ideas.'

'But, Simon . . .'

'Sorry, I'm not denigrating your suggestions, it's just that none of them is particularly pleasant.'

'Selwyn?'

The Member of Parliament knew well the world of mass

media communication, mass-media manipulation when practised by politicians, in other words convincing electors you were revealing everything whilst divulging nothing.

'I suggest the skin colour change for two reasons.' In fact he had four reasons, two of which were strictly personal. 'Firstly, Simon is right, complaining about the proposed miracles being unpleasant. We must think positive, we must not give the impression we are announcing doomsday, even if we are. Turning off the sun will inevitably be interpreted as a form of negation, almost a punishment, whereas we must make ourselves liked and trusted.'

'Like the Labour Party?' interjected Simon, getting his revenge.

'Secondly people have short memories. This can be an advantage, for example for weather forecasting and party political manifestos, but our message must register, must serve as a constant reminder we are serious, that Kylb will not conveniently disappear.' He sat back pleased with his powers of persuasion, reminding himself of his other two reasons. Firstly, he personally exuded a more than typical Anglo-Saxon tepid off-white fungus-blotched pot-marked skin that acutely embarrassed him when in the company of *señorinas* and *señoritas*, not omitting Brazilian temptresses who called themselves *meninas*. His skin either resembled the surface of the moon or an overcooked lobster, most embarrassing and excruciatingly painful when cavorting between the sheets. And secondly, his Party's re-election chances would hardly be hindered if the world changed to Tory Blue.

Margaret, resigned to having most of her clothes clash with her body, spoke up.

'Although rejecting the idea of changing our skin colour, I did consider it seriously. In fact I visited the local DIY centre and borrowed their colour chart.'

And she ceremoniously placed the cardboard display on the table. Silence ensued as the team sought the perfect tint for future mankind. Black, white, yellow and coffee were considered ineligible, so the choice was reduced to red, green and blue.

'Red's no good, we'll all look sunburned, and green will make us appear like diseased zombies from outer Venus. That leaves blue.' Selwyn doggedly pursued his promotion of the Conservative Party and, not uncoincidentally, his own. Much to his surprise everyone agreed with his choice of colour, although not necessarily for the same reasons.

'How about Côte d'Azur,' ventured Margaret.

'Shouldn't we have different shades for Africans, Arabs and Europeans? The former could be navy blue whereas we could be a nice pastel shade.'

'What about mixed race people?'

'And the Scots should be tartan.' Selwyn was still in a happy mood.

'Please everyone! This is extremely serious. At least make everyone the same colour, it will be simpler and might improve race relations.'

'Pink for girls and blue for boys.'

'What about homosexuals?'

'Selwyn!'

'Err, George, are you certain you can perform the miracles on your list?'

He smiled serenely.

'The surprise eclipse of the sun in Antarctica, that was you?'

He smiled even more serenely.

'And skin colour? Who have you being playing games with?'

'Myself of course. And my dog, Beatrice.'

There had been someone else, but he had no intention of mentioning Jennifer who unwittingly served as his personal colour chart on two occasions. Each time her skin had changed to every shade found in the rainbow, plus several that were not, at a speed that would make a chameleon turn green with envy. Most of the attempts were ghastly, akin to Hieronymus Bosch's nightmare creatures coming to life. He also experimented changing hair colour, since none of his skin concoctions matched her auburn tresses, but the results made a Barbie Doll downright dowdy. So he gave up in disgust, on both occasions Jennifer climbing into bed having been returned to her customary mottled pinkish off-white. And he had gone to bed concluding his nymph-like neighbour looked most adorably perfect as nature had previously intended she should.

'I rather like Ocean Mist,' said Margaret more to herself than the others.

The others studied the little square of colour until Margaret screamed, Simon shuddered, Jeffrey crossed himself and Selwyn muttered 'mouldering Maggies'. Their bodies had turned blue, Ocean Mist blue to be exact. Only he remained unperturbed.

'There's a mirror in the hall if you want to have a better look.'

The final choice was Caribbean Sunset, a glowing and friendly reddish-orange.

'That's about it, then,' he announced to the others. 'I'll contact this Jacky person and Carstairs Welsh. Oh, by the way, Selwyn, one last question. What does 'mouldering Maggies' mean?

But the utterer of the words was not letting on.

'GEORGE!'

Gladys hurtled into the lounge and, as was her wont, omitted bothering to enquire of her husband whether she might address him a few words. This time she was so incensed at his potential skulduggery, conspiring with anarchists disguised themselves as roof repairers, she failed to verify his presence. Present he indeed was not. Gladys muttered something very rude, an excruciatingly horrendous forbidden word she had learned at Girl Guide camp.

'Damn!'

She was about to set off in search of the cause of her aggravation when the object in question ambled into the room.

'Yes, dear?'

'Don't you 'yes dear' me'.

'Yes, dear. I mean no, dear.'

'What is this roof repair committee up to, it apparently has nothing to do with roofs. It's a sham, a shameful sham, isn't it? How dare you.'

'Yes, dear.'

'Well, has it or hasn't it?'

He was flummoxed. He knew in such circumstances the best, or rather the safest course of action, was to reply to Gladys' questions promptly, but he had lost track of her positives and negatives. Silence fell momentarily on the McHendersons, Gladys finding herself as grammatically disorientated as her husband. However, such considerations were fleeting irritations to her.

'What are you up to?'

'I've promised not to tell anybody. We have all promised. Don't worry, we are not planning a bank robbery, but we must be discreet if we are to ensure the success of the mission. And I promise to tell you before anyone else. Scout's honour!'

'You can tell me now, I promise not to mention a word to anyone. Also, perhaps I could be of help.'

Having in the space of a mere seven words convinced her husband he must never, never, never utter a single word about Kylb to his wife as long as he lived, Gladys launched into another attack. Her husband was being extremely stubborn.

'No! I've made a promise and you know that I must keep it. Guide's honour. How was the bowls?'

He sighed, listening to ten minutes grumbling about the British climate was better than domestically re-enacting the Spanish Inquisition.

Now it was evening. He was sitting in his favourite armchair whilst the generous glass of Jack Daniels was warming to perfection in his right hand. He was not given to consuming

Yankee whisky but the bottle had been graciously offered by one of his American clients. Showing pleasure when receiving the gift had been an effort, but after several tastings he was starting to admit, strictly to himself, that he rather liked the stuff. Meanwhile the gramophone was playing one of Gladys's records. The owner of the piece of vinyl had just heaved herself into bed, the thudderings and shudderings plus intervening scrapings and grindings ceasing abruptly as a mattress and set of bed strings took on their nightly burden of maintaining her suspended in slumberland. He was feeling weary, his brain hardly fit to cope with the intricacies of Mozart or Beethoven, so he had glanced through his wife's musical selection. Having grimaced at Barry Manilow and Celine Dion, 'Italia Mia' caught his eye. Yes, the cascading strings of Mantovani would suitably soothe him.

Who the bloody hell on earth had told Gladys of the surreptitious activities of the Church Roof Repair Committee? And from whom had she found out? He assumed it was a 'she', women ran the Esher gossip Internet. So far he had successfully fended off his wife's attempts to wring the truth out of him, but Gladys was not one to renounce. Her stubbornness made the average mule suspiciously feckless. And who else knew, or rather knew that they did not know what the Committee was really up to? Or really did know, for that matter?

Apart from his fury at the Esher gossipmongers, he was pleased with the latest Kylb Committee meeting. Things should soon start moving. The following morning he would organise meetings with Jacky Hufnizcwck and Carstairs Welsh. He had already announced to the office his special assignment was entering its preliminary stages, he would consequently be absent from time to time. Only Janet was suspicious. There was no correspondence for her to type, no memos or reports to file and no *rendezvous* to confirm. Nothing. Just what was her boss up to? It was undoubtedly something important. He had been acting distractedly the last few weeks and had absent-mindedly forgotten several appointments. She was used to his scrawling *Balance Shit* when he doubted the accuracy of a client's inventory valuations and *Vat 69* when discussing Value Added Tax, he was after all a whisky connoisseur, but twice recently he had written *Prophet and Loss Account* in his audit reports. No doubt she would be informed sooner or later but her mothering instinct, common to many secretaries, resented her being kept out of the picture.

Mantovani was returning to Sorrento when a flash of light warned him Jennifer was on her way to bed. He adored gazing at her unadorned body, its simple beauty relaxed him, there were no longer erotic or licentious thoughts to accompany her nudity, just admiration and pleasure. People spent hours studying the *Mona Lisa*, Botticelli's *The Birth of Venus* or Michelangelo's *Pietà*, so why shouldn't he gaze at a living statue sculptured so perfectly it made Rodin's efforts gawky and amateurish? In any case there was business to attend to tonight, he needed to test run Caribbean Sunset.

He peered expectantly at Jennifer's window, his plans cascading into tatters as he caught sight of the latest addition to his youthful neighbour's bedroom furnishings.

Curtains.

'Please come in, Mr McHenderson.'

It was the woman who had answered the phone. He recognised her voice but this time he equally appreciated the warmth of her smile.

The previous Monday he had set about contacting Carstairs Welsh and Jacky Whateverhernamewas, anyway whatever her name was it was unpronounceable. According to plan, he presented himself at the latter's office. She had categorically refused to meet him at her home or anywhere else, no doubt conjuring up visions of being kidnapped or something despicably worse. There was no welcome, there was no warmth. The harsh, scrawny business-person facing him had precious little time to spare and was certainly not going to waste it on high-society visitors, however polite they might be. It took three minutes before he was forcibly ushered out of her office, accompanied to threats of calling the police and taking legal action.

Thus the following morning, in the entrance hall of the house of Carstairs Welsh, he was more than relieved to be greeted with a warm smile. Selena, Mr Welsh's personal assistant, showed him through to the study where the scientist was watching television, a wildlife documentary of course.

'Good morning, Mr McHenderson, do take a seat. Coffee?'

The man offering him refreshment looked so normal, anything but an absent-minded professor. Genial but not genius. He started relaxing until he realised the grey hair adorning his host's head signified the server of his coffee belonged to a potentially endangered species, the senior citizen.

Five minutes later his jovial, relaxed and friendly host was no longer jovial, he was decidedly unrelaxed and he was anything but friendly.

'Mr McHenderson, I do not appreciate cranks coming to see me under false pretences and wasting my precious time in the process.'

He admitted his pretences had been false, in fact he had lied blatantly to Selena when requesting the meeting. But truth and business have little in common, apart from their tendency to constantly interfere with each other.

'Mr Welsh, that is a remarkable butterfly collection, what a shame to keep them stored under glass panes.'

'The glass serves as a necessary protection. For your information, Mr McHenderson, they are dead. Very dead. And my butterfly collection is my affair, not yours.'

'They don't look dead to me, Mr Welsh, they seem to be desperately trying to escape from their cages.'

His host's sun-tanned exterior returned to Anglo-Saxon normality as enraged winged creatures fluttered desperately against the glass frame of their prisons. Those unprotected by glass, with a pip-popping of pins, were soon winging their way around the cluttered study of their keeper and one-time assassin. A horrendous sound of shattering glass, greenhouse glass, transferred the stupefied nature-lover's attention to his garden. Carstairs Welsh had gained prominence in the late 1960s with his studies of the African rhinoceros. These can weigh several tons and, living in the sparsely populated savannah, are unused to navigating their bulk around suburban gardens. Being accordingly unfamiliar with greenhouses, and never having encountered a dodo, the fully grown male in question had inadvertently failed to appreciate that, transparent or not, one walked around greenhouses and not straight through them to inspect interesting objects flapping their wings the other side. The dodo, if it could have flown, would have flown. Instead, highly suspicious of the intentions of the approaching animated armoured carrier, it trampled through the goldfish pond and plantation of daffodils so carefully tended by Mrs Welsh.

In exchange for a promise to send the rhinoceros back to Zimbabwe and return the butterflies to their glass frames, Mr Welsh, with the dodo eating bread-crumbs out of his hand, sat down to listen to his visitor's tale.

'Mr McHenderson, I am prepared to admit you differ from the normal nutcases I episodically encounter in the course of my professional duties. However insanely impossible your story might be, it has a certain logic that intrigues me. I propose a stroll to Pen Ponds in nearby Richmond Park. There is something I would like you to perform for me. If you succeed, I am prepared to take you seriously. On the way I will discuss what must be accomplished if we are to respect this fellow Kyleeb's demands. Not that I am prepared for the moment to believe in his existence.'

So he and his eminent acquaintance walked across Ham Common and entered one of London's most natural and beautiful parks.

'You must understand, Mr McHenderson, that nature is a genius at achieving an equilibrium, an order to things. We humans produce excrement. Flies feast on it, only to be eaten by spiders or birds. These are in turn consumed by cats or rodents, whose carcasses are eaten by worms who enrich the soil which nourishes the grass that feeds the cows which produce the milk that nourishes the children who create the excrement and so on. There are innumerable variations to these food chains but the basic principle is always the same, something dies so that something else might live. It is vital that food chains remain intact otherwise species risk extinction from famine, inevitably placing in jeopardy other species which depend upon them for food.

'Evolution progressed unaffected by artificial influences for millions of years, until mankind became industrialised a couple of centuries ago. The dodo is one highly visible although relatively minor example of man's ability to exterminate by unrestrained hunting. However, the desecration of virgin rain forests in South America, to a lesser extent in Asia and Africa, is far more serious a threat. By ruthlessly cutting down these natural reserves we are eliminating complete eco-systems, entire food chains, some reasonably well known, others never scientifically studied by mankind. Being self-supporting it, could be said their removal will have little effect on life as we know it. But what unknown treasures are being wantonly wiped out of existence by greed and short-term stupidity? No one knows.

'However, pollution is the greatest threat, by far the greatest menace to life on earth. Pollution in the air, in the ground, in the water reserves, in the stratosphere. Everywhere. Heedless of warnings from the scientific world, mankind is reshaping his environment, changing it for the worse, mindlessly altering the delicate equilibrium that took millions of years to evolve. Marine life is being trawled to extinction. Breeding fish in immense industrial farms with not replace the intricate biological world existing in the depths of our oceans, furthermore their waste is polluting Scottish lochs and Norwegian fjords to the point of turning them into toxic cesspools. The recent outbreak of lethal drug-resistant measles in Brittany is, in my opinion, linked to untreated waste from genetically altered pigs. Agricultural chemicals used for intensive cereal and livestock farming are reducing topsoil to a sterile powder before infiltrating the Earth's crust. Untainted drinking water will shortly become one of the world's rarest commodities. Mankind knows what is happening, yet the destruction continues unabated.

'Even more alarming in the long-term are global warming, ozone holes and disturbed climates, phenomena all closely connected to man's flagrant disregard for the planet on which he lives. Mankind may successfully adapt and survive, but no other species, from elephants to minute bacteria, have the same ability to save themselves from a tragic fate unilaterally enforced upon them by humans.'

'How long until we eliminate ourselves?'

'Impossible to say. Always assuming we do. No one knows how existing life forms will interact with the changing environment. Evolution is remarkable, for example if you were to place a seventeenth-century person in Piccadilly Circus, it is believed he would choke to death within minutes. Our lungs, in fact our entire bodies, are constantly adapting to cope with the incessant onslaught civilisation flings at them. But evolution is excruciatingly slow and the environmental devastation caused by humans is accelerating out of control. I would not take out an insurance policy on life on earth lasting beyond a hundred years, unless we rethink our very concept of civilisation. However, no one can be sure, I certainly am not. But can mankind afford to take the risk?'

He did not know whether to be relieved or depressed at his companion's gloomy edicts. At least his own tentative and simplistic summarisation in the *Mission Document* had been validated by this knowledgeable scientist.

'So what is the answer?'

'I support your theory that man's actions, not his total numbers, are the fundamental cause of the enfolding catastrophe. Halting deforestation is one key action to be implemented. Replanting trees would be practically pointless, forests would be recreated but not the precious ecosystems they sustained. Prohibiting hunting would be overreacting. However, we do need strictly controlled quotas. Of course, as you so rightly point out, or should that be Keylib, reducing pollution levels is the primary objective, drastically reducing them. This imposes government action that will rock our fragile economies to their foundations. It is sad to admit but our advanced societies can no longer afford to eliminate the noxious by-products of their industrial complexes. Either we sink steadily into a chemical quagmire of our own making, or we halt the pollution and self-destruct capitalistic civilisation as we know it.

'But enough hypothetical theorising.'

The speaker simultaneously stopped talking and walking.

'Mr McHenderson, we have arrived. Welcome to Pen Ponds.'

He admired the scene, open tracts of bracken interspersed with solitary twisted oak trees facing the elements like wizened old men. A herd of deer grazed peacefully, oblivious to being a mere dozen miles from Hyde Park Corner. And there before him were the twin ponds they had come to visit. The grey water reflected the grimness of the clouds streaking overhead on their endless journey from the Atlantic to the Urals, or wherever clouds went after visiting Britain.

It was stark and desolate, yet too beautiful to be depressing. Flashes of colour from the water and surrounding banks of reeds signalled the presence of ducks and geese. It was a scene straight from a wildlife documentary.

'Now, Mr McHenderson, its my turn to make a request. To be honest I've enjoyed talking to you but I don't believe a word of your extraterrestrial visitations. Either I am going to enjoy watching you make a fool of yourself or I'm about to experience the thrill of a lifetime. I want three *Tyrannosaurus Rexes*, two *Apatosauruses*, four *Triceratops*, six *Dimetrodons* and a *Cetiosaurus*. In other words a local version of *Jurassic Park* without any help from computer simulations.'

'Can you please repeat the list?'

He was unable to reel off the names with the same easy

familiarity as his botanist companion. His botanist companion obliged.

The wind continued to ruffle the surface of the ponds, forming minuscule wavelets that slapped incessantly onto the shore. A couple of geese fluttered gracefully to a landing on the opposite side of the lake. This was nature at her most inspiring, simple and unspoilt. Then it arose out of the water. He had no idea which of the requested varieties it represented, but it was gigantic and ugly. And terrifying. He desperately hoped he could return it to the Jurassic era, assuming it had been borrowed from then, before those evil jaws crunched him to shreds. More forms emerged from the turbulent waters of the lake, equally horrific although thankfully smaller. Then, demolishing a couple of oak trees, it was clearly too lazy or stupid to bother walking round them, the largest of them all emerged from the nearby wood and shuddered its way down to have a wallow in the mud. With a roar that made a Pink Floyd concert hushed in comparison, two of the behemoths engaged in a ferocious combat, one apparently taking objection to being eaten by the other. Sheets of muddy water sprayed the lakeside, soaking the two awe-inspired observers. The ducks and geese had long departed, emitting screeches of indignation at the effrontery, the inexcusable invasion of their privacy.

The combating animals suddenly paused in mid-fight, the others stopped feeding or glaring ferociously at everything in particular. British Airways Flight 768 from New York was in its final approach to Heathrow. As the Jumbo roared overhead the dinosaurs scattered in unholy panic, unused to visitations from Boeingosaurus Rex.

Before they demolished the remaining trees surrounding Pen Ponds he sent them hurtling back from whence they had come.

'How about the Loch Ness monster?' he asked his companion.

Carstairs Welsh may have been a normal human being, at

that precise moment an extremely petrified one, but he had the burning curiosity of the true scientist.

'Och aye mon, a wee bit a'yer Nessie'll do me fine.'

Scientist he might have been, character actor he was not.

The two of them waited and watched and waited and watched.

'There!'

A half-submerged tree trunk beached in front of the two disappointed monster watchers. It started to rain.

'George, may I call you George? Perhaps we had better return to my place.'

Professor Welsh was damp and mud-splattered, his pulse was racing, but he was better off than his counterpart in Jurassic Park who had only reared two-dimensional computerised holograms. His accountant companion duly experienced an intense interrogation whilst walking back, regrettably being unable to answer many of the more scientific questions pouring forth. He did, however, manage to interject one question of his own.

'Carstairs, would you agree to become our spokesman?'

All he could wring out of his companion was a non-committal, 'I'll think about it,' before the interrogation recommenced with renewed vigour.

Back in the safety of the botanist's study, sipping an aperitif to restore their nerves, he did obtain a commitment from his host to accept or reject the position of spokesman within three days. This was in spite of refusing the scientist's request to be allowed to keep the dodo as a pet.

'Sorry, but we must be discreet. I've mended the greenhouse and replanted your garden. And thanks for the books.'

If he read the volumes proffered by his host he would be an expert on botany, biology and the remaining vast paraphernalia of natural sciences. A few minutes later, as he walked out of the front door, he heard from within.

'Selena, cancel the rest of the day's meetings.'

'What are all those books?'

Trust Gladys to be in evidence when he was transporting them discreetly into the lounge.

'Brought home some work, dear. Might have a zoo as a new client.'

Once again it was evening. At least twice during supper he sensed Gladys was about to enquire into the dubious activities of church roof repair committees. Twice he glared at her, imitating one of the meaner versions of the morning's assortment of dinosaurs. And twice Gladys never quite dared raise the subject.

'This is the BBC from London. Here is the nine o'clock news read by Martin Walsop.'

Delightful accent he thought to himself, but why did he have to look quite so morbid?

'Police are investigating claims of dinosaurs being sighted in Richmond Park.

'Palestinian snipers kill two female Israeli soldiers as Middle East peace talks fail to make significant progress.

'In Georgia rebel soldiers have occupied an army missile site. It is not known if live nuclear warheads are involved.

'A chemical plant in Venezuela has exploded, pouring highly toxic resins into the nearby Guardalara river.'

Pause whilst the newscaster stole a not very discreet glance at the tele-prompter.

'John Hoskins, retired policeman and amateur ornithologist, claims to have sighted numerous dinosaurs in Richmond Park, not far from Central London. We go over live to Richard Kelsop, our special correspondent, who is at the scene of the claimed apparition. Richard!'

'Yes Martin! I am standing near Pen Ponds, scene of the supposed appearance this morning of about twenty mammoth prehistoric monsters. I have standing next to me retired policeman

John Hoskins who claims to have watched the monsters for over ten minutes. John just what did you see?'

'Well, I was down by the ponds, not too near mind, don't want to frighten the birds away. I had just spotted some Canadian Lesser Mottled Geese, very rare so late in the season . . .'

'Yes, go on.'

'. . . when out of the water arose this gigantic scaled monster, just like in Jurassic Park. It was soon joined by dozens more. Ugly, horrible looking things, if I'd been a religious man I would have sworn Lucifer himself had risen from Hell but . . .'

'How many of them were there?'

'About thirty.'

'Could you distinguish any of the creatures, did they really look like dinosaurs?'

'Like I said, right out of Jurassic Park except there were no safety fences. Bleeding frightened I was.'

'Yes, yes.'

'Two of them started fighting, real vicious it was.'

'Thank you Mr Hoskins. The garbled ramblings of a delirious birdwatcher? Possibly, but something extraordinary happened this morning in Richmond Park. Centuries-old trees have been uprooted with terrific force, land surrounding the lake has been churned into a mass of mud, giant footprints proliferate in sinister profusion. Allen Wilkenson, Chief Warden of the Park'

'We are taking the matter very seriously. Of course, not the claim about visitations from dinosaurs, but serious damage has been perpetrated in one of London's parks. It is a serious case of vandalism, some of the uprooted trees date back to the reign of King Charles the First.'

'Thank you Mr Wilkenson. Our camera crew filmed the scenes of devastation this afternoon. As you can see, a terrifying force has turned a well-known bird sanctuary and tranquil corner of a London park into a scene straight from a war film. Superintendent Miles Sanderson of Richmond CID, was this a mini-tornado?'

'Definitely not! Tornadoes uproot trees but they do not leave footprints in the mud. Its clearly the work of pranksters, ones extremely well equipped. What puzzles us most is they would have required a bulldozer to create such havoc, but there are absolutely no tell-tale traces of the passage of any such engine.'

'Visitors from outer space?'

'The police don't believe in such things. But something arriving by air, for example a Harrier jet, could explain the damage to trees. Mr Hoskins, however, insists there was no plane, or flying saucer for that matter. He did, however, notice two men standing the opposite side of the ponds immediately before the incident and the police are very keen to contact these persons.'

'Thank you, Superintendent. Professor James Harlech of the London Zoo has been inspecting the footprints. Professor?'

'Whoever instigated the prank was extremely knowledgeable about dinosaurs. In recent years scientists have not only simulated the feet, or rather claws, of most dinosaur species but several fossilised remains have been excavated. My initial observations indicate a remarkable representation of dinosaur footprints, very convincing and I congratulate the authors of the prank.'

'Thank you, Professor.'

'I have not finished. We have discovered droppings, blood stains and even shreds of skin which could support the theory that two of the animals were fighting. These are being taken to our laboratories for examination. Probably alligator or crocodile.'

'Thank you, Professor. But that is not all. Passengers disembarking at Heathrow from a British Airways flight from New York also claim to have spotted strange apparitions in the park. In fact, it was the pilot of the Jumbo who first sighted the animals and invited his passengers to take a look, joking that some new prehistoric epic was being filmed in the heart of London.'

'Thank you Richard! Police have announced that to date there is no evidence of human casualties. We now go over to Heathrow where Katie Ediar is with some of the passengers who witnessed the scene.

'Katie!'

He, however, remained in Esher. Galloping arseholes! He had been so intent on miraculously removing mudstains from their suits, he had completely overlooked removing evidence left by the dinosaurs, evidence which was, not surprisingly, more than a little noticeable. Shit, shit and shit.

And shit again.

'Yasser Arafat told reporters today that . . .'

'The Reverend Jeffrey for you, dear,' said Gladys in a tone of voice that would have made any self-respecting *Elaphrosauros* run for cover.

'George, you weren't by any chance in Richmond Park this morning, were you?'

In fact Jeffrey was joking. He had phoned to postpone the forthcoming meeting of the Kylb committee to the Saturday afternoon; his Bishop was visiting in the morning.

'But, dinosaurs! I thought Kylb didn't take a fancy to them.'

It was several minutes before he could extract himself from the vocal claws of the Reverend Marsh. Having finally escaped, he collapsed into his favourite armchair, clasping one of the volumes lent by Carstairs Welsh.

'Simon Wizebloom for you, dear,' said Gladys, staring at her husband in a way that would make even a *Dimorphodon* quake in its scales.

'George, it's Simon. We have a problem.'

He knew they had a problem, he knew too damn well.

'It's my fault, but Jacky has gone to the police. Says she received a visit yesterday from a raving lunatic who claimed to know me, possibly a dangerous sex offender. She would not have taken further action except you mentioned dinosaurs to her. When the news broke about monsters in Richmond Park she added two and two to make five and claims she can identify the man behind the hoax. Er, by the way George, were you involved?'

'Yes.'

'Bit careless?'

'Yes.'

'Sorry. What do we do now? The police will be after both of us before long.'

Endowed with kylbian powers he might be, but he hadn't the foggiest idea what they should do.

'I'll phone you in the morning. If the police contact you,

deny all knowledge. I'll try and deal with them. By the way, Saturday's meeting is in the afternoon. At two.'

He replaced the receiver, furious at the turn of events, at his unpardonable incompetence. Well, there was nothing much he could do about it. Or could he?

He carefully chose a record, something soothing but not soporific. He had some serious thinking to do. As Beethoven's *Pastoral Symphony* glided gracefully into the first movement he sank into his armchair with an extremely full glass of Glenlivet in his hand. How could he be so stupid as to have left dinosaur droppings scattered over Richmond Park? Things were starting to get out of hand, he must be more careful in future. He envisaged two possible choices of action: enact a few miracles to squash the journalistic furore caused by his Jurassic visitors or perform his maxi-miracle without delay. The Kylb Committee urgently needed their spokesman.

Jennifer's light came on. Irritated by the glaring colour of the new curtains purchased by her mother, she flung them wide open. Having carefully placed her clothes on the chest of drawers she stood gazing out of the window, seeing nothing, hearing nothing, thinking nothing. Which was just as well. Even the beauty of her developing feminine body could not combat the garishness of Carribean Sunset. Perhaps, after all, he reflected, he should simply extinguish the sun. Or perform both miracles, in the ensuing dark no one would notice the nauseating colour scheme.

The fifth movement, *Allegretto*, came to an end. He sighed, turned Jennifer's skin back to off-white yellow, finished the last drops of his whisky, struggled out of his chair, said goodnight to Beatrice, visited his still leakless loo, cleaned his teeth and clambered into his lonely bed.

Less than 100 yards away his 17-year-old neighbour was also snuggling into bed, still totally unaware of her role in her neighbour's attempts to save mankind. She would be puzzled the following morning to awake to open curtains, even more amazed to discover several patches of orange skin disfiguring her torso.

10

Matthew

It was the month of May. Although the sun had long descended below the horizon in an immodest blaze of glory, it was still light enough to discern the elms at the bottom of the McHenderson's garden whilst gazing through the living room windows, which is exactly what George was doing at 8.55 on a balmy spring evening. The well-being of his trees was of little consequence, he was awaiting with eager anticipation the BBC's nine o'clock news. Earlier that day the Kylb Committee had finally gone public and announced to mankind the erring of its ways.

Carstairs Welsh had declined the position of spokesman, explaining he was member of a Government standing committee, which created potential conflicts of interest. He not only recommended Matthew Hodges as a replacement, he arranged a meeting between the three of them. As Messiah, he would have preferred to invite them to Esher, but regretfully his house was inhabited by a wife called Gladys who could be more than a little cumbersome.

The meeting in the study of Carstairs Welsh had been surprisingly convivial. But then he was becoming less inexperienced at initiating newcomers into the universe of kylbian visitations and prospects of precipitate hobnobbing with dodos and dinosaurs, always assuming those endowed with extinction departed somewhere, which was far from certain. For many years Matthew Hodges had been science correspondent of one of Britain's more respectable newspapers, one without page three. Well, it did contain a page three, but the spreadsheet in question was devoid of photos, no doubt explaining the publication's modest circulation statistics. It was not a paper he habitually read, so the name Matthew Hodges meant nothing to him. Carstairs Welsh was emphatic that not only was Matthew respected in the world of journalism, he also maintained innumerable contacts with research laboratories and government agencies dealing with environmental issues. Since retiring, he was busier than ever, publishing articles on such subjects as how a world of ten billion people could possibly feed itself and how to survive without an ozone layer. Apparently you could not. He was a devout churchgoer, belonging to an extremely orthodox Calvinistic Baptist congregation.

The one-time journalist was a sly old character, combining a wry sense of cynical humour with a straitjacket approach to how humans should comport themselves, both socially and scientifically. Steeped in the traditions of cautious and diligent research, 'prudence before prediction' was his motto, the wily old codger took a considerable amount of convincing. The dodo delighted their professorial host as well as Selena, who had heard unfamiliar squawks emanating from her boss's study and had allowed curiosity to risk killing the cat. But Matthew remained stoically unperturbed. Water changing to wine? No thanks, alcoholic beverages were for the sinners of mankind. Could he please instead have a glass of Malaysian iris nectar? He accepted his refreshment without indication of surprise and, after accidentally upsetting his glass, was only mildly impressed by the instant dry-cleaning of the exquisite Afghan rug spread over the study floor. Butterflies emerging from glass mausoleums left him unperturbed, kylbian poltergeists lifting books out of the bookcase to float to the ceiling only mildly disconcerted this doubting Thomas of all doubting Thomases. When a multicoloured parrot, whose photo brightened one of the walls of the otherwise gloomy study, landed on his shoulder with a loud squawk and a flurry of feathers, he started to show signs of weakening, especially when the photogenic visitor from Borneo bit his ear and deposited a damp souvenir of its passage on his jacket. He finally surrendered after having been asked to think of anyone he wished, the image of the person appearing where the photogenic parrot had been perched for the last fifteen years. There was an abashed silence, followed by a yelp of dismay from Selena, as the parrot was replaced by an extremely unethical image of herself swinging from the tree in a position never imagined by Tarzan.

Matthew Hodges closed his eyes and prayed for absolution whilst Carstairs Welsh admired the photograph with due artistic appreciation. The unexpectedly acrobatic young lady from Borneo crossed her legs and hoped to die.

'I believe you!' beseeched a highly agitated, recently retired scientific journalist. 'Please, send the infernal parrot back to . . .'

'No, wait a minute.' Carstairs Welsh had something on his mind. 'George, could I not keep the parrot and leave the pho . . .'

'No!' screamed Selena, squeezing her thighs even more tightly together.

'If you insist, but on one small condition.' There was a pause as the speaker gazed in admiration at his chubby 35-year-old demure Anglo-Saxon secretary dangling from a tropical jungle tree. 'Selena, as a matter of sheer ornithological curiosity, do you have a birthmark on your . . .'

Selena's face matched the plumage of the parrot.

'Yes I do.'

The parrot returned to Borneo, Selena uncrossed her legs and Matthew Hodges stopped doubting about Kylb.

'Mr Hodges, we are not asking you necessarily to believe what you announce to the press. It will be perfectly acceptable for you to emphasise your non-affiliation to our cause, that you have been requested by a group of people, who wish to remain anonymous, to proclaim that the following day at precisely one o'clock in the afternoon, just as Big Ben is striking, the sun will disappear for precisely one minute.'

'Will it?'

'Yes.'

He sounded convinced, he presumed the sun would disappear at the appointed hour, yet he wished it would disobey, permitting him to return to his former life. The AEX audit was running into serious problems and, without his immediate intervention on behalf of some banker clients, the draft European Community Offshore Reporting Guidelines would condemn Douglas and St Helier to respectively raising sheep and growing tomatoes.

He did not mention potential skin colour changes to the designated spokesman. After due debate and a further review of her wardrobe by Margaret, members of the Kylb Committee unanimously agreed the varying hues favoured by nature would be perfectly acceptable for the time being.

Two days later Matthew Hodges, benefiting from his presence at an international congress of meteorologists, asked to be allowed to make an announcement.

He was allowed.

As expected there was a short embarrassed silence followed by a few giggles and smirks. He did not try to convince them, that was not in accordance with their carefully contrived strategy. It would, of course, have been a total waste of time.

'The eclipse isn't until next year!' yelled one of the attendees.

He ignored the insinuation.

'For those of you wishing to receive further information concerning the Kylb Committee I will be here tomorrow evening at six o'clock precisely, five hours after the sun will have returned. That's all for now, ladies and gentleman. Thank you for your attention.'

A BBC announcer sidled up to Matthew.

'Say old chap, should I include your predictions in tomorrow's shipping forecast?'

'But of course!' riposted Matthew, his words so loaded

with sarcasm they almost failed to reach the ears of the weatherman.

And then he escaped from the humiliation.

'This is the BBC from London. Here is the nine o'clock news.'

He had stopped gazing at the increasingly indistinct line of elm trees at the bottom of his garden and was seated in front of the television. He had been building up to this moment for nearly two months, with anguished trepidation, perhaps, but also with frustrated longing since waiting is supposed to be the worst part of any assignment. All he wanted was to finish with Kylb for once and for all, as quickly as possible, whatever the outcome.

'George, the sink's blocked!'

When he finally returned to the television some agitated reporter was enthusiastically speculating on the number of dead and dying resulting from a major chemicals spillage in Pakistan, before commenting on the inability of local authorities to organise coherent action to ease the suffering, which, he speculated, was due to the Government's long-standing denial of the plant's existence, a major industrial complex whose products' pharmaceutical properties were rumoured to be highly malignant and manufactured in total disregard of the Geneva Convention on Chemical Warfare. One of the local opium drug barons was offering to clean up the mess in exchange for an armistice, an offer ridiculed by the President who was promptly assassinated by the father of one of the chemical victims.

He had missed the headlines.

He sat through twenty-three minutes of BBC news, ITN's *News At Ten* and a liberal dose of CNN, plus five identical weather forecasts promising cool showery conditions, before giving up in disgust.

The world had other things on its mind.

Extremely vexed, he chose Sir William Walton's *Belshazzar's Feast* played by the London Symphony Orchestra conducted by André Previn. An American! For once here was an Englishman capable of writing music to rival the greatest classical composers and they hired an American foreigner to conduct the orchestra. The Jack Daniels glowed in its glass. He had not chosen it in honour of the person conducting his music, it was simply the strongest firewater he possessed.

The '*Praise bes*' and '*Kingdoms divided*' were in full swing when Jennifer's light came on. He glanced listlessly in her direction as she walked across to the concealed chest of drawers. Tonight he could just not be bothered, somehow this was not the moment to be distracted by comely young maidens. So unseen, she undressed, then gazed with trepidation at the Caribbean Sunset blotches on her torso. Was it warpaint, or the result of a fertility right? She had recently watched a documentary on African tribal traditions, feeling most relieved to have been born European. She looked down at her absolute nakedness, it was rather exciting being exposed like that, so long as nobody was watching.

She pulled on some practical cotton pyjamas, cleaned her teeth and climbed between her sheets.

The London Symphony Orchestra Chorus exalted its final '*Alleluia!*' and he went despondently to bed.

He spent the following morning at the office before walking to Waterloo to catch the 11.48 fast train to Esher, members of the Kylb committee having agreed to witness together the moment of verity. Margaret had prepared coffee and sandwiches for the six people congregating in the vicarage garden. They were six because Matthew, who should not normally have been in attendance, had requested, in a tone of voice bordering on despair, to be invited to the gathering whereas Jacky, who should have been in attendance, was at that moment in the psychiatric ward of Kingston General Hospital wildly describing how she found a herd of dinosaurs in a warehouse, whose address she had forgotten, and why she had decided out of pity to let them loose in the spacious pastures of Richmond Park. Carstairs Welsh and

Selena were chatting in the former's garden, standing near a miraculously repaired greenhouse.

Back in Esher Margaret turned on the radio. The shipping forecast was promising force eight gales in Dogger, Biscay and Fastnet.

'George, is the sun really going to disappear?'

'Funny, Margaret, I was just asking myself the same question.'

'What if it doesn't?'

'Well, I imagine, having heaved an enormous sigh of relief, that I will return to being a Chartered Accountant.'

Margaret at long last dared pose the question that had been tormenting her for weeks.

'Why have you not informed Gladys about Kylb?'

'I'm not quite certain. You know the rule about not mixing the office and the bedroom, well perhaps I felt, rightly or wrongly, it would be simpler if she remained uninvolved.'

'When are you going to tell her?'

'Time will tell.'

'In woman's hour Jane Mitchell will be talking about how to brighten your home with flower arrangements and Dr Marilyn Johnston will be providing practical advice on coping with children who take drugs.'

A moment's silence ensued whilst the BBC announced exchanged pieces of paper.

'This is Radio Three broadcasting on 94.6 megahertz short wave and 1560 megahertz long wave. The time is one o'clock. Here is the news read by Dermot McDougal.'

The chimes of Big Ben dinged and donged in Westminster and, thanks to the marvels of wireless, throughout the entire world.

The Kylb Committee and their spokesman looked skywards, the cumulonimbus of a cold front protecting their eyes from the glare of the sun.

'As the Tokyo stock market continues to collapse, riots have killed three and injured more than . . .'

None of the group gathered in the vicarage garden

registered the number of injured Japanese. With a flickering, like a light bulb about to blow, the sun went out. Just like that. No fanfare, no BBC science correspondent providing a tumultuous countdown. At six seconds after one the sun was there, then it wasn't.

'The German Bundersbank announced a five point hike in interest rates. The unexpected news sent European stock markets, already jittery following events in Tokyo, into sharp decline.'

A screech of brakes and the honking of a car horn indicated the sun had also extinguished itself in nearby King's Avenue and, as witnessed by sounds of people colliding with various unidentified objects to the accompaniment of muttered expletives, throughout the surrounding neighbourhood.

'Help, someone, I've gone blind,' wailed Felicity Edwards from next door.

'Mummy, who turned the sun out?' asked little Dorothy from the other next door.

Margaret, always practical, turned on her torch. The batteries had gone flat.

'Scientists warn that if global warming continues unabated, one third of Holland can expect to be permanently flooded by the year 2025.'

He would have collapsed into a deckchair if the pitch blackness had not prevented him from locating the Marsh's garden furniture. For weeks he had been confronted with a horrendous Hobson's choice: facing the prospect of a premature forced retirement from the world of the living or becoming the fool of the century, well at least one of them. He occasionally wondered, especially when gazing at Jennifer, which choice he disliked the least, usually opting for the biggest fool alternative. Now he knew, unless he succeeded in his mission, his life expectancy could be measured in months.

He didn't want to die. Of that he was certain. He remembered Dickens's *A Tale of Two Cities* where Sydney Carton went to the guillotine to save Charles Darney. Would he sacrifice his life so Jennifer could live? The question was academic, statistically Jennifer was also doomed unless a healthy serving of compassion existed somewhere in the logic circuits on an extraterrestrial overgrown lightbulb.

'Unconfirmed reports are coming in of a surprise total eclipse of the sun in the Greater London area. I, err, well, we will give you more details in a moment but in the windowless studio where I am currently reading, speaking to you, everything appears normal.

'The death count in the Pakistani chemical disaster has now reached three thousand. Khaled Fafinhdi has been sworn in as President following the assassination of Eruhdi Khadeli last week.

'It has just been announced that the sudden eclipse of the sun has now ended and that . . . and that, well things have apparently returned to normal.'

'More coffee anyone?'

Five arms stretched out, their collective and respective owners in dire need of sustenance.

'George,' said Simon after swallowing a large gulp of Margaret's home brew. 'I know I have not always been the most cooperative of members, nor have I always been very positive, but it has been difficult for me to accept the situation. My whole life has been devoted to protecting my race, my people from a repetition of the events of 60 years ago. I was born to believe the promised Messiah would be the true son of God and that he would be Jewish. Are we the chosen race, or did we simply choose ourselves to be the chosen race? You must understand your story of being related to, no, associated with Adolf Hitler, combined with talk of population reductions . . . you must understand that three of my grandparents perished in Belsen.'

There were tears swelling in the rabbi's eyes. Although deeply moved, he found himself unable to treat Simon as a friend. It was not because he was Jewish, he had several good friends who were, it was the rabbi's physical appearance. He assumed it would be equally impossible for him to treat a Buddhist monk, Iranian mullah or Orthodox patriarch as a normal neighbour, their external trappings represented a barrier, a psychological separation that somehow, intentionally or otherwise, he assumed intentionally, created a gulf that stopped normal human relationships from forming, prevented trust and complicity from developing.

Simon continued.

'I now realise I have much rethinking to do, no doubt I have not taken the mission seriously enough. I need time to contemplate the implications, also I feel instinctively I should consult some higher authority in Israel for guidance.'

'Whom?'

'I have no idea. Most of our religious leaders are, well, to be blunt, they can be infuriatingly stubborn and highly reactionary in their thinking. One army commander recently referred to them as being hysterically historical. To some, only events happening over two thousand years ago have any relevance to life today. As for the Israeli Government, well they are too weakened by internal struggles to confront broader issues. Yatzik Rabin is dead, so that leaves no obvious choice. I just don't know, let me think about it.'

Our science correspondent confirms that no eclipse of the sun was predicted by astronomers nor did one occur, at least no normal eclipse caused by the moon. He theorises that an asteroid passed briefly between the earth and the sun. One thing is certain, the sun itself did not literally disappear for a minute.

'Here again are the main points of the news.'

Margaret turned off the radio.

The vicarage garden was once again bathed in normal afternoon light, the sun was half-heartedly shining through the clouds as if to apologise for its momentary lapse of a few minutes earlier. In the welcoming light Matthew found an even more welcoming chair to sit on. In less than five hours he would be at Earl's Court to address a band of cynical and disinterested meteorologists, except this time they would hardly be disinterested. He was going to have the press jamboree of his career. Or would they have forgotten his farcical jabbering of the previous day, so that nobody would be in attendance? Enough pontificating, it was time to start taking action.

'Can I have your attention, please? I wish to read the

declaration I have prepared for this evening's press conference. Please give me your comments, also try and anticipate probable questions so I can practise answering them.'

Whilst the committee was rehearsing its spokesman for the gauntlet he would be running a few hours later, Britain was recovering from the sun's afternoon blink. Insurance companies would take months to process thousands of claims from drivers who found themselves driving without lights in the middle of the night in the middle of the afternoon. The toll would be 74 dead and over 300 seriously injured. The committee members would be highly upset when they learned about the carnage since they had never contemplated extinguishing the sun without warning, hence the carefully prepared announcement of the previous day. Their friendly 'I'm here to help you' image had suffered a serious setback.

Trains and planes fared better since their respective signalling and radar systems worked in like manner both day and night. South West Trains continued arriving on time. London Underground passengers, when emerging into the light, refused to believe the ridiculous tales of solar blackouts, incredulous miners were equally sceptical about the furore, also night shift workers who blissfully slept through the entire commotion. It being lunchtime, few people were engaged in sporting activities. However, several cricket matches were disrupted, umpires being called upon to declare whether bad light should stop play. By the time the majority had decided it should, lighting conditions had returned to normal. In one Gloucester cricket club a bitter dispute raged, the bowler claiming visibility had been perfect when he delivered, the receiving batsman, having had both his bails and his balls demolished in the incident, insisting he could not see a damn thing when the delivery arrived his end of the pitch. The umpires, searching in their rules of play, were stumped.

Before long Britain returned to normal. After all, losing a few dozen citizens in road accidents was an everyday occurrence. The vast majority reassuringly convinced themselves an asteroid had been responsible for the inconvenience. Around the world the situation was similar, except that the sun's momentary absence upset remarkably few cricket matches. The unperturbable Asians remained unperturbed. At 3.00 a.m. one is not particularly concerned about sacrificing a minute's worth of sunshine.

An asteroid. Until certain meteorologists started remembering the senile nutter who warned that the sun would put in a disappearance the following day.

Matthew strolled into the conference centre trying to look as nonchalant as he wasn't. It was 6.01 p.m. The last thing he had wanted was the humiliation of arriving early in the assembly hall and have everybody sneaking sly glances in his direction whilst they waited. So he wandered around the block waiting for 6.00 p.m. to chime, wondering how he should handle the meeting, contemplating the impossibility of prepreparing answers for as yet unknown questions.

'There he is!'

There was only a handful of people in the hall. The majority of attendees had preferred the cruise along the Thames proposed by the official organisers or the sightseeing trip to study Soho sleaze offered by an unofficial organiser.

'Please be seated. Yesterday, to much derision, I advised you of a short intermission in the shining of the sun. No one believed me. To be quite frank, I myself had serious reservations. Your presence here today is proof that circumstances have evolved dramatically. As I explained yesterday, I represent a group of people who refer to themselves as the Kylb Committee and who, as part of their overall mission, were directly involved in the extinguishing of the sun. None of the committee members are in any way involved in astronomy, so their ability to predict an unknown asteroid crossing the sun's path would appear highly unlikely, especially as nobody else did. I will repeat the claims made by these people. There is no need to take notes, a full copy of the text will be distributed at the end of the meeting.'

Matthew read out the document he had prepared and previously submitted to the committee, the content of which was little more than an abbreviated version of the original *Mission Document*. Selwyn had advised brevity, insisting shorter is better when dealing with the press. Citing Watergate and Whitewater, he affirmed that when reporters wanted more information they screamed like hungry wolves, whereas if you immediately offered them everything they invariably lost interest. Minimum information guaranteed maximum exposure.

'To conclude,' continued Matthew, 'I am empowered to inform you, to obviate all doubt that an asteroid caused today's eclipse, that the sun will disappear tomorrow at precisely two p.m. local time for a duration of five minutes. Any questions?'

'Who is behind all this?'
'Why five minutes?'
'Why a different time of day?'
'Who is Kayleb?'
'Is your self-appointed Messiah British?'
'Is he male or female?'
'Do you feel guilty about the deaths and injuries on the roads?'
'Have you envisioned the climatic effects of extinguishing the sun?'
'Is your so-called Messiah a Christian?'
'Is this a monumental hoax, like the dinosaurs?'

'Please everyone, that's enough to start with! Firstly, I am not authorised to reveal the identity of the person who has been nominated Messiah. Secondly, the duration of the sun's disappearance will increase five minutes every day until such time the Messiah is convinced all necessary steps are being taken to meet Kylb's ultimatums. Thirdly, it should be remembered that nearly half of civilisation was unaffected by the phenomenon. By advancing daily one hour the entire world will eventually undergo the same experience, or inconvenience if you prefer. Next, I have nothing more to add regarding the identification of Kylb and I genuinely believe the Messiah himself knows no more than specified in my memorandum. As regards the next two questions, I have no intention of divulging the name of the Messiah, so please do not waste valuable time by posing questions related to his identity. And if henceforth I use the term 'he' it is simply to avoid incessantly repeating 'he or she'. Yes, he is most concerned about the tragic deaths and injuries on the roads. It was assumed my announcement yesterday would be taken seriously. Whether the Messiah is a Christian is irrelevant.'

'Is this a monumental hoax?'

'I suggest you wait until tomorrow afternoon and answer the question yourselves. In the meantime, please treat the situation with the utmost seriousness.'

'Do you realise that in several months, if your Messiah is for real, there will be practically no sun left?'

'Yes, we predict most species, including mankind, will become extinct within a year.'

There were horrified gasps from listeners, then total silence in the auditorium. Matthew was impressed with himself. He was fully aware this was a monumental bluff designed to bring the human race to heel, George had no intention whatsoever of permanently suppressing the sun, but he had spoken so convincingly that even he himself would have been fooled if sitting amongst the audience.

'But the Messiah will die as well.'

'He, like you and me, will die anyway if we do not take Kylb's demands seriously. We believe it critical that the seriousness of the situation be appreciated, sorry appreciated is not the best choice of word, be recognised without delay. We must avoid unnecessary delays. Time is a rare and rapidly diminishing commodity.'

Once again the auditorium was plunged into total silence. Brains are remarkable machines. Even working full speed they do not emit the slightest sound.

'Ladies and gentlemen, I suggest we meet here at the

same hour tomorrow evening. In the meantime, I ask you, as reporters, to give my annoucement the utmost exposure, not only due to the crucial importance of the message but also to avoid any more regrettable road accidents when the sun is extinguished tomorrow. Thank you and good evening.'

And, before he could be swamped with further questions, Matthew exited from the conference room as fast as possible without actually bolting for it. He was already late for a church meeting, whose agenda was devoted to discussing the declining morals of society. His particular argument was that the morals in question were no longer declining, they had already disappeared. People needed urgently to be brought back into the fold before it was too late. Their only hope of salvation was to join their unique band of worshippers, the only congregation to have discovered the real meaning of Christianity. But how to convince the nation's sinners of this? That was the all-important question to be debated that evening.

'George, did you see the sun go out?'
'No.'
'But you must have.'
'How could I, it was pitch dark.'
He looked straight at his wife. As Gladys's oncoming verbal eruption subsided before any words of molten lava spewed forth from her mouth, he reflected on the amazing power of the common and garden smile.
'Where were you when it happened?'
'Oh, at the office.' With modest distension of the imagination the vicarage could be considered his current place of work. 'Where were you?'
Gladys looked distressingly embarrassed.
'Well, to tell the truth, I was in the loo.'
'Better you than me.'
'Why?'
'You didn't have to worry where you were aiming!'

'George, that's not the slightest bit amusing. At times you can be exceedingly coarse and vulgar.'

Sounds of hissing from the kitchen distracted the McHendersons from their dissertation on urinary target practice.

During supper, to his amazement, he learned the real reason for the disappearance of the sun. Muriel Braithwaite had it on good authority that the Chinese were behind everything. They had placed a satellite in orbit between the sun and the Earth so the British would stop annoying them about Hong Kong and they could continue imprisoning dissidents in peace and quiet.

'Perhaps they will confirm your theory on the news tonight.'

'This is the BBC from London. Here is the nine o' clock news, read by Penelope Stewart.

'A Boeing 747 has blown up and crashed near Istanbul. Sabotage is suspected.

'Scientists are trying to explain why the sun disappeared for approximately one minute this afternoon. Preliminary theories would indicate the presence of an asteroid flying between the sun and Earth.

'There has been yet another accident in a Russian nuclear plant, major radiation leaks are probable.

'ICI announces important losses for 2004 and plans further redundancies.

After the usual baleful scenes of fiery destruction surrounding yet another jetliner reduced to scrap metal, not forgetting the tragedy of its passengers and their bereaved families, the newsreader turned to less arcane matters.

'It is estimated that nearly eighty people were killed and several hundred seriously injured in road accidents that occurred around Britain following the unscheduled darkening of the sun at one o'clock this afternoon. The worst accidents took place on the M4 near Slough and the M6 just north of Birmingham.'

George was forced to suffer images of twisted motor

vehicles and dismembered bodies being carried away in blood-splattered plastic bags. One driver was shown writhing in agony amidst the wreckage of his articulated truck, part of his steering wheel protruding grotesquely from his lungs.

'*Apart from M4 westbound, traffic rapidly returned to normal once the sun reappeared. Insurance companies warn they will be unable to pay claims from policyholders with limited third-party cover, they consider vehicle owners were driving at excessive speeds in poor visibility. Hundreds of minor incidents are reported from office buildings as people panicked and collided with doors or with each other, or fell down staircases. By the time brokers on the floor of the Stock Exchange were aware of the blackout, the situation had returned to normal. No panic selling of shares took place and by closing the share index had risen by eleven points in moderate trading.*

'*We now go over live to Katie Ediar at Jodrell Bank for an explanation of what could have happened.*'

The presentation of planets and asteroids whizzing around the sun was highly impressive. However, the Director of the illustrious establishment admitted that none of the theories so far propounded could account for the sudden, and especially the total, nature of the blackout.

Kate Ediar had reserved the best question to the last.

'*Can it happen again?*'

'*That is extremely difficult to say. As I have already stated, even today's occurrence should never have taken place, so a repeat performance is equally possible, or impossible, depending on how you view the problem.*'

'*So we can be pretty certain there will be no more eclipses in the foreseeable future?*'

'*That is correct.*'

'*Thank you, and back to the studio.*'

What in heaven's name had happened to Matthew? News broadcasts should be screaming about tomorrow's repeat performance. Infuriatingly, the errant spokesman was attending a church meeting and could not be contacted; the old-fashioned ditherer owned no mobile phone so was incommunicado. Consequently there was absolutely nothing he himself could accomplish for the moment.

Gladys arrived carrying a pile of brochures.

'George, can we discuss our summer holidays when the news is finished?'

'This is the most serious technical incident at Chernobyl since number three reactor exploded in 1989 and the first since the nuclear complex was reactivated in 2002, in spite of international outrage. A mass exodus of local inhabitants is taking place, accompanied by scenes of panic. For the moment local authorities have refused all comment on the seriousness of radiation leakage.'

Much to his wife's surprise he turned off the television and picked up a brochure.

'Where do they have the largest selection of nude women?'

'George, are you pulling my leg by any chance?'

'No, both of them!'

He enjoyed teasing Gladys. She was totally devoid of a sense of humour and repeatedly fell into his traps. However, he did not often dare, it was not worth upsetting their tenuous marital relationship. His foray into undressed sun-worshipers represented the second teasing of the evening. He had better not push his luck too far.

For half an hour the McHendersons poured over colourful glossy brochures, all of which attempted to outdo each other by printing the bluest sky, the most emerald sea and the most gloriously golden beaches. The world was one gigantic holiday paradise. He soon gave up looking for topless sun-worshippers, at least those facing the camera, surmising the relevant brochures would have been censored by Gladys. The latter enthused about Vienna and Venice whereas he pretended to set his sights on the Seychelles and Tahiti. How could he inform his wife that their discussion was almost certainly an exercise in futility?

After an animated exchange of opinions it was agreed to spend a week in Vienna followed by a few days at Cannes, where he could watch the young ladies of Europe cavorting on the beach and Gladys could soak up the Mediterranean sun, if it was still shining.

He was feeling inordinately weary. So, failing to stifle an immense yawn and leaving his untouched record collection to gather dust for another night, he retired to bed before Jennifer. For the second consecutive evening his youthful neighbour studied her discoloured torso before putting on her pyjamas, this time highly relieved that the unwelcome splurges were fading.

The news-stand seller at Esher station was intrigued. Normally that smart and polite gentleman bought *The Daily Telegraph*. Today he had also purchased *The Times*, *The Independent* and even *The Daily Express*. Perhaps there was an article about him.

In the train he scrutinised every column of every page. He had practically arrived at Waterloo before he tracked down a brief mention in *The Guardian*.

'*Matthew Hodges, retired science correspondent of* The National Reporter, *claims to have predicted yesterday's eclipse of the sun, saying it had been ordained by some new religious sect as a sign of displeasure at the way humans were polluting the earth. He forecasts a similar event this afternoon. It is a pity that people should benefit from the misfortune of others, over seventy people died in road accidents as a result of yesterday's eclipse, to attempt a hoax in such bad taste.*'

The bastards. It must be because Matthew had worked for one of their rivals. What in damnation was going on?

His first act when arriving at the office was to phone Matthew at home, in spite of the risks inherent to direct contact. Much to his relief, the spokesman answered. He had few facts to offer, but years of journalism had opened his eyes to the ways of Fleet Street. He theorised that none of the editors were prepared to stick their necks out. They had not forgotten the Hitler diaries hoax nor, more recently, the 'book' written by one of Prince William's ex-flames. There was plenty else to write about, the Boeing disaster and Chernobyl for example, and space was always a key factor in deciding what was included in each edition. He agreed *The Guardian*'s article was nothing more than a spiteful attempt to take revenge; he had never been on good terms with their editor.

The Messiah was anything but calmed by Matthew's explications.

'How dare they not take us seriously.'

'Stop worrying. If the sun disappears today as planned, I am willing to bet the hide off my backside we will monopolise every front page that exists, and many more. My meeting tonight is going to be the humdinger of all humdingers. I'll phone you just after the news. Bye!'

Matthew hung up, leaving him to face a secretary with an exceedingly long list of matters urgently requiring the senior partner's attention. Nearly three hours, several meetings, numerous phone calls, the occasional shouting match and four cups of coffee later, he looked at his pale and stressed secretary.

'Pizza?'

One could forget the pallor and lines on her face when she smiled like that.

'Janet, it's time I explained about the special project I'm involved with, not because I particularly want to, but I feel I owe you an explanation. You might have noticed I have been a wee bit distracted these past few weeks. Well things are likely to become significantly worse.'

They were seated at their usual table in the Ristorante San Remo. Having ordered a Four Seasons for himself and a Reine for Janet, they were sipping the rosé house wine. He launched gloomily into his chronicle of extraterrestrial disapproval of anti-social human living habits. Twenty minutes later, when he finally arrived at his telephone call to

Matthew earlier that morning, they were sitting in front of an empty jug of wine and two cold, hardly touched pizzas.

'Janet, I want you to accompany me to the nearby park, I would appreciate your presence when the appointed hour arrives. Depending on what the sun does, or doesn't do, you may either kiss my feet or phone the nearest psychiatrist.'

He smiled at his secretary who was delighted, overjoyed to be once again the confidante of her boss, the man she loved adoringly with all her womanly heart.

The park he referred to could only be considered as such in the broadest sense of the word. It was little more than a strip of patchy grass interlaced with tarmac paths through which weeds grew in profusion. However, it served its purpose, he and Janet could see the sky. The sun was shining brightly in spite of predictions of heavy showers. Numerous office workers wandered along the paths, no doubt counting the minutes until their lunch hour finished and they returned to their computers and photocopying machines. The constant roar emanating from the endless stream of traffic encircling the modest attempt at bringing nature into the metropolis drowned the sounds of people conversing and pigeons cooing.

At two minutes to the hour he produced a small torch from his coat pocket.

'I may be a madman, but at least I am madly methodical. Or should that be methodically mad?'

Janet forced a smile. She implicitly trusted her boss. She instinctively assumed he believed the sun was about to disappear in just over a minute, making her secretary to the Messiah. She was unable to comprehend the ramifications of the situation and had no idea whether she believed her boss's weird tale. Only one thing was evident: in about 45 seconds her life was going to change one way or the other, for better or worse. No, for worse or far worse than worse.

The other members of the committee were also gazing skywards. Matthew, on the contrary, was kneeling in the Baptist church where he spent much of his life these days, in fact the last three years since his beloved Martha departed on that never-ending journey. Whatever strange powers George may have inherited, he, Matthew, knew that Jesus was the only son of God and Saviour of mankind. He was therefore fervently praying, imploring that if Kylb existed, then Jesus would hear his own urgent warning and rescue his believers from the evil forces once again threatening God's children on Earth. Matthew was also praying for George's soul, convinced the latter was no more than an innocent victim who deserved to be pardoned for his misdemeanours. By acting as spokesman, by playing along with them, deceiving them over his real intentions, he could warn Christians of the danger looming on the horizon, also enhance the chances of saving his own modest soul from the Devil in Hades, whom Kylb inevitably represented. As two o'clock approached his glances away from the altar to the cracked and stained stained glass window became more frequent.

A few miles south, in the heart of London's throbbing Fleet Street, Jimmy Lester, science editor of *The British News*, was sitting in the senior editor's office with the big boss himself and three other reporters.

'Look, Jimmy, eclipse or no eclipse, I still think it's worth going to the meeting. Grab that Hodges fellow and squeeze from him why he is prepared to make a public ass of himself by announcing the arrival of a goddam Messiah. If he is mad we can prepare an article on the increasing occurrence of dementia in older people. If he is sane we can put something together on the psychology of hoaxers, using the Prince Willie story and, well, there are plenty of other examples you can unearth, regrettably. Try to angle the story on the danger these people present to society and how to identify them when they are living amongst you.'

'And if the sun does go out?'

There was a short silence as the big boss glanced at his watch, glanced out of the window and churned over the implications.

'You get your fucking ass out of your seat and turn on the bleeding light.'

The meteorological congress had ended and the participants were dispersing to catch trains and planes back to their various countries of origin. Another volcano was erupting under a glacier in Iceland, spewing vast quantities of ash into the atmosphere. The potential effects on North Atlantic weather patterns were enthralling and none of them wished to miss the promised drama.

Back in the park people ignored the man and woman standing rather solemnly together, looking skywards.

'Do you want the sun to disappear?'

Janet for once was unable to read his mind. Normally she knew exactly how her employer would react long before even he did. This time she was at a loss, mystified.

'No.'

And then the sun flickered and disappeared.

11

Eclipsus

As people screamed and car horns blared in frightened discord, squealing brakes confirming desperate attempts by drivers to avoid colliding with each other and the dull crunching of metal bearing witness to their failure, Janet instinctively held his hand. He was deep in thought, realising the die was now cast, that there was no retreating from Kylb. Janet was not lost in thought, she was simply lost, too overwhelmed by the sudden turn of events to register what was happening, either to her or to the world surrounding her. After several minutes of adjusting to the ominous darkness, she recovered sufficiently to realise she was clutching her senior partner's hand, but not enough to decide whether she should release it. It remained.

It was still there when, without the slightest warning, the sun returned and London was once again in the middle of a breezy afternoon. Activity in and around the small park regained a semblance of normality. He likened the scene to the restarting of a video whose image has been temporarily frozen. People covered their eyes from the abrupt glare, or struggled to their feet, vainly brushing mud stains from their clothes. Car engines burst into life, pouring forth cubic litres of the nauseous gases that were partly to blame for the sun's disappearance in the first place. People rushed to the aid of a pedestrian hit by a taxi careering out of control in the sudden blackout. A delivery van had crushed a mother and child against the park railings, splintering their bodies against the unyielding wrought iron. The mangled remains of a leg severed by a shard of metal lay immobile on the grass, still wearing a fashionable buckled shoe. A low groaning could be heard between the yells for assistance. The luckless driver had collapsed in shock, reliving the first of innumerable nightmares, recalling in vivid pitiless detail the scene of horror he had caused.

He winced in anguish, whereas his secretary, aware she was standing in broad daylight in the midst of dozens of people, unashamedly clinging to her boss, recovered her hand but not her composure.

'Let's return to the office, I need some of your coffee. And Janet, please, no cheques to sign this afternoon!'

Janet was oblivious to his desperate self-seeking attempt at humour.

'What will become of us?'

'I don't know, perhaps it's best to remain in ignorance.'

He turned to his secretary, meeting her look for a brief moment.

'Janet, whatever happens I am going to need your support and understanding.'

'Are you going to tell the others at the office?'

'No, this is strictly between you, me and the members of the Kylb Committee.'

The senior partner of Wainwright, Christie, Steinway and Company and his secretary left the park, averting their eyes from where the young mother lay twitching sporadically as life drained from what remained of her body. Her daughter lay inert beside her. Someone had respectfully placed a raincoat over her diminutive frame.

They walked the short distance to the office in absolute silence.

Jeffrey and Margaret returned to the vicarage.

'Jeffrey, what can we do to save ourselves from Kylb?'

'I've been thinking a lot, couldn't sleep much last night.'

'I know.'

'How do you know?'

'I didn't sleep at all last night.'

'We must pray that Matthew is taken seriously, that the

authorities will feel compelled to do something. I wish I could consult the church hierarchy, but you know George was adamant. Perhaps we can persuade him to send Matthew to see someone. As for finding the right solutions, if any exist, I feel utterly helpless, thoroughly useless. All we can do is support George in any way he wants.'

'Do you still pray?'

'Yes, even though I am uncertain to whom. Perhaps it's stupid, but I've prayed all my life. It comforts me. Maybe no one listens, but I feel I must continue if only for myself.'

'Do you still believe in Jesus?'

'Yes, remember Kylb confirmed his existence. Jesus did live and he was crucified. Surely, son of God or not, we owe him an enormous debt. Can you imagine society without the teachings of Christianity?'

'Will you continue to preach the gospel knowing it to be false?'

'I haven't yet decided. Jesus may have been an impostor. However, his words, his messages of love and peace, are no less inspired and meaningful. It would be calamitous if society repudiated his teachings after two thousand years, simply because he was not an accredited agent. Whatever happens, assuming we survive the next few months, I am personally convinced mankind will still require religion. Throughout history, dating back to cave dwellers, man has invented religion for his personal well-being, for the cohesion of his societies. Because it fulfilled a psychological need. Admittedly religion has taken differing forms, some far removed from the rationalism of Christianity, but whatever the message preached, however vile or illogical, people accepted religion because they yearned for something to furnish the answers they themselves were incapable of finding. In their misguided ways both Fascism and Communism were religions, secular as opposed to heavenly, but they provided people with direction not dissimilar to that offered, in many cases imposed, by spiritual doctrine.

'Traditional churches are losing countless adherents because today's highly developed societies mollycoddle their citizens from external dangers. Worshippers, feeling secure and self-sufficient, resent religion interfering with their materialistic manner of living. Youngsters often reject religion altogether, especially when confronted with conflicting gospels based upon historical facts unable to withstand scientific scrutiny. This has been exacerbated by the refusal of church leaders to evolve with the times, for example on abortion and the treatment of women, thereby inciting society's weaker elements, those least able to survive unaided, to seek solace elsewhere, not always with satisfactory results as the rise in psychiatrists, fanatical sects and drug abuse confirms.

'I am convinced most people today are intrinsically unsure of themselves and will remain dependent on some form of heavenly guidance to sustain them, whether they worship the Almighty, Jehovah or the Managing Director of the AAA Corporation.'

'Even if they do not exist?'

'Yes. So long as people believe in him, a god's authenticity is irrelevant. It's called faith. The more precarious a society, the more its members embrace some form of religion to find peace of mind. As such, I believe I will be greatly needed during the troublesome times lying ahead, even if some of the names we worship will change.'

Jeffrey smiled.

'We would have to rewrite most of our hymns, singing *Hosanna* and *Hallelujah* will definitely sound off-key. Can you imagine:

'Our Managing Director who art in the Boardroom of the
AA Head Office
Hallowed be thy corporate trademark
Thy internal procedures be done
Thy dividend be paid
Give us this day our daily lunch in the canteen
Let thy . . .'

'Stop, you're not being funny.'

'I was not trying to be.'

'Let's visit the hospital. Comforting the injured will take our minds off other matters.'

Matthew was kneeling in his chapel beseeching God's protection for himself and his fellow Christians. The situation was so desperate he had included all believers in his entreaties, hesitantly at first then magnanimously. Of course, it was for Him to decide who should be saved but he did not want Him to consider him lacking in brotherly love for his fellow humans, however far they might have strayed from the narrow path of righteousness trodden exclusively by his Baptist brethren.

There was no need to change names as far as his prayers were concerned. Yet he was highly agitated. He had initially accepted Carstairs's idea of becoming committee spokesman in the hope of creating a renewed meaning to his life, a life so empty without his beloved Martha. Also, he admitted, because in his friend's study he had been too petrified of George to refuse. It had been George, the ultimate incarnation of evil, who perverted his mind, forcing him to imagine that sluttish Selena swinging amongst the branches. He now knew his appointment as spokesman was ordained through God's divine intervention. He had been entrusted with the mission of containing Lucifer, firstly by informing everyone of Kylb's coming and then by revealing the truth about his identity and evil intentions.

'Will someone turn on the fucking light?'
  Someone did.
  'OK, Jimmy, no more bullshitting on this one. Give it the works, the full treatment, keep pages one and five available. This is the biggest story since, since . . .'
  'Mary gave birth to Jesus?'
  'Fuck you, Brian. Jimmy, grab this Matthew fellow of yours double quick, before any one else nobbles him. Get

him to spill the works, exclusive. He can name his price. The usual bank account in Zurich if necessary.'

The big boss looked at the group huddled in his office.

'Who the hell is behind this? Saddam Hussein, the North Koreans, the Russians? Hodges must know, the snivelling little anarchist quisling. If you want to be paid at the end of the month you'd better find out double quick.'

He banged his fist on the table.

'Make that treble quick!'

The Prime Minister was pissed off. He was surrounded by idiots. Nobody could explain why the sun kept extinguishing itself. Or being extinguished. Since the idiots in question were his buddies, having been appointed to high office precisely because they were his buddies, there was little he could do about it. CNN knew more than he did. What did the country pay MI5 for? Devoid of reliable information, he would be obliged to phone the successors of Bill, Boris and Helmut to discover what the bloody hell was happening. It was difficult enough maintaining his image as a world leader, being treated with the same grandeur as Disraeli and Churchill, when the country he represented on the world stage was nothing more than a rainswept island stuck somewhere between France and the Arctic Circle, an island few cared about and whose inhabitants, Scots and rock superstars excepted, were generally disparaged by all and sundry and whose Civil Servants hadn't a clue what was happening right under their supercilious snotty noses. Question time was in an hour and he had no answers to riposte the impertinently imperious interrogation he knew that weasel-faced Leader of the Opposition would launch into, displaying his usual yuppie photogenic and sadistically sardonic smirk.

The Prime Minister of Great Britain and Northern Ireland impetuously grabbed one of his phones.

'Meredith, can you please tell me what is happening?'

Meredith Fitzsimmons, one of the pompous powers-that-are of the aforementioned Civil Service, could not.

The Prime Minister sighed, then lifted another receiver.

'Lucinda, get me the President.'

'Which one, Prime Minister?'

The Russian President was jogging when the sun vanished. He was furious, his face turned rubious puce for the first time since his vodka-swigging days. His first five-minute kilometre had been practically guaranteed when his progress was forcibly interrupted. He could no longer see where the damnation he was going, although he guessed where he now was. From the thorns scraping shards of skin from his shins, he must have deviated from his intended trajectory straight into a bed of roses, where he was now currently standing. Luckily his mobile phone was still working. It should be, it had been manufactured in Taiwan.

It was not only in Moscow that elected officials were picking up phones or shouting at secretaries to do so. Until recently they would have waited, after all no world leader worth his mettle would be the first to solicit information from his counterparts. However, the delays before anyone phoned anyone else grew so protracted that Presidents, Chancellors and Prime Ministers commenced learning about world events when reading the following morning's newspapers. Finally, so it was rumoured, Hilary Clinton told her husband in no uncertain terms she would lobby to exclude males from elected office if he and the other mulish chauvinists pretending to run the planet continued behaving like pompous prima donnas. Since then it had been a competition to see who dialled whom first.

As was wont to happen in these moments of crisis, Presidents and Prime Ministers, accompanied by the occasional Chancellor and General Secretary, ended up communicating with each other on crossed party lines, never quite certain with whom they were conversing, if anyone. However, ten minutes after the sun returned to its rightful place in the sky, the lines disentangled themselves and Archibald, Stanton, Klaus and Illovich were successfully interlinked, the first three exceedingly surprised to be actually talking and listening to each other in perfect harmony. Only Illovich knew the reason, his recently acquired mobile was independent from the Kremlin switchboard ... Jean-Louis was not party to the conference, the others having long ago abandoned attempts to reach him during his extended Parisian lunch break. Premier Ministre Leon was generally more cooperative. Regrettably, his information was mostly gobbledegook handed to him by Jean-Louis, to be announced to an unsuspecting world by an even more unsuspecting political rival. Bloody French politicians, nowadays even the Italians made more sense to their harassed counterparts in London, Berlin and Washington.

The party conference call was exceedingly brief. All were equally at a loss to explain the situation. Each of them groaned inwardly. All were familiar with their informal agreement, that when no one knew what the hell was happening, the only solution was to call the Israelis. No one liked doing it, even when Simon Peres and Yatzik Rabin were ruling the roost, but this new fellow was infinitely more impossible. Stanton declined, he had phoned following the blowing up of the Boeing near Istanbul. Archibald, apart from Question Time, had a relatively free afternoon. The others hesitated. They usually only confided minor matters to the British Prime Minister and this was important, critically important. Yet they were all extremely busy that afternoon.

So Archibald set about phoning the successor to Benjamin Netanyahu, Ehud Barak and Ariel Sharon.

'Hello, Abraham.'

One did not 'Abe' the Israeli Prime Minister, even achieving first name terms was already a major accomplishment. Apparently the American president tried once in private, but having been called 'Stan' in revenge, he rapidly returned to Abraham. High-ranking diplomats fondly remembered when President Clinton and Prime Minister Netanyahu happily hobnobbed together using first names, although none could understand why wags in the British Foreign Office referred to them collectively as the Flowerpot Men.

'Ah, it's your turn. You are three minutes late.'

Which was interesting news for Britain's Prime Minister who, three minutes earlier, was unaware he would be phoning his Israeli titular namesake.

Archibald Sinclair posed his question.

'I thought you were phoning to tell me.'

Archibald was perplexed. Realising his interlocutor's puzzlement, Mr Zelkahen explained the meaning of his comment. Not out of politeness, he was in a hurry.

'After all, it was one of your citizens who correctly predicted the extinction of the sun prior to both eclipses. He calls himself Matthew Hodges, perhaps you should invite him to Number Ten for a cup of tea.' In a far different tone of voice the Israeli Prime Minister added 'We are totally in the dark and are extremely anxious to be kept apprised of any information you might obtain.'

'I promise, Abraham.'

And Britain's Prime Minister dejectedly replaced the receiver. 'Totally in the dark.' Had his Israeli counterpart been trying to be funny? With him you never knew.

He picked up another receiver and yelled at whoever suffered the misfortune to have answered.

'Who the damnation is Matthew Hodges? Why didn't I know about him, where is he and what does he know?'

The person on the receiving end of the Prime Minister's barrage of questions asked one of his own.

'About the bloody disappearance of the blasted sun.'

The panic and puzzlement being experienced around the British Isles was nothing compared to the pandemonium paralysing other nations, all of which had been pursuing typical daytime occupations until their supply of sunshine brusquely disappeared. Hundreds more were dead or maimed in automobile accidents, slightly less than the preceding day because innumerable cars wrecked in the first batch of collisions were dejectedly cluttering garages instead of proudly and dangerously conveying their owners from somewhere to somewhere else. Insurance companies threw up their hands in pessimistic bewilderment. Stock-markets plunged, excepting shares of companies manufacturing candles, torches and motor vehicle replacement parts. Workers around the world no longer invented excuses for stopping for a chat. They were even joined by their managers as factory floors and offices became the forums of debating societies. Only the medical profession and thousands of bereaved families suffered the tragic consequences of two momentary and unannounced eclipses of the sun.

George was talking to Janet in his office. This was no time-wasting recreational chat. They were desperately trying to reschedule the firm's upcoming audits based on the assumption that the senior partner would shortly be unavailable to perform his normal professional duties. They had arrived at some form of solution, a complex series of compromises, something that might just function, that is until the first unforeseen problem arose. Which it would.

He sat back in his chair, managing a wry smile.

'Well Janet, how about that *rendezvous* with the psychiatrist?'

His secretary had other matters on her mind.

'I wish you would halt future disappearances of the sun. It would save a lot of unnecessary suffering.'

'The disappearances are vital to our strategy. Without a major dose of blackmail national governments will never accede to our wishes. In any case, everyone will now be prepared, I doubt if many vehicles will be on the roads at five minutes to three tomorrow afternoon.'

'Another thing. Couldn't you please heal the car crash victims, bring the dead back to life?'

'I have already explained that curing people would open the floodgates, things would get out of hand, everyone would become distracted from the real issues.'

'Please, think of that poor mother dying in the park.'

So he relented and phoned Matthew to modify the evening's announcement. Matthew was amazed. This time Lucifer was prepared to sink to the deepest depths of trickery and underhand skulduggery in order to achieve his corrupt goals. Machiavelli must have descended to Hades and be acting as the Devil's personal political advisor.

'Thanks,' said Janet. 'If there is anything else I can do, if you feel like coming round to my place to escape from everyone?'

There, she had said it, after so many years of waiting.

He stopped smiling and looked straight at Janet.

'I might well accept your offer sooner than you think. But first, can you sneak into Matthew's press conference this evening, I would very much appreciate a first-hand report on what happened.'

And then the telephone rang.

The Archbishop of Canterbury was barricaded inside his Lambeth Palace office. Canterbury was inconvenient, too far off the beaten track, so he only popped down at weekends to officiate at the Saturday evening and Sunday services. Alone, Dr Auldley Huett was ruminating upon the never-ending problems caused by inducting women into the church hierarchy. After centuries of simple straightforward sexism it was difficult for his quaintly medieval institution to adapt to God having created women alongside men, admittedly only as an afterthought, but that hardly solved the problem. If only He had designed them to use the same toilet facilities, plumbing conversions were costing a major fortune. Furthermore, instead of easing the suffering of mankind, his teams of clerical scholars were being forced to waste invaluable time scrutinising the church's voluminous edicts to de-sexify them, paying lip service to a handful of rampaging feminist activists. Some leftist agitator neophyte from Sheffield, why couldn't her parents have been Catholic, was rejecting the use of the term 'dog collar'. He nearly told her she deserved a 'bitch collar' round her neck, preferably to throttle her, but desisted in case she negotiated the adoption of 'canine collar'. Another budding suffragette trainee claimed that since males wore frocks for worship, why should women not be allowed to wear jeans? Yet equal or not, (well everyone knew they were not the slightest bit equal but one was no longer permitted to state even the obvious), women could no longer be treated as non-citizens. The magnitude of church collections increasingly depended on feminine generosity.

However, women apart, his main challenge at that moment was trying to talk sense into the Protestants of Ulster. Never had he witnessed such unforgiving mistrust and contempt for one's fellow countrymen. Apart from a few brave deacons who unfalteringly not only preached reconciliation from the pulpit but practised it in their daily lives, the only true Christians in that hell-hole of insular insanity were the women of the various peace movements. During yesterday's meeting his theologian elite had argued in concentric circles, stubbornly digging their mental heels ever deeper into the quicksand of sectarian dogma. The meeting had not been helped by the sun's disappearing for the second day in succession.

The Irish excepted, he was making some real progress towards harmonising relations with other church leaders. At the current pace of advancement they might instigate a multi-denominational joint working committee within the next 500 years. Unfortunately, by then, if one extrapolated church attendance figures, there would be no worshippers left to harmonise. Rome was no help. A few years previously he felt he was achieving some advancement with John Paul

II, but the new pontiff, yet another geriatric compromise candidate, was already approaching secular senility and pastoral paralysis. If only a new Messiah would return to Earth, perhaps He could perform some seriously overdue ecumenical head-banging and create the unity so sadly lacking in the world of religion.

Ah well, back to work, he had next Sunday's sermon to prepare before he drove to York to open the renovated seminary.

Earl's Court. In retaining the venue for his third consecutive evening press conference, Matthew had overlooked one small significant detail. The meteorologists might have disappeared but the subsequent group of congressional attendees had duly installed themselves throughout the building. When hundreds of shouting, pushing, shoving and yelling newsmen rampaged into the building, the quiet, orderly atmosphere so carefully cultivated by the ladies of the British Women's Institute disintegrated into free-for-all anarchy.

Matthew had been expecting a sizeable crowd but not a mob. He approached a cordon of policemen lamentably failing in its task of preventing the demure divas of the world of women's instituting from being steamrollered by the ruthless reporters of Reuters and Associated Press, not forgetting the BBC, CBS, CNN and ... in fact, you named them and they were there. He walked up to one of the policemen wearing more stripes than the others.

'Excuse me, officer, but how can I get inside?'
'Have you a special invitation?'
'No.'
'Sorry, you're wasting your time, the hall is bursting at the seams.'
'Then everyone else will be wasting their time. You see I was not invited because I myself invited everyone else. My name is Matthew Hodges.'
'Who?'

'Matthew Hodges.'

The police officer opened his mouth to speak. However, before any words materialised, he disappeared under a flurry of unladylike lady instituters. Matthew, benefiting from the vacuum left behind the surging crowd, slipped into the auditorium. One glance and he started slipping out again, only to walk straight into the cynical BBC weather forecaster he had encountered during the first meeting.

Matthew read out the abridged version of George's *Mission Document* for the third time. He then added.

'The message you have just received is hopefully unambiguous. It is your duty to report the facts to the maximum number of people, without distortion or editorial gerrymandering. It is for the elected representatives of each nation to consult their citizens, before gathering amongst themselves to debate the issues democratically, preferably using the existing structures of the United Nations. The Messiah does not unilaterally intend to impose his wishes on humanity. It is humanity which must decide for itself how to achieve the imposed targets.

'I take this opportunity to emphasise my limited rôle as spokesman for the Kylb Committee. As such I cannot personally assume responsibility for the regrettable events of the last two days. Henceforth my involvement will be to act as go-between between the elected officials of the United Nations and the Messiah, who in turn will communicate to Kylb on his return.

'I am instructed to announce the sun will disappear tomorrow at three p.m. London local time for fifteen minutes.'

There was gasps from the jostling crowd. Someone shouted 'murderer', others soon joined in. Matthew knew he had arrived at the moment he wished would never happen. It was only with reluctance he announced that those injured and killed following the sun's previous disappearances would be restored to normal health at exactly midnight local time. As he expected, the entire audience was thunderstruck.

'You mean you are going to resuscitate thousands of dead people?'

'Well, I personally am not, but that is what I have been informed will happen.'

For the first time since the beginning of the conference there was a hush as the enormity of the implications sunk in. Hundreds of millions of television viewers paused momentarily in amazement, the meeting was being beamed throughout the world by satellite. Then, as disbelief took over, the decibel level in the hall rapidly returned to its previous cacophonic level. Question time descended into a deregulated shouting competition and was soon abandoned.

Matthew escaped half an hour later, thanks to the valiant efforts of a cohort of policemen whose main leisure activity was the playing of rugby football, in the scrum. Encircled by the mighty men in blue uniforms, he failed to notice Janet standing on the pavement opposite the conference hall, the nearest she had been able to approach. Of course, he would not have recognised her, nor she him.

'George, a Lucas Hollings for you.'

He looked blankly at his wife, he did not know a Lucas Hollings.

'George, it's Matthew. Did you watch the news conference on television?'

'Most definitely. Congratulations, it went perfectly.'

'It most certainly did not, I was almost lynched. George, are you serious about curing the road accident victims?'

'Matthew, making miracles is rather like playing golf. When you hit the damnable ball it should theoretically fly straight towards the green, you are convinced it will, some pray that it will, in all logic it should, but until it actually does you close your eyes and hope.'

'If they are not all cured I'm going to be hung, drawn and quartered tomorrow.'

'Don't worry, I'll make sure nothing happens to you.'

'How?'

'No idea for the moment, but trust in me.'

Which was the last thing Matthew was prepared to do.

'In any case, we cannot continue with the same format of press conference. From now on they must be dignified, conducted like those at the White House. A few selected journalists, security checks and preprepared questions. If that is fine with you?'

'Go ahead, you're the expert. Let me know what you have organised, but if possible maintain the six o'clock time schedule for the time being. Phone me at the office tomorrow morning. And, by the way, Janet my secretary is in the picture.'

He replaced the receiver, things were advancing well.

'Woof!' agreed Beatrice.

'Ah, Beatrice!' he whispered in inaudibly hushed tones since Gladys, in the adjacent kitchen, possessed ears considerably more acute than a hawk's optics. 'You can relax, even if you were capable of comprehending the mess we're in, you could still be as carefree as a cuckoo. Kylb is only interested in eliminating us humans, not nice pollution-friendly dogs. Wait a minute! If all your masters and mistresses are zapped to the happy unpolluted hunting ground in the sky, who will take you walkies, open you cans of Doggifood?'

Gladys, hearing no sounds from the lounge, did not realise her husband was in deep discussion.

'What did Mr Hollings want, dear?'

Gladys was convinced she could be of boundless service to society, but only if she knew everything that was happening around her. Everything. Absolutely everything. Plus just a little bit more, just to be on the safe side.

'Someone phoning from a client.'

'The cheek of it, calling you at home!'

'Don't get excited, dear, I asked him to. Where were you sitting when the sun went out today?'

'I was not sitting. Well, to be honest I was, but not where

your dirty mind is thinking. I was having a drink with Muriel and Doreen.'

'So what is the latest on the Messiah?'

'I told you yesterday, the Chinese are behind it all. We should bring back Maggie and sent the navy to Hong Kong, show them who is ruling the waves.'

'So how are the Chinese going to cure thousands of injured and bring hundreds of dead people back to life?'

'What?'

'Haven't you heard about today's press conference?'

'Of course I have, but I was tied up at the Bowls Club. What happened?'

Gladys hated asking her husband for anything. However, to be permanently better briefed than everybody else, she occasionally had to beg him for information updates. He made the most of the occasion.

'It's impossible! No one can resurrect the dead. That Matthew Hodges fellow must be a phoney and deranged to boot.'

One of her committee members had trodden on a doggy dung during the latest blackout and twisted her ankle. It would be interesting to see if she was cured by Chairman Ding Dang Dong. She could never remember Chinese names.

'Tonight's news should be interesting.' He immediately sensed the tension mounting across the room. 'Don't worry, dear, we'll wait and tune in to the BBC at nine o'clock. What's for supper?'

Whilst the McHendersons were having a domesticated dinner in sedate Esher, the salmon was delicious, much of the rest of the world was in turmoil. Matthew had not dared return home, nor even visit his chapel, in case journalistic sleuths deduced where he might seek refuge. Instead, he found a haven at his sister's home in Beckenham. No one could possibly imagine looking for anyone down there. He found a haven, but hardly a peaceful one. His elder sister

Ethel compared her younger brother to a feeble, easy-to-be misled libertine weakling when it came to treading the paths of heavenly righteousness.

'Well, if your are the agent of the Almighty Himself, you can cure my varicose veins.'

'I keep telling you, Ethel, I am the spokesman of Lucifer.'

Not surprisingly, his sister refused to be mollified by her unruly baby brother's latest proclamation. Matthew realised he could have described his new assignment with a little more lucidity.

'I will pray for your soul.'

Which she promptly did, for two and a half hours.

During the praying for his soul Matthew phoned George. It was strange, unnerving, how natural he sounded, quite unlike an emissary of the Devil. But anyone who could make him conjure up visions of loathsome harlots swinging with legs spreadeagled . . .

However, now the entire world was beaming into his press conferences, he could finally announce the truth about Kylb. Tomorrow the power of Good would once again repel the forces of Darkness.

Janet lay back on her bed. The waves of excitement flowed round her body, always returning to that unique spot before starting their journey again with renewed intensity. But only in her imagination.

She had done her utmost to attend the press conference. At least she had recorded the broadcast on her VCR. She could invite him round tomorrow evening. The television was in her bedroom . . .

She did not resent his involvement with Kylb. On the contrary, it was the latter's visitation that had broken the ice, shattering the social barriers separating them from the shared joys they so deserved. In the park, and later in his office, he had acted so naturally, precisely like the warm-hearted and vulnerable person she knew he really was. Perhaps in a mere 24 hours he would be there with her.

'Brian, I'm listening, and I want to hear something worthwhile.'

Brian was an unscrupulous, arse-licking, cunning, conniving, mean-minded, lying and fly-by-night mathematical genius, so he had inevitably been appointed Chancellor of the Exchequer. The Home Secretary, who should have been in attendance, was visiting his Lancashire constituency. He insisted the trip had been planned weeks earlier, but with him you never knew. Brian at least had the disadvantage of living next door.

'Archibald, from what I can gather there is absolutely no plausible explanation as to why the sun repeatedly goes on the blink.'

With the Prime Minister, at least this one, it was wiser to debut with the worst and build up to the good news. If the latter was in short supply, not an infrequent occurrence since the dramatic dissipation of their election victory euphoria, then you promised it would be forthcoming. By the time it did not forthcome, the Prime Minister had usually forgotten that it should have been forthcoming. Unaware of any silver linings he could announce, the Chancellor of the Exchequer in desperation presented his not quite so bad news.

'It would appear that nobody has any information not already available to us. The Chinese are most upset at the accusations being flung their way. Foo Xyong, our Chinese affairs expert at the Foreign Office, surmises that for once they are genuine. The Ministry of Defence boffins are stymied. Apart from lamenting about budget restrictions preventing them from acquiring the equipment necessary to solve the mystery, they have absolutely nothing to offer. Informally they are unhappy with asteroid theories. They are convinced someone would have pinpointed the offending objects and issued timely prior warnings. Keith Moles suggests you read Fred Hoyle's *The Black Cloud*. It's a science fiction story about a monster inadvertently blotting out the sun.'

'Brian! I am Prime Minister, not your ten-year-old son. In other words, you are telling me you have nothing to say?'

'Yes, Prime Minister.'

'That will be all.'

Alistair Sinclair did not speak the words, he sighed them. He was beginning to understand why John Major always looked so forlorn and harassed during his years at Number Ten.

'There is one point to keep in mind. You have presumably been informed this Hodges bloke promised the restoration of the accident victims to normal health.'

The blank look of stunned amazement on the face of Alistair Sinclair informed Brian Daintree that the Prime Minister had unquestionably not been informed.

'If his prediction does come true we can forget about the Chinese. It might also be advisable to stop committing adultery, stealing and coveting thy neighbour's wife, or whatever you are not meant to covet. However, if nothing happens . . .'

'Yes?'

'We are no worse off than now.'

The Chancellor departed, leaving the Prime Minister attempting to remember the seven other commandments and whether he had transgressed any of them. On second thoughts, how many he had transgressed. On third thoughts, how many times he had transgressed them.

'Gerald?'

'Hello?'

'It's Auldley.'

'Good Lord, its the 'arch' villain himself. Long time no see. How's your diluted version of the true Catholic gospel doing? Collections booming? Don't ordain big-breasted women. Good singers but their boobs get in the way when leaning over the font at christenings.'

Gerald and Auldley had attended the same Cambridge college, they even shared the same girlfriend, although not concurrently. Auldley seduced her away from Gerald, partly explaining why the latter decided to take the sacramental oath. Auldley then promptly lost her to his athletic younger brother when the latter joined Cambridge as a fresher. As fellow members of the not very exclusive *Ex-lovers of Amanda Association*, Auldley and Gerald retained a bond of friendship that overcame their working for competing organisations.

'Gerald, since we are buddies, I'm phoning to give you a scoop. The new Messiah is confirmed C of E and hopping mad at you Catholics for paying too much attention to its mother.'

'Before He burns me at the stake, I confess everything!'

'He?'

'Oh gawd, not a flipping wee lassie?'

'No. Bisexual.'

'No problem. Why didn't you say so?' Gerald cleared his throat. 'Talking about confessing, well we who live in sinless boredom on the banks of the Tiber know nothing about Kylb. He is apparently not one of us.'

'Well, that's a relief.'

The time for verbal jousting had ended, the two friends had some serious talking to accomplish. Thanks to Amanda, bless her soul, a soul that departed prematurely due to an irritating attack of venereal disease, Canterbury and Rome had a very unofficial and extremely important link that served to pour oil over troubled waters and keep unnecessary diplomatic incidents to a minimum.

'But what if he does cure these people?'

'Apart from creating unemployment in Lourdes, I have no idea. The implications are far too incredible to contemplate.'

'In other words, the Messiah really has returned?'

'Well, can you think of another explication?'

'We'll talk tomorrow. At least things should be less confused.'

Stanton Forbes was in a foul mood. His ratings were plummeting, the electors disapproving his failure to respect certain election pledges. They must be joking. Election pledges were, well they were election pledges, made solely to get oneself elected. Did they believe Al Gore and the Bush brothers would ever keep theirs? Unfortunately, since people never understood what his current opponents were mumbling, nobody ever confronted them with failing to respect their pledges, if there had been any. Then his wife was acting even more obnoxiously than usual, as if she was suffering from a double-dose of pre-period pains and post-menopause depression. What the shit was bugging her? He hoped she had been joking when she screamed the sun going on the blink was his punishment for putting his hand inside that waitress's knickers. It was a lie. She hadn't been wearing any. Lawyers! Women!

One of the array of telephones in front of him rang. It was none of them. He pulled the mobile phone out of his pocket and pressed the answer button.

'Yes, I watched the press conference. A riot, most un-British. So no one knows? Still no word from Jean-Louis? Let's see, midnight in London is six p.m. our time, meet me in the Oval Office five minutes before with Cy and Sol. Oh, and Walter had better be in attendance.'

The President of the United States hung up and returned to reading the bulky file containing his election promises. Had he really said that? And they had believed him?

Deep in the crumbling depths of Belfast the pub was overflowing with a combination of thirsty Irishmen, smoke fumes and the stench of beer. But the usual raucous laughter was absent.

'But if we ain't be no longer neither Cathlics an' Protstants, then what'll we fight about?'

It did not take them long to conjure up alternative causes of conflict, veritable justification for butchering each other, and the laughter once again flowed as furiously as the beer.

The Israeli cabinet was in full session. It was inevitable, if the world believed the claims of this Matthew Hodges, miracle cures or not, that the Arabs would unite to oust the Jews from Jerusalem, if not the whole of Israel. The mullahs would, of course, conveniently forget that Moses, also a duly appointed local agent, had led the Jews to the Promised Land, situated somewhere near Tel Aviv airport. However superior the technical ability of the Israeli armed forces, not forgetting the fighting spirit of the nation's 4,000,000 citizens, there were nearly 200,000,000 Arabs to contend with. It was not the Arab governments that would cause the problem. Some had started to see reason in recent years, Israeli reason of course. It was their religious leaders, who knew exactly how to inflame their populations. The real danger came from them. And Arabs needed little inflaming before they would embroil the entire region in total warfare. It would be Iraqi chemical weapons against Israeli nuclear warheads. Nobody would survive, which, in the warped minds of the fundamentalist mullahs from across the Jordan river, represented a glorious victory for Islam.

One of the ministers spoke.

'It would appear that the . . . for want of a better word I will call him the Messiah, all right, the 'claimant', is George McHenderson, a reputable Chartered Accountant living in the suburbs of London. We have it on good authority he has recently been endowed with extraordinary powers. One of our agents, Samuel Weisenblaum, has a direct contact to a member of the Kylb Committee. Claims being made by their spokesman, Matthew Hodges, are apparently valid. The 'claimant' would appear to have no strong religious or political convictions, nor any criminal ones. He appears to be acting under orders from this Kylb person and is not motivated by personal gain. As to the identity of Kylb, from the information available it would appear that . . .'

'For pity's sake, Ariel, please stop repeating 'it would appear that'. Do you or do you not know?'

'Of course I personally do not know. I am merely relaying information transmitted to my department, information available to no one else.'

'Well, the British certainly don't have it. So what is going to happen at midnight their time?'

'From what I have been told, and I repeat, from what I have been told, the miracles will take place as promised.'

'And Israel with be in a state of siege,' one of the other ministers added in a grim voice.

'One other point. Our contact has advised that the potential danger to Israel has been discussed with the Messiah, who is not necessarily opposed to intervening on our behalf.'

'But this Messiah person, the 'claimant', he isn't one of us?'

'No.'

'So why would he help us?'

No answer was forthcoming and the Israeli cabinet turned its attention to other matters.

In Tripoli, Libya's eccentric ruler was in a malicious mood. Unlike the occupant of the White House, he was not experiencing wife trouble, he did not have any. How dare they not consider him the prime suspect behind extinguishing the sun? He had been infuriatingly absent from world headlines, having failed to blow anyone or anything up for ages. Even that Boeing disaster near Istanbul had not been one of his achievements. He loved being insulted by the Great Yankee Devil itself, if only they would fire a few more rockets at him. Blaming the Chinese, the ignominy of it all!

If Mohammed was the chosen one, as of course he was, and if that illegitimate Jewish peasant was not, as of course he never had been, then there must be some way to exploit the situation, stir up rebellion somewhere around the world. Infuriate the Americans. But he could not think of anything.

So in a monumental huff he departed for his tent in the desert.

Kawa, having consulted with his brethren, fetched his knife from the hut. Inside his wife was breastfeeding their latest child, no, not breastfeeding, holding her shrunken mammary to its mouth. Their goat was the only source of milk for all nine of them, yet it had to die. The Gods were upset. They were extinguishing the sun as a warning that they wished to be appeased. He carried the struggling animal to the ceremonial spot and quickly sliced its throat. As he returned to the village flies swarmed onto the blood and vultures hovered overhead in expectation. That night, as the giant birds were feasting, his child would die of malnutrition. But the Gods had been appeased.

The young man exited the council house carrying a suitcase. Inside were white robes. None of his neighbours suspected anything but he belonged to the Order of Druids. At last here was an excuse to organise a ceremonial mass that would outdo all their previous manifestations. Tomorrow, as the sun extinguished itself over the desolate coastline of Cornwall, they would pray and dance and shout in ecstasy. With a little encouragement from the Grandmaster they would organize an orgy in honour of the Almighty.

'This is the BBC from London. Here is the nine o'clock news, read by Margaret Simmons.

'Over sixty deaths and a thousand injuries are reported in road accidents following the extinction of the sun for the second day running.

'*The Japanese Government has resigned as a result of the Tokyo stock market crash and accusations of bribery and corruption amongst ministers.*

'*Over sixty thousand inhabitants of the area surrounding the Chernobyl nuclear reactor are thought to be dying from radiation exposure.*

'*India and Pakistan are threatening nuclear war following border skirmishes which left hundreds dead.*'

Pause whilst she glanced at the teleprompter.

'*At two o'clock precisely the sun disappeared for five minutes, once again creating chaos on Britain's roads as drivers suddenly lost all visibility. Seven deaths occurred on the M1 near Luton in a forty vehicle pile-up.*'

'If they ever catch the Chinese responsible, I hope they shoot them.'

Gladys not infrequently added her own comments to those of the BBC announcers.

The scenes of carnage, mutilated bodies trapped in crushed vehicles and body bags being carried away lasted slightly longer than the previous day. The world was starting to take Kylb seriously.

'*The reason for the sun's double disappearance is still mystifying scientists around the world. The passage of a second asteroid is being taken seriously in some quarters but attention is focusing on claims made by a sixty-four year-old retired newspaper correspondent, Matthew Hodges. Mr Hodges predicted both yesterday's and today's eclipses of the sun, claiming it was ordained by an as yet unknown person calling himself the Messiah. We now go over to our special science correspondent, Terence Bishop, who is standing in the Earl's Court conference hall where Matthew Hodges made his predictions. Terence!*'

'*Yes, Margaret! Behind me the auditorium is empty, in stark contrast to the pandemonium of earlier this evening.*'

The McHendersons, plus millions of other viewers, relived the highlights of the press conference. He remembered Matthew pessimistically predicting the humdinger of all humdingers. The poor chap had not been exaggerating.

'*The crux of the matter, the question on everyone's lips, is what *is going to happen tonight? There are of course two possibilities, either a miraculous mass healing and resurrection occur, or nothing whatsoever changes. If nothing happens, we are back to the theories of asteroids or Chinese space piracy, neither of which has found favour in official circles. If the miracle cures take place then, well I think we should be speaking to our religious affairs correspondent.*

'Thank you Terence. Religious leaders, including the Pope and Dr Auldley Huett, Archbishop of Canterbury, have so far declined all comment. Naturally the BBC will interrupt its programmes if anything of note takes place during the evening. Our scheduled programmes have been modified to make way for a special edition of Panorama. This begins at eleven forty-five p.m. and continues throughout the night, obtaining reactions from people once it is known whether Matthew Hodges is a monumental fraud or the twentieth century's equivalent to St John the Baptist.

'Japan is in a turmoil . . .'

15,000 miles away from Tokyo, back in Esher, George and Gladys sat in silent contemplation. Not surprisingly Gladys's share of the contemplation did not remain silent for long.

'John the Baptist? How does he arrive at that presumption? Anyway, if those people are cured, I'll eat my hat.'

'Which one, dear?'

'All of them.'

'Will you still believe it's the Chinese if the miracle cures take place?'

'Well, whom else could it be?' And Gladys Joyce stalked off to bed.

He consulted his collection of records, which one would have the honour of being selected on such an important occasion? After much hesitation he placed on the turntable Ravel's *Bolero* played by the Paris Conservatoire Orchestra conducted by Albert Wolff. Why had he so dramatically chosen midnight as the hour of resuscitating those poor victims. He would have to stay awake for hours before discovering what happened. Not that it would change things if he benefited from a good night's sleep, catching up on events in the morning. Especially since tomorrow he would be with Janet and, well sleeping would not be high on his list of priorities. For the moment the solo flute was pirouetting the music gracefully around the turntable and he could enjoy relaxing after a long stressful day.

Jennifer's light came on. As the rhythm of the music slowly yet relentlessly built up towards its crescendo, he gazed fondly at his angelic neighbour. Jennifer, staring sightlessly at the stars, yawned in a manner most indelicate for a young lady. He smiled to himself. She had not even placed her hand to her mouth. However impolite, her yawn sent ideas rushing to those parts of his brain deciding short-term behavioural patterns. They concluded the body they inhabited should go to bed. So it did.

The casualty ward of Luton General Hospital was full to overflowing. The pitiful rows of mutilated bodies groaned as pain seared though their damaged limbs. The lucky ones were too drugged to feel anything, unable to appreciate they were the lucky ones only whilst remaining unconscious. Some of the night nurses were hardly more awake than their patients, last night had been a terrible ordeal and tonight was promising to be worse. The medical staff had tried to keep news of promised miracle healings from the injured since nothing was worse than building false hope before dashing it into smithereens of despair. However, hospital wards are well equipped with the means of distracting patients during days of interminable waiting. Television and radio sets were installed at many of the bedsides. Everyone who was conscious knew of the Earl's Court press conference yet, much to the relief of the doctors and nurses, few, if any, seemed to care. Pain and misery dull the powers of reasoning. For patients and staff it was just another night in another ward of another hospital somewhere in England.

Midnight struck. The night nurse looked up, everything was normal. Bloody miracles indeed! And without a second thought she returned to her textbook. Her final examinations were scheduled for next month. Miracles and medicine did not mix. The sick could visit Lourdes if it kept them happy, but when the health chips were down it was more sensible to rely on the NHS, even better the private sector if you could afford it, which as a nurse she couldn't.

Her thoughts returned to the diagnosis of skin cancer.

Someone stirred in the ward. Then someone else. Then everyone seemed to be moving. The nurse looked up and closed her book, the whole ward was coming to life. Patients were stretching their limbs, heaving themselves into a sitting position. Mr Jones clapped his hands together in glee, causing Nurse Jenkins to reflect for a moment that something was not as it should be. Then she recalled he was one of the amputees, his left arm. As the noise level increased she turned on the lights and rang for assistance. Mrs Calstairs had not been expected to last the night. She was now vigorously scratching a leg abandoned in the mangled remains of her Datsun a few hours earlier. Mr Fascher was asking where he was, using a brain declared moribund by the surgeon who had stapled his skull together. Laughter broke out, wild unnatural laughter. People clamoured for telephones to announce the extraordinary news to their loved ones.

Two hours later the ward was empty except for 18-year-old Johnnie Greaves, who thrilled the girls with daredevil exploits on his Honda motorbike. Linda, who had taunted him to overtake the Mercedes, was lying in the morgue, whereas his mess of twisted limbs lay congealed to the bandages that held him together, limbs torn beyond recognition when he hit the car emerging from the driveway.

Linda had dared Johnnie precipitately. It had only been five minutes to two when he caught sight of the Volvo.

12

Publicus

The Messiah arrived at Esher Station at 7.59. The 7.58 had of course departed at precisely 7.58, carrying its load of compacted commuters towards Waterloo. He muttered something most unmessianic under his breath, considered then abandoned the idea of recalling the train to Esher, then ambled to the kiosk to purchase his papers. It was his own fault. First he had listened attentively to the morning news instead of shaving, then he waited until Gladys finished her bathroom ablutions before misinforming her of the 'business' engagement he was 'obliged' to attend that evening.

The platform was still empty when he returned clutching *The Daily Telegraph* and *International Herald Tribune*, the latter because he was intrigued by how recent events were being reported beyond the shores of Britain. Another commuter joined him on the platform. It was none other than Miss Prick-teaser. The previous week's knee-hugger had been discarded for a mini as her hemline, which had been successively rising of late, abandoned her knees altogether and ascended towards the apogee of her femininity. Noticing his admiring glance, she turned away, pointed her protruding yet safely packaged posterior in his direction, and honoured him an ever so discrete little wiggle. The little bitch still hadn't learned her lesson.

Incensed, he momentarily forgot his promise to forsake personal miracles in case they resulted in his being identified.

> 'Miss Prick-teaser, you sleazy young flirt,
> You think you are safe inside your thick woollen skirt.

Things, however, are not so apparent.
Don't look now but it's turned quite transparent.'

And transparent it had become.
Completely.
And absolutely.
But not her panties.
Because she was not wearing any.
The suburban slut, travelling to work knickerless. No wonder she had waved her backside at him in such a provocative manner. He scrutinised every rounded contour of his fellow commuter's posterior, not so much out of masculine interest but more to wreak his revenge on this pubic public nuisance. He then returned to his newspapers. As he read, admittedly with frequent interruptions to admire his handiwork, the platform filled up with those arriving to catch the 8.16. They gathered around the young miss in a crescent, cherishing the three-dimensional double magnificence of what their imaginations had only previously managed to imagine. On the opposite platform, passengers waiting for a southbound train were extremely vexed when it arrived without warning, one old man decided it was worth waiting for the following one. He had spotted her wedding ring, unusual place to wear one. No, it couldn't possibly be a wedding ring. Image the best man trying to slip it on during the church service.

The young miss sensed the glances. She knew full well she was been admired by those drooling City executives, damn their supercilious male chauvinist guts. She waggled her pelvis in their direction, ever so slightly but ever so effectively.

The 8.16 arrived. A couple of passengers checked their watches, one indicated 8.14 and was duly advanced by its owner. Thirty seconds later, after the habitual pushing and shoving, especially outside the compartment chosen by Miss Prick-teaser, the train pulled out of the station leaving behind a deserted platform.

The prick-teaser of all prick-teasers discovered her predicament when she sat down, glanced at her lap and saw something that should not have been there. Well, it should have been there, it simply should not have been in evidence. The train had already left Esher. There was no escape. With her acutely developed instinct for feminine self-survival, she placed her handbag over the offending object and fought back the tears of humiliation. She was never again seen at Esher Station.

He learned nothing further from the newspapers. The BBC morning news had thoroughly reported his midnight miracles, including surrealistic scenes of resurrection in municipal morgues. Many road accident corpses went home with streaming colds due to lying naked in cold storage chambers, most inconsiderate of the municipal employees. Some, encased in plastic bags, were brought back to life only to suffocate in their airless tombs. Administrative personnel had the unusual task of tearing up pathologists' reports so meticulously prepared the previous day. Employees were not unused to being thanked for taking good care of their charges, not, however, by the corpses themselves. Life insurance companies celebrated the good news whereas relatives gleefully planning to spend their unexpected inheritances displayed less enthusiasm. Most of the born-again travellers showed boundless thanks for their revival, although some, ever hard to please, regretted the Messiah had not repaired their smashed cars.

Similar occurrences were taking place around the world. Both the British and American press hailed the miracle as a sign that Kylb was undoubtedly the messenger of God, a reincarnation of the Angel Gabriel, and that something remarkable was happening. Italian newspapers, especially those printed in the Vatican, were considerably more muted in their proclamations, applying a 'wait-and-see' attitude. All attempts to blame the Chinese were abandoned and, much to the disgust of its neurotic leader sitting in his desert tent, still nobody thought to accuse Libya. There were some partly disguised attempts at speculating on the identity of the Messiah, newspapers reiterating Matthew's formal statement of the previous evening that he himself was no more than a spokesman. There were vague references to the reason for Kylb's visit and his list of demands. However, for the moment, little thought was given to events other than the joyous homecomings of the dead and injured, including a mother and child who had been cruelly crushed against metallic park railings adjacent to the offices of Christie, Wainwright, Steinway and Company.

'Good morning!'
'Good morning, George. Heard the news?'
'Morning!'
'Good morning, Richard. You must tell me about your trip to South Africa.'
'Morning, Janet! When the coffee's ready I would be delighted to see you in my office.'

And he looked straight at his secretary in a way never done before. And she returned the look in a way never dared before.

'How was the meeting?'

Janet explained she had been unable to penetrate into the conference centre, but she provided a vivid account of the pushing and shoving witnessed from across the street.

'I recorded the conference on my VCR in case you wished to watch it again.'

He did not particularly want to, he was far more interested in that evening's conference.

'That's a great idea. Could I come round to your place after office hours, we could watch it together.'

'I think that should be possible, I have nothing special planned for this evening.'

Which was untrue. She had something very special planned for that evening.

'Janet, I propose we concentrate our minds exclusively on the business affairs of C.W.S. and Company. Clear the decks so to speak.'

'If I might be permitted to say, Mr McHenderson, it's one blooming big deck that needs clearing!'
'I'm ready for the worst. You'd better verify that coffee is in plentiful supply.'

Whilst Janet and her senior partner were ploughing through piles of papers, the world was waking up to the realisation that a new era could well be dawning. An eminent guest on the Jimmy Young Show suggested it was no longer 12 May 2005 AD, but 12 May 1 K.

The senior editor would normally have flung his reporters to the verbal lions for failing to trace Matthew Hodges. However vastly increased circulation, sales were up 30%, had temporarily mellowed his tempestuous temperament. He instructed a colleague to delay printing the 'scandal of drug-taking student prince' article, telling him to wait until the Kylb bonanza was finished, in about a couple of weeks.

The Archbishop of Canterbury decided the York seminary could be opened another day and flew back to Lambeth. He was huddled in his office with a couple of bishops who had driven from Guildford and Gloucester respectively in order to consult with their Commander-in-Chief.
'Gentlemen, I would be much in your debt if you enlightened me on the nature of the miracles performed last night and the identity of the person claiming to be the Messiah.'
'We were hoping you could tell us.'
An ecumenical checkmate descended upon Lambeth Palace.
'Who does know?'
'How can we be certain this is indeed the promised coming? It could be a monstrous fraud, visitors from outer space, anything.'

'Kylb is a visitor from outer space, where else do you believe the Angel Gabriel would materialise from?'

'I thought he resided in heaven.'

'Have you phoned the Vatican?'

'Not officially.'

The bishops knew what that implied, both having been informally informed about Audley and Gerald, although not the *Ex-lovers of Amanda Association*.

'Rome is as perplexed as us. They are delighted one of the earlier Messiah's was Catholic, even more so that we Protestants toasted her for tea.'

'What about the competition? You know, Mecca, Lhasa, Jerusalem.'

Blank faces stared at him.

'How can we be certain the new Messiah has returned as a Christian?'

'Is not that remark more than a trifle blasphemous, my dear Bishop?'

Auldley was making a feeble attempt at joking. Yet they repeatedly preached that God moved in mysterious ways. Imagine Him pulling a fast one, for example anointing a Maori witch doctor as the new Messiah. They would all have to trundle off to New Zealand, that is if they were invited and if they could afford the air tickets.

'Let's try Rome again.'

The phone rang somewhere deep in the catacomb of offices considered indispensable to run the Vatican. It was answered by one of the administrators of that unique and complex organisation.

'Hello, the Archbishop of Canterbury speaking. Can I please have a quick word with his Holiness? Oh, I see. Do you know how long he is likely to be? Well, can he please call me back, it's rather urgent. Thank you.'

Auldley Huett looked at his two bishops.

'He's busy on another line. Whom on earth could he be calling?'

'Did you say "on earth", Audley? How can we be certain it was a terrestrial communication?'

The Archbishop's personal assistant interrupted the meeting.

'A Mr Matthew Hodges for you on line three.'

Elisabeth Fielding took a taxi home. Her car had been a total write-off. So had she. The clothes lent by the Red Cross fitted her atrociously, the styling was abysmal. But anything was preferable to the embarrassment of waking up stark naked surrounded by gawking males. How dare they undress her without permission, she would take them to court for sexual molestation. She still felt uncomfortably stiff from lying on that marble slab. However, her neck was fine, considering her head had been retrieved from the back seat of her Vauxhall and thrown into the wrong body-bag.

'Been identifying a deceased relative? Must be a terrible experience.' The taxidriver was a cheerful and chatty character, although tact was low on his list of personal attributes. 'Your Mother?'

'No, it was me.'

The taxi stopped in front of her home. The second part of the journey had been significantly less comfortable than the first. The driver seemed to be having excessive trouble changing gears.

Elisabeth opened the front door.

'Hello, I'm back!'

She went upstairs to find her husband Gerry sozzled out of his mind in bed with her sister, Agnes.

'But I thought you were dead, darling.'

The divorce judge was obliged to rule against adultery on the grounds that coitus occurred when the claimant was dead so that, technically, the defendant had not been married at the time of the misdemeanour. He awarded a *decree nisi* all the same.

'Ssssh! That's it, clear as anything. Using a telephone card from a call box. Pathetic!'

'Death to Satan America, death to Satan Britain!'
　'Death to Satan America, death to Satan Britain!'
　'Death to Satan America, death to Satan Britain!'
　The crowd had lost count of the number of incantations. In fact, it had reached 2,767, excluding rehearsals. They had struggled over the word 'Britain', usually Satan only infested America. The captain of the Iranian religious police explained that Britain not only harboured Salman Rushdie but another of its heretical citizens was now daring to denounce Mohammed! Most demonstrators were uncertain their shouting would be heard in Britain, wherever it was, but as full-time members of a spontaneous crowd they were accorded preferential living quarters. So they dutifully and enthusiastically shouted and gesticulated in unison with each other.

As the crowd passed in front of an imposing building, none of the choristers noticed a bearded face scowling down from an upstairs window. The face turned towards the interior of the room, still scowling. Someone had just entered the expansive yet sparsely furnished office, bringing the number of its occupants to seven.

'Ayatollah Kasmiklani, did you order this manifestation?'

He had.

'I suggest you wipe that foolish grin from your face. You have sinned against Allah.'

All six attendees gaped in surprise. Surely their spiritual leader, the Ayatollah Yasmlani himself, had misunderstood the situation?

Their leader's icy glare softened, yet his black-brown eyes still bored into Ayatollah Kasmiklani with feudal ferocity.

'Let me explain. But first, please be seated. I am convinced the person claiming to be the Messiah, although living in infidel Britain, is the true messenger of Allah, the successor to Mohammad.'

Six faces stared in open-mouthed amazement. They implicitly respected and trusted the wisdom of their leader. Yet how could he possibly be so informed? Had he also received a visitation?

'You are aware of the contents of the Aakzra scroll.'

Everyone instinctively gazed downwards in respect. The scroll was the most precious and one of the most secret parchments concerning the origins of their religion. It was kept in the vaults of a Qum mosque, in fact only several hundred yards from where they were meeting.

'The scroll, as you know, describes Mohammed's first meeting with Allah's messenger.'

'*First* meeting?!'

'Yes, there was a second meeting, more a confrontation. The messenger criticised Mohammed for failing in his duty, firstly by restricting his preaching to local tribes and secondly by deforming sections of the heavenly philosophy to suit his personal ambitions. Due to the blasphemous leanings of the message contained in the scroll, whose authenticity is unquestionable, our ancestors agreed it should be suppressed, that only the senior Ayatollah resident in Qum should know of its existence, let alone its contents. The text names the messenger as Alaap, the same as during the first visitation. One phrase is crucial, it is a quotation of words spoken by Alaap to Mohammed: 'I should punish you severely for your irresponsible actions, but I will spare you. Be relieved it was I, not Kylb, with whom you were dealing.''

'Kylb!!'

Yes, the very same. Now do you realise why ordering thousands of peasant cretins to chant 'Death to Britain' is not only foolhardy but detrimental to our very survival?'

World leaders of all shades and varieties phoned and met, met and phoned, phoned and phoned, all in a desperate attempt to understand what was happening. As frequently occurred in such circumstances, people with little or no information filled in the gaps with suppositions which became rumours which became hypotheses from unnamed sources which became facts from informed sources. As the day advanced, the world became ever-increasingly confused as more information led to less understanding and greater speculation. Stock markets remained stable because no one could envisage how the sudden arrival of a Messiah would affect interest rates. Church shares would probably have risen, but they were not quoted. The media procrastinated, concentrating its coverage on the homecoming of the crash victims and on debating whether the Messiah was Protestant, Catholic or Methodist or, heaven forbid, a Jehovah's Witness.

By early afternoon reports warned of mammoth street demonstrations throughout the Arab world, with hundreds of thousands of demonstrators chanting the same message: 'Death to the Zionists'. Street battles erupted spontaneously in the Occupied Territories, by evening the Palestinians were compiling yet another long list of valiant martyrs. In the turmoil nobody noticed that one zealously reactionary Moslem country, after some initial minor disturbances, returned to being a haven of tranquillity.

In Germany, shortly afterwards in Austria, members of the Neo-Nazi parties took to the streets, violently expressing their latent desire for recovering their rightful superiority. The *Zieg Heils* grew in number and in intensity throughout the afternoon, sending shivers of apprehension down the spines of Poles, Czechs, Danes and Alsatians. However, the greatest fear was experienced by the vast majority of Germans, normal decent citizens who wanted nothing whatsoever to do with their Fascist countrymen.

In the United States, sanctuaries of the country's paraphernalia of sects and religious communities were besieged by frantic people imploring to be saved from the forthcoming Day of Judgement. Frenzied parishioners ransacked several more traditional churches when their ecumenical representatives admitted having no message of hope to offer, apart from praying for salvation. Life insurance companies stopped issuing new policies.

In France, protesters dumped over-ripe tomatoes in various places associated with Britain, including the square in Rouen where Joan of Arc had been cremated alive.

Then, as 3.00 p.m. approached, the half of the world enjoying daytime slowed, then progressively ground to an eerie silent standstill. The Messiah had been right. At five minutes to the hour roads were practically devoid of moving vehicles. River transport also came to a halt, barges had demolished several locks and bridges the two previous days. Planes continued to fly normally, even taking off and landing, airport authorities having turned on their night-time guidance systems. The military world, on the other hand, went onto progressively higher alerts, not because of threats of surprise invasions from Mars, but to observe the sun in an attempt to discover what was wrong with it. The scientific world was in a similar state of turmoil. No boffin worth his salt was going to miss the opportunity to solve the mystery and collar one of next year's Nobel Prizes.

At precisely 3.00 p.m. the sun disappeared from view. The world waited, watched and wondered. Who or what was causing the phenomenon? What did it signify? The mention of Messiahs was extremely vague, only that grey-haired spokesman announced anything of interest and he was not always intelligible. Church leaders and governments refused to divulge anything. The Pope had been invisible for days. There had been vague mention of eliminating pollution and ceasing to launch satellites, but why? Anyway, reducing pollution was hardly innovative. World leaders had been promising to enact stringent measures for over 20 years, during which time the pollution had omniously and progressively worsened. So why all the fuss? There had also been vague references to population restructuring, whatever that meant, but bringing the road accident victims back to life was fantastic. If this self-proclaimed Messiah could revive all those people, then logically he could bring others back to life, like Mother, Kevin and darling Rosemarie. Plus cure invalids. Myself for example?

At 3.15 p.m. the sun returned. People smiled, children danced and sang. In northern countries strangers politely shook hands whereas in more southern nations inhabitants gaily embraced each other and joyfully opened bottles of Asti Spumante or Champagne. Millions crossed themselves, churches were packed as believers arrived *en masse* to give thanks for their deliverance from the momentary darkness. Doubters joined the believers as a wise precaution, just in case God really had arrived on a tour of inspection of Planet Earth.

As the spontaneous celebrations died down, as people returned to their everyday occupations, as twilight replaced afternoon brightness, it was a significantly more thoughtful human race that sat down to their evening meals. People became increasingly puzzled. They started asking themselves numerous questions. When no answers were forthcoming, they realised how little they understood. Before long the main topic of conversation was to what extent the authorities were withholding information from them. Also, where was the Messiah and how could one pay him a visit?

The aforementioned authorities were, in fact, censoring only one extract of Kylb's message; nevertheless it was undeniably the most momentous. By tacit agreement between Matthew, the media and national governments, no direct mention of population reductions was made. There was no point risking needless panic until world leaders fully understood the implications of what was happening.

Selwyn Broadstairs sat in the House of Commons acting as unnoticeable as possible. His heart missed a beat each time one of his Conservative colleagues hailed him. An American congressman had introduced him to the philosophy of 'when the shit hits the fan, hide under the table'. One almighty dollop of extra-terrestrial excrement was waiting to be sent flying towards dozens of fans at any instant and tables were in short supply. Sonjia, his Swedish bedmate, owned an isolated retreat somewhere amongst the tundra of Lapland. The Kylb Committee could surely manage without him for a while. Meanwhile, the Party Whip was calling everyone to vote. It was embarrassing having forgotten what the motion had been, but that pompous authoritarian party twit let it be known he was in complete agreement. The 'ayes' would have it.

'So, Mr Hodges, you are convinced Kylb is a messenger of the Devil. Can you please explain how you arrived at this most interesting conclusion?'

Matthew obliged, but the distinguished persons in the office at Lambeth Palace remained none the wiser. Auldley Huett, hopelessly perplexed, tried vainly to further elucidate matters.

'If bringing the accident victims back to life is a trick to deceive us, then what does ... what exactly does Lucifer want?'

'You should be telling me, milord.'

Samuel Saunders, titular head of the Baptist movement in Great Britain, fidgeted in his chair, an outward sign of his inner embarrassment. 'If we could at least talk to the person claiming to be the Messiah, perhaps...'

'Never! We must not warn him we know his real intentions.'

'But what are these intentions, Mr Hodges?'

'Sending us all to Hell!'

Matthew was unwilling to provide additional arguments to reinforce his chilling hypotheses.

'And how can we prevent this?'

'Pray to the Almighty, stop him from succeeding when he returns.'

The others assumed he was referring to Kylb.

'Mr Hodges, I suggest we do nothing rash. Let us keep this matter to ourselves for the moment. I need time to carefully consider your very important information. I would equally wish to consult, very discreetly of course, with several of my colleagues. How about meeting again the day after tomorrow?'

When Matthew had left Auldley Huett turned to the others.

'Take your pick, gentlemen, the Devil or the deep blue sea. Have any of you experienced dreams, visions or visitations, or does this Messiah and his sidekick Hodges have a total monopoly of the diffusion of heavenly information?'

'Wouldn't the good God, sorry, I mean the true Almighty, the one we pray to, only perform pleasant miracles?' suggested the Bishop of Guildford.

'Three thousand years ago he was rather keen on droughts and hordes of locusts.'

The meeting concluded, choosing neither the Devil nor the deep blue sea.

He and Janet were drinking tea in the office. They had made excellent progress, the in-tray was almost empty. When the sun went out Janet turned on the lights and they continued unabated with their labours.

'Don't think for a moment, young lady, that I'm going to pay time-and-a-half for working nights!'

'Mr McHenderson, I find your attitude reprehensible and I henceforth announce my intention to strike.'

'You mean you are revolting?'

'Yes!'

He eyed her body in a manner bereft of the slightest modicum of professional probity.

'After due consideration, dear Janet, I find myself in almost total disagreement with you. You are anything but revolting.'

Both laughed. Both were thinking about some other night work they would shortly be performing together. However, unknown to both of them, their aspirations differed fundamentally. Janet had years of bottled up frustration and pent-up passion to release in a night devoted to endless wonderful lovemaking. He, however, was looking forward to relaxing with her, talking, sharing her most intimate thoughts, kissing affectionately, caressing her body, cuddling up on the sofa before tenderly making love in her bed.

Someone banged on the door and poked his head into the inner sanctum.

'Come on you two workaholics, it's Belinda's birthday and we need you to sing happy birthday so she can blow out the candles before the sun returns!'

They decided to leave the office at 5.30 p.m. in order to reach Janet's flat before Matthew's press conference began. Matthew phoned as planned at 4.30 p.m. Both agreed the evening's meeting should be used to inform reporters and public alike of the true nature of Kylb's demands and the importance of acquiescing, however distasteful this would be. Emphasis would be given to the immediate protection of other species and improving pollution controls. For the time being population reductions should be limited to feasibility studies. It would then be for the United Nations in full session to vote which measures should be enacted before Kylb's return, if any. Tonight there would be no bowing down to government pressure to withhold key information.

As 5.00 p.m. chimed yet another audit manager was sent scurrying back to his office with an extended list of directives from the boss. The phone rang. Janet answered.

'It's your wife.'

'George, there all sorts of people milling around the house, some have even dared enter the front garden. They say they are reporters and want to interview you in connection with the Messiah. Some have even taken photos. I'm frightened. Shall I call the police?'

'No!'

'But what shall I do? When are you coming home?'

'There is my meeting . . .'

'George, drat your meeting. If you don't come home immediately I'll call Inspector Landerson.'

'All right, dear. I promise to cancel,' George looked at

Janet, 'postpone the meeting until tomorrow evening. I'll come home straight away. Be brave!'

He left the office without speaking to Janet. Each knew exactly what the other was thinking. Words were redundant. In the train he read the evening newspapers. They provided no clue to the sudden presence of reporters in Esher. It was surely impossible for anyone to have found out his identity. None of the Kylb Committee members would denounce him. Matthew? The old boy was doing a great job, it could not possibly be him. Miss Prick-teaser? No, one does not phone the press to proclaim one's predilection for travelling knickerless on South West Trains. There must be some mistake.

He was horrified at the sight of his house surrounded by agitated people with cameras and microphones. They were reporters, no doubt about that. He recognised Katie Ediar, plus someone who usually seemed to be shouting to viewers from far-distant war zones with mortars zooming over his head.

With a loud hoot of his horn he forced a passage into the driveway.

'Mr McHenderson?'

'Yes.'

'Is it true that you are the Messiah, a member of the Kylb Committee?'

'I have nothing to say. This is surely a hoax. Who told you to come here?'

There was total silence, reporters are instinctively averse to revealing their sources, especially in front of other reporters.

'Well, you are wasting your time. If you wish to be useful, go and pester the blighter who gave you this false lead.'

'Do you personally know Matthew Hodges?'

'That's enough!'

He made his escape by entering his house through the front door. It was, however, an escape only in the most relative of terms. He was simply transferring his allegiance from the frying pan to the fire. Gladys, he knew, would be waiting for him in the hall.

She was.

He had to be lightning quick.

'I don't care where you take me, where you lead me, so long as it is straight towards the cocktail cabinet.'

Before his wife had sufficiently gathered her wits to ask the questions poised somewhere between the front of her brain and the back of her mouth, he was gulping a gin and tonic that contained an exceedingly meagre helping of tonic.

'George! They were saying you can provide information about the Messiah. One even asked if it was you! He must be out of his mind.'

'Yes, dear.'

'George, has the Church Roof Repair Committee anything to do with this Kylb fellow?'

'Yes, dear.'

'They must be crazy, out of . . . what did you say?'

'Yes, dear.'

'No, before that.'

'Yes, dear.'

Not for the first time the McHenderson attempts at communicating were prone to confusion.

'For your information, dear, the Church Roof Repair Committee is a front for the Kylb Committee. As such, the reporters are not exactly out of their minds coming to say hello to us.'

'So it's Jeffrey?'

'What is Jeffrey, dear?'

'The Messiah.'

'No, dear.'

'It's that Simon fellow. I knew it, the Jews have done it again.'

'No, dear.'

'Well, it can't be Selwyn Broadstairs. No one would choose a politician even if he is a Tory.'

'No, dear.'

'It cannot be Dr Zhigani.'

'Why, dear?'

'Because . . . Well, is it him?'

'No, dear.'

'It's not Margaret and that Matthew Hodges chap is only the spokesman. There must be another member you have not told me about.'

'Why can't it be Margaret?'

'Because she's a woman.'

'So what?'

'You know what I mean.'

'No I don't.'

'GEORGE!'

'Sorry, dear.'

'Well, is there?'

'What?'

'Another member of the committee.'

'No, dear.'

'Well, who is it?'

'Me, dear.'

'Don't be stupid, you're the Treasurer.'

'Actually, dear, I'm the Chairman, also known to the world at large as the Messiah.'

'George, that is enough of your stupidity. WHO IS IT?'

He gave up.

'Go and ask the folks waiting outside.'

A brief pause ensued.

'Prove it.'

'How?'

'Do a miracle. And no cheating.'

'Yes, dear.'

'Well, go on.'

'What miracle would you like me to perform?'

Mrs McHenderson was inhabitually but only momentarily nonplussed. She looked round the room.

'Mend the tear in the curtains.'

And the unsightly gash that had been disfiguring her beautiful flowered lounge curtains obligingly mended itself.

'Gladys, I think we had better have a talk, but first can we please watch the broadcast from Earl's Court?'

The McHendersons sat on the sofa, not quite huddled at

opposite ends as was their habit, and watched events unfolding 15 miles away in the heart of London's West End. Matthew spared no one. He announced the list of Kylb's reclamations as if he were Lucifer reincarnated, briefly outlining the satellite and pollution requirements before launching into population control with zealous gusto. His fire and brimstone presentation was reminiscent of the *Führer* addressing Nazi rallies in the 1930s or Billy Graham inviting sinners to repent, only the language was different. The specially invited audience of correspondents was cowed into silence, stunned into subjugation at the implications of what was being said.

'Are there any questions?'

Those attending had been ready with their previously vetted pre-prepared requests, ready to scream into action the moment Matthew finished speaking. However, for a few seconds, there was stupefied silence before the audience disintegrated into howling abuse. One question was heard above the pandemonium.

'Are you serious?'

'Yes!' screamed Matthew to the whole world.

Back in Esher he was aghast. Matthew could not have better sabotaged his mission if he had been trying. Trembling he turned off the television and sank into his favourite armchair. But, before he could proceed with telling Gladys of his involvement with Kylb, shouts erupted from outside the house. The journalists, having followed the conference via their satellite links, were hungry for further sensations.

Realising there was no way he could bluff his way out of the situation, he looked at Gladys.

'Sorry, dear, but our *tête-à-tête* will have to wait.'

He opened the front door and invited five of the hovering crowd to enter his house for a quiet exchange of information, no cameras (Gladys was there) but tape recorders were acceptable. When they were seated, having been first introduced to Mrs McHenderson, he made a brief statement.

'All Matthew Hodges has announced these last few days

is the truth. I apologise for my earlier refusal to answer your questions, but I wished to consult my wife before speaking with you. I formally admit to being the person Kylb communicated with on Sunday twenty-first of March, the person he requested should transmit his message to humanity. For want of a better appellation, I am the Messiah.'

'You took a long time to come out into the open.'

'There was preparatory work to be accomplished. I do not intend to restate what Kylb told me, everything has been enunciated by Matthew Hodges on three separate occasions. I genuinely believe Kylb was serious when he talked about eradicating the human race. In the conference room there were cries of 'murderer'. Even though Mr Hodges could have presented the facts a little less dramatically, he did communicate what was required of him. In other words, precisely what Kylb announced to me. I am quite happy to leave our civilisations unchanged, but Kylb, well, he gave the impression wiping out six billion humans was a normal afternoon's work for him. Whatever your colleagues at Earl's Court might have shouted at Mr Hodges, Kylb does not consider that his demands constitute murder. He views it as molecular restructuring. I cannot be certain, but he seems to consider the molecule as the basic life form. Death, as experienced by humans, is therefore no more than, than . . . than shuffling a pack of molecular cards.

'I would emphasise I am not imposing my own will on society, I am merely Kylb's messenger. As such, I encourage mankind to take appropriate actions to comply with his demands.'

'By 'encourage' you mean performing miracles like extinguishing the sun.'

'Exactly.'

'When will Kayleb . . . ?'

'Kylb.'

'. . . come back?

'From what he told me, we can expect a reappearance sometime next spring.'

There was a brief respite, a stillness in the room.

'How do we know you are telling the truth, that you are not a mass serial killer?'

'You don't and there is no way for me to prove it apart from performing miracles.'

'What are the extent of your powers?'

'I do not know.'

'What will you do supposing governments refuse to accept Kylb's conditions?'

'At the present time I have no idea.'

He benefited from a pause in the questioning.

'May I ask you, and your colleagues, to kindly stop implying that I am a potential mass murderer. I am far from enjoying the current situation, being insulted only makes matters worse. I assure you that I personally have no desire to harm anyone.'

There were nods all around.

'Would you like a scoop?'

They were practically drooling.

'In exchange, please will you leave my wife alone, stop pestering her? Now that my identity is known I promise I will cooperate with you, consequently there is no need to come visiting me in Esher. We have a deal?'

There were more nods.

'The dinosaurs in Richmond Park were no hoax. I arranged the apparition. I offer you a repeat performance tomorrow at ten in the morning. Bring your cameras! If the Park authorities are unhappy, tough luck!'

'But the retired policeman and that Jacky woman?'

'I did a little rearranging of their brain circuits. That reminds me, I must return them to normal. Perhaps we should invite them tomorrow?'

The reporters agreed. All were beaming with childish rapture. Any reticence concerning impending mass molecular redistribution had been eclipsed by the promised meeting with dinosaurs.

'One last point. I feel it my duty to personally present tomorrow evening's press conference. I look forward to meeting you again at Earl's Court!'

Five of the toughest journalists of the world's multi-media industry filed out of the McHenderson house, utterly charmed by the Messiah. He himself was pleased and relieved. It had been far easier than a Charles Dewey audit meeting.

'What's for supper, dear?'
  'Haddock.'
  'For me, you mean.'
  'No, for both of us.'
  'But you have your hats to eat, dear.'

And that is the end of the news.
He switched off. The question he had been expecting to come, came.
  'Why didn't you tell me? I could have helped.'
  'I didn't want to worry you, you were extremely busy with the church fête and all your other social activities. Also, it's rather like my accounting work. When I get home I want to escape from it all, not have to restart the discussions all over again.'
  'What other miracles have you been performing?'
  'Professional secret, dear.' He smiled at his wife impishly. 'However, if you promise to never again pester me with that question, I will accord you the right to three personal miracles. Only this is not Hans Christian Andersen and I reserve the right of veto.'
  There was a lengthy silence.
  'Please, can I think about them?'
  Gladys looked as thrilled as a young girl delving into her Christmas stocking.
  'Yes, I graciously accord twenty-four hours to compile your list.'
  Gladys nearly entered into the spirit of things, riposting with 'thank you my Lord and Master', but she desisted. After all it was only George.

He had some urgent phoning to accomplish, starting with Matthew Hodges who was thanked for his services as spokesman. He then contacted the other members of the Kylb Committee, to warn them they were heading for instant stardom. Selwyn mentally tried to remember flight times to Stockholm.

Night had fallen, Gladys was stomping around upstairs. He chose Mendelssohn's *The Hebrides* played by The Royal Philharmonic Orchestra. Perhaps, if he was extremely lucky, he could escape to a Scottish island with Janet during the summer. He doubted he and Gladys would manage to spend their summer holidays in Vienna as planned, or anywhere else for that matter.

He waited in anticipation for Jennifer's light to come on but the neighbourly nymphet was at the school concert with her parents. She sang contralto in the chorus. Should he conjure up a substitute? No, the time of after-dinner cabaret miracle-making was ended. Life was about to become deadly serious.

The record clicked on the turntable, Mendelssohn's trip to the Scottish islands had been of brief duration. He yawned. Tomorrow was going to be horrendously exhausting, he had better benefit from a good night's sleep.

As he carefully climbed into bed, he did not want to wake Gladys, his wife said, 'I've decided on two of the miracles already. And, George, even if you have made a terrible mess of things so far, well, I'm proud of you.'

13

Panicus

He glanced at his watch. He still had 15 minutes before the appointed time of his meeting, except one did not attend meetings with the Queen, one was convoked to audiences. His car was stopped at a traffic light in Eaton Square, Buckingham Palace was less than a mile away, slightly over a kilometre for foreign tourists. Even allowing for further red lights to hinder his progress, he would arrive on time. He languidly watched a couple of casually yet exclusively dressed young yuppies walk by. No, yuppies were American. He smiled, the terribly upper-class pedestrians holding their Harrods shopping bags were none other than Sloane Rangers. He had just driven through Sloane Square. This was upper-crust London, Britain at its true-blue ultimate aristocratic best. There were unquestionably more Rolls Royces than Ladas driving around.

He eyed the traffic light, still haughtily commanding all and sundry to stop, Rolls Royces and Ladas alike. Very democratic institutions, traffic lights, and obstinate. He sat and fumed with impatience. If the light did not change promptly, the area, true-blue British or not, would soon qualify as a red light district. The driver, supplied by the security department of the Home Office, engaged first gear and he was again advancing towards Buckingham Palace. There would be no need for a teeny-weenie little miracle after all.

He did not habitually worry about his proximity to the Queen's official place of residence. They could have moved it to Arizona, reconstructing it next to London Bridge, for all he normally cared. Today, however, was somewhat different. He had been invited to have tea with the Queen, not a garden party with three thousand other discerning citizens, but alone. Just her and him. Tea for two.

Forty-eight hours had passed since his return home to face the crowd of reporters and then Gladys. Only two days, yet it seemed an eternity.

The Kylb mission was going badly, extremely badly, disastrously badly. He doubted he was being invited to receive polite compliments from Her Majesty, with a knighthood into the bargain. On the contrary, the audience was a strictly unofficial encounter to enable them to evaluate the situation and determine the best course of action to pursue. In other words, to sort out the shambles.

Funny, he had never considered the Queen as a businesswoman. Of course she opened Parliament and signed decrees, but her regal responsibilities were surely restricted to walking her corgis, attending Ascot, marrying her children, she did not attend their divorces, launching ships, not many of those these days, and reading the Christmas message. Her main justifications for existing were to increase the circulation of the scandal tabloids and boost the British tourist industry. At least theoretically, because today's meeting was strictly business, business of world-shattering importance. Was he awed at the prospect of meeting her? Not really. She had a reputation for making people feel at ease, the antithesis of Charles Dewey. So did he, so they should get on famously together, each making the other feel perfectly at home. There she had a slight advantage. The meeting was at her place of abode, not in Esher, so he could hardly make her feel at home since she was already there. Although, of course, he owned his mansion at Esher, whereas she was only a tenant at Buckingham Palace. Or did her family personally own the place? If not, what rent did she pay? And if she was in arrears, would a bailiff come to turf her out?

His mind stopped wandering. He wondered if all those on their way to meet Her Royal Highness suffered similar bouts of stress-induced idiocy.

Ceasing his contemplation of homely matters, he cast his mind back to recent events.

The reappearance of the dinosaurs in Richmond Park had been an enormous success. Living in a world of cyber space and virtual reality, viewers were too *blasé* to be impressed by the eerie images ricocheting from communications' satellites into their parlours, kitchens or wherever people installed television sets. But the 300 spectators actually in attendance, surrounding Pen Ponds at a very respectable distance, were simultaneously thrilled, awe-inspired, thunderstruck, amazed and terrified. Parkkeepers experienced an extra panoply of emotions as their peaceful idyllic nature reserve was again transformed into a heaving fetid mudbath. Carstairs Welsh had invited some of the world's foremost zoologists, who spent most of the time in earnest discussion or scribbling illegible notes. Selena stood alongside her boss throughout the performance in a state of suspended petrifaction. She still had not fully recovered from the Messiah's resuscitation of a brightly plumed parrot.

John Hoskins was invited, but the retired police officer had witnessed sufficient Mesozoic Age monsters for one lifetime. Jacky Hufnizcwck, however, was in attendance. Whilst walking to the ponds he sidled over to her. He expressed regret for upsetting her thought patterns whereas she, fully briefed on events subsequent to his visit to her office, was full of remorse at having threatened legal action against a Messiah.

'No problem, I would have won the court case.'
'How can you be so certain?'
'Easy, I would have "fixed" the judge.'

Jacky glared at him, then burst out laughing. They shook hands, absolving themselves from past contradictions. She agreed with alacrity to incorporate herself into the Kylb Committee, accepting special responsibility for minimising social disruption if and when population reductions were implemented. On returning to her office she would commence gathering statistics on existing and predicted global population levels, providing committee members with summary reports as relevant data became available.

When two of the bulkier members of the dinosauric cast discovered that uprooting centuries-old oak trees was great fun, the park superintendent pleaded to have the prehistoric vandals returned to the past.

'But I have no intention of returning them, I thought you might wish to keep them as a tourist attraction.'

The assembled parkkeepers looked aghast.

'All right, how about London Zoo?'

There were no takers.

'Disney World?'

An American displayed signs of interest until a playful *Tyrannosaurus Rex* converted yet another oak tree into a pile of splinters.

'Not to worry. The lady on my right claims to have a warehouse where dinosaurs can be stored.'

He glanced towards Jacky, his mischievous grin giving the game away.

'By the way, how do you pronounce your family name?'

'Hufnizcwck.'

He was none the wiser.

The seance was brought to a sudden close when two of the nastier looking *Ankylosaurusess* caught sight of the spectators and ambled over to obtain a closer look. They ambled remarkably quickly, approaching to within 20 yards of the nearest humans before they, plus their less inquisitive comrades, were zapped backwards to the dawn of prehistory.

His next port of call was the office. He was driven there courtesy of Richmond Police. As the driver activated his siren and hurtled at 80 miles an hour down the wrong side of the road, his passenger pleaded there was no desperate hurry. The driver kindly slowed to a sedate 60.

'I suppose I'll soon be unemployed.'

The police driver was a remarkable fellow. Not only could he negotiate the labyrinthine roads of Greater London at breakneck speed, he could also engage in a friendly chat.

'Sorry, but I do not quite understand.'

'Well, I imagine you will soon be solving crimes, probably even preventing them from happening. No more murders, no more arson, no more bank robberies, no more muggings, no more police radar traps.'

His passenger was silent as he contemplated the implications.

'And consequently no more police,' added the driver as he calculated that on Putney Bridge it was possible to overtake a London bus overtaking a London bus whilst a third London bus was negotiating the bridge in the opposite direction.

'To be honest, I had not thought about such matters. Please remember my mission is not to regulate society. This is not 1984. I believe British police are doing a fine job, I have no intention of usurping their rôle in society.'

'Why not? It makes sense.'

'Pardon?'

'Well, we could all be made redundant on full pay. Instead of busting our asses chasing serial killers and harassing drivers who forget to put coins in parking meters, we could luxuriate in Spain, play golf and really enjoy ourselves.'

Long before arriving at his office they knew something was terribly wrong. The streets were clogged with cars, many parked in a way that would make even the average Roman blush. Their initial apprehension at being dangerously noticeable was soon dispelled. So many other official vehicles were rushing around with sirens blaring, they probably had the safest cover possible. They stopped alongside a Metropolitan Police squad car.

'What the hucking fell is going on?' asked his driver,

revealing either a love for Spoonerisms or a tendency towards dyslexia.

In view of his difficulty in distinguishing left from right when overtaking other vehicles, his passenger concluded the second option was more likely.

'It's that freaking Messiah. Since his identity has been known and, if I may say so, his bleeding extermination plans have been announced, the population has gone crazy. Most of them want to butcher him, although others have arrived in ambulances and wheelchairs hoping to be cured. They can't make up their minds whether to worship him or burn him at the stake.'

Neither of which was very comforting for the senior partner of Christie, Wainwright, Steinway and Company.

'Turn round. I'll try and phone the office from somewhere.'

The driver promptly turned round in a fashion unarguably efficient if you overlooked wear on tyres.

Hauling himself into a sitting position, he ordered the driver to head for the Savoy, surmising that hotel staff familiar with the whims of oil sheikhs, rock superstars and Elizabeth Taylor would be well prepared to welcome an errant Messiah.

They were. Their discretion was so discreet one failed to notice it.

Safely installed in one of the hotel's suites he phoned the office. Janet herself answered. He had used his private line whose existence was known to few.

'Janet, what's happening?'

'We are totally besieged. For the moment no one can either enter or leave the building. The police have promised a helicopter to evacuate us.'

'Are you all right?'

'Put it this way, if anyone ever dares insinuate that working for an accounting firm is routinely boring, I'll thump him one good and proper.'

'Atta girl, that's the spirit! You're not frightened?'
'No, it's you they are after.'
'I am deeply honoured. No phone calls?'
'Plenty, you have been in great demand this morning. The Chinese Ambassador and the Libyan *chargé d'affaires* are desirous of meeting you in their respective official residences. Selwyn Broastairs left a message confirming his departure on a parliamentary commission to Scandinavia. The Institute of Chartered Accountants would like you to call back and the BBC wished to know if you were available for tomorrow morning's Terry Wogan Show. Ah, yes, I almost forgot, a gentleman by the name of Charles Dewey rang. Says he now understands why you reduced his inventory valuations, so he plans to take legal action if you do not accept his original figure.'
'Bugger Charles Dewey.'
'If you say so.'
'Janet, when can I see you?'
'I'll be home all evening.'
Both knew what she meant.
He gave her his number at the Savoy.
'Good luck!'

Mr Forrest of G.E.T. Well Cards Plc was sitting in his sumptuous office. The sales manager and financial director were both in attendance.
'Does anyone know the new Messiah's birthday?'
No one did.
'How many Christmas cards have we currently in stock?'
'Approximately fifteen thousand remaining unsold from last year and a further three thousand printed in February, ready for next December.'
'Is there any way we can remove the 'Happy Christmas' and replace it with . . .'
Mr Forrest was stuck.
'Happy Kylbmass?' ventured the sales manager.
The managing director sighed. At least the Messiah had

waited until after the seasonal Easter rush before manifesting himself.

'Everyone, let's please get down to business!'
In the boardroom of Maiden Records a relative hush descended on those present. Zylac Hinterstein, like his counterpart Mr Forrest of G.E.T. Well Cards, had convened a meeting of senior management to devise ways of successfully exploiting the current situation. He had come a long way since serving as errand boy to Fontana Records, where in 1962 he narrowly escaped dismissal for assuming Joan Baez's recording of *Banks of the Ohio* was a protest song attacking capitalistic exploitation of the workers by America's financial institutions.

'November, you said. Who the blazes wants to be born in November?'
Apparently none of those attending the meeting did.
'So what recordings in our back-catalogues could be made into a compilation of Christmas, Xmas, bugger it . . . seasonal songs?'
Silence. No composer of popular refrains seemed to have been inspired by the eleventh month of the year. There was 'September Song' and 'September in the Rain', one could croon and spoon endlessly in June, watch 'April Showers' and swoon in 'Apple Blossom Time', but there was nothing much to do musically in November. The month in question was clearly out of season in the world of popular melody making.
'How about "Autumn Leaves"?'
'Or "A Foggy Day In London Town"?'
'"Jingle Bells" doesn't actually specify its taking place in December.'
'And I suppose the sleigh will be effortlessly sliding its way through rotting leaves?'
'I've got it!'
Everyone turned to hear what the youngest element of the team had 'got'.

'Morrissey recorded a song about November!'
'What was it called?'
'"November Spawned A Monster".'
Pause for brief embarrassed silence.
'In any case Morrissey records for HMV.'
'Damn the Messiah for being born in November.'
'Messiah?'
'We'll call him whatever he wants, so long as it boosts sales.'
A long pause ensued.
'Keep thinking, I refuse to market a compilation containing one song.'
An even longer pause ensued.
'What about "St George and the Dragonet"?'
'Rick, Stan Freeberg's wacky irrelevant humour is not exactly suitable for Christmas. I mean the festive season. Although, having seen photos of the Messiah's wife, there is some topicality to your idea.'
'Gentlemen, please! Let's maintain proper decorum. Remember we do happen to be discussing religious matters.'

Fenella Hawkins, the only woman at the gathering, was personally responsible for sacred recordings. It was a minor appointment, extremely minor. Her lifelong ambition had been to create her own subsidiary label, which she would name *Virgin Mary Records*. Now, thanks to this Kylb incarnation, her ambitions appeared destined for the mausoleums of music.

'Well, everyone?'
Silence. The silence of desperation.
The compilation project was shelved.

The ayatollahs of Qum were having problems. Domestically, the Iranian population was fulminating over the recent prohibition of street demonstrations. One such gathering had been illegally convened to protest about no longer being able to protest. On the international forum, Iran's lack of fervour concerning the final glorious elimination of Israel was seen by neighbouring Moslem countries as a despicable turncoat attempt to undermine Arab dominance of the Middle East. In the equally convoluted world of religious politics, the ayatollahs' efforts at interconnecting with other religious denominations had encountered stiff resistance. Not only was their carefully nurtured pagan image little conducive to forging links with their pious analogues, but religious officials successfully contacted were too preoccupied dealing with rumours of a new Messiah to make themselves available. However, through diplomatic channels, essentially ambassadors and cultural attachés, the ayatollahs eventually established telephone liaisons with several high-ranking religious functionaries.

Within the Christian world the success of the Iranian overtures had been depressingly mitigated, especially in America, but two ex-lovers of Amanda sensed there was a genuine willingness to communicate. Auldley boasted connections with the military, his brother, the younger athletic one, was a NATO general. Consequently, shortly thereafter, a Royal Air Force plane flew secretly to Tehran carrying an intriguing array of ecumenical officials, including two distinguished rabbis known for their progressive preaching, three European Moslem leaders, a senior representative of Britain's Hindu community, the European Commissioner responsible for religious affairs and specially selected interpreters. Auldley and Gerald jointly represented the polymorphous patchwork of those practising the varied and various variations of Christianity.

The series of meetings in Qum were a revelation to those attending. They drew lots to appoint a chairman, someone had to administer the meetings. The sight of a rabbi and ayatollah in earnest discussion on procedural matters was amazing enough. Their resulting agreement was as near to miraculous as one can achieve without divine intervention.

There were points of discord, but the collective will to succeed overcame pride. The more they learned about the fundamentals of each other's doctrines, the more they wondered why they had been bitter enemies for centuries.

An internal communiqué summarising their joint conclusions highlighted three issues:

* Kylb existed. His wishes, however disagreeable, must be taken seriously.
* A gathering, a synod or whatever, of leaders from all religious denominations would convene in Geneva to debate the taking of measures necessary to meet Kylb's demands. The Messiah would be invited to attend. In fact, as the rightful representative of all world religions, George McHenderson should chair the assembly. The Archbishop of Canterbury would contact Him without delay.
* Religious leaders would work closely with national governments and international organisations. Without one global effort on behalf of the entire human race there would be little chance of achieving anything constructive.

It was implied, in contrast to statements made by the newly-appointed Messiah, that they should not hesitate to apply less than democratic means to advance with their mission. The ayatollahs announced their admiration for Christian theology, privately admitting many of its teachings were superior to the Koran. However, they disparaged Christianity's innumerable weakling subdenominations for ineffectively controlling their congregations, excepting Jehovah's Witnesses and the First Church of Christian Science, who both received praise for the dynamic management of their devotees. Auldley received bitter criticism for according almost equal rights to women, also for allowing social progress in Britain to distort the already tainted teachings of his organisation. He was especially miffed at the Ayatollah Yasmlani's assertion that the Reverend Ian Paisley, he from tyrannically puritanical Ulster, would have made an excellent Archbishop of Canterbury.

The visitors were invited to tour the impressive religious monuments of Qum, before bidding farewell to their hosts and flying back to Europe. As he watched the barren mountains of Armenia glide beneath the wings of the plane, Auldley was comforted. After centuries of clutching at historical straws when defending the church's outmoded and occasionally irrelevant dictates, he now represented an influential movement battling for relevant, contemporary and vitally important issues.

The Messiah decided to remain at the Savoy until that evening's press conference, which was to be held near Fleet Street. He phoned Gladys, who was sitting at home watching police install a security barrier around their house. Surprisingly, she had other matters on her mind.
 'George, I've chosen my three miracles!'
 'Tell me tonight, dear.'
As he replaced the receiver he remembered his other plans for that night. With Janet.
 He switched on CNN, with more than a little trepidation.
 '. . . my has been put on maximum alert. Government spokesmen insist this is to forestall aggression by the illegal puppet government of Taiwan, following recent heinous propaganda attacks falsely accusing China of causing the sun's disappearance. Our Far Eastern correspondent believes China's move is primarily designed to quell internal unrest subsequent to news of the Messiah's arrival infiltrating into the country via internet. Peking authorities fear this could be interpreted by dissidents as a sign to liberate nations living under the totalitarian yoke of communism.'
 'Thank you, Ginnie!
 'Tens of millions of Arabs have paraded in countries as far flung as Pakistan and Morocco, all brandishing the same war cry 'Death to the Zionists.' A summit meeting of leaders representing the entire Arab world is planned to take place in Cairo tomorrow. It will be the first time all Arab leaders have met together simultaneously, that is if Iran sends a delegation.
 'Meanwhile Israel is in a state of extreme tension as the country prepares for war. The Prime Minister, in a television broadcast to his nation, reiterated longstanding government policy that never,

whilst a single Israeli was living, would they surrender the city of Jerusalem to their Arab opponents. Our Middle East correspondent theorises that without direct military intervention from the United States, Israel could inflict colossal damage on Arab forces and their civilian populations, but would be unable to survive a sustained attack. The main concern is that the Israeli government would resort to tactical nuclear weapons, a horrifying prospect knowing Pakistan and possibly Iraq also possess nuclear arms. Connie Schwietzer, United States Secretary of State, will visit several of the region's capitals tomorrow in a desperate attempt to prevent all-out war.

'Over to you, Chris!'

Chris commented images of howling street demonstrators brandishing slogans little different from those waved at television cameras for decades.

'In Europe, literally millions of demonstrators have poured into the streets as people realise the Messiah has been instructed to eliminate billions of lives. Most national leaders have made statements affirming the determination of their governments to protect their citizens by all possible means.'

Images of European demonstrators brandishing slogans little different from those being waved by their Arabian counterparts were followed by statements from several government spokesmen, each swearing their citizens had nothing to worry about. None appeared the least concerned about the fate of humanity living beyond their country's boundaries, in other words practically everyone in the world.

'International airlines have reported a sudden surge of passenger bookings, all with the same destination: London, England. The would-be travellers are either invalids or terminally ill. Their final destination? Esher, approximately twenty miles south-west of London, home town of George McHenderson, the self-proclaimed and apparently accredited Messiah. In England itself, hundreds of thousands of sufferers plus a multitude of pilgrims simply wishing to see the Messiah, have been amassing in the previously quiet community of five thousand inhabitants. However, far more ominous, are the gangs of mostly young people, many on motorbikes,

chanting 'McHenderson murderer!' and whose intentions are anything but peaceful. Monstrous traffic jams have formed, for there is nowhere for the visitors to park when they arrive in the vicinity. Overworked police are in the process of installing a network of roadblocks throughout the region, thereby preventing vehicles from approaching the town. In Esher itself, violence erupted as visitors met with stiff resistance from local inhabitants furious at the invasion of their town and increasingly frightened for their safety. Local schools have closed. Looting is reported as famished visitors seek food by any means available.

'George McHenderson has not been seen since this morning's display of dinosaurs in Richmond Park. His house has been cordoned off by a special army unit, access within five hundred yards is impossible. It is rumoured that the Messiah, having relieved Matthew Hodges from the position of spokesman for the Kylb Committee, will personally present future press conferences, commencing with this evening.

'Our reporter Kenneth Simpson was one of the lucky five personally to interview George Henderson, sorry McHenderson, last night in his spacious mansion near Esher.'

There was a view of the McHenderson house in the background as Mr Simpson launched into his presentation. The subject of the report listened in acute embarrassment.

'George McHenderson is a polite, affable and highly intelligent British Chartered Accountant. After the strident announcements of Matthew Hodges, it was a pleasure to listen to the calm measured tones of fifty-six-year-old Mr McHenderson. Even if his message was no less disturbing. It is clear that George McHenderson believes in the threats of the extraterrestrial Kylb and is determined to ensure the latter's demands are implemented. I repeat that this could result in the reduction of world population from seven to one billion. Mr McHenderson emphasised that if appropriate efforts were made to save other terrestrial life forms, essentially by reducing pollution and halting the desecration of forests, then it might conceivably be possible to negotiate a settlement with Kylb. This, he insists, is the responsibility of national governments and international authorities such as the United Nations, not himself. He does not know the full extent of his miracle making powers, although they are *clearly awe-inspiring, but warns he is prepared to use them without compunction to convince people to take Kylb seriously.*

'Is George McHenderson the new Messiah? Does Kylb really exist? Is the so-called AAA Corporation really God or some other civilised life form attempting to conquer our planet by devious means? Is George McHenderson telling us the truth? It is not for me to say, it is up to world leaders to decide whether to comply with Kylb's demands or prepare for an intergalactic battle straight out of H.G. Wells' War of the Worlds.*'*

'Thank you Kenneth. At a press conference yesterday evening President Stanton Forbes commented on the situation.'

'My fellow Americans, I can assure you nobody dictates to the United States what we should or should not do in relation to the supposed visit of the alien Kylb. I promise you there will be absolutely no reduction of our population levels so long as I am President. We will not be blackmailed into concessions and I refuse to enter into any discussions, however informal, with anyone claiming to represent this Kylb creature until the sun is permanently returned to its rightful place in our skies. I have been consulting with other world leaders and I can assure you there is no question of bowing down to totalitarian external forces, wherever they might originate. Thank you and God bless America!'

The broadcast returned to the studio, where the announcer, whose name he did not know since he had missed the beginning of the bulletin, turned her attention to Europe.

'Millions of Germans have taken to the streets as Neo-Nazi protesters demand the resignation of Chancellor von Gildhein and the installation of a coalition of right-wing parties. Important yet considerably smaller counter-demonstrations demanded immediate action to outlaw extreme right parties and imprison their leaders. Hundreds were injured in Frankfurt when rival demonstrations attempted to hold meetings in the same square.

'In London, British Prime Minister Alistair Sinclair confirmed his government was carefully reviewing the situation and would not be pressurised into taking hasty actions which could be regretted later. He emphatically denied having met the Messiah and confirmed no such meeting was scheduled.

'*Over to y . . .*'

Then the telephone rang with the invitation to Buckingham Palace.

He had hardly replaced the receiver when the phone shrilled again. The whole Fleet Street area was under siege by thousands of people waiting for him to arrive. Consequently, it would be impossible to organise the conference as planned, even dangerous. He would be lifted by helicopter from the roof of the Savoy and flown to a secret air force command centre, from where he could broadcast his message and answer questions phoned by reporters installed in the Fleet Street conference centre.

Before being escorted to the hotel roof he decided the American President was a public menace, someone who should be taught a lesson before his obstreperous nationalistic incantations turned everyone against himself and Kylb. Furthermore, it was the Americans, back in June 1997, who effectively sabotaged the New York international meeting organised to introduce world-wide anti-pollution legislation. Under pressure from business interests.

Had not the CNN reporter, when referring to their meeting in Esher, described his host as 'affable'? Stress and tension, plus suffering the blinkered actions of those with more power than sense, can play havoc with affability. So Mr Forbes accused him of blackmailing? He had been right, yes, he, George was going to perform some blackmailing. Or rather 'black-maleing'. He closed his eyes and turned the White House black. A very dark black, inside and outside, in the furthest recesses of every nook and cranny, a black that made coal insipidly dark grey in comparison. Feeling especially piqued at the insolence of the President himself, he changed Stanton Forbes's skin to a shiny deep ebony, entering him into the history books as America's first black President. Convinced that obnoxious wife of his was stirring things from behind the scenes, she also turned black. Highly appropriate, she had recently been overheard proclaiming her distaste for mixed marriages. Nothing racist, of course, as she had embarrassingly explained the following day, but as a means of preventing America's rich polygot cultures from merging into one boring homogeneous nonentity.

When flying to the military base something else turned black, the sky. He had completely forgotten his ordaining of daily eclipses. The pilot had not. The helicopter continued its journey as if nothing had happened.

'Fellow citizens of the world . . .'
From the depths of a military bunker he broadcast the speech prepared during his enforced isolation at the Savoy. He considered his presentation satisfactory, although there was little to say other that restate the messages previously communicated by Matthew.

The reporters' questions, however, had changed in nature: aggression replaced curiosity.

'Your announcements have caused riots around the world, how are you going to stop them?'

'That is for the authorities in the countries concerned to solve. I am a messenger. It is not my responsibility to police the world. That is what governments are for.'

'Did you turn the White House black?'

'Yes.'

'Why?'

'Because the message given by the President was seditious. It was a flagrant attempt to undermine my entire mission. Such talk can only increase the threat of mankind's extinction by Kylb.'

'Are you going to cure the sick people congregating around Esher?'

'No.'

'Why not? would it not be a gesture of goodwill, a step to build trust, stop the riots?'

'I am here to limit population. That is, you must understand that I am following instructions to that effect and it is not in my intention to get involved in matters other than those outside the scope of my instructed mission.'

Many Americans thought that he sounded like a presidential election candidate.

'Surely that is extremely selfish?'

'Err . . . perhaps it might considered to be, but I have a duty to perform in which selfishness must be overruled by an immediate patriotic sense of universal mission.'

Even recent presidential election candidates thought he sounded like them.

'What are you going to do next?'

'I do not know. I am waiting for national governments to take the lead, to formulate and then put into operation their action plans.'

'Do you think they will?'

'Of course.'

'The American President is not very enthusiastic.'

'Perhaps he will now see things differently. At least he will be seen in a different light.'

'What do you mean by that?'

'Has no one told you? Like his place of residence, the President has also turned black.'

And so on. After nearly an hour of intense interrogation he noticed, as was often the case in such circumstances, that the questions were becoming progressively irrelevant. When one female reporter asked whether he consulted his wife before making miracles, also why were they childless, he gave up in disgust.

'What's for supper, dear?'

'Lasagne.'

'Not too cooked if possible, dear.'

'George, next time you arrive by helicopter can you tell the pilot to be more careful. He landed right on top of some of our rosebushes.'

'I promise, dear.'

The McHendersons sat down to supper.

'Sorry, there is nothing fresh to eat, I was unable to go shopping.'

'That's all right, dear.'

'George, I'm frightened. It's horrible being surrounded by soldiers. They keep looking into the house and watching me.'

'You didn't do anything you shouldn't have?'

'George!'

'Sorry, dear.'

'They said on the television the whole of Esher has been invaded by hordes of people wanting to see you. Some have apparently committed horrible acts of vandalism. Hundreds are camping at the golf club. The police sergeant told me they have been digging up the greens as souvenirs of where you played golf. Please, George, do something.'

'We live in a democracy. It's the responsibility of national governments to act on behalf of their citizens, not me. Regrettably, elected officials have so far achieved nothing, except sit on fences or issue proclamations trying to sabotage my efforts.'

Gladys said nothing. There was so much George could be doing, should be doing, to force those feeble-minded politicians to treat the matter with due seriousness. Oblige them to get up off their . . . well, whatever they were sitting upon. Normally she would not have hesitated, she would have told George in no uncertain terms what should be done, giving him the benefit of her considerable experience in organisational matters. However, things were far from normal, so she remained silent. If only Kylb had chosen *her* as Messiah.

'Did you hear that some five-star general has told the Prime Minister to resign, so the army can run the country? He insists, in troubled times like these, that countries need strong leadership and a military junta should therefore be installed.'

'Perhaps he is right.'

'On the other hand, I am surprised the country's religious leaders have been so quiet. One Anglican bishop did plead with everyone to stay calm, insisting Jesus was the true Saviour and that they should do nothing to aggravate the crisis. He promised to organise special church services so worshippers could pray for guidance. A Catholic then mumbled something about it being for Rome to decide on such matters, that people should humbly pray for forgiveness instead of interfering in areas that did not concern them.'

'Has the Pope said anything?'

'He is still in hiding. The reporter said there were rumours circulating about his health.'

'Fine time for him to be out of action. They should replace him.'

'They are not allowed to, he has to die first.'

He was about to say something exceedingly cynical, but stopped just in time.

'George, please let's go away from here. Anywhere.'

He smiled at his wife.

'That is the best idea I have heard for ages. I will ask the army to escort us to a quiet hideaway, somewhere in North Wales or Scotland.'

'Couldn't we go somewhere sunnier, like the South of France?'

'I think we should stay in this country. I doubt if the French would appreciate us disembarking at Nice airport with a battalion of SAS troopers, and I personally don't fancy being escorted by dozens of *gendarmes*. Let me think about it. Perhaps we could ask to be installed with Salman Rushdie. At least he should be interesting company.'

There was a brief respite in the conversation as the McHendersons tackled one of Gladys's apple and blackcurrant crumbles. Whilst she was making coffee and tidying the kitchen, he suddenly remembered something.

'I have been invited to have tea with the Queen tomorrow.'

'Good heavens. Whatever for?'

'To discuss affairs of state, no doubt.'

'Am I invited?'

'Err, well nothing was mentioned.'

'Can you phone to make sure?'

'No, it was just me.'

'Oh.'

He hated people who changed subjects in order to squirm out of an awkward impasse, but this was not the moment to be squeamish.

'What about your choice of miracles?'

The moisture forming in Gladys's eyes evaporated.

'You won't be cross?'

'No, why should I be? You can request whatever you like and I can veto whatever I like.'

'Well, firstly, well, it doesn't count as a miracle, although it sort of will be one. I need your agreement to advance some money to pay for the cost of the other miracles.'

'How much?'

'About a thousand pounds.'

'Granted. Now what are your wishes?'

'The first is not for me, it is for Mother. Can you please cure her arthritis?'

He sighed. He was not a saint, however Kylb's instructions did not specifically prohibit curing the sick. And what the hell, thanks to his apparently misguided efforts, Lourdes and Fatima had already been supplanted by Esher. Before very long the Thames would supersede the Ganges for pilgrims wishing to cleanse their souls.

'Granted. But tell her to keep 'mum' about it. If word gets out we will have the whole neighbourhood pleading to have their ailments cured. Our house will become a witch-doctor's surgery.'

Gladys promised.

'Next miracle please!'

'I . . . oh George, please, I want to have a child.'

He sat in stunned silence. He should have guessed, but he had been too preoccupied by other matters.

'Not now, not with all the chaos going on around us. Let's wait. We need time to consider it. I am not saying no. Please try and understand this is a long-term proposition, something to take very seriously.'

'I have been taking it very seriously, for the last twenty years.'

He had nothing to say.

'And finally, please return me to how I looked when we were married. Even more than having a child I want to be like everyone else, instead of a massive hulk loved by no one.'

Silence. He could not bring himself to lie to his wife, console her by avowing that he at least still loved her.

'Please, George!'

He wilted under his wife's tear-stained gaze. He would never have guessed, never for a moment imagined this was what she wanted more than anything else.

'But why the thousand pounds?' was all he could mumble.

'I will need a complete set of new clothes,' she replied, displaying a very ungladyslike and impish grin.

He pondered. Returning Gladys to normal might take her mind off her desire to have a child . . .

'Gladys Joyce McHenderson, I . . .'

'Stop! Only my body, not my mind.'

'Gladys Joyce, I return your body to its shape on the day of our marriage.'

She looked awful.

Her tough tweed clothes hung limply around her body, forming a shapeless mass. As she walked with trepidation towards the mirror her girdle fell around her knees, tripping her up. But then, one by one, the offending clothes were discarded to reveal a vision straight from a *Playboy* centrefold, both Jayne Mansfield and the Venus de Milo were completely outshone by the woman who stood in front of the mirror and gazed at herself in wonderment. Gladys turned towards her husband and everything else was forgotten.

Two hours later in the guest room, it was the only bedroom with a double bed, Gladys placed a very tender kiss on her husband's forehead, a husband who was sweaty, exhausted and aching all over, a husband wishing he had rejuvenated himself as well.

'Let's have a shower together as we used to!'

As he slowly, delicately and quite unnecessarily wiped the soap suds off Gladys's breasts, they were truly amazing not only for their size but also for their shape and consistency, he suddenly remembered where he should have been spending the evening, and his promise to phone Janet. Failing to respect a promise is a serious lapse of social etiquette but, momentarily, he had a handful of other matters that required his attention. He would contact her in the morning. He supposed he was being unfaithful to his secretary, a form of inverse adultery. Although, in his defence, he had not exactly made love to Gladys. She had made love to him, well, at least to begin with.

'George, a tiny bit lower down, please.'

Back in bed, once again sweaty and exhausted, both were pausing to think. He wondered whether this could really be Gladys, the woman with whom he had been living without touching for nearly 20 years? He sensed her personality had also changed. She was lively, laughing, and relaxed. Tomorrow morning at breakfast, would she return to being the same obnoxiously bossy cock-pecking wife? Perhaps the ideal would be Janet in the body of Gladys? No, his secretary in the body of his wife would no longer be Janet. The biggest challenge would be the baby. The prospect of their becoming parents was inconceivable. No, start again, wrong choice of words. He recalled some words of wisdom from a schoolfriend who had fathered five offspring. Having children, he confided, was ten minutes ecstasy for the father, nine months discomfort for the mother and 20 years hell for the parents. In 20 years' time, when Junior would be setting off to university, his father would be pushing 76.

Gladys, lying next to him, converted her thoughts into words.

'George, couldn't you please stop the sun disappearing every day, it's only annoying everyone.'

'But we must prove how serious we are.'

'Well, I suppose you know best.'

Gladys had indeed changed, even her name no longer suited her.

He thought for a moment.

'If it will make you happy, I will temporarily stop it going out.'

'Thank you, darling.'

And Gladys Joyce snuggled even closer to her husband, as close as her breasts would permit.

Slowly yet steadily the passion subsided, the clutching and clawing weakened, became caressing, the French kissing that had nearly sucked his tongue down Gladys's throat calmed into friendly pecks until finally, sweat intermingling with sweat, his head came to rest between the two halves of his wife's abundant bosom, nestling in its comforting cleavage as he slowly sank into deep contented sleep. Gladys lay awake a little longer, her hands gently holding her husband's head as she recalled lonely wasted nights of marital emptiness. Then, leaving his head exactly where it was, she also drifted away into the night.

In Earl's Court Janet lay alone in her double bed.

Breakfast, a late breakfast. The soldiers outside were relieved at spotting signs of activity from within as a curtain was drawn. Strange, that was not the McHenderson's bedroom window.

The Messiah treated himself to pancakes oozing with maple syrup whilst listening to the news. World events were much of the same, only worse. He invited the army captain into the house to be reintroduced to Gladys. The look of perplexity and amazement and then admiration on his face was hilarious to watch. Even her voice had changed. It still had the same tonality but it was less booming. The dirty old man, converting his wife into a sex symbol. Must be part of his publicity stratagem. His Celia could do with a bit of rearranging, she had never returned to her original shape after the birth of their son Shaun.

They reviewed details of his trip to Buckingham Palace:

helicopter to Chelsea then a chauffeur-driven car. Her Majesty had protested at landing in the palace gardens, contending this could draw unwarranted attention to the encounter.

The army captain had kindly brought some newspapers and a pint of milk. He confirmed that passengers on South West Trains had identified him as the Messiah, something to do with altering the consistency of a woman's clothing.

Furious at his mini-skirt indiscretion, he sat down at his desk and thumbed through the accumulation of bills to be paid.

'George!'

Gladys was in the bathroom, officially to clean her teeth, but there was a large mirror and . . .

'Yes, darling.'

'My right breast is smaller than the left!'

'I beg to disagree. The left one is bigger than the right.'

Gladys, admiring her contours, could only but concur with her husband's diagnosis. Strange, she had never noticed back in her hockey playing days that her breasts were asymmetrical. After another lengthy visual inspection she concluded that if that is how she had been created, then that is how she was going to remain.

The breast's owner's troubles were, however, only just beginning.

'George, I've nothing to wear.'

'Well, surely your bras still fit. After all, your breasts did not shrink, they are just slightly more elevated than yesterday.'

'George!'

'Sorry, darling.'

'Please George!'

'It's simple, I will return you to normal size, sorry your previous size, so that you can dress and go shopping.'

'No! Please let me stay as I am! Anyway, if I went shopping as I was, I couldn't try on the clothes.'

Finally, Gladys unearthed an antiquated sports' outfit, a souvenir of her reign as captain of the Surrey County

Hockey Team. He thought she looked exceedingly stunning in white bobby-socks and a tight stretch jumper, plus a pleated mini-skirt that would have done justice wrapped around the thighs of Miss Prick-teaser herself. Gladys, ever ladylike, nearly died of shame. Braless, her nipples protruded provocatively through the material, a problem some gentle caressing from her husband only aggravated.

Beatrice could not understand what the fuss was all about. Down where she was standing nothing seemed to have altered, both her master and mistress smelled exactly as the previous day.

'Woof!'

'Ah, Beatrice! Miracles really do happen. Do you realise your mistress said 'please' twice during our last conversation?'

Whilst Gladys, accompanied by an army escort, was shopping in one of Esher's trendier boutiques for the younger generation, he visited the Mother Superior. He prevented her from kneeling before him, instead he clasped her with unabashed affection.

'Please forgive me for revealing Jesus was not the son of God. It was never my intention.'

'You have nothing to be ashamed of, much to be proud about. It is the message that counts, not the identity of the author. Do you think our children care whether Jesus or Kylb is our guiding light? It is the love we share together that is important.'

He visited the children. Their shouts of welcome had not altered. Accountant or messenger of God, they screamed with equal pleasure when 'Uncle Georgie' played hopscotch and pushed them on the swings.

'There is one upsetting factor,' the Mother Superior announced as they escaped from the clamour of pleas to continue playing. 'I, and all the sisters, work unceasingly for the children. Between ourselves we always assumed a long and restful retirement awaited us, but apparently no longer.'

'Why not?'

'Because our retirement was to be spent with Jesus in heaven!'

Her smile was angelic. If anyone deserved the accolades of sainthood it was the diminutive woman standing next to him. If anyone deserved to be included in the surviving billion it was the Mother Superior and the other sisters. And the children.

The car pulled into Buckingham Palace Road and approached the gates of the Queen's official residence. What, he wondered, did Her Majesty have on her mind?

14

Regina

The car was stopped outside the wrought-iron gates by some very officious officials. Thankfully, one offhand glance at the occupant was sufficient. They recognised his face, and the car was permitted to proceed towards the main building. To his surprise he was not searched, although no doubt he was being filmed, X-rayed and otherwise genetically dissected by hidden security devices.

The driver parked alongside a delivery van. Although not expecting the Horse Guards, a 21-gun salute and the Queen waiting at the front door, the tradesmen's entrance was pushing things beyond the limits of propriety. At least there was a lackey to open the car door and usher him through the very modest access into the Palace itself. He had no coat so the attendant, dressed like a chorus singer from a Transylvanian opera, had nothing to do except gape gormlessly at his visitor.

'Please wait here. Someone will fetch you.'

So he was going to be 'fetched', reduced to the status of a corgi waiting for its mistress to throw a ball. 'Fetch boy! fetch boy!' He noticed, however, that the Palace authorities had exhibited some consideration for their guests. Toilets were accessible for petrified citizens about to pee in their pants at the thought of imminently encountering Her Majesty. He stood up, prepared for action, when footsteps echoed from one of the corridors.

'Mr McHenderson?'

He nodded. The person fetching him superciliously looked down his nose, haughtily signalled his visitor to follow and strode down the elongated corridor from whence he had materialised. After a walk, sufficiently long for him to conclude Buckingham Palace needed electric golf caddies for internal transportation, he was shown into another room. There was no Queen, so he assumed this was another waiting room, referred to as ante-chambers in posh circles. He could not be bothered to sit, so he gazed out of a window at the gardens. Houses had a garden, whereas palaces had gardens. Pretty stupid, there was still only one of them. Only it was bigger. About 50 times bigger.

'Mr McHenderson.'

This time there was no question mark so he assumed his identity had been duly established. Things were looking up.

'I am led to believe you have not previously had the honour of being presented to Her Majesty?'

The question marks were back again.

'That is correct.'

'On meeting her it will be correct to bow slightly and take her hand if it is offered, but only very briefly.'

He was then inflicted with detailed instructions worthy of his initiation to preparatory school. It was insulting, he was no longer a ten-year-old greenhorn wearing shorts. When the official, who had divulged neither name nor function, finished articulating he had a question of his own to pose.

Fulminating, he asked, 'May I be informed whether Her Majesty has previously been introduced to a Messiah? If not, could you please appraise her that when greeting me it is customary to kneel and kiss my shoes, only briefly of course, since I am a busy man with little time to spare.'

'Mr McHenderson, I trust you appreciate the honour Her Majesty is bestowing on you, that you will behave with due decorum whilst in her presence. Her Majesty is occupied for the moment, so will you kindly please wait here.'

The lack of question mark was grammatically correct. He was being instructed and not invited to attend Her Majesty's pleasure. So he waited, impatiently. And waited and waited and waited. And in the process of waiting, in spite of being offered no refreshment, he became increasingly fed up.

Furthermore, to add insult to potential injury, he experienced sensations from down below signalling his hydraulics were agitating for access to a loo, sorry toilet. Such facilities were inevitably and infinitely conspicuous by their absence.

The supercilious twit reappeared. As he was being escorted across the threshold into an expansive and luxuriously decorated chamber, he remembered he had completely forgotten the royal *mode d'emploi* so meticulously dictated minutes earlier. It was too late, there She was sitting at an escritoire.

'Your Majesty, Mr McHenderson.'

Curious, the manner of speech had altered, the superciliousness had evaporated, his chaperone was actually playing humble, perfectly portraying Charles Dickens' creepy-crawly Uriah Heap.

Her Majesty rose, her hand held out graciously and a friendly smile adorning her face. He instinctively bowed and held her hand, briefly.

So far so good.

'Tea, Mr McHenderson?'

'Err . . . yes, please. Your Majesty.'

Much to his disappointment, she did not propose foregoing formality, converting to first names, so he presumed he was lumbered with 'Your Majesty' whilst remaining himself a nondescript 'Mr McHenderson'.

'Please be seated.'

As he installed himself onto a settee of stylish grandeur, probably on loan from the Victoria and Albert Museum, he remarked his hostess had not even excused herself for keeping him waiting. Extremely bad manners.

'I believe that you live in Esher?'

'Yes, indeed, Your Majesty. Not far from the golf club.'

'And you work in London as a Chartered Accountant?'

'That is correct, I am senior partner of a firm in the West End, in fact near to Aldwych.'

'A most interesting profession. We have to deal with accountants almost every day.'

'Well, as life becomes more complex, the need for qualified advice becomes increasingly necessary in everyday life.'

As he stumbled over his words he wished, for the umpteenth time in his existence, that people, Queens included, would stop implying they 'had' to deal with accountants. Accountants were neither lepers nor lawyers. Working with them could be a rewarding experience, except possibly when fees were billed.

Mercifully, tea arrived. The waiter, or whatever they called themselves in palaces, was a real flunky. A professional pouf. Perhaps, following the logic of hiring eunuchs for harems, no eunuchs were not readily available on the employment market, you hired normal males and then performed some judicious snipping, the palace only engaged queers in order to protect the Queen from inopportune encounters. On second thoughts, perhaps the person pouring his tea was a randy athletic and virile stud, pretending to be a pouf to facilitate his access to the chambermaids.

The moment of verity had arrived. Gladys insisted he find out. Did Her Majesty or did she not? He had promised to report back, providing the unabridged facts. Did she or did she not?

Her Majesty picked up her cup, advanced it delicately to her mouth. No, she did not, much to his surprise. The small finger of the right hand, that which held the cup, remained altogether uncocked. However, again much to his surprise, she slurped her tea, quite a commotion was to be heard. He decided to demonstrate the proper Esher manner of proceeding, aimed badly and emitted a slurp that left an elongated dribble of Earl Grey slithering down his chin.

'Mr McHenderson, apparently, according to my advisers, you are able to perform unusual feats?'

'Yes, Ma'am.'

He had completely forgotten the 'Your Majesty'.

The Sovereign of Great Britain pursued her train of thought without indication of upset at her change of denomination. He recalled she was an adept of Shakespearean drama, she was assuredly familiar with Romeo's 'What's in a name?' philosophy. Even so, he should be more careful.

'Would you be so kind as to perform one for us?'

What on earth could she want? One of her horses to win a race, Camilla to enter a convent??

'Of course, Your Majesty.'

'There is an empty glass on our desk. Without moving from your chair we would wish the glass to become full of water.'

'How about whisky?'

'Mr McHenderson, we are quite capable of deciding such matters for ourselves.'

After a moment's hesitation he decided against enquiring whether gaseous or flat and filled the empty glass.

'Mr McHenderson, you might be endowed with special powers, we are, however, most unhappy with your interference into the daily lives of our people. You must realise that proper authorities exist to administer such matters. It was improper of you not to insist that Kylb consult with us.'

'I did not choose him, he chose me.'

'Mr McHenderson, we did not give you permission to speak. As we were saying, your interventions have been clumsy, inappropriate and most regrettable. We therefore request you communicate to Kylb our desire that he attend our pleasure, either here or at Windsor, without the slightest delay. Although our programme is busy we are prepared to make every effort to accommodate his schedule. Have we made ourselves understood?'

We had. He wondered if Kylb would qualify for the 21-gun salute and manage to drink his tea without slurping.

Her Majesty proceeded.

'It is our command that you cease your so-called messianic activities, apart from contacting this Kylb entity. Likewise, you will publicly apologise for inconveniences consequent to your unsanctioned meddling in matters outside your jurisdiction and, to put things bluntly, return to your accounting. You will be replaced by a team of experts fully competent to handle such assignments. Please remember that you are no more than a professional accountant.'

'I have been personally nominated the Messiah.'

'Mr McHenderson, that is quite enough of such blasphemous talk. Please note that we are not making a request. We are commanding you to comply with our wishes.'

'I am already under orders from elsewhere.'

'MR McHENDERSON! Enough of such sedition. You will stop the disappearances of the sun forthwith and . . .'

'It has alr . . .'

'We do not appreciate being interrupted. You will henceforth stop extinguishing the sun and declare that Jesus was the true son of God, also that the other persons mentioned in your preposterous press conferences were not ordained messengers of God, especially as concerns Herr Hitler.'

'And if I refuse?'

'You will not, that is our decision.'

The Queen rose from her chair. She had terminated the meeting, audience. He had no choice other than to stand himself. Whilst leaving, he was not even proffered a royal hand to shake. He turned towards the short, dumpy and determined woman standing across the room.

'Mr McHenderson, you may turn us black if you wish. It will achieve nothing other than demonstrate your true state of mind.'

'I have no intention to harm you.' Looking at the glass poised on her desk he continued. 'All I can say is that I hope you enjoy your whisky.'

As he hurried though the antechamber he espied a squat huddled figure studiously reading in a corner. The face looked familiar, but not the business suit, because he normally wore white robes and worked in the Vatican. So he was not ailing. The cunning little Pontiff was working hand in hand with HM The Queen. What devilish plans were they concocting together?

He was ushered out of the palace with as much courtesy as one would proffer a Mafia *Padrone* with a double dose of bad breath and leprosy. So much for friendly teas for two.

'How did it go?' inquired his driver.

'Not too bad. To be honest, strictly between the two of us, things could have advanced a wee bit better,' replied a somewhat depressed although well-intentioned apprentice Messiah. 'Oh well, back to Esher. Could we please visit a W.H. Smith? If I am destined to be cooped up at home for some time, I had better purchase some books and videos.'

The driver stopped the car in Sloane Square, on a double yellow line, whilst he made his purchases. It was always difficult to choose when in a hurry. Finally, clutching a couple of Jeffrey Archers for Gladys plus a Jack Higgins and Tom Clancy for himself, also a few 'family viewing' videos neither of them had seen, he queued to pay. Through habit he had eyed the selection of Sharon Stone movies, plus one with Demi Moore showing a lot of leg on the cover, but he left them on the rack. Who needed Sharon and Demi when Gladys, the new Gladys, was waiting for him at home?

A couple of the customers glanced curiously at him, but his simple disguise of a hat, moustache and glasses held up to their scrutiny. He paid in cash. Credit cards displayed one's name. No point in broadcasting his arrival.

The car was still waiting. The driver was in earnest conversation with an aggrieved traffic warden whose unique *raison d'être* for existing at that precise moment was to defend his yellow lines from unsanctioned intruders. The driver looked extremely relieved at seeing his passenger emerge from the shop.

Then there was a blinding flash, unbelievably intense, which expanded exponentially until the brightness completely enveloped him. The mighty # must be visiting in person. And then the brilliance dimmed, became more distant, gloomier, darker, finally incredibly black as the surrounding world faded from view.

Selwyn Broadstairs MP was not at ease with himself. His one-man parliamentary commission to observe the fornicating habits of Swedes, in fact not study them but actively participate in them) and there was only one Swede he planned to actively participate in), was not advancing according to plan. To start with, he had assumed fine weather, permitting some exhilarating outdoor activities to supplement his indoor indulgences, but the weather was inordinately execrable and you cannot indulge continuously and consecutively for days, not forgetting the nights.

His mind wandered. He was sitting outside the log cabin, shivering, concluding that flat endless tundra was as about as exciting to watch as a blank TV set. Sonjia had wandered off in search of firewood. In fact, in search of anything that allowed herself a respite from her benefactor's marathon groping and groanings.

Without her omnipresent sensuality to distract his mind from more pragmatic and less enviable considerations, his reflections returned to events taking place in England. True, he was well distanced from the Party Whips who, in common with many of his local constituents, were screaming for his blood. But he knew from experience that he who is absent inevitably reaps the blame. It was his own favourite strategy for self-survival. Unfortunately, this time he was the absentee, the one shouldering the disapprobation of the entire political world. He remembered the saying that when the chips were down, the waitress in McDonald's would shout out your number. The chips were down all right and he was the one being fried. He must return to England, use every devious means devised, plus numerous others not yet imagined, to save his political hide.

He reconnected the telephone and phoned SAS reservations in Stockholm.

The light was dim in the office and the curtains were drawn although it was already 10.00 a.m. The lamp was pointing away from the person sitting behind the desk, rendering him practically invisible. The Chief of Staff of the White House recognised the voice. His boss and President of the United States of America was addressing him.
 'Can you get hold of Michael Jackson for me?'
 Michael Jackson? The Chief of Staff thought Stanton Forbes's predisposition was country and western, not Tamla Motown.
 'Should be possible, although I don't believe he performs at political functions.'
 'I don't want him to sing. He was born black and has somehow managed to turn himself white, so I was hoping he could provide some useful advice.'

'Prime Minister, Margaret Thatcher for you on line five.'

'Gentlemen, our greens are mud-infested swamps, our bunkers are used as public toilets, seven people were killed and twenty seriously injured when those wishing to be cured broke into the sports shop and stole our stock of number three irons, before proceeding to annihilate those planning to lynch him. And you still entertain doubts whether we should retain George McHenderson as Treasurer?'
 'Not forgetting the fifteen grand I invested in a new electrical system which has been rendered ... which is no more than a mangled mass of wires and smashed appliances.'
 Cirus B. Howenberger had not the slightest intention of letting anyone forget his generous donation.
 By a unanimous majority Eunice Gallaway was elected

Treasurer. The decision whether to cancel George's membership was postponed. His annual subscription was paid until the end of the year and, considering the state of the greens, it was impossible to play golf anyway.

'Come in Simon. Jeffrey and Margaret are already here and Aziz is arriving shortly. Selwyn, as you know, is in Scandinavia on important parliamentary business. George has not yet returned from Buckingham Palace. It's unlike him to be late but one should be condescending in these troubled times.'

Simon faced the buxom bombshell standing before him. She had advised him to expect a change, but this was ridiculous. His rigid upbringing warned it was sinful to even cast eyes on a female of her physical disposition. He must ensure he was not sitting opposite her during the meeting.

Meanwhile, the Vicar and his wife were installed in the lounge enjoying a quiet palaver.

'I assure you she really looked like that, perhaps her chest did not . . . was not quite as prominent, but she really was stunning when young.'

'And did she dress the same?'

'Of course not, fashions were different in those days. Jeffrey, would you want me to become like on our wedding day?'

'No, I love you just the way you are. On second thoughts, if I was also converted back to being twenty-eight, perhaps it would be worth it. We could organise a second honeymoon!'

Gladys entered with both Simon and Aziz, the latter having been held up at the security barrier, the army officer conscientiously protecting his messianic *protégée* from an attempted assassination by Islamist fundamentalists.

Gladys opened the proceedings.

'Firstly, thank you for braving the dangers outside to attend. Secondly, it really is me. My body may have changed but not my mind. Thirdly, George should be here any minute. Surrey County Council is in emergency session so Jacky, regrettably, cannot participate. However, she promises to phone.'

'Why did George visit the Queen?'

'I have no idea. It was at her suggestion.'

Silence.

Simon spoke. 'I see little point in continuing with the Committee. It was conceived primarily to advise George with establishing his Action Plan and has served its purpose.'

The other members had already reached the same conclusion. There were a couple of 'mmmmmm's of agreement.

'Of course, if George has specific questions we will be more than willing to oblige, but he must surely be receiving all the advice he needs.'

'Probably more!'

Gladys studied her guests. Were they chickening out? Possibly, but she could only acquiesce to their simple logic. Country vicars and general practitioners were out of their depths, it was for national governments and religious authorities to assume their full responsibilities.

'We will discuss your concerns with George as soon as he arrives.'

The phone rang.

Listening in to Gladys talking in the hall, they sensed something was wrong, terribly wrong. She returned to the lounge in a daze, white as a sheet. She collided with the standard lamp, her eyes no longer focusing properly.

'There has been a bomb, George has been injured, others have been killed.'

'How serious is it?'

'They say there is no hope. He has been pronounced brain-dead.'

And Gladys collapsed in a heap of tears.

It was evening. She had half-heartedly eaten some frozen fish fingers and the remainder of the apple and blackcurrant crumble. She had been saving it for him. Now she was sitting in the lounge, in the dark, alone.

They had flown her by helicopter to Hammersmith Hospital, expecting her visit would merely serve to identify the corpse. However, the patient was showing remarkable resistance, quite remarkable. Medically, he should have been shredded with the others. But his body was intact. Admittedly, it was a ghastly mess, not much skin remained, although the negative reading from his brain was considerably more serious. He was not medically dead, nor was he alive: a living corpse as opposed to a dead one.

She sat in silence in the hospital room, alone with him. Thankfully, bandages hid the worst from her. The scene recalled *Carry on Doctor*, George had insisted they watch the film together. She had gritted her teeth in grim silence whilst he roared at the smutty humour. Now he just lay there. If only he would move, even laugh that raucous dirty guffaw of his.

A doctor entered the room.

'Will he live?' she asked.

The woman reeled off the clinical facts in an equally clinical voice. She then manifested minor signs of being human.

'Please understand his body may still be breathing but his mind, the person you knew, is no longer there. Whether the body continues living depends predominantly on our life-support systems. You are certainly aware of the importance of the will to live, mind over matter, which has resulted in some remarkable recoveries in the past. Your husband, regrettably, has no mind and therefore no ability to fight the forthcoming battle he faces. To be honest, you must accept that your husband will never return.'

She continued to sit at the bedside. Then, concluding there was nothing she could achieve in the hospital other than get in everyone's way, she asked to be taken home.

It was nearly nine. She switched on the television.

'*After the news Matthew Bryan introduces a Sports Special from Toronto where the World Ice Skating Championships are taking place. There are great hopes that Britain's twelve-year-old prodigy, Abulla Uqaziba, will clinch a medal, although competition is extremely tough.*'

Short silence.

'*This is the BBC from London. Here is the nine o'clock news read by Francis Bookham.*'

She suffered the spinning globe and fluttering flag accompanied by music that forewarned of catastrophes and crises to be announced.

'*George McHenderson, self-proclaimed Messiah, is in the intensive care unit of Hammersmith Hospital following a bomb attack in Sloane Square. Five people were killed, including a Home Office driver and traffic warden, and numerous pedestrians were injured.*

'*Much to everyone's surprise, the sun did not disappear at five p.m. this afternoon, as had been predicted by Matthew Hodges, recently fired spokesman of the Kylb Committee.*

'*The area around Esher is still under siege as tens of thousands of visitors clamour to see the man who claims to be the new prophet.*

'*Several soldiers have been killed in border skirmishes along the Israeli-Lebanese border. All-out war still threatens, in spite of valiant efforts by US Secretary of State Connie Schwietzer to negotiate a last minute settlement.*

'*Twelve-year-old Abulla Uqaziba will be skating tonight to bring home a medal for Britain at the Toronto World Ice Skating Championships.*'

Pause.

'*It was nearly five p.m. this afternoon in London's exclusive Sloane Square when a bomb exploded. In the ensuing panic nobody immediately understood what had happened, nor why. We go over live to Katie Ediar who is standing outside the booksellers where the assassination attempt took place. Katie!*'

'*Francis!*

'*Behind me is the shop visited by George McHenderson this afternoon. No one knows why he visited the area, nor exactly why he should have stopped at the bookseller. I have been informed by the store manager that he acquired Jeffrey Archer's Shall We Tell the President? and Twist in the Tale plus Jack Higgins's Touch the Devil, also the videos of Titanic, Four Weddings and a Funeral, and Sense and Sensibility starring Emma Thompson. He was walking back to his car when the bomb exploded. The driver of the car, a traffic warden, two passers-by and a shop assistant were killed instantly. Eleven others were injured, three seriously. Two of these were women. I have standing next to me John Dermont, the store manager. Mr Dermont, what happened?'*

'Well, it was just like any other day, quite busy, when without warning there was a terrific blast. The plate glass window smashed into pieces as a body came hurtling through. There was smoke and screams and the shop was severely damaged. One of my cashiers was decapitated by flying glass.'

'Did you see anything suspicious prior to the blast?'

'No, but one of the cashiers, not the one who was killed, said afterwards that a customer had been acting strangely, paying over sixty pounds of purchases in cash. She thought perhaps the notes were forgeries, although we have subsequently verified they were genuine. Otherwise, I do not believe that anyone saw anything untoward.'

'Thank you, Mr Dermont. The entire area has been cordoned off as experts sift through the rubble for clues. It was only after his arrival at Hammersmith Hospital that the identity of one of the injured was confirmed and, no doubt, the reason for the attack explained.'

'Thank you, Katie. We now go over to Georgina Grafton who is waiting outside Hammersmith Hospital.'

'Yes, Francis! I am standing in front of Hammersmith Hospital, situated in Hammersmith, West London. Somewhere inside this red brick building lies George McHenderson, fighting for his life. I have with me Doctor Meredith Carlisle who is responsible for the hospital's Intensive Care Unit. Doctor Carlisle, how badly hurt is George McHenderson?'

'The patient is alive in spite of very serious injuries. At present his condition is stable.'

'Will he live?'

'The question is academic. George McHenderson is brain-dead.

Whether his body continues living is irrelevant since his mind has ceased to function.'

'So George McHenderson, to all intents and purposes, no longer exists?'

'That is correct.'

'Thank you, Doctor Carlisle.'

'Thank you Georgina. Claims for the assassination attempt have been pouring in to Scotland Yard and press agencies. So far they include the IRA, Libya and a Trappist monk from France said to be acting on orders from Jesus himself. Police say they are taking all claims seriously.

'This afternoon millions of motorists stopped driving, prudently preparing for the promised forty-five minute disappearance of the sun, announced for five p.m.. Nothing happened, in Britain and throughout the world the sun continued to shine normally. Was it a coincidence that the bomb exploded in Sloane Square at almost precisely the same hour? For the moment we have no answer but it would appear that George McHenderson, alive or dead, has lost his powers of miracle-making. We will bring you further information on his condition during our late-night news update.

'Meanwhile, Europe and much of the world is still in turmoil as violent demonstrations disrupt life in numerous countries. Nearer home, most of South-East England is still in a state of siege as tens of thousands of fresh arrivals, one could refer to them as pilgrims, attempt to converge on Esher and the surrounding countryside. We now go over to Brian Dermott who is somewhere in the midst of Esher. Brian!'

'Hello! I am speaking to you, not without difficulty, from one of the hotels situated near Esher Golf Club. It is becoming clear that police efforts to prevent further people from reaching the area are showing signs of relieving the dramatic situation here. But only marginally. As crowds camp or simply bivouac on any open space available, including the golf course and residents' front gardens, the numbers of people wandering around the streets has diminished. However, matters have become increasingly ugly as food supplies start running out, resulting in looting and clashes between those with and those without victuals. Much of the area has been turned into a litter dump and is awash with human excrement. Numerous

houses were ransacked when local residents turned down pleas to provide nourishment.

'Hundreds of visitors have been scouring nearby Claremont Woods in attempts to locate the clearing where Kylb is supposed to have made his visitation. Several spots have been identified, but for the moment no one can be certain, always assuming you believe the story of Kylb in the first place.

'News of the assassination attempt started filtering through to visitors in the early evening. It is clear the mood is changing. Isolated groups have even started to leave the area. Ironically, police barriers designed to prevent new arrivals from invading Esher are hampering their progress.

'I have with me Jason Blunt, one of the visitors. Jason, why did you come to Esher?'

'Well, it was like this. Me an the missus, well we don't like this talk about being extermoinated and the sun going out, so we come here to tell the Messiah bloke to stop all his bloody miracles and leave us in peace. My Moana, she be pregnant and there ain't no point in her giving birth if this Messiah only then kills us all.'

'Would you be prepared to kill the Messiah in order to save yourself?'

'No need, some bloke's already gone and done it. Now we can go home and live in peace and quiet like.'

'Thank you, Jason. In fact, this seems to be a common attitude amongst those arriving with, how to describe it, with aggressive intentions towards Mr McHenderson. Scuffles broke out as groups, no longer united in a common cause, relieved their frustrations on each other. Police Superintendent Wilkinson of Esher Constabulary, what is going to happen?'

'We will be making every effort to facilitate the departure of the visitors in an orderly manner. We hope news of the bomb attack will convince those still trying to approach Esher that there is no longer any reason to come. Once the flow towards the area has subsided we will be in a position to convey those already here to other areas, preferably to their homes. In the meantime, I plead with visitors and residents alike to remain calm. If residents could show some consideration for the visitors' plight, by offering cups of tea and making toilet facilities available, I am certain this will ease the tension and prevent further damage to property.'

'Thank you, Superintendent. Mrs Rosalie Witherson arrived here with her daughter Melanie, who is suffering from leukaemia. Mrs Witherson, what will you do now?'

'Try and see the Messiah in hospital.'

'In Hammersmith?'

'Wherever He may be.'

'You are convinced he can cure your daughter?'

'He brought those road accident victims back to life, so He can cure my Melanie.'

'Thank you, Mrs Wilkinson. Thus, although the situation is still critical, it would appear the worst is over in Esher. By tomorrow morning things should start returning to a semblance of normality.'

'Thank you Georgina! Our attempts to interview Mrs Gladys McHenderson have been refused. Rumours abound that she has undergone plastic surgery and now looks twenty years younger. Other members of the so-called Kylb Committee have also refused to comment on the situation.

'A state of emergency has been declared in Germany as millions of demonstrators engaged in street battles. In some towns the situation has been compared to civil war. Hundreds are thought to have died, many thousands injured. A dusk to dawn curfew has been imposed in over twenty cities as troops patrol the streets. Chancellor von Gildhein has scoffed at ideas about bringing representatives of extreme right-wing parties into a government of national unity.

'Arab leaders are still attempting to thrash out a common policy on how to deal with Israel. Connie Schwietzer, in spite of vigorously criticising Israeli actions, was injured when stones were thrown at her in Damascus. Syrian president Assad Imbrahim insists the incident was caused by over-enthusiastic crowds and confirmed no criminal charges would be forthcoming.

'Pakistani airforce jets have bombed targets in India and Kashmir. Many deaths are reported and troops are preparing for battle.

'Reijke Boovermann, a recently retired Amsterdam prostitute, claims George McHenderson was one of her customers several years ago. She refuses to provide details, but is offering to sell the full lurid story to the highest bidder. No one has come forward to collaborate her claims.

'An Italian football referee was seriously injured during a match between Juventus and Fiorentia, when supporters engaged in pitched battle with players. The game was abandoned after seventy-three minutes with Fiorentina leading one-zero.'

She half-listened as tragedy followed disaster to be succeeded in turn by declarations noteworthy for their arrogance and mercenary approach to solving the world's problems. Or, more appropriately, not solving them. A marine biologist tried valiantly to warn viewers of an impending ecological disaster that could exterminate ocean life. He affirmed in a note of desperation that if global population reached ten billion by the year 2050, as forecast, there would be no fish to nourish the teeming populations unless stringent measures were immediately taken to control industrial pollution. Whether or not you believed in his existence, the message attributed to Kylb made sense and should be heeded.

He was followed by a smarmy economist-cum-political lobbyist who assured viewers that recent comments pertaining to the ozone layer were unduly alarmist. The economic and social cost of overacting to a highly theoretical and unproven danger, exaggerated out of proportion by hysterical fringe politicians, would far outweigh any hypothetical inconveniences. Surely viewers did not wish unemployment to rise dramatically? In any case, government actions taken in consultation with industry leaders, had the situation fully under control. There was nothing to worry about.

A second, more earnest colleague had differing views:

'Do you realise that over one hundred million items of rubbish are discarded every single day in Britain alone? Where is it all going? There is no escape, we are systematically destroying our planet. The only question is whether we suffocate from air pollution before or after being poisoned by toxic chemicals.

'Just one example. It has been estimated the annual consumption *of toilet paper in Japan, if joined together, would reach to the moon.'*

'It's all that raw fish they eat,' interrupted the interviewer.

'That is irrelev . . .'

'Thus in the last fifty years the consumption of Japanese toilet paper must well be on its way to Mars!'

'That is hardly the point. If . . .'

'Mars would look rather pretty wrapped in pink and blue ribbons.'

'Please, I am trying to be serious. Chemicals used to manufacture the toilet paper, especially . . .'

'Unfortunately, the toilet paper would have been used, so the Martians might not be pleased after all!'

'Please, the point I am trying to make is that the toilet paper remains on Earth, putrefying our planet.'

But the viewers were no longer interested in domestic pollution, visions of planets encased in colourful gift wrapping were considerably more amusing than terrestrial cesspools. The interviewer was overjoyed, his image as an entertainer must have improved enormously. It was only a question of time before they offered him his own talk show.

'After early morning rain, skies will brighten from the west. Fresh breezes will keep temperatures low for the time of the year. Heavy showers can be expected in Scotland during the afternoon, although these should die out by early evening as cloud once again thickens from the west, heralding the arrival of another frontal system.'

Depressed, she switched off the television. Was there nothing good happening or did television only report disasters and catastrophes because that is what most interested viewers? Did audience ratings replace the impartial judgement of the news editor? There must surely be some good news occurring around the world, although possibly not since George started his meddling.

She went upstairs and into the guest room. The double bed had been made, she had even changed the sheets which had endured intense wear and tear the night before.

The top sheet had been turned down in anticipation of tonight... She replaced it in its normal position and went into the main bedroom. She had washed their other sheets although, not expecting to need them, had omitted making the beds. Slowly and methodically, she made her own, hesitated, then left his undone. He would never be returning home to Esher.

Downstairs she passed their wedding photo. Should she put it away? No, he was not yet dead. It was worse, he was breathing, his body was breathing, but not him. She wandered aimlessly around the lounge. She picked up the pile of holiday brochures, Vienna, Cannes and Venice, and threw them in the dustbin. She tidied away his pile of records, worn relics from the days of Edison and Marconi. And yet he so loved them, scratches and all. What on earth could she do with them? No one would buy them. They were so worn it would be an insult to take them to Oxfam, but she couldn't just discard them. It would be like throwing away part of him. She rearranged his bottles of whisky, he had been drinking more than usual these last few weeks, but she supposed he could be forgiven. Did he ever stop to wonder how his glass, left lying dirty on the table every night, was always returned spotlessly clean to the cocktail cabinet by the following evening?

She stopped in front of his desk. No, she would not touch his papers until he really was dead. She noticed the Sharon Stone videos tucked away. How could anyone be attracted to that tasteless hussy? But millions were. Hussy or not, she was unquestionably endowed with what men wanted in a woman. There was his tiny lens, placed so he would see the neighbour's light come on. And the binoculars hidden in his desk. What in heaven's name did he see in her? She was surly, stupid and dim-witted, nothing much to look at, and suffered terrible acne. She supposed he was only interested in her buttocks and breasts. Poor George, there was not much choice for him in Esher. Had the young woman been sufficiently careless to undress in front of the window? She surmised, however unattractive the girl might be, that she must have been infinitely more pleasant to admire than herself, at least until yesterday's transformation. For many years she had hidden her hulk from her husband, ashamed of what she had become. She had never actually explained that she did not wish to be seen. She never locked the bathroom door, yet he never entered. Was he embarrassed, did he not wish to embarrass her, or did he no longer care to see his wife undressed? Did he still have any feelings for her? Would he give a damn if she suddenly disappeared, apart from having to cook his own supper? Did he have anyone else? There was Janet. All those business meetings up in town, they must have been having sexual relations behind her back. It was her own fault for being so huge. How could she blame him for seeking relief elsewhere?

Admittedly, they did communicate. She always looked forward to their Sunday lunchtime exchanges of gossip. Then there were the occasions he teased her. She pretended to disapprove but in reality she enjoyed it immensely. It was an indicator she had not been entirely forgotten, that something still remained between them.

How would she cope? She was not worried about the Esher side of things, she handled that anyway. It was the office and the Kylb affair. Who would take on the responsibility, assume the rôle of Messiah? Perhaps she should try and communicate with George, understand what he wanted. There must still be thoughts stored in his brain. Had he chosen a successor, or should she offer her services? She would visit the hospital tomorrow, try to obtain some response from him.

Jennifer's light came on. She watched with morbid curiosity as the young girl walked out of sight to get undressed, put on her pyjamas and clean her teeth, before returning into view to draw her curtains and climb into bed.

Was she herself condemned to remain childless? Of course, there were other men in the world. She was fertile, although only just. She knew from the signs that it was beginning. It was like a death warrant. A stupid pernicious name, only blasted unthinking males could have chosen it:

'menopause'. 'Womenostop' would be more appropriate as far as her maternal ambitions were concerned. Terminus. Sterility until death do us part. She had only ever known George, she could not imagine doing it with another man. Was it fear of failure or her Christian beliefs? How on earth would she cope being a widow, especially now she was endowed with the stunning body George had given her?

She sighed, chose one of her Barry Manilow CDs, placed it in the hi-fi and slowly cried herself to sleep to the accompaniment of the music.

15

Terminus

They were in the hospital room, alone and silent. George lay exactly as the previous day, motionless, showing not the slightest sign of life other than an intensely slow almost indistinguishable breathing. Like hibernation, except he would not be waking up in time for summer. She tried to communicate with him. She held his hand, then in desperation shook him, attempting to access the thoughts still stored within his brain. It was useless. He continued to lie immobile, living yet dead.

Would he want her to replace him as Messiah. What still required accomplishing concerning Kylb? Ordinarily she found it easy to denigrate his ideas, propose her own vastly superior solutions. At times he could be remarkably dimwitted. But the organisational genius inherited from her father had momentarily forsaken her. If only George had confided in her earlier, surely she could have avoided the global mayhem he had unwittingly unleashed. She glanced at the pile of newspapers. She was anxious to read them, not to determine what had already taken place, she knew all too well, but to ascertain what people were saying, were thinking, were expecting to happen. She hesitated. She felt it would be detestable to ignore him, read the editorials with him lying alongside her. But did he know she was there. Did he know he was there? Finally, she selected a journal from the untidy heap. If he were upset at her display of social indecorum, her husband only needed to demonstrate his displeasure.

If only he would.

The front page announced in block capitals the assassination attempt, showing a gruesome photo of Sloane Square with the almost naked remains of one of the victims lying amongst the rubble. It was shameful, little more than abject voyeurism, presenting that poor man's mangled legs and blood-soaked undergarments. Had editors no sense of decency, no respect for people living or, in this example, someone indiscriminately slaughtered for simply being somewhere at the wrong moment? They practically gloated when announcing a sixth person had succumbed to her injuries. A small inset showed a smiling face, it looked like an old wedding photo. Twenty-three claims for the attack had been received, although the newspaper implied none were totally convincing. The preliminary report from police anti-terrorist experts surmised the bomb was highly sophisticated, tending to confirm the premeditated involvement of professionals. The Trappist monk was soon forgotten. The real mystery was the purpose of George McHenderson's visit to Sloane Square. Was it really to purchase books and videos or was his shopping spree designed to camouflage other intentions? Also, who could possibly have known he was there? A member of the team sifting through the debris commented unofficially that parts of a radio transmitter had been found amidst the wreckage of the car, which was registered with the Home Office.

There was speculation as to why someone who could bring thousands back from the dead could not perform a similar miracle on himself, also whether the sun would disappear at 6.00 p.m. as announced previously by Matthew Hodges, also what would now happen concerning the so-called Kylb mission? The remainder of the newspaper was filled with stories of rioting, strikes, imminent wars and actual conflicts. The Secretary General of the United Nations had convened a special session of the Security Council to debate the implications of the sun's disappearances. He rejected any link between the planned session and Kylb, whose existence he refused to acknowledge, stating competent authorities existed to process extraterrestrial sightings.

She glanced through the other newspapers. Although their presentation changed radically, the reported facts were depressingly repetitive. In general, apart from the occasional veiled reference to impending world population reductions and two brief editorials speculating whether Matthew Hodges would replace the injured George McHenderson, the British press was more concerned with the previous day's sordid sensations than evaluating future problems facing humanity.

And Abulla Uqaziba had won a bronze medal for Britain in the ice-skating championships. Her victory had more coverage than how to save six billion lives.

She sighed. World events sadly reflected upon the self-proclaimed affirmation by *Homo sapiens* that it constituted the ultimate civilised life form.

'Good morning, Mrs McHenderson.'

It was one of the doctors responsible for supervising George's medical treatment.

'Have you noticed any change, any signs of movement since your arrival?'

'No, nothing at all. Please, doctor, I have one question. In television documentaries and *Casualty*, sorry I did not mean to be insulting, the patients have all kinds of tubes sticking into them, or should that be out of them. My husband, apart from bandages and the wires attached to his heart, has nothing.'

'Let me try to explain. The tubes are linked to life-support systems, used to maintain vital organs until the patient recovers sufficiently to survive unassisted. The case of your husband is unique. Any normal person suffering his injuries would have died instantaneously. But he did not. His body continues to function without help, almost as if he were in suspended animation. His body does not require our machines, consequently there are no tubes. The wires you noticed are attached to a cardiogram measuring his heartbeat, merely measuring, not in any way assisting it. It is a unique situation, but then your husband was endowed with unusual powers. Are these powers keeping him alive? Is this another miracle? Who knows?'

'What will happen to him?'

'Medically speaking, either he continues in his current stable condition, or suddenly deteriorates. If so, unless we couple him to a life-support system, which is obligatory unless we receive authorisation to the contrary, he will die a natural death.'

She instinctively shook her head in disagreement.

'For practical purposes we suggest he be transported to Kingston Hospital. It would be more convenient for you to visit him there. Well, to be honest, there are two other reasons. We are short of beds and, well the hospital administration would appreciate being rid of the crowds hanging around outside. Police say their numbers exceed a thousand and more are expected, many arriving from Esher. Kingston Hospital has a place available, a young mother knocked down in a road accident a couple of months ago. Well, she is in an irreversible coma and her family have recently given instructions to disconnect her life-support system.

'We plan to transfer him tomorrow tonight, very discreetly, of course. Is there any point in your remaining constantly at his bedside? Possibly, I just do not know. You must decide for yourself.'

His bleeper bleeped and he excused himself. She was once again alone with George.

After nearly two hours doing nothing, achieving nothing, not even expecting to achieve anything, she decided she should recreate some of her former life. She suddenly remembered Esher Squash Club was holding its Annual General Meeting that afternoon. As Club Secretary, they would require her presence. That Ullswater woman who was President was utterly hopeless at organising anything. She would return home to Esher and start making herself useful.

Before leaving she asked to be seen by a doctor.

'Mrs McHenderson, not unnaturally yours is a most interesting case. Without the results of our analyses I cannot be certain but, to put it bluntly, you may look twenty-five but medically you are nearing fifty in the preliminary throes of menopause. It is as you described, you asked your husband to make you look younger but not literally convert you into an athletic hockey player in the prime of her youth.'

Was she relieved or disappointed? She did not know. Whilst walking to the police car the omnipresent crowd, pushing forward to catch a glimpse, shouted for news about the Messiah. Several gasped in amazement, others recoiled in disbelief at the Hollywoodian vision before them. Involuntary wolf whistles were heard over the general commotion.

In exchange for not being endlessly hounded by the pack of journalists encircling her, avid to gather any titbit of information however noxious or nauseating, she agreed to attend a press conference that evening in Earl's Court.

Arriving back in Esher she was amazed at the scenes of desolation. What had recently been a sleepy select suburb of the stockbroker belt now resembled a war zone. The armies of pilgrims and would-be assassins had departed, to be replaced by residents, municipal workers and commercial enterprises repairing and cleaning the area, which was slowly converting back into a select, if distinctly soiled, part of suburbia. The army team commissioned to protect their house was withdrawing, although the officer, eyeing her no less lasciviously than the previous day, promised that a small unit of commandos would remain as long as was necessary to guarantee her safety.

Having asked to be escorted to the squash club at two, she sat down to a pitiable meal of tinned tuna and yoghurt. She recalled George jesting 'the company was more important than the cooking', so 'if the bird', he meant female, 'was physically unattractive then select a good restaurant and at least eat in style, whereas if she was inspiringly beautiful you could choose any old cafeteria since you wouldn't notice what you were eating.' Accordingly, he would say with a cynical smile, taking his wife to a self-service canteen would be a great compliment whereas

Mario's *haute cuisine* was a gross insult, also an expensive one. She smiled at her husband's lunatic logic. He certainly possessed a vivid sense of humour, even if regrettably only a distorted male one.

Meanwhile, the only company on hand to help her digest the unappetising tuna was Beatrice, who appeared morose and in deep depression. Not the slightest wag of her tail had greeted the return of her mistress. Did her canine brain understand what was happening? Was she in mourning for her master?

As she sipped her instant coffee she sensed it would be a tremendous relief to be surrounded by her squash club cronies, excepting nincompoop Ethel Dalgleath and her nebulous notions about proposing the courts on Wednesdays, free of charge to boot, to unemployed labourers living on the council estate. That kind of poppycock radical nonsense must be nipped in the bud.

'Floriano, it's Charles. Charles Dewey. Can you hear me? Incredible, London must be over five thousand miles from Caracas. Look, now that this pathetic fuss about Messiahs is dying down, I would like to resuscitate our Orinoco project, urgently. Last time we spoke you confirmed the Forestry Commission, or whatever you call it down there, would have no objections. Didn't you say the Commissioner's wife suffers from euthanasia, you know that breathing disease? Can't remember its exact name. That's it! So presenting her with a chalet in the Swiss Alps, plus of course some spending money, will ease her discomfort. A noble cause, one to which my company will be honoured to contribute.

'Delivery dates for road construction, did you say? No problem! The funds are available in the Bahamas. We can shift the equipment from Houston within two weeks.

'No, of course our operations in Mozambique are not going to be abandoned. However, there will be considerable shipment delays due to the floods, so the timber will not be arriving in Europe as per our original schedule.

Which is why our Orinoco project is so important. If we ship before London commodity prices return to normal, we'll make a fortune, pay back our investment within eighteen months.

'To hell w ... Please, Floriano, don't get so wrought up over the problems of several hundred Indians. All we request is the shifting of their villages higher up the valley. The mountain air will be good for them. Remember, if the timber does not start arriving in Europe this autumn our housing programmes will be delayed, thousands of mothers and children will risk freezing to death in our harsh winter climate.

'Lumberjacks and bulldozers destroying insects?! You must be joking! Come on, an educated man like you surely doesn't believe in flying saucers! By the time the project's finished the only unhappy people will be manufacturers of mosquito repellent!

'That's more like it!

'See you soon in Miami.

'Bye!'

The Baptist chapel was hushed. More precisely, no noise emanated from inside the building. However, the perpetual rumble of London's traffic invaded the modest structure, even into its inner sanctum where two members of the congregation knelt in prayer. They could be mistaken for man and wife but were, in fact, brother and sister.

They were praying silently. They knew God was able to probe their minds, He would undoubtedly understand the reason for their gratitude. Their prayers for intervention had been finally heard, the messenger of Lucifer had been struck down by the Forces of Good. Christians could once again live in peace and harmony. They, the humblest of mortals, thanks to their incessant pleading for Divine intervention, had helped save the children of Christ from the Fiery Furnace.

If God was receiving their message he was not letting on.

This did not perturb the two figures beneath the altar, they were not expecting signs of recognition. They had faith. They were true believers. That was all that was needed.

The group of people sitting in the restaurant, consuming *choucroute* and Riesling wine, not surprising since they were in Strasbourg, were unusually excitedly and animated. Members of the European Parliament, militants of an assortment of minority Green parties, habitués to the humiliation inflicted on fringe activists, they sensed their moment of glory had arrived. Thanks to this new Messiah their policies were now being discussed seriously in the staterooms of power. At the next elections they would assuredly achieve a working majority. Nuclear power was doomed. International business would pay for cleansing the face of the earth, eliminating over a century of shameless chemical spillage. Environmentalists would soon hold the strings of power and reap the glory.

But that had been yesterday.

Today, the same group sat in stunned silence, realising that in the ongoing battle to impose their noble ideals the powers of capitalism had two major advantages over them: access to limitless funds and a total absence of scruples. A possible third advantage failed to occupy their thoughts, that their capitalistic adversaries did not live in Utopia.

The whale was confused, disorientated. They should be approaching the sanctuary, that wondrous place where the cold waters they usually inhabited met warmer flows full of plankton. The sanctuary was naturally far more than a feeding ground, it was a place where the presence of God was felt, where they could communicate with Him, pray for deliverance from the mundane life they had to endure before rising to reside with Him in heaven.

More than ever they needed His help and guidance. For generations the monsters, they that floated where the friendly waters ended and the hostile unknown emptiness commenced, had massacred their brethren, reducing their numbers to pitiful levels, populations well below those necessary to sustain the cultural richness of their societies. But now an even more sinister enemy was threatening their existence. The enemy that was within them, dulling their senses, deregulating their navigation sensors, effacing their means of communication. It was something that had infiltrated the oceans from elsewhere, some invisible microscopic aggressor that progressively entered their bodies and destroyed them from inside.

The signals became even more confused, indicating they were straying into unfrequented shallow waters dangerous to their survival. The water was becoming warmer, in fact far too warm, and it was no longer possible to see clearly. Where was the sanctuary, what was happening to them?

And then he felt the rough sand on his underbelly as he ground to a halt. He was stuck, so were many of his brethren. When the tide receded they would be doomed to slowly suffocate in the emptiness that existed above the water.

The murmur of female voices was pierced by the strident tones of Juliet Ullswater, President of Esher Squash Club.

'Ladies, we are all present except Gladys. Has anyone seen or heard from her? No, well it is now five past two so I suggest we commence the proceedings without delay.'

The door opened and the Secretary walked into the room.

'Sorry I'm late. Acacia Terrace is still blocked so we were obliged to make a detour.'

She looked around the room. Everyone was staring, some with mouths agape others attempting to smother a smirk. They had all seen her on television but few were prepared for the real-life apparition standing before them. She studied those seated around the table. The whole committee was present, but where was her chair? There was no empty place awaiting her arrival.

'We assumed you were not coming, what with all the upsets.'

And the President, in a tone of voice singularly lacking enthusiasm, instigated a musical chairs without musical accompaniment in order that Gladys might recover her rightful place. The proceedings then proceeded to proceed, with Gladys guiding the ladies skilfully through the various items on the agenda.

At least to begin with. She tried to act herself, formal and authoritarian. Such behaviour was expected of her. Someone her size should boom, impose her presence with her voice. Besides, it was the only way to achieve anything when handling the ladies of Esher. But today things were different. Her voice had altered. The boom was absent. Her vocal chords must have been remodelled at the same time as her waistline. She carried on, struggling with increasing difficulty to maintain a grip on the meeting. She remembered another of George's pearls of wisdom: 'Democracy is divine but doomed to disintegration, dictatorships are dire but designed to deliver'. She must not lose control. If she allowed the ladies to take over, however democratic the innovation, they would never complete the agenda. She became aware of fidgeting in the audience, the occasional clearing of throats. Ordinarily she would have called the meeting to order without hesitation, in a voice that instantaneously bespoke compliance. But today her inborn self-assurance was absent and the frequency of whispered comments steadily increased.

Mercifully, she came to the last item on the agenda, re-election of the Committee. She felt the tension mounting. The nervousness was explained when they arrived at the position of Secretary. She realised there had been some informal behind-the-scenes manoeuvring prior to the meeting. Surely they couldn't be so asinine as to replace her with Gloria Gunnesbury? Yes they could.

'Please, Glady's, it's nothing personal, but we thought

you would be too occupied. And, following George not being re-elected at the golf club, well we assumed ... Perhaps another time.'

Juliet Ullswater stopped talking. It had been done, without pronouncing what everyone was really thinking: that Gladys no longer looked the part. It was nothing personal. If Margaret Thatcher had resembled Samantha Fox she could not possibly have ruled the country as the Iron Lady. Appearances were important. Imagine the Queen looking like one of the Spice Girls. Until Gladys returned to being Gladys there was no place for her on the Committee.

On the way home she asked the driver to stop at Tesco's. The place resembled San Francisco after the recent earthquake. Wooden hoarding replaced windows and entangled debris littered the parking lot. She was not refused entry, nor was she hissed. Nor was she welcome. Clutching her purchases, she practically ran to the safety of the army limousine.

'Angus, could you please be more precise. We have agreed George McHenderson's conduct these past weeks has hardly corresponded to what the Institute normally expects from its members. But I insist that to remove him, and I would appreciate your refraining from using the term 'defrock', we must receive unequivocal evidence of serious misdemeanours.'

'Misdemeanours! Announcing publicly he has unilaterally decided to annihilate six billion people and you call that a misdemeanour! It's a crime against humanity.'

'Angus, that may well be the case. If you are convinced of this, then perhaps you should address your grievances to The Hague. Our function is to impose disciplinary action when members disregard the Institute's rules which, not surprisingly, do not extend to population controls.'

'But he claimed to be the Messiah.'

'Angus, however unusual his behaviour, the Member's

Handbook does not specifically prohibit such actions. And we have previously agreed that none of his public statements could be interpreted as unauthorised advertising.'

Angus McPherson, Scottish son of an ecclesiastical family from Perth who married delectable debutante Diana, daughter of a Church of England bishop, sought vengeance on his fellow member whom he considered a self-seeking, blasphemous racketeer who was desecrating the reputation of the accounting profession.

However, as the meeting progressed he recognised the futility of convincing the gabble of money-grabbers, seated surrounding him in the Institute's conference room, of the inescapable gravity of George McHenderson's crimes. Why? Because, thanks to the latter's recent public crusade to save the world, applications from those wishing to enter the profession had soared. The Chartered Accountant was finally accorded the social acceptance he merited, no social gathering was complete nowadays without one in attendance. The BBC was planning a situation comedy based on the daily life of a provincial accounting firm and had asked the Institute to act as technical advisor, all thanks to George McHenderson FCA, the Institute's most distinguished member.

'Ladies and gentlemen, as agreed, Mrs McHenderson will first read a pre-prepared statement before answering your questions.'

She stood up. The hall was bursting with hustling jostling reporters, some of whom she recognised, including those allowed into their house for the informal chat. What amazed her most were the cameras, the array of microphones and the brilliance of the lights. Even though the millions of viewers to whom she was broadcasting were mercifully invisible, she could somehow sense their presence. She was not scared, just highly impressed.

'I have a brief message to read out. I visited my husband in hospital this morning. I was, regrettably, unable to communicate with him and the hospital recently confirmed there has been no improvement since I left. He is not dead and, remembering the edict 'while there is life there is hope', his return amongst us cannot be ruled out. However, we must accept his temporary inability to act as the appointed Messiah. The Kylb mission will therefore continue without him.

'Despite what happened to my husband, we must assume Kylb's message remains unaltered. We should, therefore, pursue the introduction of measures to ensure compliance with his demands. I personally requested that the daily disappearances of the sun cease. My husband acceded to my wishes, which explains the absence of blackouts these last two days. The original strategy behind these was to spur governments into action, not to cause suffering to innocent individuals. I sincerely hope that elected authorities will continue to accord the mission due consideration, in spite of no longer being threatened with eternal night.

'I will temporarily replace my husband as Kylb's Local Agent but I insist it is for world governments, not me, to take whatever actions are necessary to respect Kylb's instructions. I propose weekly meetings in this hall for information updates, unless of course something dramatic occurs. Thank you.'

Hands and voices were raised in a bedlam of confusion. It took several minutes to restore some semblance of calm and establish a sequential order for the asking of questions.

'Mrs McHenderson, what do you mean by 'dramatic'?'

'I don't really know. My husband regaining consciousness, Kylb returning.'

'Have you replaced your husband as the Messiah?'

'No. Yes. Well, not really. I am proposing my services for as long as required.'

'Why did you have your shape altered?'

'I fail to see why that should interest anyone. It was a joke.'

'Will you return to normal?'

'I . . . I cannot answer. I mean, well, I do not know. So long as my husband is unconscious, well I suppose I have no choice.'

'Do you prefer you current physique?'

'What has that to do with Kylb? All I can say is that it feels different.'

'Mrs McHenderson, do you know when Kylb will return?'

'No.'

'Will he visit you personally now that Mr McHenderson is incommunicado?'

'I have no idea.'

The questions continued unabated for 20 minutes, then the intensity of the reporters' zeal began flagging. She had just decided to terminate the proceedings, some of the questions were becoming embarrassingly pathetic, when one of the less experienced reporters posed the question no one else had dared ask.

'Gladys.' He really was inexperienced. 'Are you able to perform miracles?'

The hall hushed into total silence.

'I do not know.'

'For example, have you tried bringing your husband back to life?'

She had not.

'Would you perform a miracle now for us?'

'I can try, but I have no idea what will happen. What shall I attempt?'

Fifty voices shouted simultaneously.

She overheard several suggestions above the pandemonium. Selecting the least stupid, she announced she would attempt to make George walk onto the stage.

He did not.

She tried another.

The sun did not start shining.

She made a final desperate attempt.

The jug on the table remained full of water.

The meeting drew rapidly to a close. The reporters, moving towards the exits, had lost interest.

'Gladys!'

It was Selwyn.

'I'm just back from my mission in Scandinavia and I could not resist the temptation to come and see you, ask after George. Are you free for dinner?'

She had little faith in the social integrity of the venturesome Member of Parliament. It was a strange time to vanish into the backwaters of Northern Europe, but he was good company and company of any kind was in exceedingly short supply. She accepted.

Selwyn was delighted. Firstly, in his quest for self-survival he had decided, following his poorly timed disappearance, that he should forthwith be seen actively participating in everything. If he was going to be mixed up with Kylb, and he was, even the Chairperson of the Conservative Party had told him in no uncertain terms, then he should give the impression of being really and truly mixed up, not quite taking charge but providing a steadying hand, acting as overall coordinator, ready to reap the accolades of success whilst remaining poised to substitute a scapegoat if things worsened. Considering George's shambolic mismanagement of things, the situation would undoubtedly improve and he wanted to be recognised as the inspiration behind the return to relative sanity. There was another factor guiding his actions. He enjoyed living, he was especially eager to be included with the surviving one billion. Furthermore, of course it was of no real consequence, but he had seen photos of the new Gladys. With Sonjia's monthly headache degenerating into migraine, well why not? Dear Gladys would need consoling, appreciate a masculine shoulder to cry on.

In view of the circumstances, the dinner was surprisingly relaxing and successful. Selwyn played the gallant suitor and Gladys not only pretended to enjoy the attention, including the corny compliments and slightly suggestive comments, she really did appreciate his company. For the first time in decades she was being wined and dined like a woman. She was reminded of Freddie Fender, the boring imbecile who had been necessary to render George jealous, spur him into matrimonial action: the spider and the fly.

She gladly accepted Selwyn's invitation to drive her home. She accepted with equal alacrity his offer to remain in contact. With the demise of the Kylb Committee she would need advisers, Selwyn and Jacky for example, to keep her informed of progress made by governments.

Her politician chauffeur halted the car in front of the McHenderson mansion. The omnipresent security guards made any motorised moonlighting a non-starter, so Selwyn suggested being invited inside to help finish off George's whisky.

Two minutes later Gladys was phoning the hospital for the latest bulletin on her husband whilst he was driving himself home, trying to bolster his morale with Robert the Bruce's philosophy of 'If at first you don't succeed then try, try and try again'.

The head lay on the ground where it had come to rest. The blood that had initially spurted from the severed neck was soaking into the desert sand. Only a few drops now oozed from where the throat had been. Most of the spectators preferred to study the spasmodically twitching limbs, the last time her body would stimulate male interest, but the more astute gazed at the head, the beautiful face, especially the eyes. They were looking at you, not with fear or pain but with puzzlement, as if not expecting to be beheaded. Could she still see? Medical researchers believed the brain functioned for a short while, theorising the last view of guillotine victims was not looking down at the basket but staring upwards as the blade was hauled skywards ready for the next victim.

If she were still seeing what would she be thinking, how would she be reacting to the gloating faces of the spectators? What would be her final emotions as eternal darkness bore down, knowing her very existence was being extinguished for an eternity?

Some of the spectators regretted the sacrifice of a lithe young female, who would consequently never again provide pleasure to a male. Others thanked Allah that justice had been done, one spitting on the head as it lay in the sand.

The eyes glazed over, the expression of puzzlement dimmed. A couple of flies eagerly feasted on the blood congealing under her chin. Another landed on an eye. There was no reaction. She had not noticed. She was no longer there. Her body was nothing more than a decapitated corpse.

However beautiful she might have been, Allah's will had to be imposed. Adultery, the most reprehensible of crimes. And with a non-believer. Admittedly she had sought out the mullah in order to confess her sins. Actually she had boasted about them, claiming she was the chosen wife of the new Messiah. At first no one believed her, but then she divulged the union had been consummated in a Swiss ski resort and evidence was forthcoming that the so-called successor to Mohammed had indeed been resident in the very same hotel. They had initially hesitated over her punishment. What if he really was the Messenger of Allah and had chosen her as claimed? But all doubts dissipated when he was blown up by a bomb. The desire for retribution rapidly rose to fever pitch.

A municipal worker picked up the head by one of its ears, disturbing the flies, and dropped it into a plastic bag.

Allah's will had been done.

The ceremony of molecular redistribution was over.

'*Mais Madame, je suis desolé*, I am so sorry, but the hotel is full. You must wait, let me see, until the month of *Septembre*. September.

The hotel manager replaced the receiver for the twentieth time that afternoon. He groaned as a group of optimistic pilgrims entered the lobby from the street, ignoring the *Complet* sign.

The Hotel Splendide at Lourdes was indeed full to overflowing and would remain so for many months.

She was contented. The hive was filled with nourishment, the larvae could grow without fear of starvation. Nor had they surpassed their quota. Her disciplined brain, programmed with impulses transmitted from her genes, dictated behavioural absolutes never to be disregarded. Climatic conditions frequently prevented population targets from being reached, but that was the law of Nature. Exceeding the limits was different, unpardonable. The mathematical equilibrium between different species must be respected for the good of all, in order to conserve the wondrous environment in which they inhabited. It had been difficult to prevent her workers from halting their flights to the rising ground, where the yellow blossoms spread in profusion, but the nectar was needed by others.

No more than the expected number of her colony had been lost to predators. She felt no resentment for the giant creatures. Nature had created her species to feed them, it was the sacrosanct reason for their very existence. The survivors, now the food-cells were over-flowing, could engage in colony activities. Not only did the buzzing sessions socially bind them together, they were enormous fun and ensured that their unique culture would propagate.

The hive suddenly shuddered, tilted, then crashed to the ground. Before the community members could exit their home, it was crushed out of existence by the whirling feet of a behemoth monster which roared and belched fumes, not from its mouth as dragons, but from its extended anus.

Manuello Gomez changed gear, the bulldozer reversed away from the shredded remnants of tropical jungle. He was satisfied, Pasqual could torch the mound of mangled plywood, transforming the useless vegetation into ashes that would provide welcome nutrients to the soya beans he would sow before the rainy season.

Yoki sat alone in her hotel bedroom. Never had she skated so dismally, she had humiliatingly failed to reach even the semi-finals. Far more mortifying, the new champion was younger than herself and that dark-skinned English girl who won the bronze medal was only 12-years-old. She gazed at the mirror. Her ethereal grace and beauty were still intact but inside she was nothing, never had been anything. From infancy she had skated. The world existing beyond ice rinks was an enigma, a no-man's-land she had never belonged to. And now the only asset she possessed, her skating ability, was abandoning her, condemning her to an irreversible downhill decline from fame to ignominy.

She believed in reincarnation. She had been an eagle in her previous life, hence her graceful genius on skates. Should she escape towards another existence, something very different? True she was still a woman, but if that was womanhood, the sooner she commenced her onward journey the better. He, her trainer, had started by placing his hand there as a punishment. Then it had no longer been his hand. And he always found fault, always an excuse to punish her. Then a second man, amongst the snow and skiers, another man had punished her. She could not recollect it happening, but the discomfort the following day told of the nocturnal chastisement. She had seen him on television. He was the new messenger of God. Even God himself had seen fit to condemn her.

How should she die? She had no access to poison, nor a sword. Jumping from the window was quick, but she shuddered when imagining her crumpled body lying surrounded by photographers. Dying was private. The belt of her pyjamas would extinguish her life if tied around her neck. It was quick and simple.

There was no point in delaying. She would deny him the satisfaction of tonight's punishment. She hesitated between donning her skater's outfit or remaining dressed in her sweater and jeans. Who was about to die, the person or the skater? The skater, there was no other person. She undressed and carefully stepped into the delicate fabric of her tunic. She stood on a chair, looped the belt round the hook to which the bedroom light was fixed, then tied the other end tightly around her neck.

Everything was ready. Her future existence would soon be revealed to her. She kicked over the chair and felt herself falling.

The belt harshly clutched at her neck, scorching the skin. She screamed in agony, but couldn't. She instinctively breathed in, and could not. She saw the walls of the bedroom moving, she was spinning on the end of the belt. She tried to stop, clutching the hanging rope with her hands. But still she turned, no longer able to control her destiny. Her lungs hurt, her throat ached agonisingly. She wanted to live, she wanted to die: anything other than the pain she was enduring. Her head started throbbing, her eyes were being squeezed from their sockets. Although the spinning slowed, the walls remained blurred, out of focus. She choked, but the air remained trapped in her lungs.

Then everything faded, the pain subsided, her lungs ceased trying to breath. Her brain muddled the individual messages of hurt into one feeling of discomfort. The walls stopped turning, she saw herself indistinctly in the mirror. And the stretched material of the pyjama belt, which her hands were still holding, as if clawing themselves back to her previous existence. But she knew the deed was done, there was no returning. She lowered her arms in resignation and waited, dispassionately watching her legs twitching. And then her image dissolved into nothingness as she escaped from her current existence and journeyed towards something far superior.

'Something's bothering you?'

Gerald and Auldley were strolling along the shores of

Lake Geneva. Its French shores. Hotels were cheaper than in Switzerland and churches were grudgingly adjusting to the sad realities of diminished offerings from their worshippers. Also French cuisine was vastly superior to Swiss.

'When we were organising the seminary I received every possible encouragement from Rome. Archbishop Luccini was to accompany the delegation, always an indication of papal involvement. As you know, he cancelled at the last minute. Attempts to communicate with Rome, well there is no specific difficulty, nothing I can pinpoint. It's just their attitude. Something has changed, their enthusiasm and support are no longer in evidence. When phoning, I feel I am interrupting them.'

Auldley experienced no such inconveniences. He was his own Pope. The Queen, as titular head of the church, was admittedly his boss, but she delegated most decisions to Lambeth Palace. Throughout the crisis he had briefed her about Kylb. She had remained conspicuously non-committal, politely deferential, which, on reflection, was strangely out of character.

'Perhaps they prefer to retain a safe distance. Much of our agenda could justifiably be considered bordering on the heretical.'

Indeed, the discussions had entered philosophical domains in stark contrast to the homilies of Sunday sermons. As one participant proclaimed, when a king dies people hail his successor. Today there was a reborn Messiah with a renewed message. His disciples on Earth should unquestionably accept His authority, which was not a changing of allegiance since God had not changed, only his emissary. Furthermore, if all religions united behind the same Messiah, they would regain the all-powerful influence they once wielded so beneficially over human society. No one knew whether to smile or groan, when one of the participants wondered whether such a merging of interests would have to be approved by the Monopolies Commission in Brussels.

News of the assassination attempt had initially brought the proceedings to a halt, but they agreed unanimously to advance as if nothing had happened, a decision reinforced when it was announced the Messiah was only injured.

'Have you noticed there are fewer reporters, especially cameramen. Where are they going?'

Auldley considered his friend's puzzlement.

'Who cares? The main thing is that we are making remarkable progress.'

His statement could not be contested. The United Counsel of Religion, as they planned to name their organisation, was well-advanced with its proposals. These constituted a powerful statement of their faith in humanity, a commitment that societies and civilisations, from African tribal communities to the G7 nations, would amalgamate their industrial and intellectual resources, mend their wayward ways, seek to recover the dignity mankind merited.

There were two provisos, simple and lucid and non-negotiable:

- Human civilisation would introduce necessary measures, as soon as feasible, to protect other life forms inhabiting the planet, both animal and vegetable, at whatever cost, however this affected economies and unemployment.
- There would be no imposed population reductions. Kylb either accepted humanity's desire to amend its misguided ways, or he eliminated everyone.

There was a determination, a motivation to succeed. If democracy had to be momentarily sacrificed in order to advance rapidly, then so be it.

Far from the shores of Lake Geneva, the more senior and more traditional world religious leaders were desperately searching scripts, scrolls, parchments, anything to validate the *status quo*, anything to confirm Kylb was an impostor and should be repudiated. Let their more irrational younger brethren brainstorm themselves together, form intellectually idealistic solutions. They might even produce something of practical use, but nothing was going to undermine the foundations of the world's polymorphous religions, each of which was the unique, sole and only truly authentic representation of God on earth.

Business leaders and trade unionists were in complete agreement. Population reductions would destabilise national economies, stunt economic growth and risk triggering a depression, also reduce operating profits and create unmanageable levels of unemployment. Imposing stricter pollution controls would have equally dire consequences. Industrial societies simply could not afford it. In any case, such measures were wholly unjustified. Everyone knew scientists were shamefaced pessimists who only vaunted the dangers of pollution to gain publicity and insure government funding. No mad-hatter English accountant straight from *Alice in Wonderland,* nor cloistered dreamers in back-to-front white collars, were going to dictate how to run the world economy.

Elected officials foolhardy enough to mention acceding to Kylb's demands had witnessed their ratings plunge. Consequently, very few politicians had remained foolhardy for long. President Stanton Forbes, although no longer seen in public, was a visionary and formidable ally. Government agencies, working in consultation with press barons and television moguls, deftly guided the editorial tendencies of their multi-media outlets towards a more reasoned vision of society's real priorities. Reporters covering the misguided attempts of rebellious religious radicals in Geneva were recalled, as a necessary precaution.

Although none of the above-mentioned public figures would officially voice such an outrageous opinion, many were privately congratulating the unknown hero who had blown the so-called Messiah to soggy smithereens.

The two engineers huddled together in the disaffected storeroom, ignoring the outside world. Which made sense since the endless permafrost wastelands of Siberia were best ignored. No one wished to be reminded where they were when they were there. Passionately nationalistic to the very pores of their communistic selves, both accepted isolation from normal society as part of serving their glorious fatherland. In order to make it glorious once again.

The metal containers filling the warehouse, oxidised and identified only by torn, partly illegible labels, were Russia's safeguard from outside attack. The innocuous-looking depot cumulated sufficient lethal germs and bacteria to annihilate the entire world, its very existence providing foolproof security against misguided plans of aggression from unfriendly powers.

With a slight twist of logic, an insignificantly minor question of timing, use of the stockpile could be advanced to pre-emptively wipe out potential aggressors before they aggressed, leaving Russia dominating the world, something the Russian President had not overlooked when considering the implications of population reductions imposed from outer space. Russia would generously select the six billion volunteers, without consulting them beforehand, no need to unduly upset them. A special convoy was due shortly, the precious cargo would be shipped to the launching pads. And Kylb's will would be done.

She was making her way to the river. The shining ball of life in the sky was still higher than the tree-tops, there was no hurry. She had stubbornly insisted on visiting the uplands where the vegetation was richer. But the others could not be bothered. So she had feasted alone, criticising her cousins for their lack of enthusiasm for bettering their contemptible existence.

Now she was thirsty. Also, well she had missed their company, especially Huura the young bull. He was not only handsome, his size now gave him a good chance of expelling his father from the tribe and mating with some of the females next season. Nothing would please her more, she was certain he was interested in her. Giving herself to him, of course only after pretending to refuse, would be extremely exciting, far more so than with his father.

She arrived at the river, stumbling onto the scene of carnage. None had survived, all lay amidst their blood, unmoving. She knew who must have attacked them, only the black two-legged midgets pursued them, not for their meat, which would be understandable, but to remove their tusks.

She had survived, but she was alone. Very, very much alone in the world.

Two weeks had passed since Gladys's first press conference and dinner with Selwyn. She had just returned home from her third conference, at least she had returned home from the conference hall, the planned meeting had not taken place. Well it had, sort of.

Only 50 reporters had attended the second conference. There was no live television coverage. The questions had soon dried up and in an atmosphere of slight embarrassment she had left the hall with Selwyn. Luckily, their dinner had been as enjoyable as the previous week's, possibly even more so. It was a relief to discuss things other than George and Kylb, and Selwyn was charming company. His flirting was as hilarious as it was outrageous. She entered into the spirit of things and reparteed with enthusiasm, After all, it was nothing other than childish fun. A couple of hours later, driving home after delivering Gladys to her house, Selwyn reflected upon having consummated two of Robert the Bruce's 'trys' without so much as receiving a goodnight kiss. Ah well, Sonjia had announced she was once again operational, so life could have been worse.

The third conference had been a fiasco. There had been less than a dozen reporters, all female, representing such publications as *Woman's Own, Cosmopolitan* and *The Daily*

Starlet. No, she would not pose for page three. The questions ranged from: would she be accepting any film offers, what were her vital statistics and how had plastic surgery affected her sex life?

'I have not had plastic surgery, merely a weight reduction, if you please.'

'Will you remarry?'

'I am already married.'

'What sign of the zodiac are you?'

Gladys gave up and walked out. Her police escort drove her home. Selwyn was otherwise occupied and had not attended the conference.

The moving vans were crammed with the multitude of objects a family considers itself unable to survive without. Aziz and his family were moving once again, this time to Bradford. A surgery was desperately short of practitioners and could he start immediately? With a bit of good fortune his new associates and patients would fail to recognise the former member of the Kylb Committee.

The sound of the District Line train faded into the distance as it rumbled its way towards Ealing Broadway. All was quiet in the block of flats near Baron's Court. The tenant of a third floor apartment was sitting in the dark, deep in thought.

Janet's new boss, senior partner of Christie, Wainwright, Steinway and Company, was inordinately infuriating. For the third consecutive time they had worked late into the evening, endlessly discussing matters of excruciating technicality and mind-numbing complexity. But she admitted he was efficient and dynamic and had already introduced time-saving innovations to the office organisation. The backlog caused by recent events was all but eliminated.

She had watched the new Gladys on television. It was evident, even if George recovered, that there was no future for their romance. One of the audit managers had invited her sailing next Sunday. He was recently divorced and obviously searching for feminine company. Should she accept, or remain faithful to his memory?

After yet another lonely meal, Gladys turned on the television. During the last few weeks she had frequently contemplated the problem of George, arriving at some preliminary conclusions. So long as he was alive, well, she was married and that was that. But if he died, well, she needed male company just like anyone else. Several female friends had invited her for drinks, but was it out of friendship, curiosity or pity? The only persons she had confidence in were the Marshes, the bond of the Kylb Committee somehow overcoming the invisible barriers that prevented normal socialising. She had once invited Simon over for a drink. He had some papers to return and did not stay long. In fact he was clearly desperate to exit as rapidly as social etiquette would permit.

For the moment there was little she could accomplish except show patience and fortitude, await events, see what happened to her life, George's life.

And await the return of Kylb.

'This is the BBC from London. Here is the nine o'clock news.

'A peace agreement has been signed in Washington between Israel, Egypt, Jordan and the Palestinian authorities. Other Arab nations refused to attend, but have informally indicated they will cease all hostilities.

'European leaders, meeting in Dublin, emphasised their continued commitment to the Treaty of Maastricht and the importance of strengthening the European Parliament in Strasbourg. Following unavoidable delays, resulting from matters outside their control, a new timetable would be established in time for their next scheduled gathering in Madrid.

'The Tokyo stock market gained a further three per-cent as

Japan's new government introduced rigorous measure to combat the economic crisis.

'*A giant petrol tanker has gone aground on sandbanks near Le Havre, starting to break up in high seas. French authorities expect a major ecological disaster.*

'Fifty more cases of bovine spongiform encephalopathy have been reported in Belgium, increasing pressure on Britain to slaughter its few remaining herds of cattle.

'Peking has announced an immediate lifting of the decree limiting families to one child. A spokesperson explained that the change in policy resulted from recent vicious attacks on China from decadent capitalist regimes. Due to the resultant increased threat to national security, it was regrettably necessary to augment the country's population, thereby ensuring China remained not only democratic but strong and independent.

'The Islamist government in Kabul has executed eleven women for leaving their houses without male escorts and for failing to be attired in accordance with Muslim tradition. Respecting ancient custom, the women were buried up to their necks in sand, then stoned to death by the crowd of males who had been invited to participate.

'Princess Stephanie of Monaco is to remarry for the fifth time.'

Pause for a shuffling of papers.

'United States President Stanton Forbes has achieved his biggest foreign policy success to date. Amidst due pomp and ceremony, the peace accords so laboriously negotiated were finally signed today in Washington. We go over to John Chapman at the Black House.'

She, however, stayed in Esher, listening dispassionately until the weather forecast promised warm sunny weather for the British Isles. They had not once mentioned George or Kylb, nor why the White House was now black, including the President who lived and worked there.

Despondent, she switched off the television. After a moment's hesitation she walked to the cabinet containing her CDs, selecting Neil Diamond's *Jonathan Livingstone Seagull*. She had adored the film, although George infuriatingly commenced snoring long before the end. Her eyes closed, she recalled the beautiful images of the desolate, wild and unspoilt coastline of Greenland where life was so simple, assuming you were a seagull. And there were no oil tankers in the neighbourhood.

The music ended, Gladys slowly and sadly mounted the stairs and entered her bedroom.

Across the garden the nubile young neighbour finished cleaning her teeth, spread an anti-acne cream over the spots disfiguring her face, walked to her bedside wearing her cotton pyjamas, climbed between the sheets and extinguished the light.

The Pope was extremely fatigued but satisfied. He was kneeling in prayer at the side of his bed. In spite of his aching muscles, there was a immense smile of contentment on his face. God's will had been done. The future of the Catholic church was assured. Amen.

The dim light in the aseptic room at Kingston Hospital hardly penetrated the gloom. This was of little consequence since no one was in attendance. All was peaceful. However, if you listened very carefully, extremely carefully, it was possible to distinguish a very low breathing originating from the motionless shape lying on the bed. In five months, three weeks and four days the motionless shape would be receiving a visitor.

The Council meeting chamber had lost its customary harmonious hum. Electrons, neutrons and mega-molecules vibrated with unusual intensity in spite of the protective magnetic vacuum. Kylb, however, remained calm.

'Well, Kylb,' boomed the mighty #, 'give us your latest report on Bl-zzziii-5.'

Kylb irradiated with increased intensity (the nearest equivalent in human communication terminology would be to 'stand up and address the meeting').

'I am pleased to report the situation is fully under control. In spite of efforts by isolated specimens of the offending neobiological life form to respect Zy-eecep, it was clear they were unprepared to respect our authority. Applying biophysical neuron separation, considerably more efficient than deviating asteroids and easier to apply than molecular redistribution, the species was eliminated without damage to either the planet or other life forms. I have appointed a new permanent Local Agent to oversee the planet, a member of the Formicidae species which is better disciplined and less polluting than the self-proclaimed Homo sapiens.'

'It was regrettable about the previous Local Agent. I hear he valiantly attempted to save his subspecies from elimination.'

'That is true, Mighty #. In consideration of his noble efforts, I spared both him and his sex-reproduction partner. His cranium logic processor required major reprogramming, having sustained severe ruptures to its neuro-circuits, also his outer covering had to be reconstituted, but I am of the opinion that he has been satisfactorily restored. Since both surviving specimens are sterile, they may live the rest of their temporal existences without risk of activating their self-inflicted 'procreation' process.'

Meeting adjourned.